NO MAN'S ISLAND

Susan Sallis

LARGE PRINT

Oxford

First published in Great Britain 2006
by
Bantam Press,
a division of
Transworld Publishers

Published in Large Print 2006 by ISIS Publishing Ltd.,
7 Centremead, Osney Mead, Oxford OX2 0ES
by arrangement with
Transworld Publishers,
a division of
The Random House Group Ltd.

British Library Cataloguing in Publication Data
Sallis, Susan
   No man's island. – Large print ed.
   1. Inheritance and succession – Fiction
   2. Island people – Fiction 3. Large type books
   I. Title
   823.9'14 [F]

ISBN–10 0–7531–7698–X (hb)
ISBN–13 978–0–7531–7698–6 (hb)

ISBN 978–0–7531–7699–3 (pb)

Printed and bound in Great Britain by
T. J. International Ltd., Padstow, Cornwall

For Jane and Mike

CHAPTER
ONE

It happened on a Sunday morning. Daniel Casey — if that was his name — had thumbed a lift to the Manor, before the bottom of the hill. He remembered the hill: the road climbed steeply up the side of the wooded rock face and then dropped suddenly to the sea. He got out of the car, thanked the driver and strode out past the old grocery store and the Edwardian houses on the right, then gradually shortened his steps as the road ascended sharply to the church. It was seven forty-five on September the seventh. As the wind rose — the place was famous for the prevailing south-westerlies — little scuds of leaves blew from the trees and eddied in the road. Dan knew he would be grateful for the cooling wind by the time he reached the church at the top.

Weariness weighted him down. He had caught a train from Paddington to Bristol the evening before, then walked round to the bus station and waited for a bus, dozing now and then, feeling cold and rather sick. The cleaners had started at five in the morning and one of them had said to him — if you're still here at seven, I'll give you a lift. When they had got into his unexpectedly sleek car, the man had explained that the bus services to outlying villages did not start until midday on Sundays, and Dan had been deeply grateful to him.

He reached a little plateau, rather like a half-landing on a staircase, and paused to look through a gap in the trees on his left. Just as he remembered, the Victorian houses spilled down to the flat lands, but now the moors were no longer empty. The housing estates marched on across the Somerset Levels. Nowhere was safe from the developers.

He tried to gauge where the tide was. There were a couple of fishing boats bobbing close to the shore so it must be fairly high. He felt a little surge of excitement. He wasn't too old to take off his walking boots and awful old socks and paddle down the slipway. He started walking again with more spring in his step. The church would be round the next corner, or if not, then the one after. Beyond the church it was downhill all the way to the sea; he thought he could just about make that.

There would be people along the beach: parked in their cars reading the Sunday papers or walking their dogs; perhaps the hardier still swam in the tide, over-arming themselves out to the pier so that they could catch the current as it changed and whirled them back into the shore. Or perhaps it was a little too early in the day for that . . .

The church was not round the next corner, nor the next. Dan paused again to get his breath and rejig his elusive memory. He put a hand on the rough stone wall and looked across at the sea. He remembered the tall old houses on top of the quarry, and the famous tiled clock, though not the long low buildings that flanked it. It was so quiet — a ghost town. He hadn't wanted to see people. Apart from the obliging cleaner with the beautifully kept Jaguar car, he had shunned everyone since leaving London. Now, quite suddenly, he needed another human being; a face, the sound of a shout, or a gun bagging rabbits up in the woods. But no-one was about. Surely there were still church services at eight o'clock on Sunday mornings?

He clung to the wall as the view began to tilt and slide sideways. He refused to panic. It was absolutely natural. He hadn't had enough money both to pay his bus fare and to buy food on the train so he'd gone without the food. Now he was hungry and unbearably tired.

Then a terrible thought shook him back to steadiness. Supposing he had already died and this was some crazy memory flashing through his mind before the actual void? He clung to the wall desperately. He remembered he'd been in hospital, but surely there'd been nothing physically wrong? He'd been there for other reasons . . . He squeezed his eyes shut, trying to remember. He could not.

Then, at last, he heard a sound: an engine. A car was coming down fast from the top of the hill. Dan turned his back on the view and half sat on the wall. He needed to see who was driving the car.

It was a woman, white hair flying in the gale coming through her wound-down window. She was going much too fast; some of the leaves on the road were wet.

She flicked him a glance as she sped past, then suddenly jammed on her brakes. Sure enough the car skidded slightly, but then stopped safely. She shot back in reverse until she was level with him, then pushed her head through the open window.

"Are you all right?"

He was so pleased to see her that he smiled much too widely. "I am now," he said.

She looked slightly startled and he realized he might have sounded as if he were coming on to her. He added quickly, "I haven't seen a soul yet and I was beginning to think I might have died without noticing it."

She flung back her head and laughed. She was younger than the white hair suggested. Her throat was beautiful.

She said, "I know what you mean. But everyone's in church by now. Except me and I'll be late to my own funeral. So I'd better be off." She waved through the window, drove on round the corner and was gone.

Dan, feeling a sense of loss, began to walk uphill again. And the very next corner revealed the church — to which she obviously had not been going. He wondered why she had said she was.

He got to the gate and clung to it. Above his head the church clock began to strike. He counted carefully; sure enough, it was eight o'clock. He thought suddenly that he would go in and sit at the back and listen to the familiar liturgy and rest for a while.

He lifted the big latch on the gate and pushed, then saw it was padlocked. There was a notice board fixed to the wall further on and he read it slowly. It said that

Holy Apostles was now closed but that services would be held at the usual times in the parish church on the sea front. As if confirming this statement, distant bells rang out. The clock on the parish church had always been slow, and was still. Dan smiled; that was reassuring.

Binnie Cash drove more circumspectly to the foot of the hill and turned away from the parish church towards the tiny chapel built on to the end of the Manor. It was opened for morning services for the family and staff. She drove very slowly indeed along the tree-lined drive because the aptly named Mr Parkes, who looked after the grounds, was quite capable of refusing her admittance to the service if she ploughed up his gravel. She parked outside the old kitchen, next to Miles' Jag, then left dignity behind her and ran hell for leather across the lawns to the chapel, trying to re-pin her hair up as she went. They'd left the door open for her in spite of the wind, and Lady Barbara's sonorous voice could be heard quite plainly reading the first lesson. Binnie thought, my God, I really have done it this time. And she cursed the poor old devil of a tramp, who would have fallen down if he hadn't propped himself against the wall around Holy Apostles. She'd thought she was being some blasted Good Samaritan going back like that, and then he'd turned out not to be a tramp at all but one of these crazy coastal path walkers or something similar.

She slid inside the Manor chapel and closed the door. There were seats for thirty but just six people there; no escaping notice, except from Sir Henry, who was taking the service and appeared to be asleep in the pulpit. Lady Thoroughgood — Lady Barbara to the staff — stepped down from the lectern and gave Binnie a frosty look. Miles turned and winked broadly. He must have been doing an early shift for Thoroughgood Cleaners and arrived home just in time to be nobbled by his parents.

Sir Henry announced the Gospel so he couldn't have been asleep. His voice was so soporific that Binnie felt herself slipping away. She stood up with some difficulty and, after the Gospel, stayed standing for the Creed. There were no prayer books, but Miss Sinclair, Lady T's secretary, held her typed paper well up so that Binnie could read it. Gratefully she sank to her knees for the prayers.

Afterwards, she was invited to the house for breakfast, but as it was invariably cardboard toast and cold tea she declined with the excuse that the children were coming to lunch and she must get cracking. Will, her nineteen-year-old, was in Leeds "fixing up" his next term's accommodation, and Lady Barbara knew that, but there was always Dorrie and her new partner. Lady Barbara pursed her lips but said nothing. She had been introduced to the partner, unsuitably named Gabriel, and told him immediately that she was one of those strange people who still had standards. Dorrie had called her an old cow, though not to her face.

Miles accompanied Binnie to her car and nodded approvingly at the smooth gravel around it.

"You will be top of the pops with old Parkes," he commented. "You should have heard him moaning at me! Dammit, I left here at four ack emma! I can't be expected to be mindful of the gravel at that hour!"

Binnie frowned. "I thought it was agreed that if someone didn't turn up to clean on Sunday mornings, I would fill in?"

"And *I* thought you needed your beauty sleep," Miles said with a grin. "Didn't mean it, Binnie — you will always be beautiful to me." He laughed and ducked as she swung her handbag in his direction. "And there was me thinking I would be earning a few Brownie points."

"Sorry. Sorry, Miles. It was marvellous not to have to get out of bed in the small hours — thank you."

"Quite. Especially as you couldn't even get here by eight o'clock!"

"I met some old chap halfway up the hill. Thought he was a down-and-out. Turned out to be a walker or something. But it just tipped me over the eight o'clock deadline."

Miles raised an eyebrow, James Bond style. "You too? I noticed him when I was working — he was waiting at our stop. I offered him a lift. He didn't know where he was going but reckoned he'd know when he got there. I dropped him at the front gate and sure enough he started off at a good whack."

"What time was that?"

"About seven thirty, I suppose. Not sure."

"He must have slowed right down when he got to the hill. He didn't seem lost. I thought he might be ill, though."

"For God's sake, Binnie! No more lame ducks."

"What on earth d'you mean?" She looked at him, annoyed.

He raised an eyebrow again. "Will and his awful friends. Dorrie and her prisoner-reform efforts —"

"Gabriel has not been to prison!"

"Not yet."

"And neither of my children is living in the cottage any longer." She heard her voice break slightly and cleared her throat. "If I didn't live in tied accommodation you would have no right to say that sort of thing, and just because you have a right does not mean you should exercise it. In fact, just the opposite."

"Why don't you simply tell me to shut up?"

"Shut up, Miles!"

"That's better. And you're right, of course. Except that I did not mean to exercise any possible rights I might have. Just to offer friendly advice. Allow me." He tried to open the door of the beaten-up Mondeo, but it was stuck as usual, and eventually he had to put his foot on the passenger door and wrench it wide. It screamed a protest.

He was unable to maintain his Bondian sophistication and she laughed at his expression. He wasn't much older than Will, but already hung around with the responsibilities of the Manor and its grounds. And, after all, he never minded turning out when one of the cleaners failed to put in an appearance. Lady Barbara ran an industrial cleaning company that was unexpectedly successful. Sir Henry had landed contracts with Bristol City Council, First Great Western Railways and two shopping malls. They called the business "Thoroughgood Cleaners", using their family name.

Miles leaned into the car and fastened Binnie's seat belt. She pressed herself back. Miles enjoyed flirting with her because their age difference made him feel safe. She never wanted it to go any further, Brownie points or not.

He withdrew and said, "All I meant was — take care of yourself. Put yourself first for a change." He grinned. "It just took rather a long time to say it!"

She shook her head at him and turned the car carefully.

When she got to the top of the hill she should have turned right and gone on up into the woods where, since the early 1900s, Thoroughgoods had shot anything that moved: rabbits, foxes, birds of all kinds. But she turned left instead and headed for the sea. She knew she would not see the walker-cum-tramp again but . . . well, you never knew. She did not intend to ignore Miles' concern completely but he had no idea of the real Binnie Cash. The old gamekeeper's cottage, in the middle of all those trees, was not inviting but it had been home for the past fifteen years at a peppercorn rent. It was what tied her to her job as administrative clerk to the Manor house and grounds, and made it impossible for her to say no to Thoroughgood Cleaners when she was needed to fill in for an absent employee. When Miles referred to her "lame ducks" she knew it was because he saw her as someone who had been hurt — damaged even — and naturally turned to helping others. Miles had always put her on a pedestal. But she had welcomed the numerous friends her children had brought home with them. Now that William had gone to university and Dorrie was living with her boyfriend, Binnie was very lonely indeed and knew she needed her lame ducks more than they needed her.

She drove down slowly, telling herself she simply wanted to look at the sea and then return home via the newsagent's, get herself a Sunday paper and settle down with a crossword or the supplements or even the obituaries. She must be getting on if obituaries were part of her must-read. It was surprising how interesting they were. A picture of an old buffer obviously in his nineties, and then the peeling away of time: he was an officer and a gentleman . . . he had the DSO for his gallantry in North Africa in 1942. His wife had turned their stately home into flats for disabled soldiers . . . his children had worked in Zimbabwe . . .

Binnie parked the car and got out into the September morning. The breeze was stiff. The flags along the front were at attention, pointing to the north-east, the prevailing south-westerlies still going strong. Binnie, wearing a skirt to be smart for Lady B, had to hold it down. She ran across the deserted promenade and leaned on the railings. The little beach was enclosed by the arm of the pier on one side and a stubby headland on the other, with a Victorian bandstand at its base. She flung back her head and breathed deeply.

She was often mildly surprised at herself. Her ability to be happy in the face of so much sheer unsatisfactoriness probably revealed that she was a shallow character. Her husband had dumped her and only two days ago she had heard he might be dead; her children were wild; her financial affairs were chaotic. Yet this happiness insisted on creeping up on her now and then for no reason at all. And anyway, he couldn't be dead — not Theo. Natalie must have got it wrong.

She took another breath as if she were drinking from a chalice of the gods, then opened her eyes to smile at the unlikely view: grey sky, grey sea, grey pier and rocks, the slipway disappearing into the solid and unfathomable sea . . . and there she stopped. Because, waist-deep, fully clothed, her tramp-cum-walker was wading slowly but inexorably out of his depth.

CHAPTER
TWO

Binnie shouted several times as she negotiated the stone steps to the slipway. The wind was coming off the sea and the walker did not hear her. She kicked off her shoes, wriggled out of her skirt and ran down in her tights. The water was bitter, even at ankle depth. She kept shouting, "Hey! Hey — you! Hey — man! Stop! Stop this minute! D'you hear me?" And at last, when she was knee-deep and wondering where the edges of the slipway were, he did hear her and he did stop and turn. She stopped too. Again, there was that split second of near-recognition, just as there had been on the hill when she was driving to the chapel. His face then had at least smiled. Now it was a complete blank and she knew quite certainly, and with a shock, that he would have gone on walking. Whether he intended suicide was another thing, but he had vacated his body with all its natural instincts for survival and would have submerged himself and probably drowned.

Binnie waited for him to speak, and when he did not she snapped, "What the hell do you think you're playing at?"

He blinked and looked around him. Then he said, "I wanted to paddle. We came here. Before. And we paddled. In the rain."

"You've paddled up to your armpits!"

"Yes. I felt unclean. The train . . . then the bus station . . . you know how it is."

"Come out now. Move slowly because the slipway is not completely straight and you could go over the edge. Take my hand . . . that's right. Come on. Your clothes are weighing you down but once we're on the concrete apron . . ." For some reason it was necessary to talk. "This is where they unload the boats from the trailers at full tide . . ." She led him to the steps. "Sit and let some of the water drain while I . . ." She peeled off her tights and scrambled into her skirt. Behind her the tide crept insidiously in. She shivered.

He watched her as she stamped her wet, unwilling feet into unsuitable Sunday shoes.

"I'm sorry. Did you come in to rescue me?"

"Obviously." She spoke tightly. If he was going to carry on the pretence of the nostalgic paddle she might well lose her temper.

"Well. Thank you. That was very . . . kind."

"It was, wasn't it?" Her voice, sarcastically pleasant at first, sharpened to a knife edge. "Especially as I have probably ruined my best shoes!"

"I'm so sorry. I'd better . . . go."

He stood up and water poured from folds in his clothing. He leaned against the wall.

Above him, someone looked over the railings and a male voice called, "Are you all right? Do you need help?"

The man, still dripping freely, did not reply.

Binnie said quickly, "Shall I ask for an ambulance? You're not well."

He shook his head vehemently and she looked up and called, "No, thanks. We're wet, that's all."

"Slipway's not straight, you see. Easy to fall off the edge. You're lucky you didn't break something on the rocks."

"Quite."

"All right then." The passer-by moved off.

Binnie said, "Look. My car is at the top of these steps. Can you make it?"

"I'd ruin the upholstery. I'm wet," he said with a ghost of a smile.

"So you are. Come on."

She ran ahead of him, unlocked the passenger door and opened it wide. He walked very slowly up to it, then stopped.

"I can't. Really."

"Well, what else can we do?" she asked impatiently. "If I leave you here you'll probably collapse and then someone will call an ambulance anyway. Maybe that would be best —"

He got in, stumbling, knocking his head on the car roof, squelching water from his boots, oozing it from his clothing. "You're like a giant squid," she told him. He didn't laugh.

14

She got the driver's door open with difficulty, as usual, and drove carefully back up Sea View Road and straight over the crossroads into Woodshill Lane. The smell of seaweed was overpowering. Halfway up she realized her passenger had gone to sleep, chin on chest, head lolling with the watery roll of the car. She edged across another road, wide, an enormous shelf in the hill, lined with luxurious houses overlooking the sea. Then they were in the woods proper, untended since the Thoroughgoods had gone into business. A few dog walkers kept half a dozen footpaths open but it was not easy-going for humans, and the track to the gamekeeper's cottage was the only one that would take a car.

The house was like a child's drawing: four-square, a front door plumb in the middle with a window either side and three above it. The middle window upstairs had been at the end of the landing, which had been partitioned to make a bathroom. Dorrie had parked a row of plastic ducks along the middle sash. All the windows were thickly netted. Binnie had no fondness for nets but she had a horror of being seen by someone . . . lurking.

She parked across the front door, another statement to any day-time lurker, and got out with difficulty to open up. Her Sunday shoes must be shrinking, she could hardly move. She glanced back. The man was still asleep, which gave her a moment to whip into the room on the left of the door and check that she hadn't left anything that could be tripped over or knocked down. She picked up a pile of books from where she'd left them last night and drew the best armchair towards the windowsill, lifting the net to check on the car. The man seemed to have collapsed into the driving seat. She clicked with annoyance but it was too late to try to keep part of the car dry. She ran to the bottom of the room, which was the kitchen, and switched on the immersion heater. At some point she would have to get him into a hot bath. Her heart sank at the prospect.

It sank further when, having collected all the clean towels she had, she woke him and tugged him out into the open. He was shivering and seemed barely able to stand.

"You should have let me have my paddle," he muttered through clenched teeth, then smiled as if it were a big joke.

She propped him against the car and pulled off his jacket and sweater, and wrapped a towel around his upper half.

"When we get into the hall, I want you to take off everything else and use these towels, then give me a shout and I'll help you into a chair."

He said, "Oh God . . ." but let himself be led through the front door. She closed it and pushed the bolt across. If Dorrie and Gabriel arrived unexpectedly they would simply walk in. She didn't want that. She kicked the stranger's discarded clothes into a heap and waited with her back to him.

When she turned, she saw that he was sitting on the stairs and had tugged off his boots and trousers. He was trying to pull the top towel over his knees. She put two bath sheets on his lap, and gathered the clothes up and took them through to the washing machine. She could hear him fumbling after her and rushed back to pilot him into the chair.

He gasped, "That's good. Thank you so much. If I could just . . . I'll soon be out of your hair."

She couldn't see how. He was in what Dorrie would call "a state". And the "state" had included a suicide attempt.

She said briskly, "We'll talk about it later. Some food now. And then a really decent sleep."

He was still shivering so she fetched a blanket before she put bacon on the grill pan. Then she filled a hot-water bottle. Then, biting her lip, she lit the first fire of the autumn. She was beginning to wonder whether he would ever get warm again.

He wasn't interested in the food; he did, however, begin to turn pink, and it was obvious all he wanted was sleep. She kept him awake long enough to eat a slice of bacon broken into pieces and hand delivered. Then he had two sips of tea and his head slipped back and he was asleep. Binnie stood eating the rest of the bacon because, after all, she hadn't had time for breakfast. She watched him all the time, frowning, wondering how she was going to get him into the bath and then out of the house. And then what would he do?

She moved slightly away from the fire, drew up the other chair and picked up a book she had been reading last night. It was a history of the Skalls, the Lost Land, an archipelago fifty miles west of the more famous Scillies. She frowned again, wondering just why she had looked it out from Theo's old books. The Skalls had been his stamping ground. He always returned there from wherever he had spent the summer, going back to Trapdoor Island and beachcombing and living like a hobo.

Binnie sighed sharply. The pain of losing him had long gone and should have eased the news that he was now reported dead. But it had made a new pain: a terrible ache of a loss that now could never be recovered. He was gone. He was not in this world, messing about with his beloved boats, behaving like an irresponsible schoolboy . . . hurting people . . . damaging his children . . . He had drowned while crewing for a charter in the Tyrrhenian Sea. There had been an unexpected wave and he had been swept overboard. A ridiculous accident for such an experienced man of the sea. And Binnie would not have even known about it if it hadn't been for his second wife, Natalie.

He had left Binnie and gone to Natalie and eventually married her. And then he had left Natalie and gone off with an Italian girl, and Natalie had ranged herself alongside Binnie and the children. But they had nothing in common except Theo, and Theo was not — never had been — enough. Natalie had visited once and had thrown up her hands at what she called the "primitive conditions" of the gamekeeper's cottage.

"And you actually have to go out *cleaning*?" she had asked.

"Well, now and then. I show people around the Manor . . . invitation only . . . but the family runs an industrial cleaning business and if they're let down . . ."

She looked at Natalie's sceptical expression and said lamely, "The son of the house helps out too . . . It's a case of all hands to the pump."

"Sorry, but I think it's disgraceful that Theo has made no effort to support you or his children. Thank God I never wanted a family. It was bad enough that he just walked off with bloody Violetta . . ."

They had not heard from Natalie again until she married Ernest Broadbent, the chairman of a grocery chain. And then had come the news of Theo's accident on the last day of August . . .

Now, Binnie flipped through the book, finding the illustrations. The Skalls, originally called the Skallaswag Islands because of their usefulness to smugglers from France, were now beloved of bird-watchers and holiday-makers. Twitchers and tourists, Theo had said. That had been before he had dumped her and gone to live with Natalie on his very own Skall: Trapdoor Island. The island nearest France, with one tiny landing beach, and nothing to warn shipping of the knife edge of rock that protected it. Like the Cornish wreckers, Theo had edged his dinghy around the rocks and dived after the remains of cargoes from years back, some of it sea-spoiled, some of it still saleable.

"He simply wanted to play — like an overgrown schoolboy!" Natalie had said angrily. "And he had that lovely old house on the mainland . . ."

But not, it seemed, any longer.

Binnie put down the book gently so as not to wake the man and went to the kitchen end where Natalie's letter still lay in separate sheets, weighted by the sugar bowl. It was dark down here, the trees pressing almost against the back windows. She put on the light, bent over the open pages and read them yet again. She knew the words almost by heart, yet still found them difficult to accommodate.

The notepaper was embossed; Natalie now boasted an address in London as well as Plymouth.

"Dear Benita . . ." Nobody called Binnie by her full name and no-one had ever shortened it to a racy "Ben". The story went that her father had wanted his baby girl to be Benita after his own mother, and his wife had simply made a face, cuddled her protectively and said, "All right. My own little Benita . . . little Binnie . . ." And she had been Binnie ever since. Except, it would seem, to Natalie.

Dear Benita,

Sad news but probably as much a relief to you as it is to me. Theo drowned last week. One of his silly charter things in a calm sea — sudden wave — off he went. Simple as that. Bit like Theo himself, really. I always told him he'd have to grow up one day. Proved me wrong yet again. Anyway, the solicitors have written. No will, of course. Typical. I'm next of kin, believe it or not. But obviously that's not fair so I'm suggesting to you that I sell up everything I can get my hands on — mostly the house in Cornwall and his boats — and we split it fifty-fifty. What say you? Can't do anything about the island, apparently. The so-called owners hold them on leases of hundreds of years but they can't sell them except to the lessors and then only for a valuation dated the year dot — ridiculous, of course, but cast-iron apparently — I've been into it. Theo always told me that Trapdoor was for his family. And by family he meant you. Sounds crazy but I know it's true because I asked him once who he meant by "family". And he told me: Binnie. So you see, you were always the one. I've passed all this on to the solicitors. I guess you'll hear from them with a cheque for your half of the house — in due course, as they say! Hope you are all fighting fit. I have never been happier. Keep in touch?

Fondest . . . Natalie.

Binnie stared through the windows at the trees. The proceeds from the house on the mainland would be very useful indeed. But the island . . . that was something else. If it turned out that it was legally hers, they could all live there for part of the year. She felt a small jump of excitement. And immediately quashed it. Theo would turn up again. He always did.

She began, slowly and methodically, to clear up. Behind her, the man, the would-be suicide, shifted and snorted and then slumped into unconsciousness again. She could leave him there, of course, but what if . . .? He might be fighting fit when he had had his sleep. And he might turn out to be a raving lunatic. She remembered Miles' words about lame ducks. Should she ring Miles and ask him to spend the night up here? Certainly not — a crazy thought. But she could ask

Dorrie and Gabriel to come up. She wasn't keen on that idea either but she had to do something.

She went to the freezer, which was round the corner behind the "front parlour", as Miles called it. It might be more tactful to invite them to Sunday lunch. There were lamb chops. And she still had cabbages in the garden, which pushed into the woods by the back door.

She sighed, put another piece of wood on the fire and took the phone as far away from the sleeping man as she could. Gabriel would be able to get him up the stairs and into the bath, surely? And she must ask him to bring some spare clothes too. Unless she could dry off the wet ones. They were still in the washing machine. She'd have to get cracking . . .

There was no reply from Dorrie's house. Binnie stood there, waiting, looking at the chops lying on the draining board. And then her eye was caught by movement at the back window. No-one came that way. The woods closed in around the hill on the north side in tangled thickets of fern and thorn. But someone was there.

She replaced the phone carefully and stepped to the side of the window. Then there was a tapping on the glass and a hoarse shout.

"Binnie! It's me — Gabe! Are you there?"

She looked out and sure enough it was Gabriel. Gormless Gabriel. Gabriel Mackinley. Good-looking, charming in a weak sort of way and, presumably, in love with Dorrie. Certainly Dorrie was in love with him. Like her mother, she had fallen for someone who — in Lady Barbara's terms — was highly unsuitable.

He looked terrible, his hair on end, scratches already streaming blood from his hands. She opened the back door.

"What on earth . . .? Why didn't you come along the track, for God's sake? Look at you! Honestly, Gabriel . . ." She ushered him in and led him to the sink, even turned on the tap. That was how he was; he would have simply stood there. She passed him some soap and made washing motions with her own hands.

He said, "I left Dorrie to cover for me. I'm sorry, Binnie. It was nothing. Really. Just that I owe some money and I can't pay it and they keep giving me extra time and now it's run out and they've come after me! Dorrie made me come — pushed me out of the window and told me to go the back way up to you and you'd know what to do."

At one time Binnie would have been shocked and horrified by this blurted story. Now she was not. Gabriel believed that gambling was his God-given profession; he had been in all sorts of trouble before. He was absolutely hopeless. No wonder Miles had prophesied prison for him.

She said, "What about Dorrie? Is she going to be all right?"

"I don't know."

"I've just phoned. No reply." Binnie was already pulling on her jacket. "How could you leave her there? Why didn't she come?"

"She said she could manage. Bluff. Tell them I'd gone abroad. Something." He looked helplessly for a towel and she thrust one at him. He twisted it around his wet hands. "Oh God, Binnie. She'll be all right, won't she?"

"I don't know. I'll take the car. Lock yourself in and don't make a sound if anyone knocks." She made for the front door and came up short at the sight of the man asleep in the chair. "I'd forgotten . . . Gabriel, listen. This man is ill. I fished him out of the sea a couple of hours ago. Make tea and give him some if he wakes." She went into the tiny hall, then came back again. "I've put the immersion on. If you could get him into the bath it would be good. Warm him up. Keep the fire going."

She left Gabriel standing helplessly, staring at the sleeping man swathed in towels. She thought viciously that it would give him something to consider other than his own stupid skin. And if anything had happened to Dorrie, she would personally hand him over to his unsavoury creditors, whoever they might be.

She got into the car, then got out again, fetched a plastic dustbin liner from the boot and laid it over the soggy driver's seat. Then she drove back the way she had come earlier, veered to the left and descended the hill again towards one of the recent housing developments, which stretched predatory fingers over the Levels. She glanced at the clock on the dashboard: it was half past eleven. She thought of herself rushing out to drive down to the Manor that morning, late as usual but looking forward to a day to herself, no work, time to read Natalie's letter and think about Theo. And now she was rushing off again with greater urgency.

And leaving two men, both obviously inadequate, in the cottage.

She braked and took another left turn and then pulled over to the kerb. She was one street away from the terraced house Dorrie rented. The house was in a cul-de-sac, which suddenly seemed very like a trap. Binnie gnawed her lip indecisively, wondering whether to walk round or drive straight down, turn and park outside. Supposing some awful thug had been holding Dorrie down in a chair, not allowing her to pick up the phone when it had rung? At the thought, she opened the door and swung out her legs. But then she paused. If she got Dorrie out of the house, she might need the car as near as it could be.

Binnie muttered to herself, angry that as usual she seemed unable to make up her mind. Here she was, half in and half out of the car, her daughter probably in danger, and she simply did not know what to do next. A little scud of rain scarred the windscreen and irritably she switched on the wipers. At least she could take that small action. She switched them off as if she had proved a point, then got out of the car, slammed the door with a flourish and walked down to the next road.

No-one answered the bell. That didn't mean a thing, but Binnie had to behave as naturally as possible so she produced her key and let herself in. It was an anti-climax to discover that the house was empty. The open-plan downstairs area was fairly tidy: no upturned chairs or emptied drawers. She took the stairs two at a time and found the single bedroom in disarray but only from Dorrie's lack of housewifely skills. Binnie swung open the bathroom door, shoved aside the shower curtain . . . no-one was in the house.

She went back downstairs and picked up the phone. Gabriel would probably not answer it anyway. It rang twice then stopped, and Dorrie's voice said, "Is that you, Mum? Come on home, for goodness' sake. I think it's a storm in a teacup. Two men arrived, I didn't ask them in and they did not try to push past me or anything. I promised that we would get half the money by next Monday. Gabe and I can be miles away by then."

Binnie wanted to scream. All that tension and terror, and Dorrie had lied her way out of it, got into her tiny Smart car and driven up the hill as if nothing had happened. She must have taken a different side road off the estate from the one where Binnie had been parked, deliberately. And now Dorrie was proposing leaving her job and . . . leaving. And what about the man in the chair?

Binnie said, "Right. I see." She took a deep breath, then let it go. "Can you stay to lunch?" she asked.

Dorrie laughed. "Oh, Mum! You're priceless. Gabriel's upstairs with some strange man who doesn't seem to know he's alive. I'm practically on the run. And you're asking us to lunch!"

"Well, you have to eat." Binnie was going through one of those maternal moments when she rather disliked her daughter. "And if you can stay there are some chops on the draining board. Can you put them in the oven?"

She put the phone down and stared through the window at two children struggling with one skateboard.

She said aloud, "We'll go to Trapdoor. How's that for a decision? A course of action. A complete change of lifestyle. We'll go to Trapdoor and learn how to be a family again."

She went back to the car and turned it in the narrow road. She felt as she had done earlier that morning when she had looked over the sea. She had lost Theo a long time ago. Perhaps this was a way of finding him again.

CHAPTER
THREE

Dorrie did her best to placate her mother.

"Look, Mum, it's not that bad. Think of it as an illness — not even an illness! Gabe is one of those people who has the imagination to see that — that — one smile from Lady Luck will solve all his financial worries. I mean, he's trapped, isn't he?"

"By his over-active imagination?" Binnie asked in the tense hushed tone they were both using as they prepared lunch in the lower half of the kitchen.

Binnie had arrived home to find that Gabriel had somehow got the sick man out of the armchair and up the stairs to the bathroom. He had even elicited a name for him. Dan. Binnie, who had professed to prefer single-syllable names for men — as opposed to "Theo" and "Gabriel" — was now not sure. Someone with a brief, strong name like "Dan" should not be wading waist-deep into the sea at this time of year. She would call him Daniel.

She broke into Dorrie's protests about her being unfair.

"He left you to face the music on your own. All right, I know that everything was civilized, as it turned out. The 'debt collectors', or whatever they called themselves, were not mindless thugs. But Gabriel did not know that and neither did you. Otherwise you wouldn't have sent him packing up to me!" She turned down the gas jet beneath the boiling potatoes and looked round at her daughter.

Dorrie was now twenty-two and, until she had met Gabriel Mackinley, had been a level-headed, quietly attractive girl — very like her mother, people said — thoroughly enjoying her promotion to the big central library in Bristol. Mother and children had lived together in the gamekeeper's cottage and, in spite of all its inconveniences, had managed very well. Will had made the small sitting room on the other side of the front door into a cross between a study and a sound studio, and Dorrie had worked quietly for her library examinations at the kitchen table and had always found time to make her mother a cup of tea when she arrived home from work.

And then, nearly a year ago, Will had gone to Leeds on a four-year course in community education, and Dorrie had met Gabriel.

Binnie looked helplessly at her daughter and thought: my hair was that glossy brown until Theo left me. His nut-brown maid — that was his name for me. Nut-brown maid indeed.

She said, "Darling, it's you . . . I worry about you. You appear to cope with everything but you've got a stressful job and the drive in and out of town every day —"

"We thought of moving, actually." Dorrie's expression mirrored her mother's. "But rents are even higher in the city and it's good to get right away every evening."

They were both silent. The thought of Gabriel being within walking distance of the plethora of clubs in Bristol was uncomfortable, to say the least.

Dorrie tried to shift the focus by saying, "I don't want to leave you here, in this house, on your own. And the Thoroughgoods are so demanding —"

"Rubbish! They're very good to me — have been very good to the three of us for the past fifteen years!"

Dorrie turned back to the chopping board and began to chop mint as if her life depended on it. "You've never liked Gabriel," she accused.

Binnie felt suddenly weary; so much had happened already today, and it wasn't even lunch-time. She said quietly, "That's not true, actually. It's very difficult not to like Gabriel. He's so . . . honest!" She gave a little snuffling laugh because in the circumstances the word "honest" was the last to apply to Gabriel.

She took the chops out of the oven and turned them over. "These are going to be tough," she announced.

"Oh, Mum!" Dorrie too laughed. "But you're right. He's so frank about his gambling thing. He can describe his feelings in detail. He has even itemized them one by one up to the moment he says to himself — what have I got to lose?"

"That's the bit I don't understand," Binnie said, trying to take this priority list seriously. "He's head over heels in debt —"

"Gambling debts cannot be claimed legally."

"Is that true? Even if it is he might well pay with his
— his kneecaps! Or worse!"

"But you see, Mum, he's got to the stage where the
debt is so much that it has become sort of meaningless.
Monopoly money. So — to him — to lose his kneecaps
does not seem so bad when a single win would rescue
him. Can't you see that?"

"So he runs up here when they come for his
kneecaps?" Binnie tried to make it sound funny.

Dorrie said, "I made him leave. You know that."

Binnie went for the flour crock and gravy browning.
Then she said slowly, "You paid them off, didn't you?"

Dorrie laughed again, without amusement. "I could
never do that, Mum. The debt is enormous."

Binnie fetched a spoon from the cutlery drawer. "You
gave them enough to keep them on hold for a while.
When are they coming back for the rest?"

Dorrie knifed the chopped mint into a jug of vinegar
and stirred it methodically.

"Mum — for goodness' sake —"

"When?"

"Oh Lord!" Dorrie plonked the jug in the middle of
the table. "I don't know. A week, maybe two. I told
them we'd clear it eventually. In instalments."

Binnie took the chops out of the baking tin and
began to make the gravy.

"What did they say to that?"

"Nothing. That was pretty awful, actually. They did
not reply to anything I said. Simply stated their . . .
their requirements."

Binnie controlled her shiver. Dorrie had been on her own, with these two "debt collectors". "So. We've got a week." She flashed a smile at her daughter. "Well done, love. You've bought us a week." She drained the cabbage. "D'you want to go and see how Gabe is getting on in the bathroom? You see — he's coping with that very well." She paused and stared frowning through the window at the trees. "He reminds me of your father. He acts like a stereotype male most of the time, then suddenly pulls out his finger and copes with all kinds of emergencies."

Dorrie stared at her mother, then turned her face away and changed the subject. "Mum, about this man. What's going on? Gabe says you pulled him out of the water. But he seems weird to me. Is he crazy or something?"

"I'm not sure yet. Let's have lunch and talk about it." She cut into one of the chops. "These aren't a bit tough, actually."

Gabriel and Dorrie preceded Daniel whatever-his-name-was down the stairs and into chairs at the table. Daniel was dressed in his own clothes, which, presumably, Dorrie had tumble-dried and restored to him. He looked almost presentable and managed a tired smile in Binnie's direction; she felt again that faint sense of recognition. She saw now that he was younger than she had first thought; rail thin, with ginger-grey hair and beard. Probably her own age.

She said, "You look better. Can you eat something now?"

"Is there enough? I'm hungry but a sandwich would be fine."

"There's plenty. I'll cut it up for you."

She presented it in bite-sized portions, allowing him a fork and spoon to deal with it. He smiled at her, understanding her motives in not allowing him to use a knife.

"I came here from London," he said gently. "I wanted to paddle. So I was pleased to see that the tide was in."

Dorrie glanced at her mother, then back at Daniel. "You've been here before?"

"Yes. A long time ago. I can't remember exactly when." He loaded his fork and paused. "I can't remember much at all. The church. It's closed now." He frowned at Binnie. "You told me you were going there. But it was closed."

She nodded. "I go to the chapel at the Manor house." She wanted him stronger and out of here, on his way to wherever he was going. "Will you be well enough to cope this afternoon?" She remembered how exhausted he had been that morning and perhaps really ill. "I have a friend who does bed and breakfast . . . if you wanted to explore the area."

"Of course." He nodded slowly at first, then emphatically. "Yes. That is what I will do. I can't thank you enough for — for rescuing me, letting me sleep for a while. I don't think I slept last night."

"No. You were in the bus station most of the night. Apparently when you got off the London train you walked across town to the bus station."

"Did I tell you that?" He lifted his brows, surprised. "I couldn't remember ... but yes, that is what happened."

Binnie glanced at Dorrie and Gabriel. Gabriel was eating as if he hadn't a care in the world.

"Miles was cleaning this morning and brought Daniel to Cherrington. Miles told me about it at church." She shook her head gently at Dorrie before anything could be said about lame ducks. "Miles Thoroughgood," she said to Daniel. "His family run an industrial cleaning business and he filled in for an absentee this morning."

He frowned again and she realized he was making a physical effort to concentrate and find sense in what was said to him. She frowned too. What on earth was the matter with him?

"I see." He glanced at Gabriel, who was still eating. "I want to thank you all for helping me. Your mother first, of course. But then you, Gabriel. I needed that bath!" He laughed unconvincingly.

It was Dorrie who said, "Are you ill? I know that a night in the bus station is enough to make anyone feel grotty! But if you're really ill, you should let us take you to see a doctor."

Daniel turned his gaze on her and then back to Binnie. She had thought his eyes were colourless and now realized they were the slate grey of the sea. He had a wide mouth, long jaw, beaky nose. He said uncertainly, "I don't think I'm ill. I don't feel ill. I'm sure you won't catch anything from me."

Dorrie made a sound of exasperation. "Not what I meant at all!" She glanced at her mother again. "Perhaps I can drive you down to Sea View Road — I take it you're thinking of Nancy's place, Mum? Shall we have a cup of tea first?"

They did that and then Gabriel made up the fire and they sat for a while, expecting Dan to explain himself a little more. When he was silent, apparently quite content to watch the flames, Binnie became fidgety. If she really wanted to go to Trapdoor Island she had to tell Dorrie that Theo was dead, and she had no idea how Dorrie would take that news. It must be ten years since Theo had last visited the children. They had been to see his island twice, and had loved it and probably adored him too. Children fantasized about absent parents — that was well known. Dorrie — and Will, of course — might well be heartbroken at the news.

The autumn afternoon darkened. Gabriel was asleep in one of the chairs, Binnie was clearing away the lunch things in a desultory way and Dorrie was at the sink. She was saying something in a low voice, wondering whether they should phone Nancy about their unwanted visitor, when there was an enormous explosion from the front of the cottage. Then a sheet of flame lit up the woodland, revealing Binnie's old car parked next to the door and the outline of Dorrie's treasured Smart car as it was swallowed by fire.

Dorrie screamed, Gabriel woke with a cry, Dan jerked round and half fell out of his chair, and Binnie ran for the front door.

Dorrie yelled, "Mum — come back! You can't do anything. Don't open the door — for God's sake!" She snatched at the phone and punched in three nines. The sound of the fire, the smell of it, the garish light, all combined to make a hellish scene.

Dan held Gabriel away from the window. "It could blow, old man. Keep back."

Behind them, Dorrie was asking for the fire service and giving a number and directions.

Binnie said, "If mine goes, the house will be in danger. Get ready to go out of the back door."

Gabriel was gibbering now. "That's what they want! They're smoking us out — don't you see? Where's the fire engine, for God's sake?"

Binnie said grimly, "Get your shoes on, Gabriel. This is nothing to do with you!" But Dorrie said nothing so Binnie knew that this was in fact all to do with Gabriel. She could have wept suddenly; Dorrie had been so proud of her little car.

Binnie's Mondeo remained intact. The woodland was too wet to burn and by the time the firemen reached the scene, the Smart car was reduced to a metal skeleton, which they thoroughly soaked. The blackened trees steamed dismally as everyone drank tea and Binnie's family told the fire-fighters what they knew. The fire chief did not like it.

"New car like that, hardly likely to be faulty. Afraid I'll have to report it to the police. Are you going to be all right?"

"Of course," said Binnie. "Do you think it was some kind of sabotage?"

"It's a possibility. The police will want to know if anyone has a grudge against your daughter. Our investigator will be along tomorrow. We must be thankful it did not happen when you were driving, miss."

Dorrie swallowed. "Yes," she said.

They watched the fire engine bucket slowly back through the woods. When they went inside again, Gabriel positioned himself by the window where he could keep an eye on Binnie's car.

Unexpectedly Dan said, "This is not a good place to be. It is too secluded."

They all looked at him; unless Gabriel had poured out his heart in the bathroom, Dan could have no idea of the so-called debt collectors.

He shrugged. "I think it might be better if I stayed here tonight. I'll sleep in the chair down here. Just to keep an eye on things."

Binnie said, "We'll all stay here tonight. Are you working tomorrow, Dorrie?"

"Not until three. But then until closing at nine."

Binnie glanced at Dan. "I need to talk to the children, Daniel. Family stuff. Would you mind going into the other room — just for half an hour?"

"Of course not. But I think I'm going for a walk. I need some air. And it would be good to reconnoitre, don't you think?"

Gabriel spoke up. "Listen. I'll come with you. You don't need me, do you, Binnie?"

"Not at first, I suppose." She smiled at him; sometimes he was very understanding. They couldn't very well let Dan wander around on his own. She found wellingtons belonging to Will and a dry anorak too. She watched them tramp off very slowly and begin a circuit of the cottage. Already it was beginning to get dark. One thing was sure, she could no longer live here.

Behind her Dorrie was making more tea. "It's one of those days when the teapot is going to be in constant use," she forecast with a tiny smile. "Oh, Mum, I'm so sorry, bringing all this trouble with me." She brought two mugs to the fireplace and put them on the mantelpiece. "My car . . ." she said, and began to weep.

Binnie gathered her up. "Darling, cars can be replaced. Remember what that fireman said. Let's just be thankful."

Dorrie sniffled into a handkerchief and at last pulled away and sat down.

"Mum, what on earth is going on? Those men — the debt collectors — were polite enough. They couldn't be responsible for this — this atrocity. Could they?"

Binnie leaned on the mantelpiece and inhaled steam from her tea. It was instantly soothing. She said, "I can't think of another explanation. If we were in the city we wouldn't question it. That they should come here — to our quiet little town by the sea . . . it's terrible." Dorrie said nothing and Binnie passed her a mug and kneeled beside her. "Darling, there's more bad news. I should have told you before but I thought it was all a mistake." Dorrie's eyes were full of new fear. Binnie said quietly, "I had a letter from Natalie and you know she is not always reliable. But . . . it's likely that Daddy is dead. I'm so sorry, darling."

Dorrie closed her eyes for a moment, then opened them and gave that small wry smile again. She said, "Oh, Mum, I'm sorry too. But I thought it might be you. Some horrible illness or something. I couldn't take that. I can take Dad's death somehow. He's always been like a legendary hero and most legendary heroes are dead!" She tried for a laugh and sobbed. "I take it . . . was it cancer?"

"Oh, no! It was an accident. A charter boat, I gather. He was swept overboard. We need a bit more . . . sort of . . . proof. Natalie was contacted as next of kin and she is going into everything."

Dorrie laughed again. "Oh, Mum, that's how he would want to go. If he was alive we'd have heard." She looked into the fire. "I know what you mean. It seems incredible, doesn't it? He's always been there, somehow. We never see him but we know . . ." She stopped, took a breath, then went on, "Will and I — we worshipped him, as you know, but in the way that people who are dead and gone are worshipped. I don't think he's turned up out of the blue since I was in my teens, so . . ." She put her mug on the fender and cupped her mother's face. "Have you been dreading telling me? How long have you known?"

"Natalie's letter came two days ago. I didn't know how you would feel about it. And I certainly did not know how I felt about it. I don't think I believed it. Not properly."

"Oh, darling Mum! I didn't think . . . I didn't know! Don't tell me you still love him — are carrying a torch for him? Will thought you might be falling for Miles Thorough-good!"

They both laughed at that but Binnie did not answer Dorrie's question. Instead she took the hands so gently holding her face, dropped a kiss on them and stood up with a groan.

"You'd better see the letter. Then you'll know as much as I know. You might even think along the same lines as I have. Anyway, here it is."

Dorrie fingered the letter. "I never liked her. Is it catty?"

"Not a bit. Rather . . . well, almost . . . sweet. Really."

They both laughed. Binnie felt a surge of gratitude towards Natalie for making it possible to laugh about anything — even Theo's death.

Dorrie read and reread, then put the letter down and stared into the fire. "I see what you mean. It's direct. But not catty." She sighed deeply. "He didn't deserve to be wiped out so unexpectedly, did he?"

"That's why accidents are so frightening. They're never expected."

"I thought he'd want us again in his old age." Dorrie laughed. "I had this sort of dream — nightmare, probably. Looking after him. Hearing him say soppy things about what he'd missed in his life. Will. Me. I'm such an idiot!" Her laugh turned into a dry sob and she held up her hand. "It's all right, Mum. I'm not going to cry. Just at the moment life seems rather . . . ironic."

Binnie nodded. "It never rains but it pours. I thought my only problem was Danny-boy. I haven't told you. I just got to him in time. He was walking down the slipway. Up to his waist."

Dorrie was wide-eyed. "My God. That outgoing tide can be awful. So that's why his clothes were in the dryer." Binnie nodded. Dorrie said, "Has he told you why he did it?"

"He was paddling, apparently. He's done it before. Here. In Cherrington." She sighed. "He's totally confused about the past. But he seems so much better since he's slept and eaten and Gabriel got him in the bath."

"What are you going to do with him?"

Binnie shrugged. "Don't know. I'm far more concerned with what *we're* going to do." She picked up the letter. "I had a suggestion and, after your car going up in smoke, we might be able to . . . stretch the idea into something possible." She took a deep breath. "Dorrie, I want to go to Trapdoor Island. You see what Natalie says about it. I can look on the trip as a kind of inspection. Think what we're going to do with it. We've got some money to play with, by the sound of things —"

"It's yours, Mum."

"Not at all. It's ours. And it means I can afford to go." She hesitated. "I want to go, Dorrie. I want to see if I can lay my husband — your father — to rest. I don't expect you know what I'm talking about —"

"Yes. Yes, I do. I can remember two, perhaps three, visits from Dad. We always expected more. Now that can't happen." She leaned across and took her mother's hands. "Darling, won't it make things worse? And what about your job?"

"If I can't take a month off to see to my affairs . . ."

"Yes. Quite. Of course. And underneath Barbara's iron exterior lurks a soft centre. I think!" They both laughed again. Then Dorrie sobered and said, "It would get you away from the mess I've brought to the cottage."

"And leave you with it well and truly on your shoulders. That won't do." Binnie shook her head decisively. "We go together. You, Gabriel and me. There are flights from Bristol airport. What do you say? Quite seriously, it would do us all good. A holiday, darling. We might get the place up together enough to let it out next summer. Or to stay there ourselves."

Dorrie's brown eyes, so like her mother's, became intent as she thought about it. After a long pause, during which Binnie felt her idea grow and take root, Dorrie said slowly, "I have to admit it sounds simply marvellous. I mean — I'd love to run away somewhere, anyway. But we need a reason that has nothing to do with Gabriel's problem." She smiled suddenly. "That's what Dad's given us. A really good reason to get away. Right away."

"So he has!" Binnie smiled too. "How marvellous! He might not have left a will — perhaps he knew that Natalie would deal with everything properly — but this is the next best thing! Time . . . he's giving us time. Together." She put the letter on the mantelpiece and sat down. "What will Gabriel say?"

42

"What do you think?" Dorrie turned as the door opened and the two men came in. "Let's ask him now!" She jumped up and held out her hands. "Darling, what would you say to spending some time on an island far away from arsonists and card players and — and everything?"

Gabriel was taken aback. "It's all right, Dorrie. There's no-one out there. They've shot their bolt — if it was them. We're not going to be frightened off like that anyway!"

"Answer my question!" she demanded, drawing him to the fire. "Sit down, get warm and think about it! My father has died and left Mum his island — yes, he owned an island! And Mum has to go and look at it. Find out about . . . things." She crouched in front of him. "I can get special leave for this, darling. It'll be marvellous! An adventure!"

"You never mention your father."

"We never saw him. He married someone else and then found another someone else and then . . . Anyway, there was an accident and he was drowned. And apparently he always said that the island would go to Mum. Oh, Gabe! Come on! I thought you'd be so excited!"

"I am . . ." Gabriel looked more dazed than excited. "It's just that everything is happening at once." He looked over his shoulder. "And there's Dan. Can he come with us?"

Binnie said swiftly, "Dan has his own plans, for goodness' sake! He's come to look at Cherrington and remember old times."

Dan said nothing. The sudden silence was broken by the bell on the front door. They were all immediately alert. It was Dan who turned and opened it. A uniformed policeman stood there.

"May I come in, sir? It's about the fire earlier this afternoon. The fire chief suspects arson and I would like to ask you a few questions."

They all relaxed. Binnie stood up and pulled out one of the kitchen chairs but the constable would not sit down. He took their names.

"And you are Mrs Cash's daughter, and it was your car?" he said to Dorrie. She nodded and the constable looked at Gabriel. "And you are Miss Cash's partner? And you, sir?" He turned to Dan.

Dan said calmly, "Daniel Casey. A family friend."

"You are staying here, Mr Casey?"

"We're planning a holiday," Daniel explained.

The policeman nodded and made another note, then turned to Binnie. "It's a brief visit, Mrs Cash. We've had a spate of vandalism in the town but nothing quite so aggressive as this. And up here — well, it could have been an attempt to fire the woods." He smiled. "Luckily the miserable weather was on your side."

Binnie nodded. Vandals sounded almost innocent in the circumstances.

Gabriel was similarly reassured. "What did I tell you?" he said to Dorrie. "She thought she was being targeted, Constable!"

Dorrie tried to laugh. "Not really. It's just — my car was almost brand new."

Gabriel said, "It's insured, darling! No need to worry!"

The constable nodded reassuringly. "The investigator will be up tomorrow, miss. He might turn up something that will help us. These hooligans have got to be stopped before there's a nasty accident."

He asked them whether they needed anyone from the local Victim Support group. "As you're a family together, all adults, I don't imagine you will need an outside organization, though they are very helpful."

They assured him they were fine, he shook his head to the proffered tea and left.

Dorrie looked at Gabriel. "Did you believe what you were saying?"

"I've got an open mind, love. You yourself told me the blokes who called were civilized. I can't see them following you up here to torch your car, can you?"

"Yes. Yes, I can, actually. They did not speak. I think their silence was . . . menacing." She shook her head. "You know very well it was them."

Binnie said, "Anyway, it doesn't matter, does it? Not if we're going to Trapdoor." She glanced at Daniel. "A family holiday. That was well said, Daniel. And you are sounding much better."

Dan sat down and removed his borrowed boots. "I feel much better." He looked up at them all. "Listen. I don't know how I've landed here among you. I don't know what sort of trouble you're in. And I'm so sorry you've had this loss. But . . . will you take me with you? There's got to be a reason for me being . . . alive. Perhaps this is it."

Everyone looked at Binnie and he said to her, "Please. You must have saved my life for something."

"You were paddling," she reminded him. "And you know the area —"

"Binnie. I don't really *know* anything. I was on a train from London. I wanted to come to Cherrington. I remembered things when I got here. The roads . . . the way to the sea . . . the fast tides . . . nothing besides that. I thought I might know you, actually. And you might know me. But everything before the train is . . . grey. Foggy."

Gabriel said, "You mean you've lost your memory? You've got amnesia?"

"I suppose that's what I mean. I don't know that either. But I've got memories now. Cherrington. The sea and the slipway. You and Binnie and Dorrie and this house. And the car going up in flames. I'm part of something again. It feels right and proper."

Dorrie said, "We can't take you, Dan. Surely you can see that? If you know nothing about yourself — well, we know less. You could be on the run. You've nothing but your clothes, I take it? Mum emptied your pockets when she put your clothes in the wash. There was an old wallet with a few pounds in change. No return railway ticket. No identification —"

Binnie interrupted. "Darling, you can see he's not a criminal! And he's right, I did feel I might have known him at some time in my life. But Dorrie is right too, Daniel. We can't take you. In a way, we're on the run, not you. As Gabe and Dorrie are staying with me tonight, you can stay too. But tomorrow we'll have to

46

find lodgings for you and maybe some work." She looked at him. "I'm sorry, Daniel. You must understand."

He visibly drooped. "Of course. It was just . . . it sounded . . . interesting." He glanced at the window. "Have you got any outside security lighting?"

Binnie went into the hall to switch it on. She didn't like it — it made her feel like a sitting duck.

He said behind her, "Perhaps that's not such a good idea. I'll sleep in the chair. I can keep an eye on things. Surely if anyone tried something else they would need a torch. Shall we switch it off?"

There was more discussion on that, but it was finally decided that Daniel's suggestion was a good one. Binnie went to the kitchen and began to make sandwiches. Gabriel built up the fire. Dorrie fetched tea things. They sat together as if they were a family. Binnie told them what she could remember of the Skall Islands. She said she would see Lady Barbara tomorrow morning. Dorrie nodded; she would see her librarian and arrange for special leave.

Binnie said thoughtfully, "Perhaps the Thoroughgoods would take you on, Daniel. How would you feel about cleaning car parks and shopping malls? Or helping in the grounds? Are you up to it?"

Dan tried to grin. "I'll find out. You've got enough on your combined plates — please don't worry about me."

Gabriel pulled a face. "You sound like my aunt, who is a born martyr! Come on, talk to us. See if anything comes back. You must have been ill. Or had an almighty shock. There must have been a moment when everything kind of packed up!"

"I suppose so." There was a waiting silence and Dan began to tell them — reluctantly — about walking from Temple Meads railway station to the bus station and waiting . . . the driver of the car who offered him a lift . . . "How did he know I wanted to go to Cherrington?" he asked.

"You were waiting at the Cherrington bus stop," Binnie said. "The man who gave you the lift was Miles Thoroughgood. His parents run the cleaning business and if someone doesn't turn up for work, Miles fills in."

"It's generally you who fills in!" Dorrie said to her mother.

Binnie told Daniel about the Thoroughgoods and he said suddenly, "It was old Sir George in my day."

Everyone stared at him and he stared back.

"Perhaps I am meant to work for them," he said. "Perhaps they hold some of my memories."

Binnie said, "I remember Sir George. He shot rabbits and anything else that was edible. He started doing it in the war to keep plenty of meat on the table for the staff. And he was still doing it a week before he died."

Dan said hesitantly, "Didn't he tan the rabbit skins himself?"

"I believe he did!" Binnie smiled. "I'll speak to Lady T tomorrow. I think the Thoroughgoods may well supply you with some memories!"

CHAPTER
FOUR

Binnie slept with her curtains open that night, convinced that Daniel would fall asleep in the chair and rather hoping that he would. She knew only too well that if he had turned up at any other time she would have befriended him without hesitation. Her usual protective instincts were there, though overworked with what was happening to Dorrie and Gabriel.

Her tired mind pushed aside everything that had happened that day and concentrated on the arrangements for visiting Trapdoor Island. And on Theo. The ache of there being no Theo in the world threatened to rise up and consume her, and she had to concentrate hard on a mental checklist that began "Ring airport and bed and breakfast at Keyhole Island" and ended, almost as an afterthought, "Ring Will. After all, it's his island too". She went through it all again and inserted "See solicitor". It was probably at this point she fell asleep.

In fact, against many odds, all of them slept that night. Dan woke at first light, made a hasty patrol around the cottage and found nothing. Arriving at the front door again, he stood inhaling the damp air and surveying the bare bones of the Smart car. His conscious memory was so short that he could recall every detail of his life since he began that long walk up the hill yesterday morning; before that there were only muzzy recollections of the train and the walk across the city to the bus station. He had accomplished that without apparent volition; his legs had taken him involuntarily down the station approach and past the back of all the big department stores to the roundabout and the underpass and . . . the bus station. How had that happened? Would it have continued to happen if Miles Thoroughgood had not driven him into Cherrington? And if it had, and he had arrived in the afternoon instead of the morning, there would have been no tide offering a paddle — more than a paddle. And certainly no Binnie to rescue him from . . . from what? Would his legs have continued to move through the thick mud and into the Bristol Channel until the water covered him over and he drowned?

He lowered his head and shook it, afraid that the world would begin to slide sideways as it had before. But it stayed where it was: the encroaching woods, Binnie's old car safely outside the door, Dorrie's a burned-out wreck. And he found what he had been looking for inside his head: a tiny sliver of memory that had been knocked out by the explosion. He closed his eyes for a moment and went back to that hour after lunch . . . Binnie and Dorrie had been at the kitchen end of the living room and he had pretended to doze. Through half-closed eyes he had watched the two women, mother and daughter, so alike. But it was Binnie he wanted to remember. He had tried, consciously and carefully, to register every detail of Binnie. Already he knew she would send him away; he accepted that just as he had accepted everything that had happened that day, but he was desperate not to forget her. Why was she prematurely white-haired? Her face was still young, her brown eyes bright and full of humour. She had the look of a Regency beauty — unfashionably small mouth, rounded chin, rather patrician nose and a neck that curved above the collar of her sweater so that it was a feature in itself. Above all, she had an air of capability. She could cope. She had two children and — it seemed — no husband. So she had coped; for how long? He had watched her transfer left-over vegetables into a plastic box and walk across to the fridge . . . He found himself thanking God that she had been there when he went into the sea. And then thinking . . . how wonderful it would be to be part of her life; to look up at almost any time and watch her moving and breathing and just *being*.

He had glanced at Gabriel then, afraid that his errant thought might have shown itself in some way. But Gabriel really was asleep, feet on the fender, chin on his chest, looking good even in such an unbecoming pose — easy to see why Binnie's daughter, so neat with her glossy brown ponytail, had fallen for him — his blond hair drooped over one eye as if he had arranged it in the mirror above the fireplace. Daniel let his gaze lift to check on the availability of Gabriel's reflection and it had been then — just before the explosion — that he had seen it. The memory began to solidify . . . the mirror was reflecting the watery sun, beaming through the gap in the woods, but on the edge of the brightness for a split second, a figure had appeared. And then had gone again.

It had been a subliminal moment, unregistered until Daniel stood staring at the wrecked car. He pinned it down quickly, afraid it would disappear with all the other ephemera floating just out of reach. There had been a figure. Definitely. A male figure. And not young either. A large man. In a suit. And then the explosion and the possibility of a second explosion and engulfing flames . . .

He frowned, then turned and went indoors. No need to tell Binnie about this. She had enough on her plate. Besides, she knew — the three of them knew — that the torching of the car was no act of idle vandalism. Dan went to the kitchen end of the living room and switched on the kettle.

Dorrie woke in her usual position: some time during the night Gabriel had put his head on her shoulder and she had encircled him with her arms and held him protectively for quite some time. Her right shoulder was numb. She shifted slightly and kissed the top of his head. She thought of her father and wondered whether her mother had felt this agony of anxious loving. And if she had, how she had gone on living when he had left her for Natalie. When Natalie had visited them, some years later, Will had called her Nasty Natalie to her face. And she had been rather nasty, but not to them. She had saved all her bile for the new girl, whatever her name was. Violetta. Violetta from Naples. Dorrie smiled into Gabriel's fair hair. She and Will had been nasty too. And determined to show Daddy just what they thought of him. And then he had turned up with a car full of presents and taken them off to Trapdoor, where he had taught them to snorkel through the wrecks among the razor rocks. And they had been happy. How on earth could they have been happy with a man who had betrayed them? Twice. Probably oftener, if the truth were known.

And now she was going back and there would be no Daddy.

Gabriel stirred within the circle of her arm. "Hon?" he said sleepily.

She discovered she was weeping into his hair. He pulled her down and wrapped her tightly in his arms and told her how sorry he was, and that once they were away from here everything would be all right. And she let herself be comforted and thought bleakly that there was not much hope of a future with Gabriel. He would leave her just as her father had left her.

She whispered, "Darling. I'm going to make some tea. And have a shower. Try to get another hour's sleep." She kissed him as she would a child, tucked the duvet around his shoulders and went downstairs.

Straight after breakfast, Binnie drove Dorrie to her house to pack up her things, then went on to the Manor and her little office next to the gatehouse.

The paperwork was easy. The accounts, the correspondence with the history society who had access to the archives, the appointments — they could all be done by Miles. Binnie knew that the liaison work she did between visitors and family would be missed. She left lists of schools and private visitors for the next month and added the rota of voluntary stewards who took over during the summer months when the gardens were opened. One of them might be glad to fill in for Binnie on a part-time basis.

Then Lady Barbara arrived and went into her office upstairs from where she organized the considerable business of Thoroughgood Cleaners. Binnie followed her up and stood just inside the door.

"Sit down, my dear." Lady Barbara removed her suit jacket and donned an ancient cardigan. "Miles insisted on doing the bus station again so he's gone back to bed. He tells me you are overworked and underpaid and should not have to pitch in every time someone rings in with an excuse, so please don't stand there looking guilty."

Binnie took the chair on the other side of the desk and looked guiltier still. She was well aware that in spite of opening the house and gardens, the family could never have managed financially without Lady Barbara's cleaning business. She bulldozed her way through every difficulty, and was quite capable of donning overalls and joining her motley staff when it was necessary.

She treated Binnie to her frosty smile and sat back. "It's not the first time Miles has mentioned your position here, Binnie. You know we're grateful. But that's not enough, and now that we're established, I think an extra member of the administrative staff would be an excellent thing. As Miles pointed out, if you were ill, we would find it difficult to manage."

Binnie cleared her throat; there was nothing for it but to blurt out her plans in one fell swoop.

"As a matter of fact . . ." she had been instructed years ago to refer to the Thoroughgoods by their first names but could never quite manage it with Lady Barbara, ". . . I'm here now to ask for a month's special leave. My husband has died in an accident and it turns out that —"

"My dear girl! When did you hear about this?"

"A few days ago. I couldn't bring myself . . . I hadn't told my daughter, actually. There are complications and, as you know, I have had very little to do with him. But it seems there is some property." Her voice became hoarse. "My daughter and I have to go to the Skalls. The islands. To — to sort out . . . what is left."

"Of course. Of course." Lady Barbara was all energy. "You can fly, you know. There is a Friday flight, I believe. We can telephone. Find out. And it seems almost providential that we have this new man starting next week. I believe in people jumping into the deep end, as you well know, Binnie. You learn a job by doing it — there's no other way. Miles thought you would be here to give the new man some training. But this is much better." She nodded. "Better for you too. You've always been one to get on with things, my dear. That's the way to do it — we both know that."

Binnie began to feel she was being summarily ejected from her little office and her telephone.

As if reading that thought, Lady Barbara said, "It will be waiting for you when you want it back. But feel free of all of it for however long you need. I'll come down in a minute and sort everything out with you, then you can go." Unexpectedly, she added, "It must be hard, Binnie. After all, while there was life there was always hope. And now he's gone." She drew a breath. "But it means you can start something else. Something new. Look at it like that."

It sounded like an order and Binnie smiled obediently and stood up. It was when Lady Barbara reached across the desk and shook her hand that she felt dismissed.

She said hesitantly, "There is one thing. Did Miles tell you about the man he brought into Cherrington yesterday — before chapel?"

Lady Barbara smiled even more frostily. "He did mention it."

"I found him on the beach. In a poor state. He will need a roof and could pay for it with a job. I wondered whether Mr Parkes could do with some help."

Lady Barbara huffed at that. "We've had your down-and-outs here before, Binnie. They don't always . . . fit in."

"This one is different. He needs time. He needs to be outside. Perhaps two weeks? Three?"

"Send him along and let Parkes look him over. I'm not promising a thing. But there's always a lot to do at this time of year and if Parkes likes the look of him we'll see. Is that good enough?"

"Of course. Thank you."

She went back for Dorrie and then home, where the fire chief had returned with the investigator. They were both looking around the charred bits of Dorrie's car. It was all very discreet, but the fire chief said that there were no signs of the suspected firework that the vandals might have thrown.

"It's either a fairly sophisticated job or an electrical fault. But in that case it would need some kind of ignition." He looked at Dorrie. "Nobody with a grudge?"

She shook her head. They did not need more questioning sessions to delay their plans.

In the early afternoon, Dorrie took Binnie's car and drove into Bristol. She intended to give just a few days' notice. "If they can't accept that, Mum, I shall simply leave — walk out," she announced.

Binnie said nothing; surely it would not come to that. Dorrie was valued as a librarian. She pushed that thought aside too and told Dan what had happened at the Manor.

"It's such a small set-up as far as manpower goes," she explained. "Nobody has any idea how hard they work. And they're not working for themselves really, they're working for the estate — to preserve it for — for —"

"Posterity," Dan supplied gently. "It's all right, Binnie. For some reason, I know about the Manor. I have a feeling for it. If this head gardener chappie will take me on, I'll be all right. You can cross me off your worry list!"

She looked at him, surprised that he knew how she felt. She said, "I know you wanted to come with us, Daniel. But this is better — for you. You came here for a reason and you need to stay and try to discover what that reason is. If you're still here when we get back, we'll talk."

He nodded. "Thanks. And thanks for not trying to make me talk before now. I couldn't have done it — it's all rather hopeless, I know that. But this place . . . even these people . . . there's just some small kernel . . . I'm sorry," he tried to laugh, "I'm losing it again!"

"Then put it to one side. It's waiting there somewhere for you. Meanwhile we should talk about the near future. Will you come down with me this afternoon and meet everyone? Parkes will seem difficult but I think he will take to you. Miles is the only son and probably the only sane human being there. Lady Barbara has taken on another staff member for the organization side — I rather think he will do my job. Otherwise the open-house side of things relies on a team of volunteers. And outside help is seasonal . . ."

Dan nodded every time she paused. It was as if he knew the set-up already and was being reminded of it very gradually. She regretted that she would not be here to see him recover his elusive past. But at least she could see him installed in Parkes's rambling cottage.

They walked down through the village and, to his intense embarrassment, bought him some clothes.

"I can pay you for these when I get my first salary cheque!" He tried to make light of it, laughing at his pretentious choice of words, and Binnie reassured him by telling him about her "prospects".

"The really good thing," she said seriously, as they reached the gatehouse, "is that you are already so much better in yourself. I can't tell you how ill you were when you arrived. It was frightening. I still think I should have called an ambulance."

"Thank you for not doing that. It would have started again. The whole thing: hospitals, talking, searching . . ."

She frowned as she went up the stairs. It was all very well feeling a kind of kinship with this man, but she did not know him and it seemed he did not know himself.

Lady Barbara, however, took to him instantly in her aristocratic way. She managed to question him directly yet never personally: "Do you know a weed from a flower?" "Can you work for all the daylight hours there are?" And he answered honestly to both questions, "I don't know. I think I can and I want to work here. Very much." She made chewing movements while she looked at him consideringly, then said, "See what Parkes has to say, then move down. He'll expect you to skivvy for him in the cottage at first. That's his way of making you feel at home." She did not smile, but Daniel grinned broadly at that and nodded as if he already knew the old gardener.

As they reached the door, Lady Barbara said abruptly, "Would you be willing to do a stint at one of our cleaning sites? It's either during the night or very early in the morning."

Daniel seemed to hesitate but then said, "Of course."

Lady Barbara stopped chewing and said, "Then even if Parkes doesn't approve of you, you can stay."

But Parkes, in his normal, curmudgeonly way, seemed to approve. They found him in one of the greenhouses, potting up geranium cuttings. He grunted a greeting and said, "I've heard about you. If I'm murdered in my bed, everyone will know who did it, so I reckon I'm safe there. And if Mrs Cash says you're a worker, then you're a worker. Can you do this?" He held up his next cutting. Dan looked at the row of pots and nodded. Parkes said, "Good. Then Mrs Cash will show you where you're going to lay your head. Soon as you've sorted yourself, come back here and take over. I want to put the mower over that front lawn."

Binnie told him that she was taking a month's special leave and she hoped everything would work out. Parkes made grumbling sounds in his throat.

On the way to the cottage she reassured Daniel that the sound had tokened a welcome. She herself felt deeply grateful to Parkes who, after all, was the one who would have to share his home with this newcomer. She found the door key beneath the mat and took Dan quickly through the house. As usual it was pin neat, tea-making things next to the cooker, newspaper on the arm of a chair. Upstairs were three small bedrooms, two of them obviously prepared for visitors.

"Parkes relies on seasonal help," Binnie explained. "As I do for stewards in the Manor house. This time of year, you can choose which room you like!" She was foolishly cheery, trying to override any sense of desertion. It was ridiculous; Daniel had been a crazy stranger yesterday and today he was a friend. But she had family and other friends and he did not.

Then he said, "Looks as if I've fallen on my feet." The words jarred and for a moment she wondered whether his strangeness — the memory loss, the dizziness — was assumed. But it was only a moment.

"Parkes will expect a lot," she warned. "So will Lady Barbara. Between them you might well loose that footing."

He looked at her. "Please don't worry. You've been marvellous and I'll never be able to thank you for it. But you probably realize that the sort of problems I may well have here are nothing. I want to work hard. Then I can stop thinking about what might come out of the — the *fog*." He grinned suddenly. "It's what you do, isn't it? You keep busy."

Binnie smiled wryly in acknowledgement of this. And then they were back outside and she was on the track to the gatehouse.

Daniel tucked the key back under the mat and said, "I'll get straight back to those cuttings and settle in later on. Good luck with your island. And . . . thank you."

She turned at the gatehouse and looked back, but he was gone. And there was no time for any kind of regret. So much to do. She would have to try to see Will tomorrow. She would ring him this evening. Perhaps Gabriel would phone the airport and book their flights. Please God they could get on one this coming Friday.

Dorrie had won them one week's grace with the gambling debts. But then what would happen? Binnie shut away that thought too and shortened her steps as she began to climb the hill.

CHAPTER
FIVE

They arrived on Keyhole Island the following Friday, 12 September.

Keyhole, pronounced "Keele" by the locals, had an airstrip, a primary school, a cottage hospital, several churches and pubs, and a harbour that would take the *Queen of Skalls*, as well as a flotilla of fishing boats, luggers, cabin cruisers and anything else that would float. Shops and a huddle of houses surrounded the harbour. Beyond that, the big houses and holiday villas were tucked into folds of the small hills, out of reach of the prevailing south-westerlies. Others were perched defiantly on exposed viewpoints where they could see other islands studding the glass-green sea. Until just before the Second World War, fifteen of the islands had been inhabited — there were over fifty in all. Now just a handful were occupied, scraping a living from flower-growing and fishing. Two of them had been taken by would-be self-sufficiency groups. Postern Island was an outcrop of Keyhole and sported a luxury hotel, which had been for sale two years ago and still was. It was tiny and charming, but most twitchers and tourists tended to stay at Keyhole, where the pubs and bed-and-breakfast accommodation were much cheaper.

The local post office, which doubled up as the tourist centre, had given Binnie two addresses and she had plumped for Mrs Govern at Harbour Lights, Ditchdrain Street. Half-board, two bedrooms and a bathroom came to sixty pounds a night for the three of them. The hotel on Postern Island was sixty pounds per night per person. Binnie's solicitors had been able to tell her that Theo's property in Cornwall might realize five hundred thousand. But, of course, it might not. Binnie was cautious about anything to do with her ex-husband, and she budgeted low.

When the local taxi brought them from the little airstrip down to the precipitous Ditchdrain Street and she met Mrs Govern, Binnie knew she had chosen well. Mrs Govern was wire thin and whipped around the house, setting ornaments right as she went, popping books on to their shelves, shovelling newspapers into acceptable piles. Harbour Lights was built into the cliff, its frontage four storeys high, its rear just one. Mrs Govern dealt with its many steps by doing at least two jobs at the same time.

"You're at the top I'm afraid, my dears," she said, taking two cases from Gabriel forcibly and leading her guests to the first flight of stairs. "But there's another bathroom up there, which is handy. And, o'course the view always pleases the visitors." They reached the first landing and she indicated the window overlooking the sea. It was a still, grey day — the flight over had been perfect, with views of the islands far below. Gabriel reckoned he had seen a giant ray through the clear water. Far below them, the *Queen* was being unloaded at the longer of the quays. "About time," Mrs Govern commented as she started on the next flight of stairs. "The shop been out of sugar for near on a week." She polished the banister with one elbow and half turned. "You chose a good day, I reckon. No flights since last weekend."

Gabriel grinned up at her. "I knew this was my lucky place," he said. "I've got a feeling about Lady Luck, you know. I can tell when she's around."

Mrs Govern shook her head and hoisted one of the cases on to the next landing. "We make our own luck, I always say." She left the case conspicuously where it was as she started up to the top floor; Gabriel picked it up and marched stolidly behind her.

They had the top floor to themselves and as one of the bedrooms was the single storey at the back, they also had direct access via an exterior staircase to the street. "Fire regulations, you know," commented Mrs Govern.

Binnie nodded, smiling. The sense of being suspended in space in these rooms was amazing. It was odd to open the door at one end of the landing and discover that you could walk outside.

She said on an impulse, "When I was here before we went straight to Trapdoor Island by boat. I've never seen Keyhole."

"You've been to the Skalls before?"

"Yes. My husband — my ex-husband — inherited Trapdoor from his grandfather. He grew up there."

"Would that be Theo Cash?" Mrs Govern turned to Dorrie. "And he's your father? I thought I recognized you. He brought you to watch the gig racing when you were just a mite. And you too." She nodded at Gabriel.

Dorrie smiled. "No. Gabriel is my partner. My brother, Will, was with us. I am so surprised you remember us. I was ten and Will was seven. He's at university now."

"Don't know about your brother but you haven't changed. Not one bit. 'Cept you're taller and your hair is out of your eyes and you're tidier by a long chalk! But you haven't changed, not really."

They all laughed. Gabriel said, "Did she really used to be a tomboy, Mrs Govern? I can't imagine that."

"I only saw her the once. She looked like a tomboy but I don't know."

Dorrie laughed again. "No. I wasn't like that. Not really. Dad just didn't bother keeping us clean and tidy, so we weren't!"

"And how is your father? He hasn't been to Trapdoor for some time, as far as I know."

Binnie said swiftly, "He was in an accident. Swept off a boat. He died, Mrs Govern. That's why we're here. We have to . . . sort things out."

"Oh, my dear life! I'm that sorry, Mrs Cash. I really am. I know you were separated . . . and he married again . . ." She floundered to a stop, then concluded bravely, "You must miss him, all the same."

Binnie nodded, suddenly unable to speak. She was tired; the last four days had been busy and they had all lived with their chins on their shoulders. The police had taken no further interest in the arson and they had left the wreck of Dorrie's car in case it was needed for evidence. It had been a constant reminder of their brush with Gabriel's "debt collectors".

Dorrie said honestly, "We don't know how we feel, actually. We've come to Trapdoor to find out."

"Aaah. That's sad. But it makes sense. Poor man. He loved the sea but she got him in the end." Mrs Govern turned to leave them, then added, "I'll put a tray of tea in the downstairs room. My husband is doing some carpentry over at the Postern Hotel. We have high tea at six and a bit of supper before we go to bed. Will that be all right?"

They said in unison, "Marvellous!" And then laughed because it was so good to have left all their worries behind in just three hours.

The Governs proved excellent hosts. Mr Govern was electrician and plumber as well as carpenter to Keyhole. He was as stocky as his wife was skinny, with dark eyes and thinning grey hair. Binnie judged them to be a little older than she was — not much, still plenty of energy. He exclaimed with surprise and then shock as she told him that their new guests belonged to Theo Cash; and that Theo was dead.

"Dear God, we had no idea. He would be coming over about now to stock up for winter. I'm that sorry, Mrs Cash. And your daddy too, young lady. That is mortal sad."

Binnie murmured something and Dorrie said in a strong voice, "It's the way he would have wanted to die, Mr Govern. And we hardly knew him. That's one of the reasons we're here."

Everyone nodded; Mrs Govern whipped in with a tray of food and there came a call from the front door.

"That'll be Alf," Mr Govern announced, and went into the hall. Mrs Govern tutted but produced another plate and some cutlery.

"'Tis Matthew's cousin," she explained. "When he's late after work, he drops in for supper with us." She leaned towards Binnie. "He's a little bit . . . strange, Mrs Cash. Just take it as it comes. Heart of gold."

Binnie found herself shaking hands with someone who certainly looked strange but otherwise appeared to be friendly, warm and completely normal. He was short and as stocky as his cousin, but the resemblance stopped there. His head seemed to be set in front of his shoulders so that he was in a permanent attitude of listening concentration. And on the head was a mass of grey hair. It sprang even from his ears and met his beard so that his face twinkled from a ring of fuzz and made him look like one of Snow White's dwarfs.

He told them that his name was Alfred Trevose and he ran the school boat for the primary school children from the outlying islands.

"I land them on the short pier about half-past eight in the morning. Then I pick 'em up again between three thirty and four of an afternoon." He beamed at everyone as he made himself comfortable in the chair Mrs Govern pulled out for him. "It's a job after my own heart. No day the same as the last or the next. Lots of talk and news and laughs . . . and cries sometimes." He turned down his mouth, then upended it in an enormous grin. "And I'm always next to the sea. That's what is important to me."

They ate baked mackerel and mashed potatoes, and were "happy and chatty", as Alf said. He sobered when he heard why they were here and then brightened immediately.

"I've got tomorrow free, it being a Saturday. Just a few folk I've said I'll ferry between the islands. I'll take you to Trapdoor. You might as well get started straight away, find out about the house and the landing places — there's only the one — and what sort of supplies you might need if you want to stay over."

They were overwhelmed. Binnie said, "That is so good of you. You're right, the sooner we see it the better." Suddenly, now it was upon her, Binnie was almost nervous about revisiting the island. She smiled at Mr Govern's cousin and was reassured by his gaze, which — as Dorrie said later — was very twinkly. "Thank you, Mr Trevose."

"You call me Alf, Mrs Cash. Everyone do call me Alf. Even the children."

"Thank you, Alf," Binnie said. But she noticed that neither of the Governs offered a forename, and felt shy about offering hers. After all, she wasn't a real Skallion. She said instead, "My daughter is Dorrie. And her partner is Gabriel."

"And there's a boy too," Mr Govern put in. "Maggie were saying, he's at university."

"It's what the young lady was saying," Mrs Govern put in hastily. "We weren't talking about you, Mrs Cash."

Dorrie laughed. "We don't mind at all, Mrs Govern! Nothing much to talk about. We're fairly boring!"

Gabriel looked about to protest and Dorrie gripped his arm hard. Mr Govern smiled across the table at her. "We're the same. Most ordinary folk are, I think. Now Alf here, he's a different breed. Nothing boring about our Alf. He can talk to the sea and everything what's in it, I reckon!"

Alf did not enlarge on this but laughed and winked at Binnie. Mrs Govern was behind him serving the mackerel and she rolled her eyes and moved her serving spoon in a large circle just above Alf's head.

The next morning Binnie stood at her bedroom window high above the harbour and watched Alf leave at seven thirty. He had told them his first port of call was Postern Island, only a giant's stride away from Keyhole. He would be dropping Matthew Govern off there and picking up two passengers, and then would be off to Oriel and Portcullis Islands.

Binnie stood for some time looking down as the harbour started to come to life. Fishing boats were already chugging towards the other large island, which was Oriel. From there they would be going further west, chasing ray and ling. It was a typical September morning, golden and soft, the sea a myriad pixels of light. She opened the window and hung out, trying to see beyond the pier. The coastline dipped into a long bay and cut off the view. She closed the window. She was smiling.

★ ★ ★

70

On the way out Alf told them about his wife, Marigold. She could sing. Like a mermaid. In fact, there were times when Alf thought she *was* a mermaid and had come to live with him because he could understand her.

"How do you mean?" asked Gabriel curiously, sitting on the engine housing and leaning forward to hear above the splash of the water.

Alf turned the wheel slightly so that they met the tide head on. Binnie was standing holding the cowling and watching Dorrie, who already looked ill.

"Well, she said she weren't going to speak to me no more." He grinned. "Like Maggie says to Matt at times. But that's diff'rent. 'Cos Marigold talks to me by singing."

Gabriel said incredulously, "She sings everything to you? Like pass the salt and how are you?" Binnie flashed him a warning glance. She knew that Alf was not joking about this.

"She 'asn't sung those things, no. But everything she needs to say she sings." Alf's grin became a smile of contentment. "It's lovely. She sings all the news of the day. Sunrise and sunset, rain and storm. She sings them to me. Not many men can say that, can they?"

"They certainly cannot," agreed Gabriel, making faces at Dorrie.

Dorrie ignored him and managed to clap her hands with delight at the idea. Binnie smiled and joined in.

On that first trip, Alf took them from the bottom to the top of Trapdoor Island. He described it as a leg of lamb, the shank rising out of the water sheer and high, the long bone providing a spit of sand on which a boat could get close enough to be pulled up on to the beach. Neither Binnie nor Dorrie had thought of it like that before and they smiled at each other.

Alf launched a dinghy from the cover of the engine hatch and rowed them to the beach, pulling the loaded boat over the sand without apparent effort. Then he handed out the women with old-fashioned courtesy and pulled the dinghy further up, out of reach of the incoming tide.

The two women stood and stared at the slope that led to the summit, gentle at first, then rising almost sheer to the top of the "shank". Binnie felt as if all her perceptions were opening to the familiarity of the place. The smell of seaweed, prevalent throughout Keyhole, was surely stronger here. And before she trod it, the sandy path, winding between outcrops of rock, invited her feet to find familiar footholds. She knew what a long mile it was before the path disappeared among enormous granite boulders, which spiked the sky like battlements. For a moment an aching nostalgia threatened to bring her to tears. Then Dorrie's hand was in hers.

"D'you realize, Mum, we've never been here together? We both know it, but we haven't got a shared knowledge. Isn't that the strangest thing?"

Binnie nodded. "That wasn't Dad's doing. Not really. I had to move back to the mainland when you were on the way."

She did not add that Theo had always found an excuse for her to stay there until after Will's birth, when he had informed her he had "fallen in love again". During Natalie's reign, Binnie had gone back to her home, Cherrington, taken a flat and the work with the Thoroughgoods. When they had suggested she live in the gamekeeper's cottage she was overjoyed. She made a home there, and with Will and Dorrie coming and going with their friends, it had been fun. Nearly always, anyway. It hadn't been too good when Theo fetched the children and took them over to the island for the summer. Binnie had had a foretaste then of how cut off and lonely the gamekeeper's cottage really was. Perhaps Theo had felt the same about Trapdoor; it was only when he returned the children that she learned he was now on his own. Natalie had left him when he took up with Violetta.

Binnie sighed and glanced at her daughter. "What do you think?" she asked.

Dorrie shrugged. "At this precise moment, not a lot." She smiled wryly. "To be honest, Mum, I had forgotten what a long boat ride it is. I'm feeling a bit sick, actually."

Alf and Gabriel came up behind them. "You'll walk off the sickness, m'dear," Alf said. "It's quite a tramp to the top of the cliff. But from there you can see the Shark's Teeth very well." He glanced at Gabriel. "Them's the line of rocks that guard the whole of the Skalls."

Gabriel grinned. "Pirates' stuff, eh?"

"Wreckers, more like." Alf jerked his head at Dorrie. "Young lady's great-grandfather lived well on the wrecks. And I understand her dad used to dive down and fetch up a keg of brandy now and then!"

Gabriel was full of admiration. "They sound like my kind of people, Dorrie — no wonder I fell for you at first sight!" He raised his fist. "Let's explore!"

He led the way. The beach became dunes growing clumps of comfrey and the path, so well defined from the shore, was often lost as it zigzagged upwards.

Dorrie followed Gabriel, trying to emulate his enthusiasm. "Look for the house first, Gabe!" she called into the wind. "It's tucked into the east cliff somewhere. I remember watching the sunrise so it must be . . ." Her voice was whipped away.

Binnie dropped back, deciding she would go to the top on her own. She smiled over her shoulder and said, "Don't feel you have to come with us . . . Alf. This is the first of our trips and I don't expect we shall be very long. We need to take things gradually."

"Catches you unexpected, doesn't it?" Alf said.

Binnie did not look at him as he caught her up. "What does?"

"Times past. Times that can't come again. Maggie Govern was telling me about your husband, Theo Cash. We didn't know. Not proper, like. He doesn't come back to the islands till about now each year. Then we only see him when he stocks up his stores. So we didn't know." He paused and seemed to withdraw even more into his hair. "We're sorry," he concluded.

"Yes. Thank you, Alf."

74

"I'm glad you've slipped into calling me Alf all natural, like. I would like to think we're going to be friends."

Binnie was touched by his directness. "I was a bit shy about my name last night," she confessed. "It's Benita. But I'm called Binnie. And of course you already know Dorrie and Gabriel."

"Yes. Gabriel. Named for an angel." Some white teeth appeared. "Some proud parent made a mistake, I reckon."

Binnie grinned and began to walk up through the dunes. It seemed Alf had summed up Dorrie's partner in a very short time. And then she wondered whether it was a family trait, choosing unsuitable mates.

The wind increased the higher they scrambled. The "thigh" of the island was protecting them from the southwesterlies; it would hit them with gale force when they reached the top.

Halfway up, Dorrie hailed them. She and Gabriel had discovered the house that Theo's grandfather had built into the east side of the cliff, and wanted to explore that first. Binnie called back to them to go ahead, she would climb to the top and then go into the house for a rest on the way back down. Alf followed close to her heels. The slope was now very steep, the thin grass covering strata of rock and forming giant steps. She stopped now and then for breath and to take in the widening view.

Memory was washing her back and she wished she could have been alone. Theo had brought her here the day after their wedding, and they had puffed and panted their way up, laughing, pausing not so much for breath as to hold each other. She had been pregnant — that was why he had married her, she now supposed — and when they reached the top, just short of the sheer drop down on to the Shark's Teeth, he had turned her to face the endless ocean and put his hands across her abdomen and whispered in her ear, "This is your place, Binnie Cash. And the place of our children. Don't forget that, will you?" And she had stretched her arms to infinity, laughing, nearly crying with such ecstatic happiness, and said, "Never! I'll never forget that!"

Now she had to get on all fours for the last "stair" and as she pulled herself above the final jut of rock and the wind hit her face, she knew she was weeping. She thought: what happened? Dear God, what *happened*?

Behind her, Alf said, "You all right there, Mrs Binnie? I'm d'reckly behind you in case you miss your footing!"

She could not speak so she reached behind her and found the collar of his jacket and tugged as a sign for him to join her. He scrambled up, not looking at her.

"Low tide, look. There's the rocks — hardly a space between 'em. No wonder this is called Trapdoor Island!" She nodded and he went on, almost shouting into the wind, "See, if you knew just 'zackly where they was and you came in at high tide, you could do it. Otherwise . . ." He lifted one hand and pointed the thumb downwards.

She shivered. Theo had told her the stories of the wrecks — boats lured inshore by waving lights on a dark night. She remembered her horror and his voice, light, unconcerned: "It was the way they lived then, darling. Doesn't do to be squeamish about the past. It's done with now, anyway."

Alf said, "Best be getting back. You'll want a fair old time in the house and I have to pick up some folk later this afternoon." He added, as if comforting her, "We can come back tomorrow. Bring some stores. Have a bit of a picnic, p'raps."

They went back down in sitting positions, almost sliding along each grassy "tread" and then scrambling down the riser to the next one. She thought what a kind man he was. Almost as if he knew about her failed marriage and understood things she did not understand herself.

There was a flight of stone steps that led down into the side of the island; Theo had called it Jacob's Ladder and had insisted that the steps were part of the threshold so had carried her down them and then pretended to collapse when they reached the bottom. This time Alf preceded her and commented over one shoulder that the Victorians knew how to build, then added something about slave labour.

Dorrie ran across what had been the vegetable patch to greet them.

"Mum! We couldn't get in, so Gabe had to force the kitchen window and climb into the sink! It's the size of a bath actually, and was half full of water and of course he fell into it!"

Binnie laughed. "How nice and normal," she commented. Then she went to the well, which was outside the kitchen window, lifted a stone and produced the key. "Sorry Gabriel! I'd forgotten until just this minute! No reason to think that might have changed!"

She opened the front door and went into the hall, then stood very still. It was over twenty years since she had left this house and she had thought it would hold no emotion for her; not now, not when Theo was dead and the awfulness of his betrayal was dead with him. She was not prepared for the sheer familiarity of the big square hall, with its stone-flagged floor, candle sconces on the newel post and around the panelled walls. The hall stand was still facing her, with its long mirror and umbrella holder beneath. And there were the same pictures, Victorian paintings with stories to tell: two women at a window overlooking the sea titled *The Watchers*; a golden-haired child in a long pinafore, playing with a kitten and a ball of wool, *Waiting for Father*. She felt a physical clutch at her heart and laughed at herself.

Dorrie, coming in behind her said, "What's funny? It all looks as grim as ever to me."

Binnie said, "That's it. I would have thought Natalie would have gone through it like a dose of salts. But it hasn't changed a bit."

"Too difficult these days to get materials over. And he was always going to have the power brought across but he never got round to it." Alf stood in the middle of the hall. "Good solid house, this. And independent too. It's stood up to everything the elements have chucked at it — no electricity to fail. Plenty of driftwood to keep

78

the fire in, candles, paraffin. Bottled gas, I wouldn't wonder."

Dorrie nodded. "He's installed a gas cooker. And there's a gas heater too. That's probably down to Natalie."

Gabriel came down the stairs and caught the last comment. "Sensible woman, by the sound of things."

Dorrie said shortly, "She left him, remember."

Gabriel grinned. "Like I said, sensible woman."

Binnie moved out of the hall and into the sitting room. It smelled salt-damp and felt very cold. The two sash windows looked towards the Shark's Teeth and then the open sea. "Nothing between us and America," she said under her breath just as Theo had said twenty-three years ago. She moved around the room, touching the backs of the horsehair-stuffed sofa and armchairs, moving the ancient damask curtains, stiff with dust.

Dorrie came in and stood by her almost protectively. Binnie said, "They were like this when I came here first. Probably your greatgrandfather brought them across over a hundred years ago."

"The dust must have reached saturation point and after that they stayed the same," Dorrie said.

"Probably." Binnie tried to smile. "Can you imagine this lot coming over on one of the local boats?"

Dorrie said, "Everyone must have done it at some time. Lots of the islands were inhabited then. Dad said if they had a water supply someone would live on them. But it was only the folks who could live *with* them who could stick it out." She looked at her mother. "He was so *bloody* proud of being able to live with them!"

Binnie reached across and they clasped hands. And Dorrie said on a sob, "I suppose it was when he realized that Trapdoor was no good for babies that he left you."

"No!" Binnie gripped her daughter's hand hard. "No. He would have waited for you and Will to grow agile enough to live here, darling. But he met Natalie. He would have met her anyway . . . so . . ."

Dorrie burst out, "Oh God! He was such a rotter!"

"No. Not really. No-one can help falling in love. We were on the mainland and he was here for the summer season. And she was into water sports. He taught her to snorkel . . . she was so attractive, Dorrie. Really beautiful."

"I hate her!"

"No, you don't. When she found your father was having an affair with the Italian girl, she came to see us and she was very kind really. And she's the one who's making sure we have half of your father's estate. *And* she told the solicitors that Dad wanted us to have the island."

"How can you keep defending everyone?"

"Perhaps that's one of the reasons I am here, love. I need to know him again and either grieve for him properly or . . . dismiss him. I need to understand him. And Natalie. And even the Italian girl. Violetta."

"I expect there were others too." Dorrie managed a watery smile. "We could be here a long time, Mum!"

Alf came in and heard her last words. "Could be worse places to spend a winter," he said jovially. "I've looked over the house and it's right and tight. Needs paper and paint here and there, and lots of hot water and soap. You could work on it till the spring then let it out to one of the twitchers or tourists. Keep going like that for evermore. It's a good investment."

Gabriel followed him in. "Sounds like Alcatraz to me. You could pop over after Christmas and find we'd murdered each other."

Alf laughed. "Not very likely. Too much to do. And o' course you got the boat." They all looked at him. "The *Scallywag*. It's moored off the small jetty with all the others. Nothing wrong with it."

Gabriel was all enthusiasm, suddenly seeing himself as Theo's successor. "I'll buy one of those yachting caps and get an oiled sweater and —"

Dorrie laughed; Binnie noted that Gabriel could always make Dorrie laugh.

"What you won't do, darling, is take the boat out before you've had some kind of instruction!"

Alf laughed too. "Dennison wouldn't let you, anyway." He glanced at Binnie. "Was Dennison around in your day, Mrs Cash?"

"I remember him vaguely. He had a shack on Postern Island. But then the authorities housed him on Keyhole. In one of the old lookouts."

"He lived off the land and the sea. Still does. But your husband was good to him and brought him here where the pickings were . . ." Alf shrugged. "He's short of a shilling but he understands the boat and the currents. He knows the sea." He turned to Gabriel. "He'll make sure you learn about it too."

Gabriel pulled a face. "Not at too close quarters, I hope."

Alf did not smile. "You have to understand him. He looks on himself as a caretaker for the boat. He won't yet know that Theo Cash is dead. He might need careful handling. I'll have a word with him."

They continued around the house. Binnie produced a notebook from her pocket and wrote out a shopping list with gas, paraffin and candles at the top. She discovered with a strange pleasure that the old wood-burning range was still there next to the more modern gas stove. And the deal table, ridged from scrubbing, still stood by the window where she had learned to make bread and starry pies. The scrubbing brushes had gone, as had the serried ranks of cleaners and bleach. She wrote busily, then turned to the pantry and started a new sheet of paper.

"Mum's getting serious," Dorrie told Gabriel. "Let's go to the top and look out at America!"

Binnie smiled, noting that Theo had introduced his daughter to the view just as he had his wife. And then she wondered whether he had done the same for Natalie and Violetta. Probably.

Alf made investigations of his own. There were cellars built into the rock foundations and they were plentifully stocked with cases and bottles of all kinds. His face fell into lines of distaste; but then he told himself that though the Old Cash had doubtless been a wrecker — the worst kind of murderer, in Alf's view —

the Young Cash had simply retrieved what his grandfather had missed. A deep-sea beachcomber didn't sound quite so bad.

They left the island at two o'clock. Binnie was armed with grocery lists and wild plans for living there until Christmas. She knew it was crazy. Why would she "find" Theo here rather than in the mainland house, where he had dropped in to see Dorrie, then Will, and made each occasion a honeymoon? Until he had to tell her about Natalie, of course. She put her hand in her pocket and began to screw up the list. Then withdrew it. If Theo had truly loved something, it had been Trapdoor.

Dorrie sat close to Gabriel and wondered whether Trapdoor might help him to give up gambling. He did not call it an obsession, he called it a philosophy. And just as the great philosophers argued logically, so did he. The science of chance. She shivered inside her fleece jacket. Could Trapdoor show him that survival was also a science? And that living so close to nature was good for the soul? She shivered again as her mind went back to the gamekeeper's cottage and those silent menacing "debt collectors". They would never find Gabriel here. Surely.

Alf stood in the shelter of the engine housing and stared into the grey afternoon. The sea was flipping up a little outside the long arm of Trapdoor, but inside it the water slapped against the side of the boat and there was no wind. He shot glances at his passengers and saw their hope and their uncertainty. The only one who had enjoyed the trip unequivocally was the boy, Gabriel.

And that was because of the boat, *Scallywag*. Alf smiled. He was in for a bit of a shock there.

The two women were holding hands; Alf noticed it with a pang of compassion, then a twinge of anger directed at Theo Cash. Alf was of the school who believed that men should look after their women; it was obvious that Theo Cash had not done that. Or had he? Nothing was ever black and white, after all.

He half closed his eyes and looked at Keyhole's short pier as it came into sight. Out of the side of his eye he could see the woman — Binnie Cash — watching him and he turned and threw her one of his special smiles.

"I always make my own spyglass like this." He screwed up his eyes and laughed at himself. "I'm looking for my Marigold, you see. I can almost see her, right now. Lots of golden hair, and a frilly blouse what she do always wear when she's working. And I think — yes, I'm sure — that's a fish-tail I can see under her skirt!"

They all laughed, Binnie simply because she liked Alf so much.

Alf manoeuvred the boat against the short pier until the fenders bumped the wall. "She'd make every day an adventure," he said as he leaned over to grab one of the rungs on the iron ladder. "An' I reckon no-one can do better than that." He looked round and saw Binnie's eyes fixed on him. He smiled. "Your 'usband was good at that, I wouldn't wonder."

Binnie stared back. She said nothing.

CHAPTER
SIX

Within a few days they felt they were beginning to know several of the locals. They were comfortable enough with Maggie Govern; Matthew, her husband, proved to be just as practical and good-natured. But Alf Trevose was different. Alf did not simply accept them, he seemed to understand them as if he had known them for years.

Every morning, as soon as he had unloaded the last of the schoolchildren, he would run the red duster up his mast and Gabriel would giant-stride down Ditchdrain Street and look around the big old boat enthusiastically. Gabriel's insouciance seemed to amuse Alf. He called Gabriel "Dodger" and warned him that the *Scallywag* was nothing like his *Mermaid*.

"*Scally* do take the waves like a surf-board do — skips along the tops. My *Mermaid* do plough through them."

"When are we going to meet this Dennison and see the *Scallywag*?" Gabriel asked impatiently a couple of days after the first visit to Trapdoor.

"When he's ready and willing." Alf took an oil-can to the engine housing and lifted the hatch. "I bin to see him. And he's not ready and he's not willing."

"How long can he hold out?"

Alf shrugged. "If he don't like the sound of you, could be for ever."

"But the bloody boat doesn't belong to him!" Gabriel expostulated. "It belongs to Dorrie's mother, for God's sake! What's he going to do about that?"

Alf raised surprised brows. "Obvious. He'll scupper it."

Gabriel looked apoplectic and Alf laughed. "Won't come to that, Dodger m'lad! You got a lot to learn and patience is top o' the list!"

People who lived on the Skalls knew that their livelihood depended on tourists, but they did not necessarily take them to their hearts. Luckily for the Cash family, they were not in the twitcher and tourist league. Theo Cash had been a third-generation Skallion, independent, often difficult, living by his own rules; nevertheless a Skallion. It followed that his family were Skallions too. There was a certain caution — they had to prove their worth — but once they were accepted by the Polpens who ran the shop — which, as Alf had told them, was post office, information centre and grocer — they were accepted everywhere.

Two days after the arrival of Binnie, Dorrie and Gabriel, Walter Polpen hit the airwaves from his attic radio studio at eight o'clock in the morning and announced sonorously his regret at the death of Theodore Cash, and his pleasure at meeting his first wife and family. He then played a recording of "The Crafty Corsair", sung suggestively by a famous group

— "a favourite of the late Theo, who was a bit of a buccaneer himself."

Binnie had never heard the song but she knew that Theo had captured her younger self just as a pirate might have and she was touched.

It was a surprise, to say the least, when Dorrie, listening intently as she stirred her breakfast porridge, said unsmilingly, "That sums him up rather well, doesn't it? Always acting. Just who was the real Theodore Cash, I wonder."

Binnie said, "Well . . . he was your father."

"Not much of one," Dorrie came back. "And why on earth are you defending him?"

"I wasn't. Not really." Binnie heard the lameness in her voice and said, "He had his good days."

Dorrie shook her head. "Not enough. Is that why we're here? To search out his good days and forget the rest?"

It could have been the truth. Binnie steadied her voice. "We're here to clean and refurbish the house, and see how we can best use the asset he has left for us."

"Yes. Of course."

The two women looked at each other, then away.

So four days went by, during which they went to Trapdoor Island each day and worked from ten until two. Alf Trevose took them and brought them home but he did not stay with them after that first visit. His cousin Matthew was repairing roof timbers on the "fancy hotel" at Postern Island and needed his help. It sounded as if a sale was in the offing.

On the fifth day, he offered to take them to the long shallow bay behind Keyhole harbour, where a lot of the summer craft were beached for winter.

"I think it's time you met Dennison." He looked warningly at Gabriel as he whooped with joy. "No taking over, young Dodger! It's bin Dennison's boat all summer long and he's not going to take kindly to handing it over to a complete stranger." He glanced at Binnie. "Nothing to do with his Captain, either."

She smiled wryly. "I'd forgotten he always called Theo "the Captain". Well, actually Theo had his Master's ticket so I suppose it was fair enough."

"It was indeed." Alf grinned suddenly. "You might be tickled to hear that he calls you 'the Captain's lady'! He never took to the second wife. If she'd have come over she'da got short shrift. But he'll listen to you. He might even talk to you." He added soberly, "Not that he does much talking. To anyone."

It was a quiet grey day when they plodded down to the harbour and across the long jetty where the *Queen* was unloading her cargo of petrol, tractor parts, supplies for the cottage hospital, electrical equipment, cartons of groceries, school uniforms and boxes of library books. The weather had improved since their arrival and the September sun glanced off the moving water, breaking it up into thousands of dancing points. Several women lingered nearby to take early delivery of mail-order outfits; a tractor hauled a trailer of goods towards the post office; Walter Polpen stood by the open door checking bills of lading.

"It's all go," commented Gabriel with only a touch of sarcasm. So far boredom had not set in and he was excited about meeting the mysterious Dennison. He put a casual arm across Dorrie's shoulders and hugged her to him. "We could go over to Penzance once I get the hang of this boat," he suggested tentatively.

She laughed and reminded him of her seasickness.

Alf said firmly, "Don't think Dennison will agree to that!" He glanced at Binnie and added apologetically, "Sorry. I was forgetting . . . Dennison and *Scallywag* have always gone together."

Binnie was thankful. The thought of Gabriel in a small boat on the high seas was terrifying. She said, "And always will."

Gabriel said nothing but as they scrambled through marram grass to the long thin bay linking north and south of Keyhole, he dropped his arm from Dorrie's shoulders and lagged behind. Binnie knew he was sulking and wondered yet again just what Dorrie saw in him.

There were three boats moored to the small jetty. "This pier's called the Stump and you can see why." Alf came to a halt and shaded his eyes. "Practically empty now. Come summer this whole long beach is full of boats pulled right up out of the tide." He pointed. "That's *Scallywag*. Far one. White with a dark blue line."

Binnie said, "Yes. I see her." She felt a pang as if the boat meant something to her, yet she had not seen it before. She said, "It has a look of Theo. Somehow."

Dorrie said, "He used to have a real tub of a boat. Will and I used to call him Cap'n Pugwash. But it had an engine."

"*Scallywag*'s got an outboard. But she sails like a bird when there's wind." Alf scanned the beach. "No sign of Dennison. He's taken himself off. Probably watching us from the dunes." He looked round at the three of them. "He took the news bad. Real bad. Said it couldn't be true because the Captain would never let himself be swept away. We'll have to tread carefully."

Binnie said, "You three go on down and look at the boat. I'll wander along the beach. He might come and talk to me if I'm on my own."

"Why would he?" Dorrie asked.

"I don't know. He might."

Binnie had no wish to see Gabriel clambering all over Theo's *Scallywag*. She turned right along the line of dunes and trudged down to the hard sand of the beach. Nobody followed her. She was surprised at the sudden sense of freedom, then excused herself; she was, after all, used to her own company and since that Sunday — less than two weeks ago — she had not been by herself except in bed, and then had been conscious of others asleep around her.

She smiled slightly, remembering the mystery of Daniel and wondering how he was faring with the Thoroughgoods. And then went on to wonder whether her job would, in fact, be waiting for her. She nibbled her lip, pondering. It could be difficult for Lady Barbara to have to tell her there wasn't a place for her any more, but would it matter to her personally? After all, there would be half of the money from the sale of the house on the mainland — she would need to call Natalie at some point — and Trapdoor could mean an income for life. And an interest, a proper, important interest. But it could also be a millstone. If she could get it on its feet this winter, ready for letting next spring and summer, which would probably mean staying over there by herself for long periods of time, could she do that?

She had reached this point in her thoughts when something registered at the corner of her vision. She turned and looked up at the dunes: there was nothing, yet there had been something. She hesitated. If it was the elusive Dennison and he did not want to be discovered, she should respect that. And that applied to anyone else who might be dodging about in the mini-mountain ranges. Just for a second her heart leaped into her mouth at the thought of Gabriel's debt collectors. If only, if *only*, Dorrie could get over Gabriel. She sighed deeply; she was a fine one to have such thoughts. Since arriving at Keyhole she had started to wonder whether she had ever got over Theo Cash.

She was still standing there dithering when someone emerged diffidently from behind a hillock of seagrass and stood still, looking down at her. She had no doubt it was Dennison. He was short and wiry with the bony, sharp face so typical of many Cornishmen. He wore the inevitable guernsey and knitted hat pulled well down over forehead and ears. He stood, arms hanging by his sides, waiting. She hardly knew what to do. Eventually, she lifted a hand in a kind of salute and then waved. He could interpret it however he wished; as a greeting or as an invitation to join her on the beach. He chose the latter.

He arrived at a run and dug his heels into the sand to stop himself. He was wearing old tennis shoes, grey with sea water.

She said unthinkingly and without the usual polite preamble, "Have you still got that lookout building?"

He did not look even slightly surprised but he did not answer.

She said, "The one Theo — the Captain — got you years ago."

There was another pause, then he nodded once.

"And you're all right? What about money?" She waited and then sighed. "No, I suppose not. He looked after you in other ways. You must let me —"

She was interrupted by a small explosive "No!" and then a short spate of words, so fast and furious she could not understand one of them. Her face must have shown shock and bewilderment because after another few moments, he said clearly, each word separated from the next, "The Captain will come home."

She looked at the small man, weatherbeaten to the colour and texture of a walnut, the narrowed eyes that had the transparency of the sea, the bird-beak nose and inward mouth, and suddenly and quite unexpectedly tears filled her eyes and spilled down her face. His defencelessness had called out her own. She put her hands up and dropped her head into them.

"Oh, Dennison," she sobbed. "He's not coming home. Not this time. He was swept overboard . . ."

She felt his hand on her elbow drawing her up towards the dunes and she stumbled after him. When he crouched in one of the valleys, she crouched too, but she could not take her hands from her face and look at him in case she should see that he too was weeping.

But he spoke firmly enough. "Alf Trevose told me. I din't believe'n. And neither should you. He's a shilling short."

She spoke through her fingers. "I heard it from other sources. Legal ones. Proper ones." At last she removed one hand and fumbled for a handkerchief. "And isn't it the way he would want to go? To become part of the sea? You knew him better than anyone — wouldn't you say it was a right and proper end?"

The silence went on and on, and she took away her other hand and scrubbed at her face before looking at him.

Dennison was staring out to sea, considering what she had said. She watched him and realized quite soon that the transparent eyes were indeed flooded with tears. She wondered when she had last wept with someone.

After what seemed like a very long time, he stood up, not looking at her, keeping his eyes on the horizon. And he began to walk towards it.

It was like a recurring nightmare. Nearly two weeks ago she had seen Daniel walk down the slipway and into the Bristol Channel; now she watched Dennison walk towards the Atlantic and knew that he intended to keep going just as Daniel had.

Even so, she waited disbelievingly until he was knee-deep before she scrambled to her feet and began to run after him. By the time she grabbed at his shoulder they were both up to their waists in water. She panted at him incomprehensibly but he simply shrugged off her hand and took another step and she was forced to plunge fully into the water and swim around him until she blocked his way.

He did everything he could to get past her but she was always there before him and it was obvious that, like so many men of the sea, he could not swim. She prayed he would go back before she tired; her clothes, sodden already, were pulling her down and exhausting her, and he was such a determined man. With all her strength she butted him with her head and he fell backwards and actually gave a cry. She seized his shoulders and turned him on to his front and began to swim into shallower water.

When she could stand up comfortably she set him on his feet and said loudly and again instinctively, "The *Scallywag* is yours. It's yours, Dennison. Do you understand? You have to go on living to look after the *Scallywag*!"

Too much had happened and he was dumb again, looking at her wildly as if about to make another attempt to drown himself. She repeated her words again and again and could almost see them forming a pattern in his head.

Then, without another word, he began to wade laboriously up the beach and when he reached it he shook himself like a dog and then went on into the dunes and simply disappeared. She was left knee-deep in the crystal-clear, iron-cold water, watching where he had been.

A shout came from the sea and, looking over her shoulder, Binnie saw the white boat with the dark blue stripe, cutting through the sea cleanly and easily with Dorrie at the tiller and Alf Trevose dealing with the sails and Gabriel leaning out dangerously and calling to her.

She struggled out of the heavy water then and turned towards them, signalling them to go back. Alf immediately spoke to Dorrie and pushed Gabriel down as the boat tacked and the mainsail swung across. She watched them no more but tramped slowly and soggily across the beach. Alf would understand; Gabriel would not. Dorrie would say nothing for a while, then she might gently tease her mother about finding yet another lame duck.

CHAPTER
SEVEN

After Binnie had changed and Mrs Govern had made them all hot drinks and rejoiced with them that the supplies had come and there would be beef for the evening meal, Alf took them to Postern Island. He was still labouring for Matthew Govern at the Postern Hotel, and told them roundly that it would do them good to have a lunch on a plate for once and see a bit more of the Skalls.

"No point in going over this ground all the time, m'dears," he said, looking pointedly at Dorrie. "You know very well your mother done the right thing. An' you can be sure that Dennison and the *Scallywag* will be at your disposal whenever you need them."

"That's not quite the point," Dorrie said tiredly. "We came over together and I thought any decisions would be made together. This is an impulse gift, presumably to stop Dennison from drowning himself! You can't be held to it, Mum. That's all I'm saying."

Binnie had not imagined that her gift to Dennison could provoke so many emotions. Guilt made her say, "I'm sorry, darling. I really am. But there's no way I can retract now. And the boat would have been no good to us. Whereas — like Alf says — the boat with Dennison is a different thing altogether!"

Gabriel said yet again, "I would have taken it on, Binnie! You know that was the plan. That would have been my — my — role!"

Binnie said again, "I'm sorry." She wondered whether subconsciously she had given the *Scallywag* to Dennison to stop Gabriel from taking it over. She felt guiltier than ever.

Eventually they trailed out after Alf and went over to Postern for their lunch. The trip took five minutes from Keyhole's harbour to the landing stage at Postern, but the narrow channel between the two islands was deep and turbulent, and Dorrie was looking queasy by the time they scrambled up the steps in the cliff and walked through the grounds of the Postern Hotel. Alf went straight through the long foyer to join Matthew, who was working on the roof above the kitchens, and his three passengers collapsed into deep armchairs by the wide windows, which looked back at Keyhole, just a leap away.

None of them was hungry but when the waiter told them smilingly that they were guests of Matthew Govern and everything they ordered was on the house, they tried to rise to the occasion. Binnie ordered soup and cheese sandwiches. Gabriel looked at the menu and asked for roast lamb with rosemary and a variety of vegetables.

Dorrie shook her head gratefully. "I might have a pot of tea later." She smiled back at the waiter. "Thank

Matthew for us, won't you?" She turned to her mother. "I'm sorry, Mum. I'm not cut out for the Skalls, am I?"

Binnie said, "Perhaps none of us are. And yet —"

"And yet you love the house at Trapdoor!"

Binnie laughed, glad that the atmosphere was lighter. "I was thinking, before Dennison appeared out of the dunes, it will be interesting to see how I get on when I'm there on my own. I might stay around most of the year. Manage the place."

Dorrie was horrified. "You can't do that, Mum! What about your job?"

Binnie spread her hands. "That's all it is, darling. Just a job. This would be working for us — our project. It would be exciting!"

"Mum, you're serious! My God, the Thoroughgoods think the world of you!"

"Darling, they were already taking on someone else before they knew I was coming over here. Anyone can do that job. There are no qualifications necessary or anything like that."

"Mum, you're being so negative! You know the estate better than the Thoroughgoods themselves know it! The volunteers come because of you. You muck in with the cleaning when anyone drops out."

Unexpectedly Gabriel chipped in. "I know what you mean, Binnie. This place is yours now. You were gypped out of it before. Now you're here and it's right." He turned to Dorrie. "It's the same for you at Cherrington, honey. When we moved there, you were so settled and secure." He dropped his head. "Well, that is, until those bloody debt collectors arrived."

The food came and Dorrie accepted a small triangular sandwich from her mother's plate. They ate companionably, looking around them and admiring the hotel and the view. Alf and Matthew joined them and told them about Postern — "the back gate to the Skalls", Matthew called it.

Alf said, "My Marigold comes from Postern. They're all related to mermaids. That's why she can sing."

Matthew rolled his eyes. "Sing? She couldn't hold a tune to save her life! She sounds like a cat whose tail has been trod on!"

Alf said comfortably, "If you wasn't my cousin I'd throw you in the sea for that! You're jealous 'cos Maggie never sings to you!"

"Thank Gawd," Matthew said solemnly.

So they all left together, laughing. And as they pulled up the near precipice of Ditchdrain Street, Binnie knew quite suddenly that she would stay on the Skalls for this winter.

They went into the narrow hall of Harbour Lights, and as they started up the first staircase to their rooms, she said over her shoulder, "I'm going to take some groceries over tomorrow, Alf. Is that all right?"

"Course it is, m'ansom. Wondered when you'd begin stocking up."

She stopped mid-flight and looked down at him. "Did you know I would want to stay?"

He looked surprised. "It's your place, isn't it? Anyway, my Marigold sang it to me first day you came."

Gabriel's guffaws echoed from the landing above and even Dorrie was smiling as her mother joined her. But though Binnie returned the smile, Alf's words were a confirmation of her own feelings.

She said, "First Dennison. And now Marigold."

Dorrie hugged her arm. "Mum, Dennison is obviously simple. And probably Marigold is the same."

"Maybe. That could be it, couldn't it? The innocent eye — isn't that what Picasso called it? Simplicity. And they *know*. They actually know that this is my place."

"We can't leave you here on your own, Mum. And that's that."

"Rubbish," Binnie said calmly. She thought they would soon change their minds after a few nights on Trapdoor.

But they did not change their minds. They did not like living "like monks", as Gabriel put it, unable to get off the island unless Alf appeared.

"I notice the faithful Dennison has not turned up," he complained bitterly after climbing up to the ridge to look back towards Keyhole.

"I told Alf not to come for us and he has obviously passed the message on to Dennison," Binnie said. She was concentrating on the kitchen, whitewashing the walls and painting the dark woodwork navy blue. It meant that until she had finished, their meals were out of tins. "I need the kitchen to be clean and fresh. Then I'll go to it, I promise," she said as she poured white spirit on her hands. "Why don't you two get the sitting room as comfortable as possible and start bringing in driftwood for the fire?"

Gabriel continued to complain. "We're trapped here — all right, I know the idea was to get away from temptations but this is ridiculous."

Dorrie said nothing. She could remember loving it here, but then her father had always had the boat and she had never felt sick on the sea in those days. And she had made her pilgrimage; she had found it very convenient to leave Bristol and its environs for a while, but the thought of the winter here was dreadful. The more she disliked living on Trapdoor, the less she wanted her mother to do so. The whole idea was preposterous.

After a week, the kitchen was done, the sitting-room curtains had been shaken and hung out, the carpet had been beaten to within an inch of its life, the walls and paintwork had been cleaned and each evening the grate sported a small fire. Binnie was triumphant.

"We've done it! We've got beds and furniture, and everything in here is clean and fresh and — and — we've done it!"

"So can we go — as soon as Alf calls in, can we go?" Gabriel pleaded.

"Of course you can." Binnie looked at them affectionately. She had always maintained that working together made for happiness, and certainly she and Gabriel were closer now than they had ever been. "You've done wonders and I know you're not as keen as I am." She assumed a pious look. "Go with my blessing, children!"

Dorrie said, "Mum, you know very well we can't leave you here. Come back to Keyhole and see Mr Polpen about including Trapdoor on the tourist information list and then we can leave it until the spring. How does that sound?"

"Fine." Binnie smiled happily. "I'll do that. If you promise me you'll come for Christmas!"

"Of course," Dorrie said gladly. "We couldn't have left you here, darling. You do understand?"

"Well, I shall be coming across quite often. Even if it's only for a day or two." Dorrie groaned and Binnie went on quickly, "You have got to understand — both of you — that unless anything unexpected happens, this is now my home."

"Unexpected? Like a fall off the ridge? Like pneumonia?"

"Unexpected things happen all the time, wherever you are," Binnie said matter-of-factly. "Now, I'm making vegetable soup for tonight. And we need to use up the bread so it's bread-and-butter pudding afterwards — and lots of it!"

Gabriel stared at Dorrie helplessly. "Is it too much to crave for fresh milk in tea? Steak and chops and even fish and chips?"

"Of course not." Dorrie hugged his arm. "So long as Mum is based at Keyhole, it will be all right to go home, won't it?"

"Of course it will. And maybe we could find somewhere else to live. So that no-one knows we're back."

Dorrie's heart sank. In the remoteness of Trapdoor she had forgotten the terror of arson.

There were letters awaiting them on the hall table at Harbour Lights. Dorrie had one from the librarian asking about her return. She had used up her two weeks' special leave. She made a face. "I don't want to go back there at all. All this —" she waved her hand around — "has made me feel like a change!"

Binnie and Gabriel both nodded. Gabriel's two letters were from the manager of the club in Bristol. They were in the form of official-looking invoices and the interest rate being charged added up dramatically between the two although they were only a week apart. He pretended not to care and immediately screwed them up. "They don't know where we are. Someone has forwarded them."

"Who?" asked Dorrie.

"It could be Daniel. He was going to keep an eye on the gamekeeper's cottage."

"He doesn't know where we live."

"I keep your key hanging with the others. It's got the address on it."

Binnie did not think for one minute that Daniel would have gone down to the housing estate to check on Gabriel's mail but she pretended to be assured about it anyway.

Her letter was from Daniel. He made no mention of visiting either the cottage or Dorrie's rented house. He said he was getting on all right working for "old Parkes" but there was no cleaning work as yet. He added in a postscript that something rather odd had happened to him to jog his memory and he would tell her about it when she got home. She returned the single sheet of paper to its envelope and stared at the handwriting. It was big and square, confident, not a bit as she remembered the bewildered man whose life had touched hers so briefly. She put the envelope into her pocket. The writing reminded her of Theo's.

That evening she went to the red telephone kiosk outside the post office and rang the Manor. Miles picked up and was delighted to hear from her.

"When are you coming back? The new chap has got no sex appeal whatsoever."

"Be serious. That's why I'm telephoning. Perhaps I should speak to your mother. Or your father." She mentally apologized to Sir Henry for making him an afterthought.

"Both out. Ma is chairing some big Women's Institute rally in the Mendips. And poor old Pa seized the opportunity to go to his club. He's just about hung on to the membership."

"Well, for goodness' sake put it to them as best you can. I might not come back, Miles. Certainly not until the spring. If then. I'm really sorry, Miles, if I'm leaving the business in the lurch. I thought, with the new man and everything, I would be more or less redundant anyway."

"As if!" He sounded genuinely shocked and hurt. "Oh, Binnie, Binnie, life is going to be so dull and dreary."

"Well, actually, as it's you on the telephone . . . may I ask a big favour? Dorrie and her partner are coming home soon and they need somewhere to live. I was going to ask if there's a cottage anywhere on the estate, but if you mean it when you say I'm missed, it occurs to me that perhaps Dorrie could take my place in the office and live in one of the cottages as part of the deal."

He was silent and she thought she had gone too far. But then he said, "Why are you asking about somewhere else? What's the matter with the gamekeeper's?"

"Nothing. But it's rather out of the way, whereas the Manor is almost on the main Bristol road and a level walk to the shops . . . sorry, Miles, I'm putting you in a difficult position. Forget I mentioned it. I haven't said a word to Dorrie. She would probably tell me I was mad anyway!"

"No . . . no, I was thinking. Putting two and two together and probably making it sixteen." He paused. "Are you in trouble, Binnie? Seriously, you know if I can help in any way —"

"Of course not! Quite the opposite. I'm sort of . . . settling. I'm not ecstatic — I can see all the difficulties of living here only too well — but I'm getting such a kick out of it." She too paused, then said quickly, "Gabriel — Dorrie's partner — is having rather a rough time. And of course what affects him affects Dorrie too."

"Say no more. They can have Parkes's cottage with your Daniel Casey. Parkes is going to stay with his daughter for the winter and I can't see him coming back. Same applies to Dan. He tells me some 'evidence' has turned up and he might have to investigate it soon. So perhaps your Gabriel will take on the gardens for a bit?"

"Really? Actually, that would be wonderful." She felt a weight lift from her shoulders. Miles would keep an eye on Gabriel. It only remained to talk Dorrie and Gabriel into the scheme.

The next day brought another letter, this one from Natalie.

Darling, you must get email installed somehow. It's just marvellous for this sort of thing. I've been in touch with the Plymouth lot and they told me you were going to set Trapdoor Island to rights to sell or to let or something. There's a buyer for the house in Cornwall — my dear, an astronomical offer — but can you believe this? Violetta — whatever her name is — is muscling in. She can't do anything about Trapdoor, thank God, but she wants her whack of the house. Three ways isn't as good as two ways and you've got two children to provide for, so I hope you will join me in a hearty protest. I might pop over to see you. Towards the end of next month would be good, as darling Ernest is away on a conference. I described it as a grocers' get-together and he was livid! Love to Doreen and Billy.

Yours, Natalie

Binnie passed the letter over to Dorrie, who shrieked her outrage at "Doreen and Billy". "Dorothea is awful, but *Doreen*? And Will has never been Billy in his life! This is deliberate. That woman is evil." She grinned at her mother. "But at least you will have some company."

"Thanks." Binnie smiled. "Actually, I don't mind at all. Maybe Natalie will find something here too. She was so bitter." She sighed and shook herself. "Listen, I need to talk to you. Last night I telephoned the Thoroughgoods and talked to Miles at some length. It seems that Parkes — you remember, the gardener at the Manor — is going to live with his daughter and his cottage is free. Daniel has a room there, as you know, but the rest is yours if you want it. And if you were serious about a change of job, then you can have mine. Apparently you were right and they are missing me. And Gabriel can help in the grounds. What do you think? I'll have to ring back tonight and sort it out properly."

Dorrie was silent and wide-eyed. Gabriel looked from her to Binnie and back again.

"It would do as a temporary thing, darling," he said tentatively. "We can't go back to the house, and Binnie's place . . . well, they know about that too, don't they?"

Dorrie let her breath go in a deep sigh. "It's almost too good to be true. Mum, you are the best fixer ever! I was going to suggest we went up and stayed in Will's student house for a week or two but he would have hated it. This would be terrific." She bit her lip. "Miles has always wanted to help you, but what about Lady Barbara? She's the one who pays the piper, after all."

"Yes. Well, that's why I've got to telephone again this evening and talk to her properly. But if it's OK with her, then it's OK with you?"

Dorrie nodded.

CHAPTER
EIGHT

As the small eight-seater took off for Bristol a week later, Binnie had to admit to a definite sinking sensation in the pit of her stomach. She reminded herself that this was what she had wanted and everything had worked out so well that it was obviously predestined, but now, when she visualized herself in the house on Trapdoor, she no longer saw the small fortress, secure in the midst of the sea, fully stocked, safe, warm and inviting. Instead, she saw herself, an unprotected, vulnerable dot in the midst of an enormous universe.

Alf had taken them over yesterday with more supplies, and a two-way radio for emergencies. Dorrie and Gabriel had said their farewells to the house and the island and promised to be back before Christmas. It had been a happy occasion and Binnie had felt almost excited at the prospect of getting everything established properly over there ready for their return.

Now, as the plane disappeared into the low cloud, she told herself nothing had changed and this was the usual anti-climax always felt after a goodbye. She strode back along the top spine of Keyhole and took huge gulps of air.

On the highest point of the island she could see the concrete structure of the old lookout, which was where Dennison must live. He hadn't appeared at all since the day she had pulled him out of the sea. Twice she had walked around to the long bay where *Scallywag* was moored but it had not been there. Perhaps he had taken the boat and gone before the winter was on them. He was, after all, a free agent. But he had been Theo's man, and somehow she had expected he would have offered to help her. She shook herself irritably, knowing full well she would have turned him down as kindly as she could.

It was mid-morning when she got back to Harbour Lights; it would be too late for Alf to take her over to Trapdoor and she rather looked forward to sitting idly in the big downstairs room with Mrs Govern, watching for the *Queen* to arrive. Dorrie and Gabriel were not her worry any longer and, she reminded herself, she was on holiday. For today at any rate.

Unusually, the front door was closed. She opened it with the key Maggie Govern had given her and was confronted with a note written in enormous capital letters propped on the hall stand.

My dear Mrs Cash (Binnie), *Mrs Govern still had difficulty with first names*, Alf has taken me over to Postern with Matthew to measure for loose covers in the hotel. I shall be home after he has collected the schoolchildren. Help yourself to anything in the kitchen. Plenty of bread and milk. Have a good rest.

Binnie folded the note carefully and shook her head at herself in the hall mirror. It seemed that fate was determined to force her into a solitary state. She propped open the front door again, went through to the kitchen and made herself a cheese sandwich. And then, as she carried the plate into the living room, Alf came through the open front door. He stood, grinning at her, his wild hair and beard making him look like a redundant Father Christmas. She grinned back, really pleased to see him.

"You'll never guess what I've got in the *Mermaid*," he said, obviously very delighted with himself. "It's a present, if you like it. If you don't you'll have to pay me for it!"

He came down the hall and took the plate out of her hands. "Let's wrap those up and get on. I've not got very long before picking up the kids. And this will take some unloading."

She trailed after him into the kitchen again. "What on earth have you done? Is it something for the island?"

"Yes, but more for the house. Come on!"

She bundled the sandwiches into some greaseproof, grabbed her jacket and chased after him, then had to go back to lock the front door.

"Honestly, Alf. All this rushing around — it's not like you."

"Hop aboard, Mrs Binnie. Best go into the wheelhouse, wind's getting up. Good job them two went on the early flight. Plane service'll be stopped before evening, you'll see."

She huddled under the cowling and waited while he threw the moorings on board and jumped after them. And then she saw it. A great lump of machinery next to the engine casing. She had no idea what it might be but from his grin this was the surprise. And it was special.

"You don't know, do you? It's a dynamo. Works on diesel. It'll drive a pump twenty-four hours a day so you can pipe water straight into the kitchen sink. It'll manage a couple of lights, I reckon. But that don't matter so much because you've got your candles and your oil lamps. What it can do . . ." He waited tantalizingly while he set the *Mermaid* on her course past Postern and towards Trapdoor. "What it can do, Mrs Binnie, is . . . run a freezer! Milk, bread, meat, fish — you name it, you can have it. We'll order a big chest freezer from Penzance and it can come out on the next trip the *Queen* makes. Then we'll trolley it down to the *Mermaid* and get it up that hill somehow and into the house. What have you got to say to that?"

She swallowed unexpected tears. "Oh, Alf. I don't know what to say. You're so *kind*. It's absolutely wonderful. Gabriel reckoned he was undernourished without proper protein and I had started wondering how my paying guests were going to eat and drink. And you've solved the problem. How on earth did you get hold of it?"

"It's from the hotel. It was too small anyway, and now everything is being refurbished it's no good at all. But for a house, couldn't be better. You can get freezers that run on gas but this little fellow will do more than freeze!" He began to sing, his voice deep and entirely unmelodious. She laughed and he interrupted himself to say, "That was the surf then. Now comes the waves on the shore . . ." His voice went up an octave and trembled like tumbling water.

She held her sides and looked into his face with its dense framework of grey hair. There were not many people Alf sang to, she was sure of that, and she knew why. But she also knew he was doing her an honour.

The brief hour on Trapdoor was exhausting. Alf had a small trolley under one of the seats and a long gangplank; between them they loaded the dynamo on to the trolley and hoisted it over the side and down to the beach but it took the two of them to pull it through the soft sand of the zigzag path, through the dunes and bump down the long flight of steps to the house.

Alf leaned against the well, panting. "It's going to be a bit of a job when it comes to unloading the freezer," he commented. "I'll bring Matthew over. And maybe Dennison, if he's around then."

Binnie unlocked the front door and they tugged the trolley into the hall.

"Has he gone away? I looked down at the bay this morning and couldn't see *Scallywag*."

"Could've done." Alf took over the trolley and wheeled it into the kitchen. "He'll turn up when he's needed." He nudged the dynamo on to the kitchen floor. "We'll have to site this outside somewhere. Diesel fumes — and noise. Bit too much."

They pushed the dynamo into a corner and went straight out again. The wind was getting up and Alf still had his schoolchildren to deliver back to their homes.

The *Mermaid* bucked over the waves at such a rate Alf could not sing to her, though he tried again and again simply because it made her laugh.

Binnie stood to one side of him, holding the cowling, drenched in spray. She had a sense of moving on to the next phase of an adventure. And she was certain she could do it.

She said loudly, above the engine and sea sounds, "Tomorrow, Alf, I have to ring Dorrie and talk her round. Then I think I'll move over to Trapdoor for a long weekend."

He turned his head and looked at her very straightly. "Are you ready for that, girl?"

"I don't know. I'd like to try."

He jerked his head sideways. "A bit of weather on the way. Leave it for a week."

She met his gaze and nodded. After all, it was October, the end of the autumn. And they had had no autumn gales yet, so they were waiting in the wings somewhere.

In the end it was much longer than a week. The gales rolled in like fully rigged galleons, catching up the sea and flinging it around "without rhyme or reason", as Maggie put it, huddling into scarves and a knitted hat to run across to the post office for her daily chat with Gladys Polpen. Binnie found it exhilarating. She walked the length and breadth of Keyhole, from the small village of Midwatch at the other end, to the ancient St Andrew's church in Keyhole town. She talked to the vicar, John Tresillian, to Gladys Polpen and to a woman who ran one of the many flower farms in the sheltered valleys and who confessed to eating daffodils when food got really short.

There was a reading room next to the church, with a miniature library tucked into a small cubicle above a lectern. Binnie dusted the books and put them in some kind of order. Victorian tracts, beautifully bound in leather, jostled with Daphne du Maurier and medical romances. She joined Maggie and Gladys when they polished the brasses; she got a sense of belonging, of surviving. From the waiting room at the cottage hospital, she could just make out the lighthouse at Land's End.

"They're quite good binoculars," Dr Kennan told her on one of his three-day visits to the Skalls. "Left to us by one of the patients." The sister in charge said, "Nothing to do with the binoculars, Doctor. This weather lulls now and then and you get superb visibility." She looked at Binnie. "I'm making tea, would you like a cup?"

Binnie was conscious that people knew about her and she did not mind. There were some odd characters living on the Skalls and she was one of them.

And then she woke one morning to a cold and beautiful day. It was a Thursday, 23 October. Binnie was to remember it as the last normal day for a long time.

Maggie Govern, who at last was using Binnie's name, and had adopted a protective attitude towards her, rather like an older sister, said, "Well . . . this is it, I suppose? You'll want to go over tomorrow with Alf,

115

won't you?" She sat down with pen and notepad. "Let's make a list of what you will need. I can cook a chicken today and there's plenty of bread in the freezer. Milk too. Vegetables?"

"I wasn't planning to stay longer than a few days at first, Maggie."

"That will be long enough for you to know whether it will be a home for you and the children."

"Yes. Yes, you're right. I'll go tomorrow and come home . . . Monday?"

"Sounds just right."

Maggie passed down the plastic bags of food and Binnie stored them under the cowling and took her place by Alf's side.

"Do the hot-water bottles and make sure your bed is properly aired. Top up the copper all the time and keep that furnace going. Bath water, washing-up — you can't have too much hot water."

"True." Gabriel had seen to the water supply when they had been there before, and they had rolled themselves into sleeping bags each night. Binnie hugged her briefly. "You're so good to me, Maggie. Thank you. It makes all the difference."

"I'd rather you didn't go at all but I know you're looking for something and you don't know what, and the sooner you find it the better it will be, so I've got to go along with all this nonsense. But it beats me why you have to do it now. Spring and summer — that's when Trapdoor Island is at its best."

"I know. It's complicated but there are reasons."

Alf was having second thoughts about the wisdom of the expedition. "More weather will follow this last lot. And you'll be stranded out there," he grumbled.

"In a house that you yourself said was well built and weather-tight," Binnie reminded him.

He rolled his eyes and untied the rope. Binnie waved to Maggie; the engine, still idling, coughed once and settled into a steady rhythm, and they were off.

Alf came with her into the house and checked she had matches for the candles and plenty of wood for the furnace under the copper and for the grate in the sitting room. She decided to use the bottled gas and the gas cooker. He pumped up a couple of buckets of water from the well and she tipped them into the copper and then shooed him away.

"You have to get back some time. And you must leave me something to do."

"All right, all right. Remember the clocks go back tomorrow night. And I'll be over on Sunday —"

"No, certainly not, Alf! Fit me in with the school run, like you have before."

"'Tis half-term next week, Mrs Binnie. I'll come Sunday. And before then, if we have a message on that radio. It's on the right wavelength. You remember the call sign?"

"I pick up the mike and say, 'Trapdoor calling Mermaid.' Then I flick the switch and wait for you to answer."

"First off, you switch on."

"I know that!"

He caught her eye and they both laughed.

"And you will radio through at five o'clock today when I get back from the school run? Then you will know I'm safe and I'll know that you are too."

"I will. I don't deserve all this help, you know, Alf. I appreciate it more than I can ever say."

"We look after each other on the Skalls."

He would not let her come back to the beach with him so she had to wait until the *Mermaid* came into sight as it chugged back to Keyhole. Then, determined not to give herself time to feel anything at all, she went immediately to the pump and began to draw more water for the copper. And when that was filled, she lit the fire underneath it, put two or three dippers into the big iron kettle and lit the gas to make herself a cup of tea. There was an amazing sense of achievement in each small task; she enjoyed laying kindling and driftwood in the sitting-room grate and fanning the flickering flames into a blaze.

Going through the bookcase for her evening reading was a joy. There were books dating from Theo's grandfather's day — sea books, Ballantyne and Jack London; two of her own choice, contemporary novels from the sixties she had left here when she was expecting Dorrie, not knowing that it would be over twenty years before she saw them again. And, most poignant of all, there were children's books from the time Will and Dorrie came back here with their father.

She laid two or three on a low table by the fire, lugged in the radio and switched it on. It was almost five o'clock. She spent the next few minutes lighting candles and the big oil lamp in the kitchen, then she "flicked the switch" and picked up the microphone.

She felt idiotic as she began the call, but when there was no immediate reply she forgot herself and repeated urgently, "Mermaid, Mermaid. Come in, please. Alf, are you there?"

Thankfully, the reply came back. "Give me chance to get to the set, girl! I'm here. And you're there. I'm all right, how are you? Over."

"Oh, Alf. I'm fine. Really fine. I've had a lovely time sorting things out and now I'm going to get the meal Maggie made for me and just relax. Over."

She flicked the switch and suddenly Maggie Govern's voice crackled into the sitting room. "Your daughter phoned. Young Dorrie. They're staying in that cottage — all shipshape, she says. Nothing else to report from that quarter. Have you done those hot-water bottles? Don't forget them! Over."

"I had forgotten! Thank you, Maggie! Thank you. Sleep well. Over."

"You too."

Alf's voice chipped in. "Don't forget, if you want to come back, for any reason, get in touch. Over."

"Thank you, Alf. Over and out."

She switched off and stood smiling. They were such good people. She turned and went to fill hot-water bottles.

The next morning Binnie woke early after an excellent night's sleep. It was still dark and the wind howled outside like a dog. This might well be her one full day here and she wanted to make the most of it, so she got up and beamed her torch on to the clock. It had stopped at midnight. She felt for her watch on the dressing table; just before five o'clock. But she was too excited to go back to bed and it was too cold anyway. She lit two candles and made a note on her pad to bring a radio next time. It would be good to have a weather forecast and then some music to drown the sound of the wind.

She dragged on several layers of clothing, opened her bed, blew out one candle and carried the other downstairs. Then she lit the candles in the sconces and the two lamps in the kitchen and sitting room, and started on the fires. The water in the copper was still hot — Maggie had told her it would keep hot overnight — so she dippered out some for the kettle and made tea. The wind sounded not quite so bad downstairs.

She had stored bread in one of the many old biscuit tins and she cut some and made toast and carried it all to the fire. The old curtains in the sitting room were moving slightly in the draught from the window but the room was easily heated and the lamp cast a pool of light wherever she took it.

She sat in one of the low Victorian chairs, put her breakfast tray on the threadbare carpet and felt an amazing sense of being in the right place. She was comfortable here in every way; she had relaxed during the evening, slept well for seven hours and coped as easily with heating and cooking as she did at home. She looked around the faded room and said aloud, "By gum, she's done it! She's really done it!" and then laughed. And, like an immediate contradiction, there came an enormous crash from the kitchen.

Binnie was up and out of the room, forgetting to pick up the lamp, stumbling in the candle-lit hall and running into the kitchen full tilt just as another crash shook the house.

She saw immediately what it was: the outside shutter at the kitchen window, probably not used for years, had broken loose from its fastening and was slamming as hard as it knew how at the window. She would have to do something quickly otherwise it would smash the glass.

The kitchen door led into an outhouse where there was a privy, an indoor clothes line and a coal-house full of driftwood. Alf had already suggested it as a site for the dynamo and the freezer, as it was built into the rock on the seaward side and had a dirt floor.

Binnie stuck her feet into wellingtons and unlatched the door carefully. The wind opened it, pushing her aside unceremoniously and filled the outhouse so that she could hardly breathe. She grabbed the door and closed it behind her and held on to the handle with her back to the sea, trying desperately to acclimatize to the darkness and the enormous pressure and iciness of that wind driving across the ocean from the north-east. Her hair was no protection for her scalp. The wind blew her hair inside out, and as she turned into the gale the strands were blown across her face. A hat. Next time, a hat.

She edged along the outside of the kitchen wall to the window just as the shutter slammed back against the wall. Halfway up the stone frame her frantic fingers found the hook that she knew must be there. Still intact. She tugged on it and it was rock firm. She moved crabwise across the window, fighting the wind every inch, and caught the shutter as it jerked away from the wall. She hung on to it grimly while it bucked back and forth; it was heavy and unwieldy. It had torn itself away from its fastening and was now rocking madly on probably rusty hinges. She waited for another gust and then went with it, braking the shutter as much as possible, until it was tightly across the window. Then she slid the fastening over the catch and used the hook to anchor it. She had to do everything by touch because, although there was a glimmer of light in the east, the wall of rock above the house kept the lower windows in complete darkness. She waited, battened to the wall by each gust of furious wind. The shutter stayed firm without so much as a protesting rattle. Alf was right: the house had been well built.

Binnie felt her way back to the outhouse door and let herself in with a gasp of relief. The outhouse was draughty but a sanctuary after the wildness of outside. She leaned against the closed door, breathing deeply and gratefully. Her first little crisis and she had coped somehow. She went into the kitchen. It was going to be dark in there with the shutter permanently closed, but while the storm was bad she would have to leave it in place. Perhaps Gabriel could fix it during their Christmas break. She smiled to herself; impossible to picture Gabriel with a screwdriver and chisel.

From the sitting room there came a crackle from the radio; she must have switched it on before the shutter crashed in. She hurried across the hall. The candles in their sconces were not even flickering so no draughts were getting in here.

She flicked the switch to "receive" and Alf's voice came urgently into the sitting room.

"Are you there, Trapdoor? Come in, please. Over."

She glanced at her watch: barely seven o'clock.

"Yes, Binnie speaking. All's well, Alf. No need to worry. Over."

"Good. I can't get across to you. *Mermaid* would not make it. Over."

"That's as we planned. I want a day here at least. Everything is warm and weatherproof. Please don't worry. Over."

"Binnie, Dennison is coming over in *Scallywag*. I tried to stop him but there was nothing I could do. You should be able to sight him in an hour. He must be mad. I've alerted the coastguards, who are on stand-by. Can you radio me if necessary? Over."

She was horrified. The radio reception was not good but there was no doubt about the message. She pulled back one of the curtains and looked out. Even in the dim light of that overcast morning, the sea looked like a witch's cauldron.

She must have flicked the necessary switches because Alf's voice became soothing. "Look, if anyone can do it, it will be Dennison. Don't make any attempt to help him. In fact, don't leave the radio. Keep in touch. Over."

As soon as she switched off she went upstairs and pulled back her bedroom curtains. The rain beat against the glass and visibility was hopeless. Dennison might well be sufficiently skilful to sail the *Scallywag* from Keyhole to Trapdoor, but without a calm neck of sand on which to beach the boat, his beloved *Scallywag* would be smashed to matchsticks and he might well go with her. She felt a surge of anger as she remembered Alf saying Dennison would appear when he was needed, as if he had some kind of sixth sense. He certainly was not needed here and now.

There was no point in watching the grey out of doors from the bedroom window so Binnie went downstairs again, reported to Alf and cleared up her breakfast tray. She had intended to start clearing out one of the bedrooms for Dorrie and Gabriel, but though she went upstairs with a bucket of hot water and plenty of soap, she could not settle to it and after a fruitless half-hour, she marched back downstairs, apologized aloud to the radio set, put on her wellingtons and Theo's old oilskin, and let herself out of the front door.

There was a small area of calm around the pump, and she stood there for a moment, listening to the sea and the wind, and quailing at the thought of Dennison in Theo's small yacht in the throes of it. Then she started up the steps to the ridge and after that she needed all her concentration to clamber down into the dunes and on to the neck of the island. The wind blew mainly at her back, forcing her forward much too quickly, but then there were times when it seemed to go into reverse and be all around her. Breathing was difficult; the sand whipped up and stung her face. Several times she stopped and shielded her eyes to look out to sea, but each time she was forced to put her head down and go on blindly.

When she emerged on to the beach, there was a small respite again. The hummocks of the dunes protected the tiny spit of sand. It was low tide and she wondered whether there was a small chance that Dennison might be able to save himself and his boat. The north-easterly was running sideways here. If he tacked into it and then managed to come back it was just possible he could beach the *Scallywag* and with an enormous effort the two of them could pull it halfway into the dunes. Unless a big wave swamped it . . . unless it was turned over as he tacked . . . unless he was already lost . . .

He came into sight at eight-thirty by Binnie's watch. The sea would have drowned the sound of the outboard anyway but she guessed he would not use it, and sure enough she spotted the straining triangle of the foresail as he tacked away from the beach to make a final run. The sail disappeared into a trough, then rose again and was coming straight for the beach. She waved frantically but had no means of knowing whether he could see her. She waded knee-deep to where the surf was still manageable, waving all the time. If he threw her a rope now and dropped the sail she might be able — Her thoughts stopped dead. He was tacking again, this time away from her, towards the open sea and the wind and rain. Towards the Shark's Teeth.

She screamed at him, turned and dragged herself out of the water and ran towards the dunes where she might be able to see him. Her wellingtons were full and she tore them off and lugged herself up as far as she could go, clutching the tufts of grass and digging her socked toes into the sand. There was no sign of Dennison or the boat. How long she stayed there watching, she had no idea, but there came a moment when she accepted that he had gone and the *Scallywag* had gone with him. Theo's last contact . . . She put her forehead against the cold sand and knew this was the end.

Eventually, chilled to the bone, wellingtons still clasped to her chest, she let herself slide down the hillock of sand back on to the beach. She sat there, tugging on the boots, dull with overspent emotion. She had risked lives and this time a life had gone. She could not go on with whatever stupid quest she had imagined. It was over.

And then, incredibly, there was a thump beside her and a pair of dirty trainers were by her side. She looked up. It was Dennison. She began to cry.

CHAPTER
NINE

Somehow Dennison got Binnie back to the house. She supposed dully that if he had not landed at her feet like he had, she would eventually have dragged herself up over the dunes and down Jacob's Ladder to the front door. She would have had to get to the radio in case there was the slightest chance that Dennison had survived that cruel sea. It was all unimaginable and she surrendered her thoughts to the necessity of putting one foot in front of the other and hanging on to Dennison's ancient oilskins for dear life.

And life was dear. With this small wiry man beside her, urging her on with shouts that whipped away in the wind, she knew that all life was dear. She wept for the dearness of it. Her hands, wet and frozen, threatening to slip off Dennison's stiff oilskins at any moment, tightened their grip. At that moment he represented all life. She did not want to lose it.

They stumbled through the front door and into the kitchen. The candles in their sconces flickered slightly but did not go out. She saw a trail of wet footprints coming from the kitchen. Even through her exhaustion she knew that he had been through the house already, looking for her. He sat her in a chair by the deal table, opened the furnace door beneath the copper so that heat leaped out, and dragged off her wellingtons.

Binnie roused herself enough to struggle out of her jacket. Her hair, grey and heavy with water, hung around her shoulders. She hated herself, sitting there so unkempt and useless. She had imagined she was independent; she had been congratulating herself on coping so well, and now here she sat, reduced to nothing.

She scooped and twisted her hair and felt in her pocket for a rubber band. Dennison was at the cooker making tea. She reached for her slippers and levered herself up.

"I'm sorry," she muttered. She went past him and into the outhouse and the privy. He was waiting for her when she came back and led her to the furnace.

"Keep warm," he said. The chair was pulled round to face the heat and a mug of steaming tea was on the table. He put it into her hands. "Drink," he said.

She looked up at him. His bird face was creased and anxious. She said, "I'm all right. It was just that . . . I thought you had drowned. Like Theo."

"You stopped me. You did not let me drown that day. So I will not drown. That would be a waste for you."

"Oh, Dennison . . . I don't understand. How did you land?"

"I will show you. Later. You must eat. And be warm."

"I made a fire in the other room."

"I know. I will do it again." He indicated the mug in her hands. "Drink," he repeated.

He disappeared into the outhouse and returned with a basket of wood. She was surprised to see through the open door that it was fully daylight. She glanced at her watch: one thirty. Five hours since she had first sighted *Scallywag*'s foresail. She clutched her mug and went to radio Alf.

Dennison came and went without fuss, completely familiar with the house, finding tins of soup in the cupboard and opening two of them with the old-fashioned can opener, reaching for saucepans. He carried the food into the sitting room and she followed him. He had pulled back the curtains and the rain ran down the windows in an incessant stream, but the room was cheerful with firelight and the low table was cleared of last night's reading. He put the mugs on it with a basket of bread nearby and pushed her chair almost into the hearth. She sat down obediently and picked up one of the mugs.

"You must tell me soon how you landed. Where you landed. And — incidentally — why you have come."

"I will show you. And I will tell you." His voice deepened. "I had to come. And you will understand." He took a gulp of soup, wiped his mouth with the back of his hand. "We must speak to Keyhole on the radio." He nodded at the set with dislike. "They will send rescue."

She nodded but he did not move and she realized he could not work the radio.

"I'll do it, Dennison. The soup is very hot . . ." She crouched before the set, switched it on and then began the call sign. As she switched to "receive" Alf's voice crackled into the room.

"Binnie. What news? We've been frantic. Over."

She told him that Dennison was safe and they were both in the house. "I haven't got to the bottom of it yet, Alf. I'll call you again in a few hours. But we are both fine. Eating lunch. Over."

"Thank God. This storm will blow itself out by tomorrow or the next day. I'll come and get you as soon as I can. Over."

"No such thing, Alf. I will be in touch. I promise. Meanwhile, stop worrying. You were right about the house. Great-Grandfather Cash knew what he was doing! Take care. Over and out."

She smiled at Dennison as she returned to her soup. "I had to see to a loose shutter earlier. The woodwork — everything — is in such good condition."

He said, "We tar the outside wood every year."

"Ah. Like a boat?"

"Aye. The Captain makes sure everything is watertight."

"You've worked here a lot, Dennison?"

He looked momentarily surprised. "I cook for the Captain," he said.

She watched him over the rim of her mug. She guessed he had crewed for Theo, odd-jobbed for him in this fortress of a house. It had not occurred to her that he would cook — probably clean as well. She finished the soup and ate a piece of bread before she spoke again. Then she said, "You came for a reason,

Dennison. It must have been important to bring you out in *Scallywag* in a storm like this."

"She skims. That is her strength. To keep her skimming is everything." He gave a half-smile of sheer pride. He had kept her skimming.

He said, "I will show you now. Nobody else knows. The Captain would not want anyone else to know. Perhaps your son. Later."

He stood up and gathered up bread and mugs, then went back into the kitchen. Binnie followed him. At some point he had extinguished the candles in the hall and cleaned the floor. The lamp was still lit in the kitchen, which would be dark all day with the shutter across. He picked up the lamp and went straight to the door of the cellar.

She said, "I haven't been down there. Alf told me there were bottles."

"Yes." Dennison glanced up from the stone steps. "Other stores too."

She saw what he meant: plastic containers of tinned goods were wedged among crevices in the living rock. Mostly the cellar contained bottles — they were in plastic boxes too, piles of them. The whole cellar was the size of the house and supports divided it into sections, leaving the middle of the floor free. In each section the containers of bottles reached up into the darkness, hundreds of them. The whole place seemed dry and certainly did not smell musty. Probably an excellent storeroom.

Dennison went to a group of barrels. "These are full of rocks," he said briefly. He pulled one towards him and rolled it into the middle of the floor, then another. When the third rolled out it was possible to see a trapdoor. "Here is the *Scallywag*," he said briefly, and tugged the trapdoor open. "This is where the old Cash men landed their harvests." He sat on the open trap and reached for the lamp, then lowered himself carefully down and out of sight.

"There is a ladder," he called. "And light."

Binnie groped her way across the cellar floor and past the barrels; light funnelled up from the hole and showed her a ladder running sheer from the mouth of the opening. She emulated Dennison and sat on the edge of the floor opposite the ladder, felt for one of the rungs with her slippered feet and edged forward and down. The light bobbed beneath her and began to descend; she followed. It was easy enough, especially when the darkness around the lamp began to lighten. But then the rock opened up, the ladder ran freely and dipped without the support of the face, and the noise of the sea filled an enormous cave.

She stopped, hanging on with both hands, one foot above the other, gazing across the low ceiling in amazement. Dennison was standing on soft, dry sand, holding the lamp high for her. It lit an area almost the size of the house above it. To one side, the white yacht with its long blue stripe lay on its side, mast down, mooring rope tethered to an enormous iron ring further into the darkness of the cave.

"'Tis above high-water mark, but just to be safe . . ." Dennison said, following her astonished gaze.

"But how did you get in? Why doesn't everybody know about this?"

"It shows itself at low water, when the Teeth are out and ready to bite."

She glanced at him; he was not smiling.

He said, "The Teeth block the waves and make a calm pool. 'Tis why I had to sail so early. I had to be at this point before the tide turned. There's a shelf comes down — Captain always called it the Curtain. Once that's covered, you cain't see nothing of the cave and you cain't get into it neither. There's about half an hour each low tide. And that's all."

She said wonderingly, "This is where the wreckers must have waited. My God, it feels like unholy ground."

"The Captain dived outside of here. Then swam under the Curtain and brought the stuff up this way."

She gazed around, still almost mesmerized. "So Natalie will know about it."

But Dennison shook his head definitely. "No. Just him. And me. And now you. And that's how it must be."

"But why?"

"It's dangerous. It's claimed more lives than it's saved. Like what you just said, it's unholy ground."

She gave a little shiver. "Let's go back, Dennison. I'm thankful you made it in time, thankful you landed safely, but it's — it's a bit like a priest's hole. A refuge and a trap at the same time."

"Aye, 'tis that, Mrs Captain. But now you know why the gentlemen Cashes built the house where they did. And why 'tis called Trapdoor Island."

133

Binnie began to climb up the ladder. The cellar was dark and dreary but a sanctuary after the cave. She sat on the steps and waited while Dennison rolled back the barrels. Then they went up again into the kitchen and he fetched more driftwood and pushed it into the furnace beneath the copper.

"A hot bath tonight, Mrs Captain." He fetched one of the baths from the outhouse and set it by the copper and began dippering in water. She took the dipper from him.

"I can do my own bath, Dennison. Take some of the water and do hot-water bottles for your bed. I don't know where you usually sleep —"

"In here." He smiled unexpectedly. "I'll do the hot-water bottles for you and then keep out of your way."

He worked around her while she assembled towels and soap, dressing gown and pyjamas. Then she could hear him in the rest of the house, making up the fire, lighting candles. She said aloud, "You always knew when you were on to a good thing, Theo Cash!" Then she laughed. Theo had always made her laugh.

She bailed out the bath into the deep sink, remembering how Gabriel had fallen into it on that first visit to the island. By the time she had put the bath back on its hook and made tea, the daylight had gone. She went into the sitting room and said, "We must remember to put the clocks back this evening, Dennison. It's going to be dark by five o'clock tomorrow — winter has come!"

"It will be light by six thirty in the morning, though." He took a mug of tea from her and went to draw the curtains. "We could watch the tide come under the Curtain." He must have seen her reflection shiver in the window because he said, "You should know how it works. There might come a time when you need to know."

She sat down holding her mug in cupped hands. "You are actually making conversation, Dennison!" she said, smiling. "Alf told me you did not speak."

Unexpectedly Dennison said scornfully, "Alf Trevose! He is not right in the head!"

"Dennison!" she protested. "Alf is perfectly all right. You get on well with him. He came and told you about me and Dorrie —"

"I knew about you. Do you think I would not know about you? He thinks he was married to a mermaid!"

"Oh, Dennison! That's a joke because she sings to him all the time!"

"She never sang to him. It's in his mind. He thinks she is still alive. He goes to the rocks to listen to her. He is crazy!"

She was astonished again. "Are you sure? Do you mean she died?"

"Everyone will tell you. They pander to him. Just as they do to me." He blew out his deflated cheeks. "Except the Captain. And you."

She continued to stare at him, round-eyed, then sat back and tried to drink her tea normally.

"It's no good, Dennison. I can't deal with all this information. I've put Mrs Govern's casserole in the oven and we'll have that and then I'll have to go to bed. I'll think about it in the morning."

He said nothing but came with her to hold the lamp and bring in plates and cutlery.

They ate well. She was tired to the point of exhaustion and relaxed after the hot bath too.

She said, "I'm going to leave all this and go to bed. Please don't clear up — I can do it all in the morning."

He ducked his head but then said, "Mrs Captain, I'm that sorry. I have to tell you what I found out. Just in case . . . just in case . . ."

She frowned. "Is this going to spoil everything? Can't it wait?" He shrugged. She said, "Go on then. I probably won't sleep whether I know or not!"

There was a pause while he searched for words or perhaps decided where to start. She knew he found it difficult to talk and said, "Just tell me, Dennison. Straight out. Why did you have to come here in such a hurry?"

She saw his Adam's apple bob convulsively. Then he blurted, "He is dead. You were right. He is dead. And he was murdered!"

She said, "Oh, for goodness' sake, Dennison! He was swept off one of the charter boats and he drowned!"

"He was pushed!"

She closed her eyes for a moment. "Dennison. Listen. You were close to the Captain. You are angry that he is dead. And you want to blame someone. Accidents happen —"

"Not to the Captain. And he can swim like you. Better'n you. Someone hit him. Knocked him out, most likely. Then pushed him off the deck."

136

"How can you possibly know such things?"

"Violetta knows. She saw it happen. She's too scared to say anything. She told me because she thinks I'm daft."

"You've been to Italy since that day on the beach?"

"Course. Where else would I go to find out?"

"And you saw . . . Violetta? She lived with the Captain?"

"Aye. She's not a bad girl. She knew what he was doing. Smuggling them bottles in." He looked up sharply. "He could've brought in other things. But he wouldn't. Just the brandy. Like his grandfather. He thought of himself like that, d'you see. Same as Alf Trevose, listening for his mermaid."

"So you think Theo was mad?"

"No! It made him happy. Made him laugh."

"I see. Was he going to sell all that stuff down in the cellar?"

Dennison shrugged. "That doesn't matter. Not really. But I reckon they might be the reason he was murdered." He sighed. "He had a partner. He wanted to sell his share. It was him."

"Violetta told you that? How did she know?"

"Don't know that. She said she saw them fighting. And then. Bang. And he was gone."

"But . . . for a few bottles of brandy? It doesn't make sense, Dennison. You have got to accept that it was an accident and . . . he's gone."

Dennison said nothing for a long time. Binnie remembered the radio and moved towards it. He stood in front of it, blocking her.

Then he said, "The men on the boat . . . the charter. They were delivering drugs. The Captain was . . . not interested. Violetta said that the other man was. It was a lot of money. He wanted a lot of money."

Binnie said, "Listen, Dennison. I don't think we should talk about this any more. And we mustn't tell Alf or — or anyone else. There is no point." She shook her head. "Let me radio through now and then I must go to bed. I am very tired."

Dennison said, "He needs the island. He will come here. Destroy you. Search out your kin and destroy them too. The island . . . he has promised to use it for —"

"Dennison, stop it. Please. You have no proof of what you say."

"Violetta —"

"Is unreliable. She is scared and lonely and probably wanted you to bring her back with you."

"I said no. I must speak with you first. The man has disappeared. I need to tell you about him. The Captain could have — might have — told him about the Curtain."

She tried to laugh. "Well, he'd never shift those barrels from below, would he? How did *you* do it?"

"I put them there. After I had searched the house."

"Oh God. Oh, Dennison, you came to save me. I am so grateful. But nothing will happen now. Let me radio Alf and then sleep on it."

He stepped aside and she exchanged a brief message with Alf and then switched off the radio.

"Goodnight, Dennison. And thank you."

138

He said, "His name is Daniel Casey. Cash and Casey they called themselves. He will be looking for you."

Dennison turned and went into the hall. She stood with her hand on the mantelpiece, rigid with shock. She heard him moving about in the hall and as she picked up one of the candles and began to blow out the others, she could see him settling himself across the front door.

She went slowly upstairs, telling herself he had made it all up. But how would he have known Daniel's name? And where had Daniel come from?

She wedged a chair beneath the door handle of her room and got into bed. And, against all the odds, she fell asleep immediately.

CHAPTER
TEN

To her surprise Binnie slept the night through. Her watch told her it was seven thirty, which meant it was now six thirty and the curtains were outlined in light. She slid out of bed and pulled them back. The wind was still whipping up the waves beyond the Shark's Teeth, but the rain had stopped. She craned her neck to look towards Keyhole; the sea was calmer within the arm of Trapdoor. That meant that Alf would come over in the *Mermaid*. She felt relieved. She had wanted another day here but now that Dennison had turned up with his cock-and-bull story she needed to get back to Keyhole and the telephone.

She was still staring when a blob of white appeared from behind the rocks. It was *Scallywag*. She frowned watching it tack back and forth. When it disappeared she realized that Dennison was manoeuvring it for a run on to the beach while the tide was on the turn. He must guess, as she had, that Alf would be coming across this morning and would expect to find the *Scallywag* on the beach. She thought of the hole in the cellar floor and the enormous cavern beneath, and shivered.

Downstairs everything was neat, last night's meal had been cleared away, the plates washed and laid out again on the kitchen table for breakfast. There was no sign of Dennison's sleeping bag; new candles were in the sconces in the hall, both lamps refilled with paraffin. She lit the one in the kitchen and then realized that the shutter was no longer across the window. Surely he hadn't repaired the catch already?

Dennison arrived ten minutes later and accepted the tea Binnie put into his hands with a nod of gratitude.

"Not cold but the wind do take your breath." He sipped appreciatively. "I've got the *Scally* almost into the dunes. Tide's dropping fast so she'll be safe."

"I saw. Have you repaired the catch for the shutter?"

"Aye. Soon as there was enough light in the sky I did that. Cain't be all day with lamplight."

"Thank you. There's bacon. Do you want some?"

He nodded again. "I'll go down and put the barrels back over the trap. There's boxes of beans down there. Do you want a few up here?"

Binnie was going to say no but had second thoughts. She did not like that cellar. The sooner all the household stuff was up here the better. "Yes, please."

She fetched the heavy frying pan, which she had scoured several times without much of a result, and started frying the thick slices of bacon Maggie had packed for her. When Dennison came back she opened a tin of beans and added them to the pan. It looked revolting but he appeared to enjoy it immensely.

She went outside to pump some water for the copper and stare at the overgrown garden. She could have made something of this place; the back of the house was almost completely protected and she could have cultivated all the vegetables she would need. It wasn't like the gamekeeper's cottage, where the trees would hide the unknown. Here, everything was open. Or had been. She turned to the pump again and tightened her mouth. It was impossible to dislike Dennison but there was no doubt about it, he had spoiled Trapdoor for her. She could not stay here alone and there was no-one to share it with her. She tried consciously to analyse her feelings about the island but all she could think of was Daniel, and she dared not think too much about him.

She carried in two buckets of water and tipped them into the copper.

"I'll do that, missis." Dennison was wiping his plate with an enormous hunk of bread.

Binnie ignored that and sat opposite him.

"Listen, Dennison. Alf Trevose will be over some time today and I shall go back with him."

He nodded. "Safer over there. I'll mebbe stop another night. Got to find a way to secure that there trapdoor."

She said wearily, "The present arrangement seems to work."

"Aye. But then, you couldn't get in that way from below. If you needed to. It's got to be done with a key somehow."

She couldn't bear to think about that either. She said slowly, "I think I've probably done what I intended to do. The house is habitable. I'll let it to tourists for as long as I can."

He stopped chewing and looked up. "You cain't do that, missis. The Captain wanted it to be yours."

142

"It will still be mine, Dennison. Ours. We feel — I feel — that as a family we are holding it in trust. Not legally, but . . . somehow."

"That's why you cain't let strangers roam around it. This is Cash land. Only Cashes and their people can be here."

"You don't understand, Dennison. And . . . I'm afraid I can't explain. I think I have to go home —"

"This is home, missis."

She said patiently, "I have to see my daughter. And my son. Explain things."

"What I told you last night?"

"Probably."

"They will say it is all lies. Because Dennison told you. And 'e's not right in the 'ead."

"They will say no such thing. They will help me to see it all more clearly. That is all." She tried to smile. "Would you like more bread?"

"No, missis." He frowned, then said ponderously, "You were his wife. Always."

She glanced at him; of course he could not understand. Yet he had been close to Theo . . . She thought of all the heartache, and swallowed. "That's as may be, but it is good I came here, however briefly. I needed to be . . . where he had been." She smiled properly and stood up. "I reckon he loved this place better than any woman." She waited but did not get an answering smile. She said resolutely, "Listen. I'm going to clear all my muddles away. But you know very well you can stay here for as long as you like. It's more your home than mine. Use whatever you need. There's a lot of food —"

"I've got pots over the Teeth. Lobster." He too stood up and took his plate to the sink. "After I've fastened up that trapdoor, I might 'ang on for a bit. See what 'appens."

"You mean you are actually *expecting* someone to come?"

"I told you, missis. 'E's a murderer. 'E'll come all right."

She was aghast. "And what will you do about it?"

"I'll be waiting for 'im."

"Dennison, this is ridiculous. Nobody will come. Why should they? What would be the point?"

"I told you. Last night. 'E wants Trapdoor. 'E could land stuff 'ere an' 'e knows that."

Binnie said with a patience that was condescending, "So he bumps me off and just takes over, is that it?"

Dennison's wrinkled skin darkened. "I don't unnerstand the ins and outs. Maybe 'e got a bit of paper from the Captain to say 'e could have the island if you didn't want it or were dead or something. I don't know. But I do know 'e killed the Captain an' 'e won't stop at one killing. I know it, missis."

Binnie looked at him for a long time, recognizing his conviction and his championship of her.

"Look. I'm sorry, Dennison. I still don't believe you but I do know that you are completely sincere. And you were very brave to take *Scallywag* to the Mediterranean and find . . . Violetta. *Scallywag* is such a small boat —"

"Cap'n an' me — we done it often. The sea was like a millpond. I had to use the outboard a lot of the time."

Binnie began to wash up. It was good to be able to look through the window again.

"I wonder if there was an inquest," she mused. "And what about a funeral?"

"They had to swear — all of them — in front of a — a notary. What they'd seen that night. Just the Captain going over the side. They didn't say nothing about Casey. Course they didn't, 'cos he was their man. She saw 'im, though — Vi . . . letta. There weren't no body so she had a service in 'er church. People knew 'im and turned up. But no-one from 'ome." Dennison lowered his head. "We did ought to do something, missis."

"Yes. We should. In fact, we will. At St Andrew's in Keyhole. At Christmas when the children come over. Will that be all right?"

"Aye." He lifted his head; tears were still in his eyes. "I spec some of the time you 'ated 'im, missis. But you was the one. Like I said, you was always the one."

She lifted her shoulders. "I was the mother of his children."

"You was a *good* mother, that was what it was. A fair mother too."

She smiled wryly. "I didn't poison any minds against him. That's true."

"'E respected you," he maintained stubbornly.

"Ah, that's the difference, Dennison. The more he respected me, the less he loved me."

He was in the middle of protestations when Binnie spotted the *Mermaid* through the window. She patted

145

his shoulder. "You don't have to try to reassure me. We seem to be able to be really straight with each other and that is good." She smiled again; it was getting easier. "Here's Alf in the *Mermaid*. Don't come down with me, Dennison. I've got my stuff in a rucksack. I'll just . . . go." She paused at the door. "Since we are being honest . . . I don't know why I'm saying this — I did not always respect my husband, but I always loved him." She puffed a small wry laugh. "I think I still do. And that was why I came here."

She took the stairs two at a time and grabbed her rucksack, stuffing in a few things lying around. Then she was out of the door and panting up Jacob's Ladder and on to the sandy path leading to the dunes. Was she actually running away from Trapdoor when she had felt so at home there? Or maybe it was Dennison and his tales that made her plunge headlong through the dunes. Or, much more likely, was she running from her own admission? She stopped, panting and holding her sides. She could not possibly still be in love with Theo after all these years . . . surely?

She controlled her breathing gradually. *Mermaid* was still bludgeoning her way through the choppy sea; the tide was halfway up the beach; *Scallywag* leaning against one of the dunes, her sails battened to the lowered mast. Binnie turned a quarter and saw one of the Shark's Teeth exposed for a brief moment by an ebbing wave. The sheer drop to one side of it must be sheltering the cellar of the house. It was incredible to think that beneath that heaving water was the enormous cavern that had protected *Scallywag* all last night. Yet she knew that to be true because she had seen it with her own eyes. What about the rest? What about Daniel Casey?

She squeezed her eyes shut, then opened them and turned again, and there at the top of Jacob's Ladder was Dennison, his hand raised in salute. She raised hers automatically. He turned and disappeared down the steps into the house, and she stood, staring and wondering. She could have dismissed it all as the hysterical reaction of Violetta except for the name. Where had that specific name come from? And the man she knew as Daniel Casey — where had he come from?

She turned another circle, registering the views from every point of the compass as if she might never see them again. Then she faced the sea and the approaching *Mermaid* and smiled. Alf had covered the open seating with an enormous tarpaulin so that when the bull-nosed boat butted its way through the waves the water drained off the cover. It made the *Mermaid* look even more blessedly familiar, as if the boat was wearing a sou'wester.

She watched as Alf dropped an anchor in the lee of some jutting rocks and put out a dinghy from the roof of the wheelhouse. Someone was with him and helped him. She hoped it was Matthew. Whoever it was stood in the stern of the dinghy and used a single oar to propel the little boat into the shore. As a wave pushed it on to the beach, Alf jumped out and pulled it clear of the backwash, and the other man shipped the oar and joined him. It was then that Binnie saw who he was and stopped in her tracks.

Both men pulled again, lugging the dinghy right up the beach, past the high-water mark. Alf giant-strode back down to her.

"See the *Scallywag* is safe up there." He jerked his head at the dunes. "That Dennison can ride the waves like a wind-surfer. How he managed yesterday in that easterly beats me."

Binnie said nothing.

Alf peered beneath the hood of her jacket. "You all right, my maid? Don't let that storm put you off your island. You managed, didn't you?" He spotted her rucksack. "You want to get back to Keyhole quickly? I was hoping we could hang on for the tide to turn so I can bring *Mermaid* right up to unload." He grinned. "I got one of the freezers from Postern Hotel! How's that for service? Couldn't be better with Dennison here, could it? Friend of yours arrived last night and offered to come and help get it in and fixed up to the generator." He turned. The other man was loping from the dunes. He was unmistakable now. He lifted his hand in salute, his face was an enormous grin. Alf grinned too. "Useful bloke to have around, Binnie."

The man jumped from the last hummock and landed almost at her feet. She felt the sense of kinship she had felt before. As if she had known him or was connected to him in some way. It was Daniel Casey.

He said, "What a place! This is marvellous, Binnie — marvellous!" He lifted his hands and turned as she had done. "Dorrie described it rather prosaically and Gabe said it was like Alcatraz! I wanted to see you anyway because I think I've remembered something. Something curious and important." He paused and looked at her as Alf had. He lowered his arms and slumped. "Do you mind me just turning up like this? I thought . . . I thought it would be all right."

"Yes. It's all right." Her voice sounded odd; very forced.

"Are you sure? You don't feel ill or anything?"

"No. Strangely enough, I was intending to come back home as soon as I could get on a flight."

"You're missing Dorrie and Gabe. Of course. They're fine. The whole estate and cleaning firm — it comes naturally to Dorrie. And Gabe — he has promised to stay on until I come back."

Alf took her rucksack. "Let's get into the house and have a cup of tea. Dennison can come back down at high tide and help us with the freezer."

Binnie had forgotten Dennison momentarily. She almost sprinted ahead of the two men in an effort to reach him before they did, calling over her shoulder something about putting the kettle on. When she ran out of breath and looked back, Daniel had spotted *Scallywag* and was standing very still next to it. Alf shouted at him to come on and after another few seconds he moved.

Binnie held her side, breathing deeply. He had recognized the boat. She was certain of it. She reached the path to Jacob's Ladder and ran along it, her breath sobbing in her chest, telling herself that just because Dennison was right about one thing did not mean the rest of his tale was true.

She jumped the last few steps, raced around the well and through the front door. Dennison was in the kitchen. Thank God she did not have to go after him into the cellar. He was scrubbing the deal table. She stood in the doorway and he looked up, startled, knowing something was wrong.

She panted, "I'm ahead of them by about three minutes. Listen carefully. Alf has brought someone to help him to unload a freezer. It's a man I know. From home. His name is Daniel Casey."

His reaction to that name was very quick; he reached across the table and picked up the carving knife.

"No, Dennison. You have to pretend you don't know this man. His memory has gone so he will accept that." She went to him and took the knife. "We need to know whether Violetta is right. Please, Dennison."

He stared at her, not understanding; but at least he let her put the knife in the open drawer and close it.

She said in a low, tense voice, "He doesn't remember the island at all but he was staring at *Scallywag*. I don't know whether he can remember the boat. But whatever happens, just go along with it. It's the only way we shall find out anything."

He still looked stunned; she reached out and gripped his shoulder and then went back to the open door.

The two men were standing by the well and Alf was pointing out the overgrown garden, protected from the wind by the walls of rock. Daniel was silent, staring around him, frowning slightly. Binnie felt a surge of panic; he was beginning to remember, which meant he had been here before and he *was* Theo's friend or

150

partner or whatever he had been. Was he also Theo's killer?

They came inside and sat at the newly scrubbed table while she made tea and cut bread for toast. She and Dennison were almost completely silent, but Alf was full of the events of yesterday.

"What made you do it?" he harangued Dennison. "You could've lost the boat — you could have lost your life, dammit!"

Dennison shrugged.

Binnie said gently, "He goes where he is needed, Alf."

Alf shook his head, then snorted a sigh. "It were a relief when you came through on the radio. And the *Scallywag* beached and neat — this will give my Marigold something to sing about!"

Dennison caught her eye and looked away. Daniel said, "Beautiful boat. Wanted to run my hands over that varnish. You must be a terrific sailor."

Alf started to tell him that the *Scallywag* was a gift from Binnie but she butted in quickly. "Are you coping without Mr Parkes? Do I take it you are head gardener at the Manor now?"

"No!" Daniel laughed. "Can you honestly see Lady Barbara trusting me with her plants? She's advertised for a horticulturalist. Gabriel plans to ask her how haughty should he be. I don't think she'd laugh. As for Mr Parkes, I'm not sure. The cottage is damp and he's got arthritis."

It was hard to imagine the Manor and the gardens and everything that went with her life at Cherrington.

She thought of the gamekeeper's cottage in the woods and shivered. She had wanted so much to find her place here, to fit into Trapdoor as if she had never left it. If it hadn't been for Dennison she might have done that. How marvellous it would have been to be showing Daniel around the house now and taking him up to the ridge to look across the Atlantic at America.

He misinterpreted her silence and said, "I couldn't stay there anyway, Binnie. I have to keep looking for . . . something." He laughed. "Even though I don't know what it is."

"Is it on the Skalls?" she asked. She risked a look at him. He no longer looked ill but there was something careworn about his face; she thought suddenly that she must look like that too. And his hair, which she had thought gingery grey, now seemed almost as white as her own. She looked quickly at the table in case she jogged his memory. If Dennison was even half right then her real protection now was in keeping Daniel's memory well locked away.

He said, "I don't think so." He laughed, suddenly embarrassed. "I think it has something to do with you, Binnie."

She rattled plates on to the table and dropped the toast straight from the grill pan on to them. Dennison stood up suddenly and moved towards the door. Binnie knew that he was making for the cellar.

She said, "Me?"

Alf chortled as he buttered his toast. "Came in on the first flight . . . straight to the harbour, asking about a boat over here. I was coming, of course — got the freezer loaded in all that weather yesterday and —"

Daniel said, "Apparently we paddled together when we were about four years old. Did you know that?" She could not look away from him any longer. Alf continued to chortle. Daniel smiled. "Maybe that's not quite true. But I went to Cherrington on a Sunday school trip. We had a picnic tea in the gardens at the Manor. Sir Henry's father gave us all a stick of rock. I can't remember any of it but there were things I knew about Cherrington, just little glimpses and yesterday — no, it must have been the day before — Sir Henry remembered me, Binnie. The first time anyone has remembered me." His smile widened at her expression. "Yes. It all fits in, doesn't it? I wanted to come to Cherrington and I wanted to paddle. Might that have been because the Sunday school took us on to the beach and let us paddle? Might you have been there too?"

She steadied the teapot with two hands as she poured more tea.

"Is that why you got on a plane and came over here in such a hurry? To tell me that you remembered Cherrington?"

He looked slightly crestfallen. "Well, yes. But, more than that, someone remembered me. And I hoped that you might too."

She dared not let herself go back to those days of Sunday School picnics. Alf took his tea and said with sickening coyness, "I reckon he just wanted to see you again, Binnie. I reckon you got an admirer!"

Binnie started to tell Alf not to be so ridiculous but Daniel cut across her words and said simply, "I *am* an admirer. Especially since I've been at the Manor and realized how well you run the place. But it's more than that. When we met — only last month, wasn't it? — I felt we knew each other. It was just fleeting. And when Sir Henry told me about the annual Sunday school picnics . . . I suppose I was imagining things again." He shrugged. "I wanted to see you. I suppose I haven't got very good reasons but I wanted to see you."

"What did I tell you?" Alf said triumphantly.

Binnie said, "Don't be silly, Alf. I pulled Daniel out of the sea last month. Naturally there is a closeness." She stood up. "Look, can we get the freezer in? It would be good to get back to Keyhole before dark."

Alf looked suitably subdued but nodded. "Aye, we'd best not hang about. I'll give that Dennison a call and we can get organized."

The two men went out and she began to clear up. This delayed departure was unsettling, to say the least; rather like hanging out of a train that was delayed, making long farewells to someone on the platform. The trouble was she did not know who was on the platform. She had the strangest sensation that it was Theo.

CHAPTER
ELEVEN

Binnie watched the sawn-off pinnacle of Trapdoor Island slide away with a pang that was half relief and half sadness. There had been no sign of *Scallywag* as they tramped down through the dunes and Alf had been surprised and annoyed. "Blasted boat was still here when we brought up the freezer — could've done with an extra pair of hands then. But oh no, he chose to disappear on one of his errands. And now he's cleared off!"

Daniel made a conciliatory gesture. "He was thinking of his boat. Getting it back and moored before dark. It's obvious it's the love of his life."

Binnie knew very well that Dennison had pulled the *Scallywag* into the incoming tide and would be waiting for the sea to drop low enough to take the boat into the cavern beneath the curtain of rock. He wanted the place empty until he had done something about the trapdoor. She prayed he had secured that for ever. It was just possible that one day she could come back here if she knew that no-one could use the cavern again.

Alf growled something disapproving but said nothing more. He had got the message that Binnie wanted her gift to be a private one.

He and Daniel slid the dinghy over the wet sand and he jumped in and unshipped the single oar. Daniel went back through the water and lifted Binnie across. It was so unexpected she gave a small squeak of surprise and he laughed.

"I know full well you don't mind getting your feet wet. But just this once, let me do something right."

He slid her into the bow seat and gave the dinghy a final shove before swinging himself athwarts. He was so adept it was obvious he had done it often before. She was speechless. He was at home here. At home with her. With *her*. She felt red hot in the stiff breeze.

Alf laughed and settled the oar in the stern. The tide was falling fast and *Mermaid* would soon be beached herself. They all scrambled in, Alf pulled up the anchor by hand and Daniel loaded the dinghy on to the roof of the wheelhouse — again with a casual expertise — then went to the engine and started it while Alf shoved the boat away from the rocks. Binnie took her usual place beneath the canopy next to Alf, and Daniel sat on the engine casing and looked around him with obvious pleasure. The swell was no longer breaking into the enormous white horses of yesterday and the *Mermaid* rode some and ploughed through others with a kind of truculent resignation.

One wave broke on the prow and hurled itself over the wheelhouse, drenching Daniel; he laughed. She had not seen him like this. He had burst into her life — or she had burst into his — when he was sick and disorientated, then he had gradually taken control of himself and dealt with the business of the fire and the instability of Gabriel with a quiet competence — still diffident. And then there had been his experience at the Manor. She did not know about that. She looked back at him and realized that for that instant he was . . . joyous. The sea had played a trick on him and he had enjoyed it. She smiled at him. She still knew nothing about him and Dennison thought he was an evil man; but there was a side of him — no, more like a glimpse — that she liked. Yes. She liked him. Possibly more than that. Yet according to Violetta, who had convinced Dennison, he had murdered her ex-husband.

It was dark when they reached *Mermaid*'s mooring. They stretched the canvas cover over her again and clambered up the steps of the pier. Above them, Harbour Lights was indeed a patchwork of lights in the misty dark; Maggie Govern had lit every lamp in the house. She was waiting for them at the door and went so far as to hug Binnie to her thin shoulders.

"Well done, m'dear! You've took possession proper like now, haven't you? Trapdoor is yours. Your island. You've weathered your first storm!" She led them through into the kitchen, still talking. "And Alf's brought you the freezer. And your friend has come over to give you a hand. Things are working out real well, I reckon!"

Binnie had not looked at it like that at all and she felt a small gush of warmth at Maggie's assumption that she had done what she set out to do. The funny thing was, she hadn't known what she was setting out to do. She still didn't.

They sat around the kitchen table and Maggie placed a large pie in the centre of it. "The biggest pasty I could make!" she announced. "And Matthew phoned to say he was overnighting at Postern Hotel — he was stuck there last night with that wind — so that's for you!"

Binnie suddenly realized how hungry she was. She had got drinks and snacks for the others throughout the day but she could not remember eating anything herself. Alf dug into the pastry with a carving knife and began to section it up. She looked across the table and caught Daniel's eye. He was smiling. She smiled too.

She knew that Daniel wanted to talk to her about his returning memory and when he made no effort during the evening to get her to himself, she wondered again whether the sight of the *Scallywag* had opened floodgates in his mind. She told herself it wasn't likely: he was so patently happy and at ease. Surely if he realized he had killed Theo, he would not be listening so raptly to Alf's tales of mermaids beyond Postern Island?

He spoke now, his voice gently amused. "And from what you've said about your wife's singing, Alf, I wouldn't be surprised if you'd found her in the sea!"

Maggie Govern made a sound of disgust. "In the Old Peruvian. The pub on the northern tip. That's where he found Marigold Leary!" she said. "She was the barmaid there and she used to sing for the customers. Our Alf came home dazzle-eyed."

Alf laughed, unoffended. "'Tisn't everyone can recognize a mermaid, not even when they come face to

158

face!" he told Daniel. He turned to Binnie. "Didn't I tell you my maid — she don't talk — she do sing?"

Binnie nodded. "But I thought that was because she wouldn't speak to you."

"That's true too. She had to go back, you see. Couldn't stay on land indefinitely. And I was stroppy when she kept on disappearing. That was when she made her vow not to speak to me and she sung instead." He smiled beatifically. "It's a pretty sound she makes. Like when the wind blows from the south."

Maggie flipped her tea towel at him. "Stop trying to be poetic for the visitors!" She turned to Binnie. "It goes down well with some of the twitchers, you know. They hand him an extra big tip. He's getting to believe it all himself, that's the trouble." She smiled fondly. "Makes him happy. So why not?" She made for the kitchen. "I'm for bed, so lock up when you're ready."

Alf began to get up too, then sat down again and looked at them very seriously.

"I got something to say to you two. I don't know anything much about you. But I feel as if I do. As if we might have known each other . . . somewhere else. I get that feeling about certain people." He shrugged. "That's my excuse for putting my nose into your business, something I don't really believe in doing as a general rule." He smiled. "Other people will do it more tactful, I don't doubt. Maggie, for instance. I can see already she has her matchmaking cap on!" His smile became a chuckle.

Binnie glanced at Daniel. She could guess what was coming and rolled her eyes, trying to make it into a joke. But Daniel was still listening to Alf, still at home, at ease.

Alf said, "I cain't be doing with all this waiting around. I'll tell you why. My Marigold has gone back to the sea for good. I shan't be seeing her again. And if I hadn't barged in quick and married her when I did, I would have lost a whole year of complete happiness. And she left me some of it, I'm telling you. It hasn't all gone. Not by any means."

Binnie said, "Oh, Alf . . ."

Daniel said, "You don't have to tell us this, mate. You really don't."

Alf went on stubbornly. "I'm telling you for a reason, Dan. And the reason is that we have to take our happiness when it's offered. It's like a butterfly. Flutters on to your hand for just a minute, then it takes off. You two are made for each other. Don't hang about too long." He scraped back his chair and stood up. "I know what people say about Marigold and me and I don't care. I took my happiness when it was offered and I'll never regret that."

He picked up his oilskins from the back of another chair and made for the door. Binnie watched him as he struggled into a jacket and rammed on a woolly hat. Then the door slammed and he was gone. Unfortunately, his words seemed to be still there, hanging in the air. *You two are made for each other.* They gathered themselves together and settled somewhere on the table. There was an enormous silence in the kitchen; Binnie tried desperately to think of something flippant

160

to say. She did not look at Daniel but was very conscious that he was looking at her.

She cleared her throat and said hoarsely, "I'm forty-three. And I've come here to find out about my husband. To know him again."

She felt Daniel's stillness. He said quietly, "Why? Surely now that he is dead you can lay him to rest?"

"I need to know . . . something."

"Which is?"

She was going to tell him that she had no idea but then said on a kind of gasp, "I need to know whether I've been in love with him all these years. Whether I'm in love with him now."

He flinched; she could see it from the corner of her eye. It was as if she had hit him physically.

At last he said quietly, "Have you found out yet?"

"No. There hasn't been time." She did not want to hurt him. She added, "I need time. I must have more time."

He said nothing for a while and she was about to stand up and leave the kitchen when he spoke again. "On the island . . . you were frightened. I could feel your fear. Were you afraid of your husband?"

"Of course not!" She stood up quickly and made for the stairs. "I was young and he was like a pirate and it was so romantic. I was never afraid of Theo."

"But now . . . was there something on the island — something to do with him — that frightened you?"

"No." She held the newel post and looked back at him. It was amazing how close he was coming to the truth and she met his gaze defiantly. "The storm on

Saturday was pretty awful. Perhaps you sensed something of that."

"But Dennison came over to be with you. And if the worse had come to the worst then Alf would have got help to you somehow."

"I know. I wasn't frightened. Not really. The house is so solid and secure."

He took a breath. "So . . . you weren't frightened. I must have been —" he laughed — "empathizing quite wrongly!" He shook his head as if to clear it, then stood up and took his plate to the sink. She put her foot on the first tread of the stairs. He said, "I need to talk to you, Binnie. And I need you to talk to me. About Cherrington . . . anything really, to stir my memories. Let's put this conversation behind us." He tried to laugh. "It's no more than Marigold Trevose's influence!" He waited and she said nothing. "Don't put up barriers against me. Please. You are the one with the key, I'm sure of it." She climbed another stair. He turned and said with sudden decision, "Even so, Alf was right. The reason I'm here is mainly because I wanted to see you. In September, when I climbed the hill at Cherrington and you stopped your car and reversed back to make sure I was all right — that was when I knew we should be together."

She almost ran but then gripped the banister and stopped herself. He waited, saying nothing more, and after a while she spoke in a low voice.

"Daniel. I should have made it clear from the outset. I still feel married. I always have. There has never been anyone else. You could well be married yourself . . . We know so little about each other. We are still strangers."

He had been moving towards her, now he stopped and put his hands on the table as if supporting himself. He said, "Yes. All right. It must be this place. It's so . . . real . . . yet magical too. That blasted Marigold!" He laughed at himself again. "Go to bed, Binnie. I'll be up soon. Goodnight."

She said faintly, "Goodnight, Daniel." Then climbed the stairs and went into the bathroom. When she eventually entered her room at the top of the house, she took a chair and pushed it beneath the door handle. She guessed that Maggie had let Daniel have Dorrie's room but nothing had been said. She waited by the barricaded door until she heard him go past. She was trembling and found it difficult to think straight. One thing she was sure of: she had lost control of her emotions just as she had lost control of events. She wondered whether she would have gone along with Alf's advice to seize any opportunity of happiness if Dennison had not come up with his story of skulduggery. Her shaking escalated into a shiver. She had always known that Theo was larger than life, but to be larger than death was something else.

She went to the window and pulled aside the curtain. The mist had cleared slightly and there was a moon somewhere above it, silvering the surface of the sea. The *Mermaid* pushed gently against its fenders on the short pier; the long one was clear for tomorrow's arrival of the *Queen*. It was a scene of complete peace and oneness with the elements. She tried to let it soak into her mind and had almost succeeded when something white flicked from the direction of Postern Island. It was a sail. As it came into view and headed out to skirt the long pier and tack into the wide bay of Keyhole, she knew that it was *Scallywag*.

Dennison had done whatever he had wanted to do at Trapdoor; he was coming home. The island — her island now — was empty of all human life. She rested her head against the glass, feeling an unexpected yearning to go back and become part of it again. Then, suddenly, a light leaped on next to her window. Daniel. She withdrew sharply as if he might see her, though she had not switched on her own light. She was holding her breath. After a while, she began to undress and then climbed into bed. The light stayed on for a long time; the length of time it would take for Dennison to moor *Scallywag* and tramp up through the sand towards his lookout.

Binnie slept eventually and dreamed that Marigold swam into the cavern at Trapdoor Island and lived on the dry sand where *Scallywag* had been beached on Saturday morning.

CHAPTER
TWELVE

The next morning Alf went for Matthew and brought him home. He had almost done his part in the hotel refurbishment and was needed at a small clutch of cottages on the other side of Keyhole where some tiles had blown off in Saturday's gale.

"I'm always happier to work on my own patch," Matthew told Binnie as she dried some dishes while he had a late breakfast. "Not too keen on the sea. And when that damned gale trapped me over there . . . well! I thought of you, my maid. Were you all right?" She reassured him. He was a good man and a resourceful man too.

He said, "If there's anything else you might like from the hotel, now is the time to go for it. They're throwing out perfectly good stuff — a lovely bath and basin — suit you very well, I reckon."

"There's no bathroom over there," she reminded him. "And the water supply comes from the well, so I don't think we can manage a bathroom."

He made a clicking sound of disgust. "I'd forgotten how primitive it is. Still, to the visitors I suppose that's part of the charm."

"I hope so." She grinned at him. "Even so, it will be difficult to stock it each time. I'm going to have to be on hand, I think." She remembered and added quickly, "That is, if I want to advertise it for next summer."

Maggie came in, well wrapped up. "I'm going to meet the boat," she announced. "I've ordered a long black skirt and a gold top for the Christmas dance. I don't want it going to the post office and put on display."

"I'll come with you, Maggie." Matthew stood up and reached for his jacket on the back of the chair. "I can carry on over to Midwatch cottages. I'll see you tonight, Binnie. And your young man." He grinned at her. "You're a dark horse, I must say!" Maggie too grinned, then went ahead of him, leaving Binnie feeling helplessly stranded. Surely they weren't *all* jumping to wild conclusions? What had Alf been saying?

She finished tidying the kitchen then got her coat, deciding to join Maggie at the long pier. Apparently Daniel had gone for a walk as soon as it was light, and that didn't please Binnie either. She paused at the mirror in the hall stand and tucked in some stray white hairs before ramming on a knitted cap.

She said to her reflection, "What *is* the matter with you, Binnie Cash? You're a bit embarrassed still, you're a bit annoyed, a bit frightened . . . of yourself! And you are terrified at what Daniel Casey is going to remember!" She sighed enormously. "You are back to being indecisive. Pull yourself together!" She left the front door on the latch and dropped down to harbour level, continuing her homily as she went. "You actually own an island. You've never owned much before except for the car. And you own an island! What more do you want?"

The *Queen* was coming in, hooting and snorting, bells ringing, men shouting orders and greetings. It sprouted aerials and dishes on top of its old-fashioned superstructure, which gave it a foot in both the modern and old worlds. The company that ran the ferry had tried to introduce a hydrofoil service at one time but it had not been able to cope with the seas.

Binnie suddenly felt unable to join the small crowd milling around the gangplank. She kept going straight over the pier and on to the marram grass that skirted the bay. *Scallywag*'s mast was battened down and she rode at anchor in the high tide. There were other boats drawn up on to the sand — *Jenny Girl* and *Moreen*, all with the identifying S and K and their own numbers. There was someone else looking at the boats and walking close to the sea. It was Daniel. As she recognized him, he halted opposite *Scallywag* and stood staring at the slim lines of the boat.

Binnie struck inshore immediately, her indecision temporarily resolved. She would go to see Dennison.

His concrete lookout had seemed close when she walked back from the airstrip nearly four weeks ago, but in fact the going was rough and every time she climbed a rise, the gaunt building seemed to be on the next one, and then the next. She was exhausted when she got there and it was a relief to see him just inside the open door, a net draped over the wooden ladder.

He held a bobbin of nylon in one hand, stretching the net with the other as he mended a gaping hole.

He did not even pause. "It's all done. Down in the cellar at Trapdoor. I 'ad a Yale lock — three keys. Two for you, one for me. We can get in and out." He jerked his head. "Your keys are on the table."

She went past him into the bleak octagonal space of the lookout. Under one of the windows was a trestle table neatly stacked with two saucepans, a plate and mug. Next to them two Yale keys lay side by side. She picked them up and zipped them carefully into her pocket. She took a breath and let it go with sheer relief. "Thank you, Dennison. Are you all right?"

"Aye." He spared her a glance. "And it *will* be all right here, on Keyhole. He dessn't do anything here. But out there —" his head jerked again — "he can get away with it out there."

She did not pretend to misunderstand, but she shook her head as if to dismiss all the implications. "He'll have to go back to the mainland soon. He's got a job." She stared out of the window at the view of Postern Island and the hotel. "I think he might be remembering things. *Scallywag*."

"Aye. You said." He knotted the nylon and snipped it. "Will you be able to tell? If he remembers?"

"I think so."

He went to the Aladdin oil stove where a kettle was puffing steam, and began to make tea. "If it were up to me, I'd kill 'im just like 'e killed the Captain."

Binnie was shocked again. "What on earth . . .? Dennison, we have the word of a young girl who could

168

not possibly have seen all she has told you she saw! And in any case, we certainly cannot kill him, Dennison. You know that."

He poured boiling water into an ancient brown teapot and fetched clean cups.

"Reckon that's what Alf did. When Marigold said she was leaving him, he took her out in the *Mermaid* and chucked her overboard."

"Dennison!" This time she almost laughed, it was so ludicrous. Alf. The all-year Santa Claus!

"It's what the Captain reckoned too, missis. Why d'you think Alf's always going along to Postern Island to listen to the waves?"

"Oh, Dennison, please don't! You know very well Alf imagines the sound of the sea is his wife singing to him."

Dennison said nothing. He put two cups of tea on the table and went to the ladder to fold the mended net and add it to the pile in the corner. Then he climbed to the next level and she heard him walking across the wooden floor to each of the windows. He came down slowly.

"No-one about. The *Queen* is in and everyone's milling around the pier." He sat down and picked up his cup. "I can wait, missis. But the minute he remembers, he'll know he's got to pay the price. He'll know." The gravelly voice sounded like a knell.

Binnie said, "Promise me — promise me you will do nothing about Daniel. If we discover that he did indeed push Theo, then the obvious course is to go to the police. We have to leave it to the law, Dennison. Surely you can see that?"

He was silent for a long time, then said, "All I can really see, missis, is my Captain going overboard and no-one there to 'elp 'im. That's what I can see."

"I know." She stood up. "I'd better be getting back. But, whatever Violetta told you, we don't know anything for sure." She sighed and moved to the door. "Thank you for securing the trapdoor. It will make all the difference. As soon as Daniel goes back, I think I might try another two or three nights over there. Maybe a week. Take some stuff for the freezer, perhaps."

Dennison stood too, gathered the bundle of nets from the corner and preceded her into the wind. She hurried after him, deciding he must be going fishing. They tramped back over the undulating hills and dropped down towards Keyhole town and the beach. She peeled off then and made for the pier, and he stood there watching her go and then disappeared into the dunes. She fingered the keys in her pocket and wondered whether Dennison was making everything worse than it had been with his vague threats and the ridiculous notion that Alf had killed his Marigold. Had he made up Violetta's story of Theo's murder as well?

Various crates and containers were still coming from the bowels of the *Queen* and there were a few people on the pier organizing their disposal or just watching. Binnie struck up from Ditchdrain Street and past a teashop, closed until next season, and another store selling fishing equipment, then went into the fug of the Dancing Bear where she knew she could get coffee and something or other with chips. Today it was chicken; the weather had been too rough for fishing. She sat in the steamy window, gave up on the pliable plastic cutlery and ate it with her fingers. She was hungry after the long walk up to Dennison's lookout. The public bar was empty; from the other side, which served the lounge, she could hear the high voice of a woman asking for a gin and tonic. And then adding, "What about you, Billy? Another beer to wash down the chips?"

Binnie stopped chewing and listened hard. And Will's voice said, "No, thanks. I'll pop out and make enquiries at the post office. Should be able to get inside now that the mad rush is over."

Binnie squeaked and stood up, almost pushing her chair over. She rushed round the bar and there he was, reaching for his long, typically student scarf. "Will!"

He looked up. "Ma! We've been looking everywhere! No sign of you at that address — Harbour thingammy — no-one to ask — landlord here never heard of you —"

He enveloped her in an enormous hug and she held on to him, eyes closed, inhaling the familiar scent of her own washing powder — surely he had washed this ancient jersey since he had left home in August? — certain that he was thinner than before, so pleased to see him she almost wept.

"Oh, Will . . ."

"I know. Oh, Ma."

"I'm so pleased to see you. So *pleased*."

"Me too. Let's sit down."

They sat, and both looked up at the tall slim woman standing there, surveying them with a lopsided smile and a glass in her hand. It was Natalie. And she hadn't changed. Binnie had forgotten how beautiful she was, how elegant. Poor Theo, he hadn't stood a chance.

"It's all so touching!" Natalie said without a trace of sarcasm. "You two, Benita and Billy. Billy is very like his father and it's . . . strange."

Will looked at his mother and said helplessly, "I've told her I'm Will but she insists on calling me Billy. And you Benita."

"You don't mind, not really." Natalie sat down and put her glass on the table. Her voice seemed to embrace them all. "Dammit, we're practically family and here we are trying to sort out how we feel about the bloody man who is our only link. Look on it as a pet name, sweetie. The sort of name that would have been acceptable if I'd been rich Aunt Natalie!"

Will grinned. "Which I suppose you are. But then, we've got some money now, I gather." He turned to Binnie. "Ma? Natalie says the house in Cornwall is worth masses. And you're planning to let the island to the tourists and make a bomb."

"I'm not sure, Will." Binnie could not stop smiling. "I'm working on it. But . . . here you are. It's so marvellous. Let me take in one thing at a time." She turned. "Natalie, I'm delighted to see you too. You have a way of making everything seem normal. And ordinary."

"Oh, thanks. I thought I brought glamour and excitement in my wake!"

"Oh, you do that too."

"I wrote to tell you I was coming, actually. And I went up to collect Billy because I do like to have a man to see to things. You know. Well, of course you don't, do you, darling? I forgot that you are one of the few truly independent women I know!"

"Am I? I don't feel very independent. Especially since Dorrie and Gabe left. I have to be taken back and forth to the island and Maggie Govern has to stock me up with food and Alf has to find a dynamo and a freezer and even then I can't wait to get back here!"

Natalie was sipping her drink and she put the glass down sharply at that. "All I know is that you brought up two children on your own, held down a job, kept a house and home going. That's what I call independence."

Binnie said, "There are different rules here. I have to learn them."

Will leaned forward anxiously. "Ma, you all right?"

"Yes. I am. I can't imagine leaving here actually. But there are complications."

Natalie finished her drink and said acidly, "Bet they're all to do with Theo Cash. That rotten bastard left us with quite a legacy, besides his worldly goods. I had a visit from a — a gentleman last week. Very Sicilian. Asked me whether I knew where Theo might have kept his private papers." She glanced at Will. "Don't you dare laugh again, Billy!" She spoke to Binnie. "Your son thinks I'm some kind of drama queen. But this chap wasn't interested in Theo's bank or savings accounts. He was after something else. Something more tangible than a bank statement." She leaned across the table towards Will. "I haven't told you this, young man. I heard from the estate agent that the house at Constantine had been broken into and obviously searched." She sat back again. "They're looking for a trunk of money. Or some diamonds. Or something." She turned again to Binnie. "Remember, I knew Theo when he was doing all that smuggling."

"Smuggling?" Binnie said, genuinely surprised.

"Haven't you looked in the cellar yet? All right, some of those bottles came from under the Shark's Teeth but not all of them. They're stacked up to the floor of the kitchen — hundreds of bottles of cognac!"

Will was shocked but still laughing. "My father was a smuggler? Dorrie and I — we used to call him a pirate. And he really was! It's terrific. Wait till I tell Dorrie! As for your Sicilian, Aunty Nat, why didn't you tell him about the cellar, get him off our necks? We don't want the stuff and we can't start making a clean breast of it now."

Binnie said, "It might make sense —"

"It's obvious!" Natalie put in. "Of course it makes sense. I had to come and warn you — decide what we could do — just be here as support! That's why I went to get Will. It's almost the end of the term and, anyway, all students skip lectures once in a while."

Binnie said slowly, "Your Sicilian, was he very thin and fair?"

"Sicilians aren't thin and fair, Binnie, for God's sake. He was like Marlon Brando. A godfather type. A *Sicilian*!"

174

Binnie sat back. "Well, that's something, I suppose." She gnawed at her lip. "Nat —"

"Don't you start!" Natalie looked at Will and grinned. "Oh, all right then. Nat it shall be."

"Well, Nat. When you were here with Theo, was Dennison around?"

"The cabin boy? Oh, yes. What a pain. Trying to protect Theo from everything, especially me. He didn't like me."

"He's still not keen," Binnie said.

"Oh God, is he still here?"

"Yes. And he's still very protective."

Will nodded. "I remember Dennison. He was here when Dad brought us over that summer." He grinned at Natalie. Binnie was surprised how well the two of them got on. Will had disliked Natalie intensely as a child. "It was after you'd found out about the Italian girl. You weren't around."

"I should think not. I could just about swallow playing second fiddle to the three of you but when it came to someone who wore the sort of off-the-shoulder tops they wear in comic operas . . . Did I tell you she wants a share of the house?"

Binnie nodded. "I expect she deserves it."

Natalie looked glum. "I don't doubt it. All right. Leave it with me. I'll sort that out. Anyway, what about Dennison?"

Binnie said slowly, "He wouldn't believe that Theo was dead. He tried to drown himself." Will and Natalie drew a shocked breath in unison. "He just wouldn't accept that it could have been an accident and he went to Naples. To see Violetta. And came back with a — a bit of a yarn."

Will murmured, "Poor devil. He worshipped Dad."

Natalie simply said, "Dear God! He doesn't believe Theo's gone. Is that it?"

Binnie raised her brows. "No, actually it's not. Perhaps that would be even worse than his version. Or rather Violetta's version. Which is that Theo was pushed off that boat! Dennison believes that Theo was murdered!" She tried to laugh and Will joined her.

Natalie said quickly, "Could it be anything to do with my Sicilian? My God, I always knew Theo was trouble with a capital T, but this is ridiculous!"

Binnie opened her eyes wide. "Nat, you sound as if you actually believe Dennison."

"You haven't seen my Sicilian!"

Binnie made a face and told them both about Dorrie's car. Will couldn't believe it. "That bloody Gabriel! What she sees in him absolutely beats me. He thinks he's the lead in some sort of a film all the time! Oh, Ma, it's all been happening and I've been stuck miles away —"

"Well, you're here now. That's what I meant about getting back to normal. Dennison can have his little fantasies on his own and we can get on with all sorts of things. I want to dig part of the garden over and plant some spring cabbage and eventually salad leaves —"

"But, Benita! Darling! What about the stuff in the cellar and my Sicilian?"

"No-one can exactly turn up on the doorstep, Nat! Meanwhile we start bringing up the bottles and casting them into the deep!"

"Oh, Ma, what a waste!" Will mourned.

But Natalie was exuberant. "I'll dive for them again, Billy! As and when we want them. No problem!"

Binnie stood up. "Come on. Let's go and introduce you to Maggie Govern. She'll be home by now. She's got other rooms so she should be able to fit you in. And there's Alf too. We must see whether he can take us over to Trapdoor tomorrow or the day after. His boat is called the *Mermaid* and he was married to one."

She began to explain as they walked down Ditchdrain Street to the harbour. Natalie's incredulous laugh rang out often. Will looked intrigued and was about to ask questions when there was a shout from the pier head and Dennison came to join them at a desperate trot.

Natalie made a sound of disgust and Will called delightedly, "Dennison! You haven't changed!"

Dennison stopped short, staring, looking — as Natalie said later — completely mad.

Will said, "It's me. Will. Will Cash — you remember!"

Dennison nodded once and spoke to Binnie. "'E's taken 'er, missis. 'E's taken *Scallywag*! Cou'n't believe it at first. Went up and down the bay. Thought she might be beached in the dunes. Dragged her anchor or summat. But she's gone. And we know where." He was panting for breath. He hadn't spotted Natalie.

She said, "We'll see to it, Dennison. It's not your worry, is it?"

He looked wildly at her and almost recoiled.

Binnie said quickly, "The boat is Dennison's. But as he says, we know where it is." She took a step forward and spoke quietly. "There's nothing he can do there, Dennison. Come in with us to Mrs Govern's and I will make tea. You look all in." She reached behind and pulled Will forward. "You can have a good talk with Will. Old times."

But Dennison would have none of it. "I'm waiting on the pier. I'm waiting for 'im."

Binnie hesitated. Will said heartily, "Another time then, Dennison. All right? Come on, Ma."

She said, "No trouble, Dennison. Promise me —"

"Do depend on 'im, I reckon," Dennison came back stubbornly, and stumped off towards the pier.

The front door of Harbour Lights opened and Maggie Govern stood there, a smile taking up all her face.

"No need for introductions! That's Theo Cash all over again so must be his son! And you and me have met, Mrs Cash. You won't remember me —"

"Actually, I do," Natalie drawled. "You were in the gig races, 1989. Your gig beat ours by two lengths and you called me a poor loser."

"Only 'cos you wouldn't shake hands with the winners!"

Binnie realized with surprise that Maggie was loving this.

"Was that the reason? But I thought you'd just been gutting mackerel!"

"Hardly. I was rowing a boat, if you remember. I was rowing the boat what won the race!" Maggie burst out laughing. "Ah, you're still a poor loser I see!"

Suddenly Natalie was laughing too. She said, "If I'm around next summer let's do it again."

Maggie held out her hand and Natalie took it; they pumped enthusiastically. "Done!" said Maggie.

And they went inside while Binnie hung around for a while, looking out to sea for the first sign of a white sail. It was all right. Of course it was. Even if he had remembered the cavern beneath the cellar he'd never open the trapdoor. But the sea was still slapping waves halfway up the side of the wharf. Would he be able to manage the *Scallywag*? It would be dark in another hour or so.

Reluctantly she followed the others into the hall. She did not want to tell them about Daniel.

CHAPTER
THIRTEEN

Maggie Govern put Will and Natalie in rooms on the floor beneath Binnie, and there was a lot of coming and going with luggage and bedding. Binnie stood at the window and watched Dennison watching the horizon. She moved away when the others came in. Maggie brought tea and poured while they went into a kind of bantering conversation. After the semi-isolation of the last weeks without Dorrie, Binnie found it strange.

"Soon as I saw those two suitcases, I should've known," Maggie said. "If the initials had been N.C . . . but N.B. — I didn't have a clue till I saw you. You haven't changed," she said generously.

"Neither have you. Still as sharp as a knife."

Will stretched his long legs towards the fire. "The gig races weren't half so exciting the year we saw them."

Binnie could have agreed with that. She remembered watching but not really seeing them. Just Theo. Why on earth hadn't she insisted on staying on Trapdoor — or at least Keyhole — when she'd had the children? His idea of those weekends together being mini honeymoons . . . and all the time he had been falling in love with Natalie.

She finished her tea and said, "I'm going to have a quick word with Dennison. It's dark and he can't stay on the pier all night."

"Let him be," Natalie said carelessly. "He's always been like this."

Will stood up. "Actually, he has, Ma. Like a dog with a bone over everything. An obsessive, I guess."

Binnie bundled her hair back into her hat. "Is it all right if I ask him back here for some tea?" she asked Maggie.

"He won't come. But . . . all right."

Will followed her out of the door and took her arm. "Listen, Ma. Don't let Nat get you down. She's loving all this — the Sicilian business and Dad's boat going missing, everything. But all the business with the house and the legal stuff, she's been marvellous."

She squeezed his arm. "I'm fine with Natalie. Honestly. And I know she thinks we've all got parts in a film about piracy on the high seas but there has been some kind of . . . I don't know . . . skulduggery, I suppose. Concerning Dad. And I don't want us to get caught in the backwash."

They reached the pier and hung on to the rails to get their bearings. Will put his arm across her shoulders and she felt a rush of pure love for him.

She said, "Have you talked to Dorrie at all?"

"Yes, of course. She phoned as soon as they got home. That stupid Gabriel she's with — the sooner he's off the scene, the better."

"Did she tell you about Daniel Casey?"

"The man you pulled out of the sea?" He chuckled. "Never a dull moment in Cherrington, is there? No wonder you love the peace out here!"

"He's turned up here, actually. He's lost great chunks of memory but there are things he remembers about Cherrington and this place. He followed his nose when he came to Cherrington for a paddle — yes, he still thinks that's what it was — and he followed his nose out here. And now he's taken Dennison's boat and doubtless gone out to Trapdoor."

Will was silent. She gave a small laugh. "One of Dennison's obsessions is his intense dislike of Daniel. And now . . ."

Will said slowly, "Daniel Casey. Sounds vaguely familiar somehow. One of Dad's disreputable friends? I might have heard the name . . . I would have been only nine years old that time we were here. Did Dorrie know him?"

"No. I'm sure she didn't."

"She was always so buttoned up about Dad. Wouldn't let him in at all."

"My fault. I was so determined never to be a millstone round his neck. I saw him as a free spirit."

"Suited him fine, I expect." They both stared at the crouched figure on the end of the pier. Will said, "So Dennison knew this Daniel Casey. Did Daniel Casey know Dennison?"

"I don't think so. But he recognized, or half recognized, *Scallywag*." Binnie frowned into the darkness. "I'm not sure whether Daniel knows that I have given the boat to Dennison. And whether that means anything to him."

"It was Dad's boat, and you've given it to Dennison? That was generous, Ma."

"Especially as Gabe had his eye on it. Not to own but to sail. He saw himself skimming over the waves, connecting Trapdoor to Keyhole. But it's Dennison's boat, Will. If you could have seen him sailing through that storm last week — it was amazing."

"No wonder he's looking out for you." He laughed. "Never mind a white charger, he's got a white boat!" He tugged her upright. "Come on, let's go and drag him indoors."

Binnie was not surprised when Dennison refused the invitation to go back to Maggie's. It was impossible to imagine this wizened, salted man sitting next to Natalie, drinking tea.

Binnie hunkered by him. "Listen, Dennison. Go home. Please. You know very well what is happening: he's beached her at low tide and will have to wait for another low before he can get out. That's midday tomorrow. I'm willing to wager that if you go to the bay tomorrow afternoon, she will be anchored exactly where she was before."

"It's my boat, missis. You know that. He's a thief as well as a murderer!"

"Keep your voice down, Dennison," she came back sharply. "I haven't mentioned any of that stuff to Will and I don't want to. And I'm not sure whether Daniel knows that it is now your boat. Supposing a bit more memory has come back and for him it's the boat he must have shared many times with the Captain?"

"You won't believe it, will you, missis? First that he killed your 'usband. And now that he's a thief."

"He's ill — in a way he's ill. And until we know —"

"Suppose to 'ave lost 'is memory. Yet you reckon 'e knows about the cave and the Curtain?"

She took a deep breath. "He follows his nose. He may have discovered the cave, he may not. I don't know. I don't know much for sure, Dennison. What I do know is that if anything happens to Daniel Casey, the finger will point to you. And I do not want that. You looked after my husband, you were his right-hand man."

That silenced Dennison. The two of them squatted there, the sea glinting below them in the lamplight. Will, hovering around, told his mother later that they looked like conspirators.

Eventually Dennison got to his feet with some difficulty and watched as Binnie did the same.

"I'll go back tomorrow," he said. He turned to Will. "I'll say goodnight to you, my boy, and ask you to look after your mother."

They watched him lope back along the pier and disappear into the darkness of Ditchdrain Street. Will took her arm again.

"Actually," he murmured, "I'd always planned to put you in a nursing home the minute you needed looking after."

184

She looked up into the pale blur of his face, startled for a moment, then was overcome by giggles that were near to hysteria.

"You ungrateful child!" she spluttered.

They went into the house again and she ate a supper of grilled mackerel and listened to Natalie's tales of her eight years on Trapdoor Island, and felt almost happy. When they went upstairs to bed, Natalie surprised her by lingering on the landing long enough to say, "Thanks for letting me blather on like that, Benita."

Binnie smiled. "It was good for me, Natalie. Somehow the thought of you and Theo enjoying the island every summer like that makes it all so much less of a betrayal."

Natalie widened her beautiful eyes. "Oh, my dear. I never thought of it as a betrayal. I thought of us as — well, almost as sisters. That was why I came to see you afterwards." She sighed. "We've got to let it go and perhaps it's good to talk about it. I think that must be what I came for." She frowned. "I've always harboured awful feelings towards Theo. And now they seem to be melting away! Is that ridiculous?"

"No." Binnie made a face. "No more ridiculous than me wondering whether I am still in love with the wretched man!"

"That's only because of the legacies." Natalie became her usual practical self. "It's softened you up. He intended that, I expect. He wanted you and the kids to love him again. And he always got what he wanted!"

Binnie said abruptly, "I must go to bed. I'm tired."

"I should think so. You've obviously been working your socks off!" Natalie leaned forward and pecked her cheek. "Goodnight, my dear. Try not to worry. All that business about the Sicilian — just an annoyed wine merchant, I expect. He didn't even have an Italian accent!"

Binnie found she was smiling as she got into bed. Natalie was turning out to be quite a tonic.

The next morning, the rain fell gently, making a mist of the sea and sky.

"Wonderful for the complexion," said Natalie doubtfully, gazing through the window at the pier, apparently hovering in mid-air.

Matthew Govern left early for Midwatch cottages and Alf returned from Postern Island and moored his boat halfway up the pier on a falling tide. He was introduced to the new arrivals and made an immediate good impression by informing them he had spent nearly all the day before on the rocks at the northern tip of Postern, listening to the sea.

"It'd tell you things . . . what to do and where to go. Things like that."

"How simply lovely!" Natalie exclaimed. "Someone who talks to the sea. Now I've heard of people who talk to flowers, but this is something else."

Alf said, "Aye. Well, it's telling me now that if you want to go over to Trapdoor we'd better get the tide." He looked at her through his copious hair and added, "I've never talked to flowers nor the sea. I listens. That's what I said. I listens."

186

Binnie caught Will's eye and smiled. She knew he was making a mental list of the eccentrics in the Skalls; first Dennison and now Alf. And he would soon be able to add Daniel's name.

She said, "You two go over. I'd like you to see the place without me around. You can give me a proper objective view when you get back."

"In other words you want to keep an eye on Dennison," Will commented while Natalie went for wet-weather gear.

"Oh? What's 'e bin up to?" Alf asked sharply.

Will told him. "His boat — *Scallywag* — disappeared yesterday and he thinks Mum's lame duck has taken it over to Trapdoor. He was on the pier, lying in wait for him to come back and be instantly murdered!"

"What? Daniel Casey? Took *Scallywag*, did 'e? Probably don't know you gave it to Dennison, Binnie." Alf turned to Will. "He's a good one. Not a lame duck by any means. Certainly pulled his weight on Sunday when we took the freezer across." He tugged at his beard. "Wonder what 'e's up to, sailing over to Trapdoor on 'is own like that."

Binnie said, "Neither Will nor Mrs Broadbent has met Daniel. You probably realized, Alf, he has bad memory loss. He was obviously used to the sea, wasn't he? Probably took the boat out in the hope of remembering something."

"Ah. That must be right."

Natalie appeared looking improbably glamorous in oilskins and a sou'wester.

"Come along then." Alf grinned at Binnie. "Good luck with Dennison. 'E's getting worse, I reckon!"

Binnie watched them go, then went upstairs to try to catch a glimpse of the bay through the mist. It was impossible. In any case, the tide was not low enough yet for *Scallywag* to be launched from the cavern and then there was nearly an hour's sailing back to Keyhole. She thought of Daniel spending all night there, and shivered. She was so certain that was what he had done. She imagined him climbing that long swaying ladder, wedging himself against the rock and hammering at the trapdoor. She had no way of knowing how Dennison had secured it but he must have left signs of his work. Supposing Daniel did not remember that the cavern stayed above the sea — supposing he thought he was caught like a rat in a trap? She wondered whether there was the slightest possibility that it could tip him into the trancelike state he had been in that first day in Cherrington. Might he even "go for a paddle"?

Maggie called up to see if Binnie wanted coffee and she went downstairs and asked if there was anything she could do. There was no point in going to see Dennison yet and she had nothing else to occupy her thoughts.

Maggie said, "Aye. We'll peel the potatoes together. I've only got cold meat and pickles for tonight so a big helping of mashed potatoes won't come amiss!" She brought the coffee to the table. "You should have gone with them, my maid. All this worrying about Dennison is getting you down. He's not your responsibility, you know. Anyone on Skall will tell you he goes his own way. Stubborn as a mule and just as unreasonable!"

They drank coffee and peeled potatoes, and Maggie laughed at the way Alf had dealt with Natalie that morning. "But you know, he will have done just that. Gone to the top of Postern and found himself a place in the rocks and listened to the sea." She smiled wryly. "He thinks it's Marigold singing to him. Whenever he's a bit troubled that's what he does."

"It sounds sensible." Binnie cut a big potato into four. "I think that was my aim out on Trapdoor. To open all my perceptions to the place. Let it say something to me."

Maggie flicked her a glance. "Yes. Well, I'm not sure about that. I've never had the time to sit and do nothing."

"None of us have, have we? That's why it's so important. I kept busy most of the time there, when I should have been still. Alf has got the right idea."

"I'm not so sure, my maid. Alf lives half his life in the real world and the other half . . . who knows? Marigold went off with anyone who gave her a look. Finally she went off with some American — his own deep-sea fishing boat, pots of money. All that business about her going back into the sea as a mermaid — that's Alf's make-believe life. We go along with it to keep him happy." She sighed. "Only happened in the summer. He'll get over it, given a bit more time."

Binnie was surprised. She had imagined that Marigold had happened a long time ago. But at least

Maggie's version of Marigold's disappearance was better than Dennison's.

They opened a tin of soup between them for lunch, then laid the big table for the evening meal. After that Maggie announced she was going upstairs to do some cleaning. Binnie told her she was going to see if the *Scallywag* was back in the bay.

"All right. Don't forget what I told you. Dennison might be a law unto himself, but he's not your worry!" Maggie smiled. "I shall miss you when you go to Trapdoor for good."

Binnie paused in doing up her jacket. "Do you think I will?"

"Yes. It will be difficult to let. But if you're there to look after the visitors, that will be a different story."

Binnie smiled as she walked across the long pier and into the dunes. A seaside landlady. Is that how she would end up? It could be worse.

The rain had almost stopped but the mist still wrapped her in a personal space and hid the clumps of marram grass so that she constantly stumbled. As soon as she judged she would be within the arm of the long bay, she worked her way down on to the beach and the firm sand. The mist was thicker over the sea, and although the bows of one or two boats showed themselves occasionally, there was no sign of the familiar white boat with its blue stripe. She took off her wellingtons and socks and rolled up her trousers. The water was ice cold and hard on her skin. She clutched at her rolled trousers in gloved hands and called out, "Ahoy there — *Scallywag*! Are you there? *Scallywag*!"

There was no answer. She thought again of that cavern and the restless water outside. Dammit, *why* had he gone there? Following elusive memories was one thing, walking into the sea, whether it was the Bristol Channel or the Atlantic, was another. She stood still, the water lapping her calves, the mist pressing all around her, and felt again the terror she had felt when she had thought Dennison had drowned. Whatever Maggie said, she was responsible for whatever happened out here. Simply because she was here.

She opened her mouth and let out a great cry. "Daniel! Daniel — where are you?" And almost immediately the reply came back.

"Binnie? I'm here. By the red buoy. Just putting the boat back the way I found it. Call again and I'll come towards your voice."

She almost sobbed. "I'm here . . . I've got no points of reference. The mist is everywhere — everywhere . . ."

"Stand still, my love. Keep talking."

"I don't know what to say. I gave the boat to Dennison and he is going to kill you . . . and it would have been my fault if you'd drowned too. Where are you?"

And he was there, a dark shape at first and then solidly, physically in front of her, putting his arms around her, holding her hard against his oilskins. He murmured into her hair, "You're in the water. You're always coming after me in the water . . . Binnie, I love you. I've loved you for years. Ever since he told me about you. Ever since he described you, with your hair always falling out of its pins and your round face and your — your capable body!"

"What? Oh my God. You're talking about Theo!"

"Yes. I've remembered your husband. He said if ever we were in trouble we would go to you. You would help us. I loved you then, Binnie. Alf was so right." He picked her up bodily and staggered to the shore. "We must grab each other while we can. That's what Theo meant. He meant us to be together ..." He was kissing her in between sentences, frantic gulping kisses. "If we can be together everything will come together, my darling." He held her head and kissed her eyes, her nose and her mouth again. The intensity of his passion overwhelmed her; she was weeping, sobbing against his face. Even at his most ardent Theo had never been like this. She felt herself responding even as she wept.

"Don't cry," he whispered. "We will be happy. It will be all right. I know how much you loved him, Binnie. But I can make you happy if you give me half a chance. You can save me, Binnie. You can. Just as you did on the beach at Cherrington. You are the one ..."

He got no further. From behind the wall of mist, something came at them; a club, or a random plank from the sea. It hit him on the side of the head and he went down instantly and she went with him because they were intertwined. She saw no-one but she knew that it was Dennison who had wielded the makeshift weapon. A splash told her he was in the sea, going out to his boat; Theo's boat.

She stayed where she was, crouched over Daniel's inert body. His head was on the sleeve of her jacket, which was already soaked in blood.

This time her shouts were high-pitched screams that seemed to cut through the swathes of mist like knives.

"Help! Somebody, help!"

She had no idea how long it was before Walter Polpen emerged out of the mist.

"It's all right, Mrs Cash. Dennison went past the post office fifteen minutes ago and I called the ambulance before I came down. He was carrying what looked like a baseball bat." He crouched on the other side of Daniel. "He's breathing. Reckon he'll be all right. Keep him tipped sideways like that . . . well done." He peered at her in the gloom. "You all right, m'dear? Did he go for you?"

"No. Thank you, Mr Polpen. Thank you so much." She was still weeping and he was embarrassed.

"I'll go and direct the driver. You'll be all right?"

"Yes. Daniel borrowed Dennison's boat and he's gone off in it now."

"Ah . . . well." He picked up pebbles and marked his way back to the dunes.

Binnie put her head down to Daniel's and whispered, "Please don't die. I think I must love you. Just don't die."

CHAPTER
FOURTEEN

The cottage hospital, tucked into a fold of the downward-leaping hills below Dennison's lookout, had been built with fever in mind and was as far from any of the old cottages as it was possible to be. Any illnesses involving modern technology had to be dealt with by the big hospitals in Truro or Plymouth, but St Andrew's was well able to cope with injuries incurred in the sea or on boats.

As the sister said to Binnie, "We've got enough shots and bandages for an army! Don't worry about a thing."

"It's just that . . . he hasn't been well. Before this accident I think there was another. A previous accident . . . incident. He's suffering from amnesia."

"We'll see," Sister said cheerfully, and then went on to assure her that Daniel was going to be fine. He was exhausted and very cold but the head wound was superficial. "He can go home soon, probably tomorrow. Then all he will need will be frequent doses of TLC . . . tender, loving care," she translated in the face of Binnie's blank face.

Now Binnie was in a waiting room with the mandatory cup of tea. Her hands were shaking and she put the thick white cup and saucer on a magazine table.

194

Nobody had moved the magazines from their neat pile that day; on the top the *Skall Express* headlined the fishing catch for last March.

She told herself that in retrospect Dennison's attack was not unexpected. It was what went before that was so shocking. Daniel must have remembered Theo — he had mentioned him over and over again. And he had remembered her through Theo. And he had said he loved her. He had been passionate, tempestuous, and he had swept her along with him . . . she had allowed that to happen. More than just allowed it to happen — she had gone with the enormous force of it; she had reciprocated. Reciprocated — what a banal word for such a torrent of emotion. It was as if she had dammed all her feelings since Theo left her and they had burst out down there on the beach. And he had been *delirious*, for God's sake! He had been suffering from near hypothermia and complete disorientation, and heaven knows what else, given that he probably spent the night in that ghastly cavern. And he must have remembered quite a lot of things connected with how to get into it. She put her head in her hands and tried to block out the picture of herself . . . reciprocating. She felt her hands hot and damp and realized that she was crying.

There was a flurry outside in the reception hall. Natalie and William surged through the door in an aura of consternation and sat either side of Binnie, neither of them wanting to take precedence over the other so both of them patting her awkwardly.

"Have you found out what happened? Walter Polpen came over — we got back to Keyhole about three o'clock and this was about four — he said there had been an accident and you'd taken your friend over to the hospital." Natalie tried to look into Binnie's downturned face. "Are you all right? We didn't think you were hurt — are you — are you?"

"No — no, not at all." Binnie glanced up. "It's just the shock. You know. Some man coming out of the mist with a hunk of wood and knocking Daniel senseless."

Will said doubtfully, "We understood it was Dennison. And after what you told me yesterday, I assumed he was getting back at your Daniel for pinching *Scallywag*."

Binnie hardly knew why she denied this. "I think I would have recognized Dennison. This man was bigger. No-one we knew."

"But why?" Natalie said. She tried to hoist Binnie upright, then let her go with a gasp. "Darling! Was it the Sicilian? My God, I didn't think he'd follow me out here! But I told you, didn't I? I knew he was up to no good. I bet you a hundred pounds he's taken the boat! If this mist has gone by tomorrow, we'll go straight down to the bay and check. I *know* the boat will be gone!"

Will slid his arm protectively around his mother. "Of course it will be gone, Nat. Dennison has been waiting for its return. He's not going to leave it anchored in the bay where this chap of Ma's can nick it at any time."

"Darling," Binnie straightened at last and smiled at them both, "Daniel is not 'this chap of mine', as you

196

put it. And though my immediate reaction was to deny it was Dennison, I have to admit it probably was. But if I identify him, the authorities — is there a policeman on Skall? I haven't seen one but there must be — will be forced to arrest him. And that would finish Dennison for good. Don't you see?"

There was a pause. Will nodded and after another few seconds Natalie said, "Then let it be my Sicilian, darling." She thought about it. "Perhaps not. If my dearest Ernest got to hear about it, he might not let me out for a long while."

Will laughed and hugged Binnie to his side. "I think person unknown is much better anyway," he said. "If you're really all right, shall we go home, Ma? Maggie is worried sick and Matthew is waiting outside in his 1936 Flying Standard."

"Oh, how kind of him." Binnie felt some of the weight lift from her shoulders, though she knew she could not leave until Daniel came round. "Go back with him, you two. Please. I must wait and speak to Daniel."

Natalie said, "But why?"

Will replied for her. "Because he is one of Ma's lame ducks and she never gives up on them."

"It's not even that, Will. I want to know what he remembers."

"You mean this blow on the head might have kicked back his memory? Was he completely clueless then?"

"He was beginning to remember. Cherrington. The Thoroughgoods. He'd been at the Sunday school picnics, years ago. He came here to tell me about it.

There had to be a reason he struggled to get to Cherrington. But where did he struggle from? He might have remembered something else. Or, possibly, he might have lost every bit of memory again."

"What if he's forgotten *you*, Ma?"

"I think it would be a good thing. You could take him back to the Manor and Dorrie would make sure he was all right."

"Ma, now is not the time to bring it up . . . but . . . I don't want to go back."

"You don't want to go back where?" Comprehension dawned and she took his arm and shook it. "But, Will, you've got another two years to do at university."

"I know. But we need to work on the island now. Not in two years' time."

She looked at him hard. She realized how exciting it must be for Will to discover he owned an island, far more exciting than living in a rented, run-down house in a university city. She sighed.

"You're right. Now is not the time. Stay a week and see what you think then."

"OK." He smiled and looked so like Theo she could have wept.

Natalie said, "I can't stay a week. Poor Ernest can't manage without me and he'll be home on Friday. I'll have to leave then. Or Monday at the latest."

Will set his mouth stubbornly at the implication that he would automatically return with Natalie. Binnie could only feel a vague relief that she was staying no longer. Luckily, a nurse put her head round the door then and announced that Daniel was conscious and asking for "Binnie".

"That's me." Binnie stood up with alacrity and obviously either Will or Natalie stood up too because the nurse said, "Only one visitor, I'm afraid. And just for a few minutes."

The ward was upstairs and Daniel was its only occupant. The sister was standing by him, taking his pulse, her concentration on her fob watch. He swivelled his eyes when Binnie approached; his head was heavily bandaged and obviously difficult to move.

"Oh, thank God." He reached up with his free hand. "They said you were all right but I wasn't sure whether to believe them."

"I'm fine." She took the hand and glanced at the sister with raised brows. She received a brisk nod. "We have told Mr Casey what happened, Mrs Cash. Otherwise we have no explanations. But his memory is intact up to the time he received the blow." She picked up the chart from the bottom of the bed and ticked a box. "I'll leave you for five minutes only. You may bring some clean clothes tomorrow afternoon and take him home."

"Thank you, Sister." Binnie looked back at Daniel and was silent until they had the ward to themselves. She said, "When she says your memory is intact, what did she mean?"

"I remember taking the boat. I knew it, you see. It didn't seem like stealing, though I can understand Dennison is keeping an eye out for you."

"I gave *Scallywag* to him, Daniel. It seemed only fair."

"Ah. I see." He sighed. "Well, I took the boat. I looked at it for a long time and it was all there, in the right places. The blue line and the spinnaker — there's a tear and I mended it." He stopped and frowned. "Some time. A long time ago, perhaps." He was hanging on to her hand as if he thought he might fall somewhere. "I knew exactly what to do. There was no wind to speak of. I pushed down the outboard and started her first time. There's a knack, you know. You give a short pull, then a long one, and she comes up so sweetly." He smiled. "Sweetly. A good word, Binnie." Still she said nothing and he sighed again, then went on: "I went straight there — the boat took me there. And it was low tide so I went under the Curtain and into the cavern and pulled the boat on to the wet sand and went up the ladder. Took me a long time, Binnie. No light of any kind. I couldn't find the ladder, then I didn't seem to be able to climb it. And when I did, I couldn't lift the trapdoor. And when I got back down again, I was trapped myself. The tide had covered the Curtain. I had to float the boat up on to dry sand bit by bit as the tide flooded. And I think I forgot that the tide would ebb. I thought I was caught there." His grip on her hand was painful. "That was why it was called Trapdoor, you know. Because it was a trap. People died there, Binnie. They died."

So he knew about the cavern and the Curtain. "It's all right." She cupped his face with her other hand. "That was a long time ago. You got out and came

200

home. You're safe." She tried to smile. "In spite of Dennison, you are safe now."

He managed a smile in return and loosened his grip slightly. "Yes." His eyes looked heavy with sleep. "It was so cold. And the boat didn't know the way back through the fog. When I heard your voice, it was like an explosion of light. Binnie, Theo Cash — he said . . . Binnie will look after you . . . Binnie is the one . . . look for Binnie. And there you were and I knew I had loved you from the moment I saw you on the hill by the church and then in the sea. And before that. When Theo talked of you there was something in his voice. Something special. I fell in love with you then. Before I met you." His eyes closed.

She stayed very still, even when Sister beckoned her from the door. Her mind was in turmoil. She had thought he would have the answers to so many questions; but, of course, she was the only one who could answer the question she was asking. The trouble was — the real trouble was — she could not put that question into words, even in her own head. So there was not a hope of supplying herself with an answer.

She went slowly back down the stairs and out into the fog. A tiny grey car was waiting outside the little Victorian porch; Will and Natalie were squashed into the back and Matthew leaped out to open the front passenger door for Binnie. He was all concern.

"You're not hurt, my maid, but it's been a shock and the sooner we get you by a fire with a nice hot-water bottle on your lap and some of Maggie's soup inside you, the better."

She reassured him as best she could, and felt Will's hand on her shoulder and reached behind to pat it in response. "You're all so good. I'm sorry to drag you into this. I'm still not sure what is happening. But I can tell you that Dennison went to Naples to question Violetta about Theo's death and came back with a very peculiar story."

There was a pause while they all waited for her to explain but she said no more.

Matthew said diffidently, "None of my business, of course. But Alf mentioned how oddly Dennison behaved last Sunday. Coming from Alf, Maggie and I rather discounted it." He laughed uncomfortably. "We're used to oddballs on Skall. People come here who can't fit in anywhere else. We had nudists on Transom till the first winter storms."

Everyone laughed with him. There was a relief in seeing Dennison as just another "odd ball".

"The thing is . . ." Binnie took a breath, "it seems that Daniel Casey and Theo Cash had been friends — maybe not friends, but partners — for some time. I had never heard of Daniel and neither had you, Nat, had you? But Dennison knew about him and doesn't trust him. And it seems that with a subconscious part of his mind Daniel turned up at Cherrington looking for me."

"And then came here?" Natalie spoke in a low thrilled voice. This was the stuff of romance.

Will said flatly, "And Dennison tries to kill him."

"Not kill," Matthew put in quickly. "Punish him for taking *Scallywag*. He shouldn't have done it, of course, but we can understand it, can't we? Among ourselves?"

"Of course we can," Natalie said robustly. "He's an oddball — simple — you said so yourself, Matthew. Doesn't wait for explanations."

"I certainly wouldn't want Dennison to be interviewed by the police," Binnie said. "I don't think he could cope with it. How he managed to track down Violetta in Italy, I'll never know. But I'm fairly certain that Daniel won't want to make any charges, so the whole thing can be forgotten."

Will said doubtfully, "I don't think Dennison will forget." He sat back and peered out of the window at the impenetrable fog. "I could talk to him, Ma. I'm not involved. But I'm connected. And if Dennison is trying to protect you, then presumably Dorrie and I come into that equation as well." Binnie said nothing and he leaned forward again and said impulsively, "Don't you see, Ma? I can *do* things here — I can be useful!"

"Let your mother be, my boy," Matthew put in. "Like I said, she's suffering from shock."

Will subsided and there was silence in the car until they bucketed down Ditchdrain Street and parked at the head of the short pier. Then Maggie Govern arrived at a trot and took over. Binnie surrendered herself thankfully. She wondered whether she had ever been so tired in all her life.

CHAPTER
FIFTEEN

Daniel was dressed and sitting on the very edge of his bed all ready to leave by the time Will and Binnie arrived the following afternoon.

Will had found a change of clothes in Daniel's cupboard at Harbour Lights and had packed them in his own bag. He said, "How come you're dressed? They told Ma to bring clothes."

Daniel held out his hand. "My God. You are so like your father. It's a pleasure to meet you." He pumped Will's hand enthusiastically, then added, "They're just marvellous here. They've washed and dried all the clothes I had on when I arrived. Food's wonderful too. I had about five scrambled eggs for breakfast. It's almost worth a bump on the head to get this four-star treatment!"

Will looked surprised, then smiled. "You sound . . . on top of the world!"

Daniel nodded. "I feel good. Not so foggy and befuddled. I was doing things and didn't know why." He smiled at Binnie; she noticed what a sweet smile he had. "Your mother has told you I had a sort of partial amnesia?"

"We thought it was more than partial." Will's smile widened and Binnie thought with a small shock of surprise that he liked Daniel. Of course, he didn't know that Daniel had actually been there when Theo was swept off the boat and drowned. All Will knew was that this man was his father's closest friend.

Daniel said, "Well, yes. At one time it was total! Then things made a bit of a picture, rather like a jigsaw: the sea at Cherrington; the Manor and the Thoroughgoods; Sunday school outings there. I rather think I lived on a farm then . . . not sure. I came here and other bits of jigsaw seemed to be lying around. Especially the boat. *Scallywag*." He turned to Binnie and said with a kind of enormous satisfaction, "And now it's all there. Theo. The island — Trapdoor. And . . . you, Binnie."

Will said frankly, "Reckon she's been the key all along." He too turned and looked at his mother. "Haven't I always told you that whatever Dad got up to, you were always the one for him?"

She was amazed. "I don't remember you saying anything like that, Will Cash! You're making it up!"

"I'm not." He shook his head at her. "Never mind Daniel's memory, Ma. Yours is very selective!"

The men both laughed at her discomfiture and she felt suddenly light-hearted. Apart from the two of them immediately hitting it off, there was the realization that if in fact Daniel was remembering everything, he could not have deliberately killed Theo.

And then, as if responding to that very thought, he said, "I don't think I can have been around when Theo died. I would remember that. I think the shock of knowing he was gone must have triggered off the amnesia. And I blundered on to that journey to Cherrington because I must have known subconsciously that you — as Will has just said — you were the key to it all. Does that make sense?"

Binnie said nothing.

Will said, "Perfect sense. Dad probably went on and on about Ma and how she coped. So, when you needed someone you went looking for her."

"Yes." Daniel's voice was quiet. "He certainly mentioned her a few times."

Binnie pulled herself together. "Let's get you signed off or whatever we have to do. Matthew has lent us his car while he's at Midwatch cottages. We have to get you back to Harbour Lights, then go and fetch him. Natalie will look after you."

"Poor you." Will pulled a face, then said contritely, "I don't mean that. She's been marvellous. But watch out for the tall stories. Apparently there's a Sicilian following her everywhere."

Daniel grunted as he stood up and grabbed Will's shoulder but when Sister appeared with a wheelchair he shook his head and assured them the giddiness was temporary.

She handed over a prescription. "Sedatives, very mild ones. They will help you to sleep. You were physically exhausted when you came in — mentally too. Try to rest. It won't be easy but it is the only way you will get back your health."

Daniel took her hand. "Sister, I am totally grateful to you and Dr Kennan and everyone. I'm so lucky that my second hospital visit has been ... well, more than pleasant."

"Second visit?" Binnie queried.

"Didn't I tell you? I escaped from a hospital in France. A psychiatric establishment relying heavily on electric shock treatment."

"Ah." She remembered he had said something about a hospital.

Will took the prescription and went to the dispensary while Binnie settled Daniel in the tiny grey car. He held on to her when she leaned over to fasten the seat belt; she turned her face away but he had not been going to kiss her and he released her immediately she moved back.

She said, "You actually escaped from that French hospital?"

"I think that's what it was. I found myself on a train. I remember sailors getting in my compartment at Marseilles. I had stuff in my pockets. Passport, money. English money. That was odd, wasn't it? Anyway, I didn't want to go back, ever. I got on the ferry. I must have done it before because I knew what to do. Then I changed stations in London. Got on a Bristol train at Paddington and walked to the bus station. You know the rest."

"Yes." She started the engine as Will appeared. "I wish you could remember why you were in the psychiatric hospital and what happened before then." She looked at him sharply. "Are you holding something back, Daniel? *Do* you remember anything else?"

He did not look dismayed, exactly. More subdued. "Not yet. But I'm sure it's just a matter of time." He frowned. "It has something to do with Trapdoor Island. Will you let me come with you when you go next time? I need to find out."

"You went there. You haven't forgotten that, surely? You took Dennison's boat and went there."

Will swung himself into the back seat and passed over a package. "The pills are in there with instructions," he said.

Daniel pocketed the package and answered Binnie. "Yes, but I couldn't get on to the island itself. The time before, when I came across with Alf, that was when I knew it was another piece of the jigsaw."

Will leaned forward and put his head between the two of them. "Is the island a piece of jigsaw? Gosh, that would be great. We must go over, Ma. Tomorrow."

She said sternly, "Certainly not. You heard what Sister said to Daniel. He must learn to rest. After Natalie goes home . . . we'll think about it then."

The next few days were unexpectedly pleasant. Natalie went into nursing mode and laid down a regime for Daniel that was restful for all of them. On Friday afternoon he was allowed to walk with her to the post office, where she booked her return passage on Monday's *Queen of Skalls*, and in the early evening on Sunday the four of them walked to St Andrew's for the All Souls' service. Natalie was delighted with it all.

"I could live like this for ever!" She pushed her hand inside Binnie's arm. "We're like a family — a proper family! And we're going to church! I asked Mrs Govern for some potatoes and when we get back we'll wrap them in foil and put them under the fire!" She smiled round at all of them. "We always did that on Guy Fawkes' night and as I won't be here then, we'll do it tonight instead!"

They laughed at her but Binnie hugged her arm tightly. This was a side of Natalie she didn't know and it made Theo's choice so much more than just acceptable.

Inside the tiny stone church, people were writing the names of their dead relatives on a list for prayers later. Natalie and Binnie glanced at each other but went on down the aisle to an empty pew. It was a surprise when the priest read Theo's name at the end of the list. Will kept his head in his hands.

Natalie said afterwards, "I nearly cried then, Will. I'm so glad one of us was able to come out of the closet!"

The Governs had gone over to Postern Island to meet with friends and had been pressing for the others to join them, but when Daniel had cried off the visitors had all nodded, glad to have the house to themselves for once.

Daniel and Will could watch the football highlights on the television in the sitting room while Binnie and Natalie — or "the girls", as Will insisted on calling them — fished the potatoes from beneath the fire and unwrapped them from their foil overcoats.

Natalie said in a low voice, "You know I don't want to go home, don't you?"

Binnie lifted her head, surprised. "I had no idea. It's pretty low-key here for you. No bridge evenings and so on."

"Don't be sarcastic, Benita. It doesn't become you. You are well aware that I married Ernest for his money. Dammit, he's a *grocer*, for God's sake! I'm bored out of my skull most of the time!"

"But he loves you. And the way you speak of him, you must love him."

"Well, I suppose I do. And I suppose he does. But vegetables and tins and packets, they're his first love."

"Oh. That's his concern, you mean. Not his love."

Natalie ignored that and mused on. "And do I really love him? That's what I came to find out. Because if I still love Theo — dead or not dead — then I can't really love Ernest, can I?"

Binnie cut a potato in half and inserted butter and cheese into its steaming inside. She said nothing. Natalie looked at her sharply.

"Well? What have *you* discovered? You're happy as Larry here, I can see that. Does it mean Theo is still your first love?"

Binnie snorted a little laugh, arranged some cress around the potato and put the plate on to the side table between Daniel and Will.

"Of course. How could it be otherwise? There was no-one before Theo."

"And afterwards? My God, Benita, you've lived without Theo for a long, long time. There must have been someone. This Miles Thoroughgood, for instance."

"There's been no-one," Binnie said definitely, and started on a second potato. The plates were very hot and she sucked at a burned finger for a second, then wrapped it clumsily in a tissue. Natalie was taking the cooled foil and screwing it up into a ball; she squashed it viciously.

"I don't believe you. All right, no Miles Thoroughgood. We'll leave him for Do. By the way, did you know she doesn't like being called Do? What do you call her — not Dora, surely?"

"Dorrie," Binnie said briefly. She did not like the conversation being targeted at her like this. "You know that. And you also know she is living with Gabriel Mackinley, who is very like her father. So you can draw your own conclusions there."

"Hmm." Natalie threw the foil at Daniel, missed him and hit Will, who squawked but did not take his eyes from the television. "I quite fancy Do — sorry, but I'll always think of her as Do — as Lady of Cherrington Manor. Lady Dorothea. It would have been better had you had the position — one in the eye for you-know-who. But Do . . . hmm, he would have been so proud." She turned away suddenly and began on the hearth with a dustpan and brush. "Can't get away from him, can we?"

Binnie finished the potatoes and distributed the plates. She had a feeling that this might be the last proper conversation she and Natalie shared.

She said, "One good thing about coming here — the two of us, I mean — is that we suddenly are so close. And I suppose that's because of him." She smiled. "I

211

wanted to say that. You find it easy to speak honestly and openly. I don't."

"That's because of him! You've had to put up all kinds of defences for so long —"

"What I'm saying is that we are finding good things about him. And we can share them."

For once Natalie was silent, staring at her, nodding slowly. They sat down at the big table and began on their supper.

Then Natalie took a breath and said, "But we mustn't wear our rose-coloureds too often, Benita. He did ruin our lives."

"What if he couldn't help it? What if he had too much love to give?"

Natalie almost choked on her potato. "Rubbish! Sentimental rubbish!"

Will called back, "Turn down the volume, you two. They're interviewing the players."

Natalie continued in a whisper, "Loyalty. Fidelity. That's what he lacked."

"Listen. I had the children. And you found Ernest."

"Yes. And that brings us back to what happens now." Natalie swivelled her eyes and mouthed the name "Daniel" silently. Binnie made an impatient gesture with her tissue-bandaged hand.

"No good dismissing it." Natalie leaned forward, trying to whisper through a mouthful of very hot carbohydrate. "He's been sent. For you. It's quite obvious to me. Face up to it, woman."

Binnie looked up, her face wide and full of fear. "What on earth do you mean?" She was convinced in that moment that Natalie knew what Dennison knew. And believed it.

Natalie swallowed with difficulty and cleared her throat. "You know very well what I mean. Theo has sent Daniel Casey — his best friend no less — to look after you."

"Look after me?" Binnie could hardly breathe.

Natalie shook her head impatiently. "All right then. Theo has sent Daniel *for* you! To look after you — love you — be with you. Don't you see? Daniel doesn't remember, of course, but Theo — with his dying breath probably — asked Daniel to look after you. It makes sense to me!"

Binnie said, "Natalie, you've gone too far now. We've had to put up with the Sicilian. And Ernest — is he really so boring? I don't think so, otherwise you would have left him ages ago — and now Daniel. Theo wishing us well from beyond the grave! Honestly!"

Natalie shrugged. "Anyone can see he fancies you like crazy. I thought if I put that white apron on and made a cap from one of Matthew's neckerchief things, then he might go for me. But not a chance."

Binnie had to laugh. "D'you mean to tell me —"

"I certainly do. He's like Theo but he's got a sort of steadfastness about him. Any woman in her right mind would go for him. Which proves I am very much in my right mind!"

Will reached behind himself without taking his eyes from the screen. "Sauce," he enunciated.

Binnie put the sauce bottle into his hand and said, "Honestly, Natalie. You are *terrible*. I feel quite sorry for Ernest."

Natalie grinned then said, "Don't. Do you know when my birthday is?"

"August the twelfth. The Glorious Twelfth. Theo told me."

"There you go. Very easy to remember. Even by my ex-husband's first wife. Well, one year, on July the ninth, I got home from a shopping trip and found the house full of balloons, neighbours, people I'd never met before cluttering up the sun lounge, party poppers and Ernest leading the singing of 'Happy birthday'." She looked across the table, her face expressionless. "We'd already been married three years."

Binnie put her head on the table and almost wept with laughter. When she sat up again Natalie was moving the plates into the kitchen and bringing out a tray of coffee. "I'm so glad I've entertained you," she said.

Binnie wiped her eyes. "Sorry, Nat. But I bet you didn't make do with July the ninth. I bet you had something even better on August the twelfth."

"Too right!" Natalie said indignantly. "And I haven't let it drop either. Ever since then I've had two birthdays, two lots of presents, two lots of visits to the theatre. He started it and he can go on with it!"

"Oh, Nat." Binnie looked up. "I think your Ernest sounds a lovely man. Do appreciate him while you can."

Daniel came over to the table and picked up two of the coffees. Binnie thought he was looking better already. He said, "I agree. You shouldn't punish him for what Theo did, Natalie."

"You've been listening!" Natalie tried to look shocked. "How long have you been listening, for Pete's sake?"

"I heard Binnie's plea. That was when the news came on." His smile turned into a grin. "I'm afraid you two cannot hope to compete with *Match of the Day!*"

"Just as well," Natalie said. She sighed gustily. "I sort of agree with both of you — about Ernest, I mean. But only objectively. It's so much easier living with a couple of selfish so-and-sos like you and Will than it is with someone who would do anything for me. Why on earth is that?"

Daniel started to say something about living with Theo but Will interrupted. "How dare you call us selfish? We put up with all your fantasizing, we allow ourselves to be chivvied and organized —"

"You love it really." Natalie sounded sad. "You'll miss me terribly." She rallied. "Anyway, what about the Sicilian? And what about the incontrovertible fact that Dennison has disappeared?"

Will was solemn. "I think the Sicilian has got him."

Daniel said, "I think he might have gone to Italy."

"He's already done that." Binnie looked at the dark window. "I think he's living at Trapdoor. He's scared."

"Surely he realizes I won't press charges?"

"He doesn't realize that at all." She looked at Daniel. "He thinks you are his enemy." She saw his sudden frown and added quickly, "Because you stole his boat. It makes sense, Daniel."

"I suppose so . . . I must talk to him."

"And you must stop worrying," Natalie said briskly. "Come on. Off to bed. Will, you can wash up. The Governs won't want food, will they?" she asked Binnie.

"I think they intended to have a meal at the Peruvian." Binnie gathered up the plates and went into the kitchen. Will followed, rolling his eyes at Daniel, who smiled smugly and made for the stairs. As he passed the small table in the hall, the phone rang. He reached down and picked it up. They all waited, looking at him. He nodded and said, "yes" occasionally, then a more emphatic, "Of course we don't mind," then, "Listen, if we can help . . ." then, "All right. Take care." He replaced the receiver and looked at them.

"They're staying the night at the hotel. It's almost finished so it's no hardship. But they're worried about Alf. He was supposed to join them this evening and he's missing. He's done it before. He goes to Transom Island, apparently. It's deserted and he likes to be by himself. Think about his wife. But he hasn't taken the *Mermaid* — it's still tied up on the Postern jetty." He said, "Is there some mystery about his wife — is she dead perhaps?"

Will said, "I thought she'd gone off with someone else. Left him."

Natalie said, "He has to be on Postern still. Unless there was someone fishing or something and he went to Transom and now can't get back." Her eyes sparkled. "Just imagine. Marooned on a desert island!"

"There you go again!" Will flipped a tea towel at her. "D'you want to wash or wipe?"

Both Binnie and Daniel looked back at the window. It was a very dark night indeed. Daniel said, "There's bound to be a shelter of some sort over there — a ruined cottage, perhaps."

Binnie thought of Alf, small and bent and very hairy, rather like one of the Seven Dwarfs. She said, "He'll be listening to her singing to him. Down by the shore." She told them about Marigold: Alf's version first of all, then Maggie Govern's.

Natalie said, "And you call me a drama queen!" She turned to Will. "Let's get back to cruel reality. I'll wipe because my hands aren't up to the soda Maggie uses. You can wash."

They went into the kitchen and could be heard bickering amiably. Daniel said, "It's amazing. Will has allowed himself to become the son she never had."

Binnie made a rueful face. "And she's having to leave him." She shooed him up the stairs. "On Tuesday the three of us will go to Trapdoor the minute Alf has finished the school run. We'll look for Dennison and explain a few things."

"That's if we're not looking for Alf first," Daniel said soberly. "I've got a feeling about his disappearance."

Binnie said nothing and made as if to go back into the sitting room. Then she peered around the door to watch him ascend the stairs. She had deliberately allowed Natalie to look after Daniel's needs and when Natalie boarded the *Queen of Skalls* tomorrow he would be fit enough to look after himself. He could not possibly have been "sent" by Theo to look after her — typical Natalie! And of course she had interpreted being "looked after" as something quite different, so . . . typical Binnie? Even so, she was thankful Will was around. Surely it would not matter if he missed a few weeks of his course?

She began to clear up the sitting room. In Daniel's armchair was his old wallet, open, and a few loose coins that must have fallen out of it. And something else. A ring. She picked it up and held it beneath the table lamp. It was the wedding ring that she had put on Theo's finger back in 1980.

CHAPTER
SIXTEEN

Daniel was well enough to carry one of Natalie's many cases, Will and Binnie managed two each, and Natalie herself struggled with a large makeup case and a plastic bag containing sandwiches packed for her by Maggie Govern. The quay was quiet that Monday morning; enormous containers of bottled gas were being swung from ship to shore, but the parcel post was scant and no-one had come to pick up their mail orders. It was raining and if the post wasn't urgent it could wait at the post office until the weather improved.

The four of them waited by the gangplank for the personal stuff to be carried down into the waiting hand truck. Walter Polpen called a greeting and the usual "Come back soon". Natalie sniffed audibly and reached inside her shoulder bag for a handkerchief.

"We'll come on board with you," Binnie said. "She'll be another hour."

But Natalie shook her head. "It's such a wrench," she said. "That's exactly the right word. Wrench. I need to find a seat in the bar and have a quick gin, then it will stop hurting. If you come with me it will just prolong it. Like taking a plaster off slowly."

Will said, "Who would have thought, the wicked step turning out to be a fairy godmother!"

"Shut up, Will!" Natalie advised. "And listen. I shall need a phone call tonight. If Alf hasn't turned up by then who will do the school run? You heard what Matthew said — he could only manage today."

There was a pause. Everyone was becoming anxious about Alf. Although he had a reputation for going off by himself he had never missed a school run before. And there was the mystery of his boat, the *Mermaid*, abandoned on Postern Island.

Daniel said tentatively, "I could do it. The *Mermaid* is no more than an old tug. I would need a school register . . ." His voice picked up enthusiasm. "If I can get to the first pick-up — which Matt said is Portcullis Island, then the kids there can tell me where to go next and the names of the pick-ups." He said, suddenly delighted, "I can do it! I know the Skall seas . . . and it will be a job! And I'll be doing it for Alf, which makes it even better."

Natalie was even more delighted than he was. "It's a role for you too, darling! We sort of belong because of Theo, but you must feel like a sore thumb. It won't be too arduous either. I think it's a marvellous idea, don't you, Benita?"

Binnie hesitated. She needed time to think and pre-empt any snags. Would a morning and afternoon journey between the inhabited islands help Daniel or bring him face to face with what actually happened out in the Tyrrhenian Sea?

Will covered the pause. "Well, I think it's great," he said. "We won't have to look after the poor old soul any more!" He grinned and punched Daniel gently on the arm. "Ma and I can go off to Trapdoor whenever we've got the energy. Plant up the garden. Get that dynamo going."

Daniel grinned obediently and Binnie said, "I can't see any problems. Except that I do feel we should be searching for Alf."

Will sobered. "Yes. If he doesn't turn up today, perhaps the three of us can do the school home run and carry on to the outer islands to look for him afterwards."

The gangplank was free at last and they all trooped on to the open deck of the *Queen* and immediately into the bar. Will organized the luggage around a table by the window and hugged Natalie.

"This is the wrench," she said over his shoulder. "If it weren't that I like you so much, Benita, I would definitely try to adopt this boy." She leaned back so that she could see Will's face. "So like his father to look at. So unlike in other ways." She gave him a smacking kiss. "I'm glad I popped in and picked you up, Will. It was actually because I needed male protection against the Sicilian threat, but I knew as soon as I met you that it was going to be much more than that."

He guffawed. "Sicilian threat, indeed. You should be on the stage, Nat!"

"Listen." She withdrew from his embrace and shouldered her handbag. "The best of luck with finding Alf — which I'm sure you will — and please keep me

221

informed about Trapdoor, what you intend to do and what actually happens. And now go. Wrench over. All right?"

They went. Binnie led the way back to the shore, they waved in case Natalie was looking out, then trooped back to the house.

Daniel said, surprised, "D'you know, we're going to miss her. We must try not to get too heavy."

Will nodded and added, "She's fun. But now she's gone we can get down to some real work." He waited until Daniel was seated by the sitting-room window, then added, "How long can you stay, Dan? And how are you feeling? I suppose what I really mean is how much can you put into the next few weeks?"

Binnie laughed, almost embarrassed. "Hang on, Will! Daniel came out of hospital last Wednesday, remember! And he's already volunteered to do the school run till Alf turns up."

"Which means he can run us to Trapdoor every weekday and we can stay over the weekends." Will draped an arm around his mother. "Listen, Ma, I know you and Dorrie and Gabe have done sterling work there, but we need to keep it up. And we need to find out exactly what is required over there to make it into an unusual holiday home — in fact, whether it will ever be a viable holiday home. I know we can't sell it, but Matthew was saying to me that the people who are buying the hotel at Postern might be interested in taking Trapdoor on a long lease. Building two or three more houses and servicing them on a daily basis."

"Would that be permitted?"

Will shrugged. "We could try. But we have to do it ourselves first. Yes?"

"That's why I'm here," Binnie said. "And the short time I did stay over, I felt . . . all right." She looked at him. "I would prefer to keep it, Will."

He tightened his arm around her shoulders. "Same here."

Daniel said suddenly, "Theo once called it No Man's Island. I thought it was a pun on the poem — you know, 'no man is an island' — but he said he'd meant it differently. Like no man's land in the First World War. A space between all the problems and the fights." He gave an upside-down grin, half embarrassed. "I suppose he meant a sort of retreat, a sanctuary."

Binnie said doubtfully, "A lot of men died in no man's land."

"Perhaps he also meant that it was a buffer. Between the seas. Trapdoor and Shark's Teeth serve as breakwaters when the weather is bad." Will went over to the window, opened it and waved. The ship's old-fashioned hooter blared into the sitting room. "She's off. I bet you anything Nat is looking out at the house. Give her a wave."

Maggie Govern came toiling up from the pier and waved back.

The next day Alf had still not reappeared. Matthew was only too glad to hand over the *Mermaid* to Daniel. "Drop me off at Postern when you pick up the Billiton twins," he said over breakfast. "Can you manage her? She's slow but sure."

Daniel nodded. "I'm used to those engines." He grinned at Binnie. "Was it only last Sunday week I came over with Alf to deliver the freezer? Seems a lifetime ago."

She nodded, remembering how familiar he had been with the workings of the *Mermaid*. And, of course, he knew the seaways around Skall; probably as well as Theo had known them.

Daniel turned back to Matthew. "As soon as I've dropped the children at Keyhole, we'll go to the outer islands to look for Alf." He nodded as Matthew began to protest. "Yes, we know all about his sessions with Marigold, but this is for us. We're worried about him."

Matthew said, "It's good of you, Daniel. Alf does this every so often, as if he's looking for her. The only difference this time is that he left the *Mermaid* moored at Postern. And he's not come back for the schoolchildren. He could have got a lift that day with someone who was fishing. And now he's marooned wherever they dropped him. But why?" He shrugged. "Alf is different from most of us. He'd hate me for saying this, but he's got a lot of Dennison in him." He made to go through to the kitchen and paused. "And there's another deserter! Where the hell has Dennison gone?"

Binnie said nothing; she thought she knew exactly where Dennison was.

So on the Tuesday morning at nine o'clock, after a successful school run, Daniel handed Binnie into the *Mermaid* and she sat on the engine casing, her jacket hugged around her in the brisk November breeze while

Will took her place under the canopy and watched carefully as Daniel eased the boat away from the short pier. "I'll do it next time!" he called over to his mother.

"Only when I'm watching you, and certainly not if Alf is back home!" Daniel said with unusual authority.

They bucketed out of the harbour and into the weather; Binnie pulled up her hood and fastened it securely. They were headed for the nearest of the uninhabited islands. Transom first and Casement second. Neither of them was within the circle that provided relative shelter, and as they passed Postern on their left the sea started to lift beneath them in unbroken rollers. Binnie turned her back on the wheelhouse and looked at Postern and Keyhole, rising and falling, one minute invisible as if beneath the sea, the next rising above it in a repeating rebirth. Even Keyhole, with its small town and churches and the cottage hospital and the school, looked desperately vulnerable. Dennison's lookout seemed to stay above the waves — just. She kept her eyes on it. When it too disappeared behind a wall of green water she turned again and looked at the familiar backs of Daniel and Will. She wasn't exactly frightened but this roller-coaster ride was less than thrilling.

Transom appeared after another fifteen minutes. It lay to their right, or "Starboard!" as Will called back to her, his face alight with excitement. Daniel inched the wheel towards it and almost immediately it seemed that the sea dropped slightly and the *Mermaid* went into its usual pugnacious mode, pushing through the sea rather than over it. Will had borrowed a chart from Matthew but Daniel did not seem to need it. The island was not unlike Trapdoor, with a high escarpment on one side. He steered the boat into the lee of the rocky shore, then spun the wheel so that they pushed through small breaking waves, following the sheer sides until they dropped away and shingle ran up to the mouth of a cave.

"Put out the anchor, Will!" Daniel held the engine steady until he felt the anchor bite, then cut it. "We'll have to go in with the dinghy."

They launched the cockleshell of a boat and automatically Daniel stood in the stern and took them in with one oar, just as Alf did. Binnie wanted to ask whether he had learned to row like that in a gondola but knew he had not. The constant reminders that he knew Skall instinctively were frightening.

The three of them hauled the dinghy almost into the cave and then clambered over rocks, finding a way on to the sparsely green tops as best they could. It was very obvious why this island had never been inhabited, in spite of the fresh water that bubbled through the rocks from some hidden spring. It was impossible to explore every rock crevice, but they searched and shouted until they were hoarse. It was on the return scramble to the shingle beach that Will found a scrap of cloth held between two rocks. It was sodden and could have been there for a long time but he was convinced it was from Alf's trouser cuff.

"He still wears grey flannel, Ma! And it's from a turn-up — look, can you see the crease? Who else wears grey flannel turn-ups?"

"Darling, this could be from years ago when everyone wore them."

Daniel said slowly, "It could be from Dennison. What does he wear?"

They didn't know but it seemed likely that Dennison too would be wearing flannels.

They sat on the shingle and rested aching legs. Will got up and searched the cave; it was short and ended in a wall of sandy soil, rocks and pebbles. No-one had tried to dig themselves in but Will stood there shouting for at least five minutes.

Binnie said, "We'll have to get on if we're going to do Casement. It's dark before six o'clock."

Daniel frowned. "I can see him getting a lift here. But I cannot see anyone waiting for him, then taking him on to Casement Island. If it were summer and there were deep-sea fishermen around it would be different."

"How far is Casement?"

"Another half-hour in *Mermaid*. At least. It's the top of the Skall range. Just a peak above the sea and in very deep water."

"Can we land there?"

"There is one place, yes. I can moor against the rocks. Then we jump."

They were silent for a while but then Daniel stood up.

"We have to try. Perhaps we can chug right around the perimeter. If he's there he'll be desperate. There's no fresh water on Casement."

They pushed the dinghy afloat and scrambled on. They were wet anyway from the rain, but sodden feet and trousers now added to their discomfort.

It seemed an age until the promised peak came into sight and already the grey day was closing in around them. Daniel stayed well clear of the rocky cliffs and turned the wheel back and forth as he skirted the small island. It looked like a fortress. Narrow fissures in the rock face could have been arrow slits, and crenellations were clearly silhouetted against the low cloud. Will and Binnie took it in turns to shout Alf's name; their voices bounced back from the sheer sides of the island, mimicking, mocking.

They veered clumsily to port, where there was a deep and dark cleft. Daniel said briefly, "This is where we would land. See the shelf up there? Another above it, more below, like an enormous staircase."

Will said, "Let me do it, Dan. I can climb to the top from there and get a view — a downward view. Just in case . . . just in case he's fallen."

Daniel glanced at Binnie. She said, "This could end in disaster. Let's leave it to the helicopter and the lifeboat. Look at that cliff."

"Yes. But it's broken there — it's not sheer. If Dan can get *Mermaid* close enough I can hop over. I'll be ten minutes — if that."

In the face of Daniel's silence Binnie eventually gave in and they began the perilous business of edging close enough to the cliff to throw a rope over one of the rock outcrops. Daniel pushed out more fenders and began the tricky task of pulling the boat close. And then,

228

before Will could position himself for the leap, Daniel had done it. He stood on the prow of the old *Mermaid* and as she rose with the next swell, he almost stepped across on to a higher ledge. The boat descended again and he was high and dry and laughing back at them.

"Sorry, Will. Women and children and all that. I won't be long." He turned into the cliff face and began to climb. Will turned on his mother, his face set.

"You all think I'm still at school! That's what I meant about leaving university. I hate being treated like this! And it's no laughing matter!"

Binnie couldn't help herself. "It's not my fault! Daniel has proved that he knows Skall better than most — certainly better than we do. If Alf is here, injured or not, he will find him."

"And I wouldn't?"

"Possibly not."

Will said, "At least I can help him." He put one foot on the prow and leaped. He made it all right, but landed when the wave had ebbed and it immediately rose and almost engulfed him. Binnie gave a gasping scream and grabbed at the lifebelt. But Will had got a grip on the ledge above him and survived the soaking and the suction as the wave ebbed again. Choking, he scrambled on to the higher ledge and hung on there gasping and spitting sea water.

The *Mermaid* was rising and falling with each wave and Binnie called, "Will! Get back in the boat! I'll tell you when to jump! Turn and face me — now!"

He hung on, his head lowered; a wave swept up to his waist. The tide was rising. He got a knee on to the next ledge and hauled himself up, and then suddenly he was all right and got on to another ledge without difficulty. She watched him climb, her breath sobbing in her throat with terror for him. But he was climbing confidently, just as Daniel had done, and before he dropped behind the pinnacle he turned and waved to her and then pointed down the other side and put his thumb up. So Daniel was there. Binnie felt enormous relief.

She turned her attention then to protecting the boat. In spite of the double layer of fenders, it was bumping and jarring against the rock face every time a wave came. She grabbed the pole and tried to push the hull away from the sides of the island. She was exhausted within a few minutes; if she had needed proof of the power of the sea she had it then. There were no breaking waves, the sea was running alongside the island rather than into it, but the swell was inexorable. Will had been lucky to survive that dunking.

It was probably half an hour before there was a shout from above and Daniel's thin frame began the downward climb. Will was right behind him. There was no-one else. The whole thing had been a wasted effort.

They scrambled down and leaped aboard without difficulty; they did not speak. Daniel immediately started the engine and pulled off the rope. Will grabbed a towel and scrubbed at his face. His clothes were heavy with water. Under the seating, Binnie found wellingtons and he kicked off his trainers and put them on. The *Mermaid* chugged away from Casement and into the open sea again. It was then that Daniel picked up the ship-to-shore speaker and handed it to Binnie.

"You're through to the coastguard. Ask for emergency rescue. The seaward side of Casement Island. One male survivor. Broken leg, probably."

She looked at him, her brown eyes wide. "Alf?"

"Yes."

"And someone else?"

Daniel did not reply. Will choked, "It must have been Marigold." He wiped wet hands over his wet face. "He says he won't leave her again. It must have been Marigold."

Binnie breathed, "Oh God. Oh, dear God. Poor Alf. And poor Marigold."

The speaker crackled and she gave the message exactly as Daniel had told her, received the acknowledgement and handed the instrument back. She looked from Will to Daniel. They had the glazed look of people suffering from shock.

She murmured, "He always said she had gone back to the sea." And then she changed her voice and added briskly, "Home as quickly as possible, Daniel. Matthew will have to take the children back. You and Will need hot baths and hot food."

CHAPTER
SEVENTEEN

They called in at Postern on their way back to Keyhole harbour, picked up Matthew and told him almost everything that had happened before they moored at the small quay, where a group of rather anxious schoolchildren were awaiting their return. Matthew, grim-faced, took them off and urged Binnie to "make sure they two are kept warm". Binnie guessed that Daniel had probably been suffering from hypothermia after he went into the sea at Cherrington, and from the look of Will she thought he was near to it now.

She herded Daniel upstairs and Will into the Governs' own bathroom.

Maggie flew around with hot towels and drinks. "Walter Polpen came over the minute your message arrived," she told Binnie. "Dear Lord, that Alf will be the death of himself and plenty of others before he's finished with this mermaid business!" She handed Binnie two kettles of boiling water. "Top up their baths with this, m'dear. The immersion heater will boost the hot water but this will help too." Which was fine as far as Will was concerned, not so good when it came to Daniel.

Binnie pushed the door open and manoeuvred the kettle on to the bathroom stool. "Hot water, Daniel!" she called. "Keep the bath water as hot as you can stand it."

He was not embarrassed. "Binnie. Come inside a minute, I have to talk to you."

"I'd better not," she said in as cheerful and matter-of-fact voice as she could muster. "We'll talk later."

"Binnie! This is serious." He let out a sigh. "I've used your bubble bath, if that helps you in any way!"

"Oh." She stood just inside the door. The bath was oozing bubbles. He lifted the kettle and added more water. "Tell Maggie this is lovely. And stop looking worried. I'm all right. My immune system has been alerted so much in the past few weeks I'm inoculated against shocks!" She didn't laugh and he said, "Sorry, Binnie. Not in the slightest bit funny. But that's why I have to speak to you." He looked at her through the steam. "You didn't see anything. All right?"

"Of course. You know very well I didn't see anything."

"So you don't know about Marigold. Right?"

"But you or Will — I can't remember — you said he was holding her dead body."

"Forget that. He was looking for her and he did not find her."

"What are you saying, Daniel? For goodness' sake, when the helicopter winches them up —"

"Will and I, we rolled her back into the sea. Alf's leg is broken and, anyway, he could never get back over

233

those rocks. He's alone. That's all anyone need ever know."

The boiling water from the kettle had made a lot of steam and she could barely focus him. She said flatly, "I don't get it. It's all very sad but why pretend it hasn't happened?"

His voice came at her, disembodied and unemotional. "It's another can of worms, Binnie. We've got our own, haven't we? Let's leave as many lids in place as we can." He waited and when she was silent and still bewildered, he said, "Can you turn on the hot tap? I expect the immersion has done its stuff by now."

She stayed where she was by the door; she registered that he sounded different. Decisive.

He sighed audibly. "Listen, my love." She felt a physical shock at the endearment. He spoke slowly and quietly. "Alf fell in love with a barmaid who was working at Postern for the summer season. We don't know when — two or three years ago perhaps? She married him but went on with her life as if he wasn't there. Other men. She sang to him, told him she was a mermaid and had to go back to sea now and then. He loved it. He thought she was deliberately making their relationship into a romantic fairy tale. And then she told him she was going back to sea for always but she would sing for him whenever he wanted." He sighed again. "He's one of the many Skall characters. People come to live here when they can't fit in anywhere else, Binnie. Theo did it. Dennison. Alf. And me." He gave a small laugh. "Well, I was going to. Until Theo did what Marigold did, and went back to the sea."

234

She squeezed her eyes shut and opened them wide. His face was tilted towards the ceiling. She wished she could read his expression. Did she really want to take the lid off that particular can of worms?

He said, "The thing is, everyone knew she was going off with an American who was staying at the Peruvian. Nobody thought any more about her. They kept an eye on Alf instead; pandered to his self-delusion. When he went off to listen to her singing, they didn't check on him." Daniel sank lower in the water. "I think she was washed up some time ago, Binnie. The smell was appalling. He had wrapped the body in a blanket so that the birds couldn't get her. He must have gone out there fairly often to make sure she was still there."

"What you are saying is that he, Alf — we're talking about *Alf* here, Daniel — found her corpse one day, quite by chance, hauled it over those ghastly rocks and has been visiting her? You're crazy!"

"I am saying that it is quite possible the police would suspect Alf of murdering Marigold and keeping her body on Casement, which is practically inaccessible. A shrine to his own mermaid." He leaned forward and turned on the hot tap; more steam enveloped him.

"And I am saying it's ridiculous, Daniel!" She thought with a pang of terror that he knew what he was talking about: death at sea . . . he knew about death at sea. She said firmly, "No-one would think that. No-one."

Daniel said, "The thing is, he didn't take the *Mermaid*. Dennison took him out in *Scallywag*, and there were no plans to bring him back. Alf was going to go into the sea with his mermaid. And he fell. And broke his leg. So he will be picked up by helicopter any minute now, I would think."

"Oh God! Oh, Daniel. Poor Alf. Poor man."

"He's lucky. He can always go to the shore and listen when Marigold sings." He lay back. "It could have been anything, Binnie. She could have drowned — her American could have pushed her off his deep-sea fishing boat . . . But I think once questions are asked, Alf may tip over the edge. As it is, he won't be packed off to a psychiatric ward, he will be accepted here, people will still entrust their children to him — and why not? He knows Casement and people who know Casement know the sea. He will be all right. Marigold will always be his mermaid." He leaned forward again and turned off the tap. Then he said, "Just as Theo will always be your pirate." In spite of the curtain of steam she knew his face was turned to her. He said quietly, "It's all right, my dearest, I do understand."

There was a silence in the bathroom. It was as if the silence became her response to him and quite suddenly she saw his teeth flash as he grinned. He said briskly, "Tell Maggie Govern I'm looking like a boiled lobster! And then check on Will. He's a great man, Binnie. And a great rock climber too."

She went back down the stairs to the Governs' bathroom. She did not knock and Will, who was examining his foot, twisted round, shocked.

"Would you mind, Ma! Just because there are no locks around here does not mean I don't appreciate a little privacy now and then."

236

She closed the door behind her and stood against it. "Better?" She shook her head. "Sorry, darling. I've just been talking to Daniel."

"While he was in the bath? Ma, you take the biscuit!"

"He called me in. Wanted to have a word about what you found on Casement."

He went back to his foot. "Yes, I know, he talked to me too. And he's right. Forget what I said back in the boat, Ma." He picked up a pumice and scrubbed his sole. It was obvious that he was physically fine.

"Is that all you've got to say about it?"

He looked up at her, his eyes wide and clear. "What else is there? Poor old Alf. We found him just in time. They'll be tucking him up in the cottage hospital any minute now and he'll have the time of his life, if Daniel's experience is anything to go by!"

She said, "We'll have to see what Alf says about it."

"He wanted to go into the sea with her . . . it was awful." He glanced up at her and she saw that he was near tears himself.

She spoke in a stronger voice. "Listen, Will. Don't take too much notice of what he said. Yes, he probably was delirious — a broken leg and all that time without water — but even when he came to take me off Trapdoor after the storm he was always acting out a part somehow." She paused, thinking back to that first day when he had told them that Marigold never spoke to him, only sang. "Gabriel thought he was crazy from the outset. But we all have fantasies one way or another." She tried to laugh and then sobered. "Poor old Alf, at least his fantasies made him happy — you could tell that by the way he twinkled!" She laughed, properly this time, and after a moment he joined her.

She picked up the kettle and turned away. And Will must have known how she really felt because he said, "Ma, just be practical, like you always are. Daniel will still do the school runs and we'll go to Trapdoor and stay there for a bit. How does that sound?"

"Yes. We'll see." She paused. "I take it Alf was too far gone to tell you where Dennison was going?"

"Didn't even think to mention it!" He waited till the door was almost closed before he said, "Do you mind me leaving university, Ma? It seems so trivial now."

She held the door handle. "I don't think I mind. But I'm afraid you may do. Later on."

"If I did regret it I could go back."

"Keep an open mind until next term. All right?"

"All right." She closed the door just as he said, "I love you, Ma."

She did not go back in to him. She did not want him to know how amazed she was by him. And how deeply touched too.

Matthew's advice was to the point and bore out what Daniel had said. "Why don't the three of you go over to Trapdoor as you planned? I don't think we shall hear any more from Alf, but if he should start on about Marigold singing to him they might want to ask you a few questions and you could be stuck on Keyhole indefinitely."

Daniel assured him that he could take on the school run the next morning so, as soon as he had landed the children, they left with all their stores and luggage. Binnie did not invite Daniel to stay and he did not ask her whether he could. He had acknowledged in the bathroom that he too needed to keep a tight lid on a can of worms, and she recognized that he had nowhere else to go.

Binnie said nothing to him about mooring; she expected him to anchor the *Mermaid* clear of the sandspit below the dunes and use the dinghy; and in fact, that was what he did. It was high tide and the Curtain would be invisible for another six hours. Besides, the *Mermaid* was too big to be dragged up on to the sand in the cavern. Daniel rowed them ashore and he and Will ran up into the dunes with Binnie still in the dinghy. It was the first time they had all laughed together since Natalie left. Binnie, clutching the sides of the little boat, felt again that sense of homecoming. This, after all, was home.

The two men leaned over, gasping for breath, still laughing. Will got his breath first and panted, "Dad made us a sort of sled from a tea tray and we used to do this — toboggan down through the dunes. It was terrific!"

Daniel nodded. "He must have enjoyed it himself. This time last year he used a belly-board and came down at quite a rate — straight into the water!"

Will said, "I keep forgetting you knew him, Dan! Just this time last year you were here? The two of you? You remember that?"

"Almost." Daniel narrowed his eyes; there was no sun to be seen but the water struck sparks from somewhere. "It came like a snip of film — Theo face down on this old-fashioned belly-board, getting up speed between the dunes . . . he would sweep up one side and then twist the board and come down with amazing force . . . I can hear the board slapping down on the sand . . . and something else. Or someone else?"

Binnie climbed out of the dinghy and stood with one hand on Will's bent back. "Dennison?" she suggested.

"Could have been." He blinked, letting it go. Then opened his eyes wide. "It was a bonfire! It was Bonfire Night! We put potatoes and mackerel in a biscuit tin and buried it in the fire!"

Will grinned at his mother. "Thought you said he'd lost his memory — that's exactly one year ago today. Pretty good going, I reckon. You did remember it was November the fifth?"

"I'd forgotten completely," Binnie confessed. "They were building some kind of pyre up on the road to the hospital."

They tramped slowly up to the house, Will still trying to jog Daniel's elusive memories. Eventually, as they climbed down the steps to the garden and the front door, Binnie protested.

"Leave the poor devil alone, Will! He'll come up with another snippet of film when he can!"

"But, Ma," Will stopped halfway down Jacob's Ladder and stared out at the Atlantic, "it's one of the things we're here for, isn't it? Remembering Dad? I can remember him taking me right to the top of the island and telling me there was nothing else in the sea until it reached America."

"Yes," Binnie said drily. "That was one of his favourites."

But when Will joined them in the hall, exclaiming that he remembered the Victorian pictures and the curtains, and the copper with its furnace beneath, she watched him smilingly.

"What?" he asked catching her eye. "Why are you grinning at me like the Cheshire cat?"

She said, "Everybody deserves a dad as well as a mum. Just seems ironic that you are recapturing yours after he's gone." And for some peculiar reason tears sprang into her eyes and poured down her face. She was embarrassed and put her gloved hands to her eyes. "I didn't mean to do that — I'm so sorry."

It was Daniel who hugged her into his shoulder with one arm. "Don't apologize, Binnie. We're all in the same boat here, aren't we? Looking for memories in no man's land."

She forced a wry chuckle and went to connect the gas canister to the cooker. "A cup of tea first. Then we'll light the fires and have something to eat before Daniel goes back for the children."

Will unpacked one of the bags on the kitchen table and found the milk; Daniel went to look at the dynamo, which squatted in the lean-to surrounded by plastic containers of diesel. Binnie could feel the house coming alive around her. She no longer felt the terror of the cavern so far below her feet. And suddenly she knew why: because it had sheltered Daniel when he had come looking for his own personal memories. It had

241

been a cold and frightening sanctuary but a sanctuary it had been.

When Daniel had left they both felt a little bereft. She and Will had waved tea cloths from the sandspit and Daniel had "tooted" the old foghorn on the *Mermaid*, and then suddenly he and the boat were gone and they had the whole island to themselves.

Will said, "Ma, before we get started on anything at all, can we walk up to the tops and look out to sea? Dad always told us that we must climb the battlements and make sure there were no enemies in sight before we did anything else."

She rolled up the tea towels and stuffed them in the pockets of her jacket, and she and Will started up through the dunes. By the time they reached the rock itself, they were both sweating and thankful for the wind, which was cutting over the edge. They found a niche — Will called it a gap in the ramparts — and huddled inside it, looking out over the restless sea. Binnie watched Will's dark face as he stared down to the Shark's Teeth far below. He was a softer edition of Theo, open and not so wily. She did not want to show him the enormous cache of spirits below the house, but she had no fear that he would be tempted to follow his father's footsteps in that particular direction. She wondered what he would make of it. Then she wondered what Daniel would make of it. Surely more memories would surface.

Will shouted something into the wind and Binnie leaned forward to catch the words.

"Down there, Ma. Between those two last rocks. Can you see?"

"I can see the rocks. What about them?"

"It's the same sort of terrain. Where we found Alf."

She was horrified. "Such a long fall? He's lucky to be alive!"

Will turned down his mouth. "Maybe not. We don't know whether he will recover fully, do we?"

She waited until they had started the downward scramble before she panted, "Alf is very wise, Will. He's a romantic down to his socks, but he's always known . . . the truth."

They slid the last few feet and sat on the grass that bordered Jacob's Ladder, laughing together. But then Will said, "And what was the truth exactly, Ma? That he suffered delusions and believed them? Or that he made up the stories to entertain the tourists but never fooled himself?"

She made a helpless face. "I don't know, love. Truth is such an elusive concept anyway. I feel in some ways as if I've been deluding myself for the past twenty years — pretending that my life is normal." She laughed. "The strange thing is that when we arrived first of all and started coming out here, this place was where all the fairy tales happened — life back in Cherrington was still real and . . . well, true. But gradually a reversal has taken place!" She put her head on his shoulder for a moment. "Don't take any notice of me, for goodness' sake!"

He draped an affectionate arm round her neck. "OK. I know it's all hormonal anyway. Dorrie explained it to me carefully. What it boils down to, Ma, is that the past has come up and hit you in the face."

"Charming. I prefer to think I am living a fairy tale!"

"When I heard about Dad it had exactly the same effect. It was almost physical, as if Dad himself had punched me on the jaw. And then along came Natalie with her stories of Sicilian bandits!" He laughed into her hair. "It was crazy and yet . . . and yet . . . we both know that Dad sailed very close to the wind. But we don't quite know how close — whether he actually broke the law. That's why I wanted to do this, Ma. Live here again. Find out what is real and what is not." He rocked her gently. "All this stuff with Daniel. And Alf. And Dorrie told me about you pulling Dennison out of the water." He sighed. "You seem to have spent a lot of time rescuing people, Ma. And now it's happening to me. I mean, I didn't rescue Alf exactly, but Daniel and me kind of . . . well, sorted him out. Hopefully."

She pushed herself up and away to look at him searchingly. "You're all right? It must have been a nightmare."

He grinned reassuringly. "You know I'm all right. So is Daniel. But what comes out of it is that it seems real. And home seems unreal."

She let her breath go with a puff of relief then said, "Listen. We'll just have to carry on as best we can and decide what's true or real much later." She stood up. "Tell you one thing, Will. I haven't felt so alive for a long time."

They went down the steps into the house and spent time unpacking and making up beds before stopping to

244

eat a late lunch. It was already getting dark when Will said, "Let's make a bonfire! Come on, Ma — it's poor old Guy Fawkes' special night and this is the place for a beacon! We've got enough driftwood in the lean-to for starters, and then we can feed the dry seaweed on to it to keep it in."

Binnie laughed. "Why not? It will guide Daniel in — not that he needs guiding but we can pretend he does. Let's do it behind the lean-to on the end of Dad's garden where all those brambles have taken over. It will help to clear them. Shall I scrub some potatoes?"

They were like children, running back and forth with kindling, calling to each other. Binnie grabbed a rake to pull some of the brambles over on to the pyre, scratched her fingers and went indoors for gloves and some paraffin. In the last of the light they spotted the *Mermaid* bucking towards them like some old war horse. Binnie pulled the tea towels from her pockets and they waved them frantically and got a "toot" in reply. Then they lit the kindling.

It crackled pathetically for a few seconds before the flame found the paraffin and, torchlike, leaped into the air, engulfing the brambles and shooting sparks high into the dark grey sky. Binnie and Will whooped with delight as the *Mermaid* blew her horn in response. Half an hour later Daniel joined them, lugging a bag of provisions from Maggie Govern.

They sat around the fire as it died its red death. Daniel told them that Matthew and he had visited Alf in the hospital.

245

"He doesn't seem to realize he was marooned for so long. And he is saying nothing at all about Marigold. Just that he went there to listen for her singing and fell into that cleft where we found him. So obviously that's what the accident report has said and there is no question of an official investigation."

"Exactly what I told you, Ma." Will spread his hands to catch the last of the heat. "Dan, if you want to push out that tin with this branch, the spuds should be well and truly cooked."

Daniel beamed. "You have actually baked some potatoes! We used to do this on the farm — did I tell you I was a farmer's son?"

Will said, "Yeah, yeah. Push out the tin before the spuds are cinders!"

Dan glanced at Binnie in the firelight. "My parents were killed on our brand-new piece of motorway and I went to live with my grandparents. But it was when we were on the farm — that was when I used to come to Cherrington." He clawed out the potato tin with the branch, then added, "Alf sent his love and best wishes, by the way. 'Tell Mrs Theo that everything is going to be all right' — that was the message."

Binnie was still dealing with the awful fact of Daniel being orphaned. She cleared her throat convulsively and picked up on Alf's comment. "He's always called me 'Mrs Binnie', never 'Mrs Theo'."

Daniel lifted his shoulders. "He called you Mrs Theo today."

246

Binnie went to fetch plates and cheese, and thought about Daniel being a farmer's son. No wonder he could put his hand to anything.

She carried everything out on a tray and for a moment paused and watched the two men as they prised open the red-hot biscuit tin with stones and twigs. They looked so at ease together. Almost like father and son. Except that Daniel was pushing her away. Back to the delusion of Theo . . .

CHAPTER
EIGHTEEN

During the next fortnight, when Binnie stopped to think, it amazed her how effortlessly the three of them settled into a routine. It was as if Daniel had switched off the current of awareness between them and discovered an underlying friendship. It made for an easy three-way relationship between them. Life became very pleasant.

Almost unnoticeably autumn gave way to winter; the weather did not change dramatically, there were still bright, sunlit days to alleviate the typical English dullness, but the temperature dropped and the sea glittered pewter instead of silver.

Binnie steeled herself on the second day and went into the cellar with her key to the trapdoor. She moved two lightweight sacks and opened up cautiously. It was high tide and far below the sea sucked hungrily at the rock curtain in the cavern. She descended half a dozen rungs of the ladder until it was free of the rock face, then shone her torch downward. There was no sign of *Scallywag*. She raked the torch back and forth, though there was nowhere to hide the boat anyway. Dennison was not here. She breathed deeply with sheer relief. Then she clambered back into the cellar, locked the trap into place and dragged the heavy barrels over it. She stood there, panting slightly, imagining Daniel trying to lift that heavy flap not so long ago. Dennison had got a key, of course, but no way would he be able to lift the sheer weight of the barrels and get through into the cellar. She went up the stone steps, carrying a cardboard box of tinned food. No-one was in the kitchen anyway. She put the tins away in some kind of order and stood looking out of the window at the smudges that were the Eastern Isles. Somewhere out there, Marigold's body was part of the heaving Atlantic. Binnie felt she had been laid to rest.

Every morning, Daniel rose at six o'clock, and had launched the dinghy and taken the *Mermaid* off by seven thirty. His first pick-up was from Portcullis Island, where two boys, aged eight and seven, helped their parents and grandparents with an experimental sheep farm. It was one of the few comparatively level islands, shaped like a saucer — Daniel thought it might be an ancient volcanic crater — growing lush grass that supported a limited flock of very small sheep. Daniel was highly amused by them; he told Will and Binnie that they followed the boys down to the wooden dock each morning "like cuddly toys".

The next port of call was at Oriel Island. Oriel was almost as big as Keyhole, and with its three wide beaches was popular as a holiday resort. There were two deep-water quays. The *Mermaid* serviced both, picking up three at the north quay and seven at the south. Then Daniel swung across to Postern for the final six and eventually moored at Keyhole on the short quay. It was usually about eight forty-five as he lifted the little ones ashore and adjusted their backpacks and — recently — found their gloves and scarves. They accepted him without question but were disappointed that he had no sea songs for them.

"Alf makes sounds like waves. Then gulls. Then . . . mermaids," one of the younger boys explained. The older children laughed at this and the little ones looked at them reproachfully.

The boys from Portcullis asked whether they could visit Alf in hospital and Daniel told them that when Alf was a bit stronger he would visit them at school.

"A hospital visit is something their parents would have to arrange and they're all busy," he told Binnie over the washing-up the first evening. "But I reckon the teacher would welcome a visit from Alf. He's a teaching-aid in himself!"

The *Mermaid* usually anchored near Trapdoor sands before ten o'clock each morning and Daniel then had five hours until he set off for what he called "collection and delivery".

He and Will set lobster pots among the pinnacles of the Shark's Teeth. Daniel seemed to know exactly what he was doing and poled the dinghy expertly over the tops of the rocks at high tide and in among them when it was lower. Will watched and learned.

Neither of them was quite so keen on gardening. However, after the bonfire on Guy Fawkes' night, they cleared the burned brambles away and slashed at the nettles, and one morning in the second week of their stay, Will dug a sizeable plot behind the house.

"It doubles our growing area," Binnie chortled that afternoon as they sat drinking tea. Daniel was doing his ferrying. "Still time to plant winter cabbage and some roots . . ." she pored over her gardening book and noted how many hours of sunshine would warm the garden.

"Bound to be thin soil, Ma," Will warned her. "It's never had much yield, surely? When Dorrie and I came that summer after Natalie left it was just a patch of dirt. I don't remember one solitary bean or pea or lettuce or —"

"I get the message. But, actually, Will, I've got great hopes. If you look at the shape of the rocks around the house and the back, there's a chance that the wind blows soil and sand into it but not out. It's open to the southwesterlies and most of it is protected from winds coming from any other direction. I don't think it is *that* thin a covering. You were digging down a spade depth at least, and I've been forking out the nettle roots and they go down for miles!"

"Well, we can but try. It's supposed to be mild this far south. We could raise seeds indoors and plant them out before Christmas possibly."

She made up her mind quickly. "We'll go over with Daniel tomorrow morning, Will. Spend the whole day on Keyhole and come back with him in the afternoon."

Will looked doubtful. "Will it take you that long to buy packets of seeds? Or is it an excuse to gossip with Maggie Govern?"

"I'll do both, of course." She punched his arm. "But I can go to see Alf too. And perhaps discover Dennison's whereabouts."

He grinned, then sobered suddenly. "Ma. I don't want to put my great feet in it, but Daniel . . . is there something I should know?"

"How do you mean?" She closed the gardening book and went to put it back on the shelf.

"He's only remembering half a story, isn't he? Do you know the other half?"

"Of course not. I don't remember him at Cherrington as a child and I didn't know him as your father's friend or henchman or whatever he was. But then there were a lot of things I didn't know." She smiled wryly. "I think I must have closed off everything concerning your father. Perhaps that is how I deal with things, Will. I bury my head in the nearest sand!"

"It's obvious that Dad spoke of you a lot. But it's more than that." He cleared his throat and looked slightly embarrassed. "Daniel's got a thing about you, Ma." He frowned at Binnie's staccato laugh. "Sorry. I know it's none of my business but look at the facts. He has an accident, we don't know what. Loses his memory. Goes to a hospital. Runs away from hospital and makes for Cherrington. You. Makes for you. Then after you've decamped over here, he remembers little bits and pieces about Cherrington and has to come to tell you. Why? They didn't amount to much. But when he gets here something nudges his memory again —"

"*Scallywag*," Binnie said *sotto voce*.

"All right. That makes sense. Because he pinches *Scallywag* and goes to Trapdoor and stays there overnight. Comes back in a bit of a state, apparently, is knocked sideways by Dennison and ends up in hospital here. But since then, he has been . . . I'm not sure. Happy? Settled?" Will turned in his chair to watch his mother walk to the window. "I reckon he's remembered something else, Ma. About Dad. About you. I reckon you have become his — his — *mission*! Looking after you, getting this place sorted, that's his role now." Binnie shivered and Will said quickly, "Ma, you're cold. Come and sit by the fire, for Pete's sake!"

She said, "I'm fine." But she did go to the fire and stood looking down into the flames, her forearm resting on the high mantelpiece. "What's your point, Will? Daniel probably thinks he's carrying out Dad's last wishes, to keep an eye on all of us."

Will gnawed at his lip. "It's just that . . . I'm pretty sure how he feels about you — all right, perhaps he is concerned for all of us, I don't know — but I haven't got the remotest how you feel about him."

She said, "He's ill. But he's getting better."

"So . . . one of your lame ducks?"

She tried to laugh. "I suppose so. A connection with Dad too." She looked at the granite mantel and ran a finger along its surface. "I would just say, darling, don't try to jog his memory for him. I am not sure what will turn up. It might well be better if he never remembers where he was, what he was doing, when he lost his memory."

Will stood up. He was close to his mother, staring at her, making her return his look. "Ma, you know something. What is it?"

"I don't know anything, darling. I promise. Dennison made some . . . suppositions. But they were crazy. It's simply that — whatever he says now — Daniel was intending to take his life on Cherrington slipway."

"Suppositions? Crazy suppositions? Nothing to do with Natalie's Sicilian or anything?"

"Nothing." She laughed genuinely. The thought of Natalie brought her down to earth with a bump.

But Will hadn't given up. "Look at me, Ma — look me in the eye! The man is crazy for you and you know it. You won't let him under your guard, which probably means you feel . . . something. So what is making you hold him at arm's length?"

She tried laughingly to say how could she hold him at arm's length when he regularly lifted her into the dinghy.

Will would have none of it. He said, "The answer is that you know something. And you don't want him to know it. Ma, what the hell is going on?"

Binnie wondered fleetingly about showing him the locked trapdoor and the cavern beneath. Daniel knew of it — Daniel had sheltered there. Will had a right to know.

She began falteringly, "Dennison told me that when he was in Naples he contacted Violetta, who was a friend of your father's."

"I know, I know."

"Dennison said —"

The front door opened with a crash and Daniel appeared in the doorway of the living room. He was soaked but grinning.

He said, "Don't ask! Dinghy capsized. Maggie Govern gave us a leg of lamb for the freezer. I had to dive for it!"

Binnie laughed with sheer relief.

"Go and change! We'll eat early." She glanced at Will. "Shall we be really civilized and have a sherry? Do the honours, Will. I won't be long."

As she crossed the hall she heard Daniel say, "I heard Dennison's name. Don't tell me he dropped in?"

She stopped and held her breath. But Will said, "No. Don't reckon we shall see him again. Let's have that jacket, it's sodden. I'll put it over the furnace, OK?"

"You're a good man, Will!"

Binnie carried on into the kitchen. She agreed with that wholeheartedly.

It was completely dark by the time they sat around the kitchen table eating their evening meal. Binnie broached the subject of tomorrow's trip to Keyhole. "I wouldn't mind phoning Dorrie at the Manor and seeing how things are going there. But mainly it would be good to visit Alf. He must be feeling so cut off from his old life."

Daniel looked soberly into his tea. "Remember, he intended to cut himself off permanently. I think the last two weeks have probably been exactly what he needs. Besides, Matthew is still working at the Midwatch cottages and he drops into the hospital every day on his way home."

Binnie looked reassured. Will asked whether Alf had any family on the Skalls and she told him that Matthew was his cousin. "He'll make sure Alf is all right. But the sooner he can get back to his school runs, the better." She finished her coffee and sighed. "Thank God the police weren't involved with that fiasco on Casement Island. There'd have been no way he could have continued ferrying the children back and forth. Well, for one thing, the parents wouldn't have trusted him."

Daniel carried the plates to the sink. "Would you?" he asked.

"Of course! Alf is completely reliable."

Will was already dippering hot water into a bowl and looked through the steam to say, "But he wasn't, Ma, was he? You know very well that if Dorrie and I were on that passenger list, you would have been the first to withdraw."

"I don't think so, actually. But anyway, no-one knows what really happened, so it should be all right." Daniel and Will exchanged glances and she added, "There's more coffee. Shall we take it into the sitting room and sit for an hour before bed?"

"Plenty of sand in there, Ma?" Will asked with a grin. Then when Binnie looked her incomprehension: "For a spot of head-burying!"

She shook her head, smilingly, and began to load a tray. "If we go over with Daniel tomorrow, I could leave Maggie's leg of lamb in a very low oven all day. It should be well and truly done by the time we get home."

She was surprised when Will and Daniel laughed.

★ ★ ★

256

Alf looked diminished in some way, almost shrunken. His mass of hair and beard crowded around his smaller face.

"One of our auxiliaries used to be a hairdresser and has offered to cut Mr Trevose's hair and trim that beard," Sister said disapprovingly. "But he'll have none of it." She rolled her eyes. "Talked of Samson and Delilah, would you believe!"

Binnie laughed. She was visiting alone as Matthew had asked Daniel and Will for some help with fitting new windows at Midwatch. "Would you let me have a go at it, Alf? It could be working the other way round for you — all your strength is going into growing hair instead of strengthening your body!"

He twinkled up at her as he done from that first day in September.

"Don't you worry about me or my hair, Mrs Theo. Sit down and tell me how you are. Go on, sit where Sister's put that chair and just talk to me. Sensible stuff like how that freezer is a-working and what's in it and what you're going to do with all that brandy your 'usband piled in that there cellar!"

She stared at him aghast. "How on earth d'you know about that?" She sat down with a bump. "Does everyone know he was a smuggler?"

He waited until Sister closed the door of the ward behind her.

"Prob'ly. But we all thought he got shot of it as he brought it in. I'm the only one what's seen inside the cellar — went there the first day I landed you. Wasn't I meant to?"

"Nowhere was out of bounds, Alf. I hadn't realized you'd seen it all. A lot of those boxes contain foodstuffs — tinned peas and beans and soups . . ." She puffed a sigh. "Natalie thought we should throw the bottles into the sea and then dive for them and claim them as finders keepers. I just pretend they're not there. They're hurting no-one."

He nodded agreement. "So long as not too many people know about them. Otherwise you might have a landing party of other smugglers!" He chuckled and Binnie tried to smile back.

"Anyway," she said. "I've got tons of milk in the freezer. Vegetables. Bread — I'm going to make bread but not yet — butter and cheese and meat. Oh —" she clapped a hand over her mouth — "a leg of lamb Maggie sent over! I meant to get it out and cook it slowly all day while we're here. And I forgot!"

"Take it out tonight," Alf advised. "Let it thaw overnight. Marigold got food poisoning from eating unthawed meat." He looked past Binnie and out of the opposite window. "That was a long time ago."

Binnie waited but he said no more and his eyes were fixed on the window. She put a tentative hand over his. "Listen, Alf. I know it's awful. But it will get better. I promise."

"It 'asn't for you, my 'ansome." Still his gaze was unwavering. She found herself looking over her shoulder as if she might catch sight of someone peering in. They were on the second floor, for goodness' sake!

She said in a low voice, "It's not quite the same. I got over Theo a long time ago." She smiled ruefully. "Quite soon after he got over me, actually."

"You thought you did. But if you 'ad, you wouldn't be 'ere now, would you? You'd be leasing out the island to someone and seeing the lawyers about selling his house on the mainland, not trying to make a home on his island." He was looking at her now, twinkling again. "You've come to get 'im out of your system."

"Maybe." She thought grimly that she'd had enough of this kind of talk for a while and anyway she'd come to talk to Alf about his obsession, not her own. She said, "So, how soon before Daniel can retire from the school run? Will you be strong enough to take it on after Christmas, d'you think?"

"Matthew told me your Daniel were doing it. D'you remember 'ow that Daniel and me pulled that damned freezer up through the dunes and down all them steps into the house? Good lad, 'e is."

"Course I remember." She remembered Dennison grabbing the kitchen knife. "And he's hardly a lad, Alf! Older than me, probably."

"Well, you're only a girl, Mrs Binnie. Used to be a Binnie in them old musical films. Binnie Smith . . . or were it Binnie Baley?"

She said, "You've been calling me Mrs Theo today, Alf. I'd prefer to be Binnie."

"Aye. But you're not Mrs Binnie any more, are you, m'ansome? That Daniel tells me that you'll always be married to Theo Cash." He smiled ruefully. "An' there was me trying to pair you off! Better leave the matchmaking to Maggie Govern, I reckon!" He looked at her face and went on quickly, "I shan't be doing no school run again, my maid. You tell young Daniel that. He's welcome to the job if he wants it. The parents pay by the term so he'll collect just before Christmas. There's never any quibbling."

She was startled. "Alf! It's your work. It's what you do! Daniel doesn't want your job or your money! And anyway, he's not here for good. Just until you get better. He's got a job back on the mainland."

Alf said drily, "He hasn't got a job nowhere, Mrs Binnie, and you know it. He's come here to find things out. And he hasn't done that yet, so he might as well take the children back and forth while he puzzles it all out." He looked at her face and shrugged. "I cain't do it no more, anyway. If I saw my Marigold I'd be jumping right off the *Mermaid* and leaving them poor little 'uns to fend for themselves!"

She said, distressed, "Oh, Alf. The little ones miss your sea sounds so much."

He brightened. "Is that so? Is that really right?" He chuckled, well pleased. "Listen. Your Daniel was on to me to go into the school and talk to the children when I get better. That's what I'll do. I'll teach them the sea sounds and the gulls' cries and the wind coming across the top of Keyhole and blowing the thrift sideways!"

Unexpected tears pricked Binnie's eyes and she said, "Do it now. For me."

Binnie left the hospital and walked across the top of the island and up to Dennison's lookout. The door was unlocked and she opened it and peered inside. A torn net hung over the ladder and a bobbin of nylon lay by its side. The whole place looked abandoned. She closed the door carefully and walked back down to the dunes and then the hard sand. She planned to drop in to the post office and look at the racks of seed packets next to the early Christmas cards, then go on to Harbour Lights and a cup of tea with Maggie before she and Will joined Daniel on the *Mermaid*. She had looked forward to this little outing; now she simply wanted to be back on Trapdoor: home. She felt slightly jittery after her talk with Alf. Thoughts of Theo and Daniel were jumbled together in her head. And the school run . . . Daniel would not want it permanently, yet the last two weeks had been a time of routine contentment. And it need not end.

She chose her seeds and talked to Walter Polpen, who asked about the memorial service for Theo.

"I remember you mentioned it some time ago, Mrs Cash. And with Christmas on the horizon, I did wonder whether you wanted to see the Reverend. You know I'm churchwarden. I could make an announcement on the radio, if you like."

She bit her lip. "The trouble is, we can't go ahead with it until Dennison gets back and I've no idea when that will be. Have you heard anything?"

"I don't think he can write, m'dear. And phones or a radio are beyond him. Him and your husband — ex-husband, I should say — they'd go off for most of the winter. Crewing for charter boats. Bit of fishing. I thought that's what he'd be doing."

"Probably. But he was the one who wanted the service. I can't very well hold it in his absence. Can you let me know if you hear anything?"

Walter Polpen promised he would and she drifted over to Ditchdrain Street and found Will already drinking tea and watching a television programme about house decorating.

"This is what I miss!" Will declared. "We should get one, Ma. We could settle down on a Saturday afternoon and watch the sport —"

She laughed. "You haven't missed it, so don't give me that!" She hugged Maggie and poured herself a cup of tea, then said to her, "Alf seems to be getting better, but he reckons he won't be doing the school run any more."

"I know. He's said as much to Matthew several times and Matthew agrees with him! I said — what else is he going to do then? Sit around listening to mermaids all day?"

Binnie looked at her sharply; of course she had no idea that Alf had found his Marigold. She said, "Well, first of all, he's going to visit the children in school and teach them some of the sounds of the Islands. Could be quite a project he's starting!"

She showed Maggie her seed packets and Maggie said that Natalie had telephoned and sent love. Binnie remembered she had been going to telephone Dorrie and decided against it. A blanket of contentment seemed to cocoon her. They had another cup of tea and then Binnie said, "Where's Daniel? It's half past three

— the children will be coming down to the pier any minute now."

Will spoke over his shoulder. "Probably already in the *Mermaid*. He fusses around that boat like an old woman."

"Keeping it in good order for Alf," Binnie said sadly.

"Actually . . ." Will looked up, "it's getting dark. I'll pop down and make sure everything's OK. Keep an eye out, Ma, and join us when the kids start trooping across the long pier."

The two women moved to the window and gazed to their right; not a soul could be seen. The dunes humped themselves darkly beyond the long pier. Maggie said, "This is how it is until next April or May. Gladys Polpen and I tried to start some sort of fellowship in the church but it wasn't worth it." She sighed. "People who come here are the sort of people who don't want company." She put a hand on Binnie's shoulder. "I miss you already." She laughed. "Who said that, some American comedian?"

Binnie said, "Does it get you down, Maggie?"

"Now and then. This time of day when I look out like this." She grinned. "But then, along comes someone . . . look, it's that Roger Westway from Portcullis, and there's his brother. They haven't even got a television. The parents — and the grandparents — read last week's newspaper to the boys and get their opinions. You should hear what they come out with at times!"

Binnie smiled as she watched the two boys trudging across the wide apron of the long pier. She said, "Beats me how Natalie stood the loneliness for as long as she did!"

"Oh, she went off to Italy with himself every winter. That's how she found out about the Italian girl. Violet or whatever her name was."

Binnie said, "Funny. That's something the Skalls have done for me. I don't begrudge Theo his happiness with Natalie — or with Violetta, for that matter. I feel as if I know him better now. Each one of us was special to him in a different way."

Maggie laughed incredulously. "That's a very liberal way of looking at it, Binnie! Sounds to me as if you've also discovered that you are still in love with him! If he hadn't been drowned — if he'd wanted you back, would you have gone?"

Binnie laughed too. "Everyone seems to think I would! If I hadn't changed . . . maybe. But I'm not the Binnie who fell in love with Theo Cash. And he's probably not the same Theo Cash anyway!"

Maggie opened her mouth to say something then closed it and started again. "Here's your Will back again. That means no sign of Daniel."

Binnie groaned and reached for her jacket. "If Alf means what he says, who else would do the school run? I don't think Daniel will take it on — sounds as if he might have already resigned!"

Maggie gathered tea cups on to the tray. "Matthew could hold the fort for a while, but someone would come forward. We might be loners but we look after each other too. And if the school had to close, families would be forced back to the mainland. So we're looking after the Skalls — that's what it amounts to."

Binnie met Will at the door. "No Daniel?" she asked. "There's something about the Skalls that makes people disappear without even a puff of smoke!" She was joking and then saw Will's expression. "Oh my God. What's happened?"

"He's there. He was on the *Mermaid*. He's loading the kids in now. But he wants to see you, Ma. On your own. Come on." His expression was as grim as his voice. He hooked his arm in hers and almost manhandled her down to the short pier.

For some reason she pulled back. "Will, stop. I don't like this mystery. Why didn't he come up for me himself?"

"He's writing a letter to you. In case he can't speak for crocodile tears!" He shrugged and forced himself to say normally, "Wanted to say cheerio to the kids, I suppose. I'll be taking them back." He patted her hand quickly. "I can do it. I've watched him. He's a good teacher, I'll give him that."

She came to a dead stop. "He's going," she said flatly. "He's remembered. He's remembered everything."

Will said, "Yes. He's going to go out there. Naples, I think he said. Get it sorted. Kept saying how sorry he is. And that when you read his letter, you will understand."

She coughed on a sob. "This is what I was afraid of, Will. That he would remember. And the nightmare would become reality." She was almost gibbering. "If he hadn't remembered, we might have — might have —"

Will's voice hardened again. "You mean we could all have buried our heads in sand, Ma? Is that what you really want? Would you eventually have married him and settled down to Skallion domesticity?"

"Of course not! But I might have believed that Dennison's information was not reliable."

Will said nothing and his silence was condemning. Below them, the *Mermaid* rose and fell on her mooring rope, her fenders squeaking against the side of the ladder. Binnie looked down on the children; some of them waved and she waved back automatically. There was no sign of Daniel.

"He's behind you, Ma," Will's voice was gentler now, concerned. "I'm going down to start up the engine. D'you want to stay with me?"

"Give me two minutes with him, Will. It's only fair."

He swung himself on to the ladder and clambered down, and she turned and there was Daniel. She thought with terror: the lid is coming off the can . . .

He stepped forward quickly as if he expected her to run. He wore a duffel coat she had seen in the post office shop that very afternoon; a backpack was slung over one shoulder. He was ready for a journey yet he was too late for any flights from the airport.

He said in a low voice, "Binnie! Thank you — I couldn't think of a way to speak to you alone and I needed to give you this." He fumbled in his pocket and produced an envelope. He held it out to her. She did not take it.

"It's all written down here, my love. I've remembered everything. I'm so ashamed, Binnie. Agreeing to do . . .

266

what I did. I can't face you and talk about it now. There's just one way I might be able to redeem the whole thing. That's why I'm going." Still she did not put out a hand for the letter and he reached for her and folded the envelope into her palm and held it there. She felt something hard within the folded paper and thought with a huge jolt of her heart that she knew what it was.

He pulled her close to him. "Binnie, I know you will be horrified when you read this. Theo made me feel young again and I went along with him. I let it happen, Binnie. And when I found you I let it happen again, unconsciously at first. Until I realized that you loved him. You thought you might be falling for me, didn't you? I thought the same. And then I knew. You saw him in me." He put his free arm around her and held her tightly to him. His backpack pressed into her left side. She sobbed drily.

He said, "Goodbye, Binnie. Thank you for sharing . . . things. I love you and always will."

He released her and walked past her and across the apron to the long pier. And then she could see him no longer.

CHAPTER
NINETEEN

It was too dark to read the letter on the *Mermaid*, and as Binnie turned her back on the sea to clamber down the ladder she stuffed it into her pocket and felt again the hard circular shape inside. She knew that it was Theo's ring. So Daniel had remembered . . . what? How the ring had come into his possession?

She zipped up the pocket and sat down next to Roger and Colin. Will unlooped the mooring rope and jumped in after her; the engine was already idling and the boat rose and sank with the swell. She saw that her parcels were stowed beneath the cowling among the children's backpacks. She forced herself to remember choosing the seeds and talking to Walter Polpen about a memorial service for Theo; it helped to stop her crying.

Will spoke in his new hard voice: "You all right?" She nodded. The children chattered, the engine changed note as they turned towards Postern, one of the older girls started to sing "Silent Night". She thought, it's beautiful, it's wonderful, but it's no good now. Daniel's memory has come back and we have lost him for ever. What will he do? Walk into the tideless sea of Italy? And how shall *we* manage? How shall we *manage*?

Will must know what had happened; he had talked to Daniel before she had arrived. He called back now, "How was Alf?"

The younger ones stopped talking so they could hear her reply. Binnie cleared her throat. "Not too bad at all."

He said no more but then he was concentrating on manoeuvring the *Mermaid* into the quay at Postern. The hotel lights were on. Matthew ran down to greet them; he told them he was staying the night and would go home with Daniel tomorrow.

"With me, actually." Will was brooking no argument. "Daniel's had to go and see to things back in Naples."

Matthew was taken aback and started to say something about the school run but Will was determined. "I'm the school bus driver now!" he announced to Matthew, then turned to the children. "I need a special hat and a notebook and a pencil. I'm going to need some help with all this!"

Binnie sat silent and numb, recognizing he was deliberately taking over the situation. Maybe it would be all right . . . maybe they could lose their memories too. She took a sharp breath at her own thought. This particular can of worms surely had to be opened. Theo had been her husband, he deserved some kind of justice.

It was dark when they arrived at Trapdoor, and a light drizzle made it darker still. They anchored and loaded the dinghy with their purchases, jumped out too soon as usual, so were both soaked almost to the waist, then dragged the dinghy into the dunes and started to

269

trudge up to Jacob's Ladder. They needed their breath and their attention for the walk but when they eventually let themselves in and made for the warmth of the kitchen furnace, the silence between them became loud. Binnie told herself it was because the house was unnaturally quiet. As they stamped themselves out of their wet shoes and jeans, the sounds almost echoed out into the hall again. Binnie took dry clothes from above the copper and threw some to Will. She struggled and hopped her way into fresh jeans. She wanted to wail and say how wonderful it had been with the three of them here and why on earth did Daniel have to remember anything else . . . She said nothing.

Will went into the lean-to to get the dynamo going and Binnie took a taper and lit the lamps and then the candles in their sconces. The hum of the freezer partially filled the vacuum so that her voice no longer boomed when she said simple things about omelettes and lighting the sitting-room fire. Will did one and she did the other, and as he passed through the kitchen with kindling and driftwood, she risked saying conversationally, "Wasn't it wonderful when the girl from Postern sang 'Silent Night'?"

Will made a sound of assent and disappeared into the sitting room. When he came back she was turning the omelettes and grating cheese. He went behind her, rinsed his hands at the sink and fetched plates and cutlery.

"Have you read your letter, Ma?" he asked, his voice suddenly harsh.

270

She looked round, startled. "You know I haven't. I'll wait until we've eaten."

"You knew already, didn't you? You've heard about it from Dennison. That was the bit you didn't bother to tell me." He banged an old-fashioned cruet between the plates on the kitchen table. "You let me get to know him, work with him — dammit, I put him in the place of Dad, can you believe? — and all the time . . . And you knew! You let it happen, you let it go on. You probably enjoyed the fact that Dad's murderer had the hots for you, didn't you? Is that what it's all been about? Christ, Ma — it's horrible!"

She used the fish slice to dish up the omelettes, then put the pan in the sink; she was shaking all over.

She said in a controlled voice, "I couldn't believe it. The story came from Violetta who, presumably, loved Dad and was lashing out wildly at someone to blame. And Dennison was the same. He says he'd always had suspicions of Daniel but I thought probably he was jealous. Dennison was Dad's right-hand man until Daniel came along . . . oh God, I don't know." She sat down suddenly, put her elbows either side of her plate and held her head. "If Daniel remembers it then it must be true. But Daniel couldn't have deliberately killed anyone . . . could he?" She looked up through her fingers. "Could he, Will?"

It was as if she had pricked a balloon. Will actually exhaled long and loudly and then collapsed into his chair. He stared at his mother.

"How should I know, Ma? When Nat and I first arrived, he'd cleared off with *Scallywag*, if you

271

remember. That wasn't a very good start. The fact that Dennison clobbered him and he ended up in hospital didn't make it all right, did it?"

"But when you rescued Alf, and then being here and working together and doing the school run . . . watching the sport on Maggie Govern's television . . . you must have got to know him then?"

"I thought I did. Yes. But when he told me . . . when I got down to the boat he was writing to you and he didn't say a word until he had finished . . . and then he told me. It was the *way* he told me. As if it was somebody else he was talking about." He held up his hand. "I know he's not fully fit yet, Ma. Please don't start defending him. It's the whole thing — him turning up at Cherrington and supposedly trying to drown himself —"

"He was up to his waist — he had no idea where the slipway went. He could have slipped off —"

"He was there when Dorrie's car was torched — wasn't that odd? He got himself a place down at the Manor —"

"I fixed it up, Will! Just to get rid of him so that we were free to come out here!"

"And then he followed you. Honestly, Ma, it stinks of rotten fish!"

"But surely you can see why I had to give him the benefit of the doubt."

"Dad probably told him you were a soft touch."

"But he'd lost his memory — he wouldn't have remembered that!"

"Had he? Had he really lost his bloody memory, Ma? Or was he trying to move into Dad's place? Ready-made wife, came with good references, kids grown-up, his own island —"

"Will, stop it, please! I can't bear it — and I don't believe it!"

"Do you know what he said to me? 'Dennison has come to take me back to Italy. It seems I did away with your father, Will. Dennison is taking me back for some kind of trial.' He must have spent a lot of time in the boat writing the letter so he could have told both of us much sooner. He didn't even say he was sorry!"

"He did to me. That's what he said when he met me on the pier."

"He wasn't apologizing for killing Dad, he was apologizing for whatever lies between the two of you —"

"Will — please!"

"All right." Will looked at her again and said, "Sorry. You know I trust you completely, Ma. And I can see this has knocked you for six." He put a hand on her arm. "Let's try and eat. Then we can go in by the fire and you can read his letter. Perhaps that will help." He forked some food into his mouth and nodded at her own plate.

She said something in a low voice and he said, "Sorry?"

She said, "He has sent me the wedding ring. The one I put on Dad's finger twenty-three years ago. I found his wallet in his armchair at Maggie's. It was open and the ring had fallen out. It's in the letter. I can feel it."

"How the hell did he get that?" Will stopped eating.

"I don't know." She pushed her plate away.

Will said, "Come on. You must eat. He's gone now. We've always known that Dad sailed close to the wind. So it stands to reason that his so-called partner — Daniel — was a similar character. Let's leave it at that for now. Please eat, Ma. I'll make some tea and we'll take it into the sitting room. We'll manage really well without him. I know where the lobster pots are, and he's taught me how to fish and pole the boat and start *Mermaid*'s engine. We'll be fine."

Binnie nodded half-heartedly but then said, "Yes. Yes, we will. We'll be more than fine. We'll dig in here and have a great Christmas." She gave him a watery smile. "I'll come with you on the run now and then, Will. I can learn how to pilot the *Mermaid* and — and — see to things."

He forced a grin at her as he fetched the teapot. "Eat," he said.

And she did.

The letter was smudged and damp. She spread it in front of the fire and picked up the ring to show to Will.

"I knew immediately it was Dad's. I chose it, of course, and it was the same as mine. He called it a girl's ring but he didn't mind, really. See the filigree? There was no room for any engraving, but the filigree makes it instantly recognizable." She swallowed tears and passed the ring over to Will. "I expect you and Dorrie worked out years ago that I was pregnant at the time." She tried to smile. "It wasn't quite so acceptable as it is now.

Poor Dad had to marry me if he wanted to escape with his life!" She stretched the smile into a small laugh. "So all the people who have told me that I was his favourite are cooking without gas! He wanted the island to go to his family. Not his ex-wife!"

Will said curiously, "Does that still hurt? Because if it does, could it mean you are still carrying a torch for him?"

"I still don't know, Will. Natalie will doubtless enjoy telling me just how I feel when she comes over next!" Her laugh was more genuine then.

They both stared into the flames, then she gathered up the dry, crackling pages and read them.

Dear Binnie

Beautiful, practical, strong, independent Binnie. How I wish I could write *My dearest Binnie*. But you would never have been mine, I know that now. You have come to Trapdoor and are settling in there for one reason only: because it is the closest you can come to living with Theo again. I have realized that over the past two weeks when we have grown together like a family, but a family without a head.

I wanted so much to remember everything about him so that I could talk to you and you would be grateful to me and gratitude might turn to something else. But I still have just those few snapshots, just those few pieces of jigsaw which I cannot fit together. He talked of you. I know that. He wanted me to meet you. He kept saying we would go to Cherrington and see you one day. And I was happy with that because I'd been to Cherrington and I remembered it then, with its pier and its boats and its churches and its wood and the Manor. Was I insanely jealous of him then? Was I already in love with you? What made me kill him that night, Binnie? Dennison said I took a piece of wood and hit him deliberately. Is that why my memory stops dead? Am I frightened to remember that I am a murderer? Dennison says I must face the consequences and I know he is right. So I am going with him. I have asked him if we can go back to where it happened and he says Violetta will take us. She is frightened of me and Dennison hates me for what I have done. It is possible I shall pay the price for it before I reach wherever he is taking me. Just know that I love you, Binnie. You were a dream at first; a photograph Theo showed me. He kept your ring around his neck and he gave it to me in case I ever needed to identify myself. I think you must have it back now because you're not a dream any more, you are real.

Please take care of yourself and enjoy living on the Skalls. You are made for happiness, Binnie, and I think it is overdue. Look for it. It is there.

Daniel

PS. You must know about the cavern. It is the way we landed our illegal "catch". Make sure you secure the trapdoor into the cellar, always.

Binnie read it again and then again. Then she lifted her head and let the tears come into her eyes. She said, "It's rather personal in places, but please read it, Will. Daniel has not remembered that he murdered your father. Dennison has told him so, but he has not actually remembered it himself." She pushed across the sheets of paper. "I still cannot believe it, Will. Tell me honestly, what do you think?"

Will picked up the letter reluctantly and skimmed it. He put it on his knees, slammed a hand over it and closed his eyes tightly for a moment. Binnie tried to say something but he shook his head violently. Then he opened his eyes and read it again without comment. Then he looked up, and said, "Yes. It's very . . . plausible. Especially about how he feels for you, Ma. I can see that he would win you over. But read it again. He accepts what Dennison says without question. Also," he looked back at the letter, "he seems to think he deserves to be punished. And that Dennison might take that on himself. And he — Daniel — would accept that too." He leaned forward. "Doesn't that mean that subconsciously he *knows* he did this thing?"

She stared at him for a second, then scrubbed her eyes angrily. "All I know is that he's as good as dead. I follow your reasoning, love, of course I do. You can just as easily say that subconsciously he was trying to make sure justice was done when he waded into the sea at Cherrington. But Dorrie's car was a separate thing altogether. You might just as well believe in Natalie's Sicilian!" She tried to laugh, then put a hand on Will's knee. "Darling, is there anything we can do to stop this?"

He held her gaze, then put a hand over hers and pressed it against his kneecap. He said, "Well, we cannot report it to the authorities or set off in *Mermaid* to chase them." He pressed harder. "There's nothing we can do, Ma. Think about it. Dad and Daniel have been up to something illegal. Dad has already paid the price. We must let Daniel sort out the rest for himself."

She said, "We could alert the search and rescue — tell them that *Scallywag* is in trouble!"

Will shook his head. "Ma, Daniel is trying to sort something out. We don't even know what it is. But he is quite capable of looking after himself."

"But he doesn't want to, does he?"

"I think he would. If it was necessary."

She was silent. The palm of his hand was warm on the back of hers and brought instant comfort. She thought of Daniel, much too thin but incredibly strong. And just as dextrous as Dennison when it came to the sea.

She said suddenly, "I wonder if that is the answer. Was it necessary to protect himself before . . . against Dad? Could there have been a fight and Dad fell into the sea?"

Will said quietly, "I don't think we are ever going to know the truth, Ma."

They talked around it for nearly an hour. The only thing they agreed on was that they had to let *Scallywag* go.

Will fingered the ring. "At least we're talking about it, Ma. I'm sorry I snapped your head off before. D'you know, I rather think Dad wanted you and Daniel to be a match." He laughed. "I can't really see Dad as a matchmaker but why give Daniel this ring? Why extol all your excellent virtues?" He laughed again at himself and she punched his arm as she so often did.

"Stop winding me up!" she said. But it was good to talk to Will like this and she was deeply thankful for it. They could build on this. Even with Daniel on the high seas in obvious danger, they could build on it. They made more tea and sat for another hour and then went to bed. And then she looked at the letter again. Daniel had given her up. And it was clear now to her as well that she had felt something for him simply because of Theo.

She blew out the lamp and settled beneath her quilt. Here she was, in Theo's bed on Theo's island. Home at last. Daniel had been right. She was here because of her ex-husband. She had to believe it.

CHAPTER
TWENTY

Binnie went with Will the next morning simply because she could not bear to let him out of her sight. It was drizzling and the sea was flat calm but visibility was poor. Will switched on a light above the instrument panel and compared it with Alf's much-thumbed chart. She stood by him, peering past his elbow. At least Alf's navigational skills had not included such modern mysteries as radar; even she could see that they had to set their course north-east. The *Mermaid*'s engine started first time and it was satisfying to see the directional needle swing towards the east as Will turned the wheel. She almost smiled to herself, realizing that she could not believe her own son was capable of knowing what he was doing.

But she was glad to be with him. It was impossible to worry about Daniel or Theo or Dennison or anything as they chugged across this strange, almost inland sea to Portcullis and the first pick-up. There was a sense of adventure and, paradoxically, of great peace and acceptance when the children were swung aboard at Portcullis. They were so full of news and so glad to have her there to listen. She saw what Daniel had meant about the sheep. They stood on the tiny home-made jetty, calling piteously as the boys waved goodbye to them; they were the size of Jack Russell terriers and Roger assured her solemnly they were "a very rare breed".

"A man from a zoo is coming next summer to see them," he announced importantly. "Granddad says we'll have a new dynamo with the money."

Colin confided, "They have babies in December. It's warm enough here for them then, you see."

"They'd die on the mainland," Roger nodded. "They're a cross-breed and we're allowed to call them the Skall flock 'cos there's none like them anywhere else."

"Do the holiday-makers come to see them?" Binnie asked.

"Yes." Roger looked down, shame-faced. "Granddad makes them pay."

"But Mum gives them a free cup of tea!" Colin reminded him.

Binnie said, "That sounds very fair to me. I'd like to come and see them later on. Would that be all right?"

They nodded enthusiastically. "Our teacher is coming too so that we can do a project on them!" said Roger. "They're going to be famous one day!"

Will chugged slowly up to the south pier at Oriel and held the boat steady while Binnie handed down a single passenger.

"Mark can't come this morning. His tonsils are enormous and he's got a temperature. Mum said it's just in time for Christmas, as usual!"

At the north pier all the children were waiting and the tallest girl produced an ancient cap, which she said belonged to an uncle who was a bus driver. "James has brought a notebook for you," she said to Will, smiling shyly. He fitted on the cap and made some notes in the book, and the girls looked at him and giggled and blushed. Binnie smiled.

At Postern Matthew was waiting with the last of the pick-ups and told them that *Scallywag* had gone past the hotel at first light that morning. He had recognized the sails but not been able to see who was on board.

"Dennison has got a real bee in his bonnet about finding out the truth," he commented, crowding beneath the cowling next to Will. "He must have convinced Daniel too. They're evidently on the trail of something."

"Violetta perhaps?" Will said, glancing at his mother and obviously wondering what to tell Matthew.

Matthew dropped his voice. "Maggie thought Daniel was after your mother. Wrong again, it seems." He cleared his throat. "Before I go back to Midwatch, what's going to happen with the school run? There's another three weeks till they break up for Christmas. I can do it if you want me to. But I was thinking that you need a boat over at Trapdoor and if you do the run you've got the *Mermaid*. What d'you say?"

Will rolled his eyes upwards, indicating the cap. "Seems like I've been voted on board!" he said. "Besides, it stops Ma from thinking too much about me going back to Leeds. I've got a job. Up to a point, I am needed!"

Matthew looked round at Binnie, who had heard some of this and shook her head helplessly. He laughed. "All right then. I'll vote you on board too, so long as you promise to come over on December the nineteenth. It's a Friday. We have the Christmas ball then in the church hall. Maggie's got a new outfit. I'd better get you the catalogue she ordered it from. Binnie will need something, I expect."

Will looked doubtful. "We'll have to see. Ma is a bit down at the moment."

"Still some time off, lad. And it will cheer her up. If you're going to be Skallions, you got to come to the Christmas ball!"

Will tied up the boat at the short pier and they got the children out and walking across the apron towards the school. Will and Binnie went with Matthew to Harbour Lights to say hello to Maggie and, they hoped, have a breakfast coffee. There were letters for them on the hall stand: one addressed in Natalie's bold script, another from Dorrie and two for Will with Leeds postmarks.

Maggie was avid for news of Daniel and Dennison, but had to be satisfied with Will and Binnie stonewalling each question. "I am surprised that Daniel did not confide in you, Binnie. Could be Dennison found out something he wants him to see?" Maggie suggested. "Cain't think of anything else. No need to be so secretive about it all. And he could have stayed long enough to have the memorial service for the Captain. He never thinks things through, does that Dennison. Simple."

Binnie could have agreed with that. Dennison was too simple. He saw things either black or white. She shivered and Maggie hastened to put the kettle on.

Will and Matthew were poring over charts in the living room, Matthew pointing out channels through various rocks. "Nothing so bad as the Shark's Teeth, of course, and the *Mermaid*'s got a shallow enough draught. But as well to know what's where," he said. Will leaned closer, tracing seaways with his finger. Matthew chortled. "You take after your dad, don't you? Born a seafarer."

Binnie was pleased to note that Will glanced at the older man, his face alight with pleasure. She was pleased for Theo.

The drizzle gave over as they approached Trapdoor. Will brought *Mermaid* as close as he dared to the rocks that enclosed the narrow beach. "I was looking at that chart of Matthew's. There's enough water just here to anchor *Mermaid* at any tide-time." He threw the heavy anchor off the stern. "If I can get it just right, we need not launch the dinghy every time." He grinned at his mother. "Are you up to a spot of rock climbing?"

"Depends on the rocks," she said, recalling that Daniel had considered Will to be an excellent climber.

"Come on. I'll go first. Take my hand. Bring Maggie's catalogue — for Pete's sake don't drop it. Where are the letters?"

"Got them. Got the catalogue. Have you got me?" Binnie panted, leaping and scrambling and clutching all at once. They ran down the other side of the spur and on to the beach, laughing together, grateful that laughter was possible.

They ate lunch and spent an hour on the garden, and then it was time to return. That night Binnie was too tired to eat.

Will said, "Look, Ma, please don't come with me tomorrow. I've proved to you that I can do it and, without chatting to Maggie, I can be back before ten. Let's have an enormous breakfast then and forget lunch. We've got to make a proper routine otherwise we shall be nervous wrecks."

She nodded. "If I do need anything from Keyhole, I'll come over with you at three. It is a bit stupid to miss the light in the mornings. But, Will," she caught his arm, "I did enjoy this morning. The two boys from Portcullis . . . give them my love."

"Sure, Ma. Go to bed. And don't get up when you hear me. But take plenty of sausages out of the freezer, won't you?"

She punched his arm and went groggily upstairs. It never failed to amaze her that, whatever happened, she could sleep the night through on Trapdoor Island. Perhaps that night she was overtired because as she turned the wick right down on her lamp and drew the covers over her ears she found she was weeping. She reached for a tissue and scrubbed her eyes almost angrily, thinking she would now lie awake for ages. But even as the thought crossed her mind she felt her limbs relax into the mattress and her eyes close damply.

"Oh, Theo," she whispered. "We were too young. We didn't give it a chance . . ." And she was gone.

Natalie's letter was to the point.

Darlings,

I've actually persuaded Ernest to come to the Skalls for Christmas! I am so pleased! However, as Trapdoor is rather spartan, we will stay with Maggie and visit you often and you must visit us. Has Daniel said anything yet? I know I'm right, Benita, so please don't roll your eyes in that coy way!

See you soon, Natalie and Ernest

PS. Do you think I should take out an e and call him "Ernst"? Sounds distinguished, somehow. Also, is Postern Hotel finished yet? We could all stay there together. What say?

Dorrie's said,

Dear Mum and Will,

Your news is amazing. Daniel I knew about, of course. But Natalie and Will settling in like a proper family? I expect they have gone now but we will soon be with you for Christmas. I was going to make an appointment with Maggie to phone you but think I'd do better to break the news here and now (bite the bullet, Dorothea!). Gabe has left and I think for good. No, I am not broken-hearted because there is someone else. Gabe realized what was happening and took a job in Bristol. You will never guess where — the casino! He has offered to work to pay off his debts. He never will, of course,

286

but I think the owner — who is from Athens, by the way — will keep him running around like a lapdog, which he is very happy doing. I'll have to tell you the full story when I see you but that is the outcome of his visit here — the Greek chap, I mean. He brought his two henchmen and arrived at the office . . . Mum, I must tell you later. We will be arriving on the twentieth. Will phone. God bless.

Love you as always.

Dorrie

Binnie read both letters in bed with her cup of tea. She had felt unexpectedly lonely when she woke; Will had already left and the sense of being a speck in the universe came over her with a rush. The letters were a boon and she made a special treat of them by having tea in bed and rereading them again and again. After she had dressed, she folded them carefully and put them in the pocket of her jeans to show Will while he was having his "brunch". She wanted his theories on who exactly was coming from Cherrington. Dorrie had written "we" — was this the mysterious "someone else" she had alluded to, or a slip of the pen?

She went downstairs and made up the fires, cleaned the sconces and lamps, brought in wood and water, decided to let the furnace burn itself out this afternoon, then use up all the water in the copper for baths, and clean it before refilling. She paused for coffee before going outside via the lean-to and on to the rocks to gather driftwood and seaweed. Daniel had started to build a pile of weed at the end of the garden for mulching and it was important to Binnie to carry on with whatever Daniel had started — Will doing the school run and she gathering seaweed and wood.

She hauled a bleached tree branch from beneath the kitchen window and leaned it against the wall to dry off, pushed an armful of slippery seaweed over the sheltering rocks and into the would-be garden. She stood getting her breath, looking at the seaweed and wondering whether it could be useful as a fuel for the fires, then letting her gaze sweep the horizon past the submerged Shark's Teeth and out to where Casement was a grey smudge in the glittering sea. She remembered it, the dark fortress of rock rising from the surging water, stabbing the air with its pinnacles. Daniel leaping ashore expertly, Will being almost submerged . . . Quite suddenly the whole awfulness of Alf and Marigold swept over her and it was as if she saw, like the pieces of Daniel's jigsaw, pictures of Alf dragging that bloated and inert lump that had been the flirtatious barmaid at the Old Peruvian over the razor-sharp rocks of Casement, away from the sucking tide and into the sanctuary of the ravine. She watched him wrap her in a blanket and sit with her, listening to the sound of the waves and adding his own songs to hers. Coming back to her . . . how often? Once? Twice? And then deciding to go with her into the sea.

Binnie covered her face. She stumbled back inside the lean-to and closed the door with her foot, putting her back to it and waiting for the sobs to bring some relief. But they did not come. She willed them to engulf her so that she could weep for Theo and Daniel as well as Alf and Marigold. Then after a while she took her hands from her face and looked at her watch. Nine twenty. Time to start cooking the sausages.

She went into the kitchen and opened the door of the fridge. She told herself she was glad she could remain so composed; that was how she had managed all these years, first of all so that the children would not be upset and then because it was her way. She found scissors and cut the linked sausages straight into the heavy old pan, thinking back, knowing now that if she could howl and cry, there would be some kind of relief. Alf had cared for his wife's corpse; she had never had a corpse. She needed to see Theo, however disfigured he might be; she needed to grieve over him.

Her breath caught in her throat and she was conscious of her heart thudding suddenly against her ribs. She stopped snipping and dropped the scissors, holding her side, all her thoughts suddenly focused on the image of Will returning and finding her in the middle of a heart attack.

Her heart whammed again, loud enough for her to hear it, to feel it reverberating through the floor.

And then she knew it was not her heart. She gripped the edge of the old gas cooker and stared wide-eyed out of the window at the white tree branch propped against the wall. The house shook with another thud.

Someone was trying to get into the cellar from the cavern. Someone was pounding on the trapdoor.

★   ★   ★

She was so certain it was Daniel that she had snatched her ring of keys from her bag and was descending the cellar steps before the next thud. Then she had to go back for the lamp and it was as she was descending the next time that she paused, held the lamp above her head and highlighted the two barrels of rocks that she had rolled across the trap. The next thud actually lifted them nearly an inch. She put her free hand across her mouth. The trap had been unlocked. And whoever had unlocked it had used Dennison's key because she had the other two on her ring.

Another thud made the barrels bounce and crash just a little short of their original position. She gasped, not knowing whether to retreat and barricade the cellar door and then run down and wait for Will, or whether to stand on the trap herself and hold the barrels hard over the central point. They crashed again and she made up her mind and ran down the remaining steps, the lamp swinging wildly from one hand, shadows everywhere. She flung herself bodily over the biggest barrel, put the lamp in front of her on the floor and hung on grimly as the next crash thudded up through her abdomen, making her want to retch. She leaned right over the barrel again and reached down, trying to put her key into the lock. When it would not go she knew that the lock had not been broken; the key had been inserted from the other side.

There was a sudden silence. Whoever was there had heard the telltale scraping of her key. It had to be Daniel. He must have got the key from Dennison and brought *Scallywag* in during the early hours when the tide was at its lowest. She bit her lip; in which case, what had happened to Dennison?

And then a voice called hoarsely, "You there, Mrs Captain? Is it you?"

And suddenly the whole situation turned upside-down and she answered just as hoarsely, "What have you done with Daniel? Is he alive? What have you *done* with him?"

"Nuthin'! It's what he done with me! Let me up, missis — 'e's taken my boat — taken *Scallywag*! Left me food and a tarpaulin and dumped me!"

Binnie's relief was so enormous she could have laughed. And then, appalled at herself, she scrambled off the barrel and tilted it to roll away. The other one crashed to the ground as Dennison pushed up the door and hauled himself to a sitting position. He was in his usual gear of guernsey and woollen hat. His face peered up her, aggrieved. "I done it like that so we could get in and out when we wanted to!" he accused.

"Dennison, I'm sorry. I just couldn't bear the thought of it. Daniel knew about it so perhaps someone else knew as well." She put out a hand and pulled him up. "It's your fault. You put the fear of God into me. I didn't want anyone suddenly appearing, that's all."

"No-one else got a key. So they'd 'ave to get rid of me first."

She said nothing just led the way up the cellar steps and into the kitchen. She drew a chair towards the furnace.

"You'd better warm up. I'm cooking breakfast for Will and there's plenty. Make the most of the fire. I'm letting it go out so that I can empty the copper and clean it." She kept talking not only to give him time to collect himself but so that Will could join them and hear exactly what had happened the night before. She fetched towels from the airer above the copper, cocooned him thoroughly in them and put a mug of tea into his cupped hands. It was ten o'clock. She put the frying pan on to the stove and lit the gas, cut bread, laid out plates and cutlery. And Will came in.

His expression was comical but all he said was, "I can't leave this place for a couple of hours without someone arriving unexpectedly! And Maggie had the cheek to ask me whether we were lonely!" He flung his coat over the newel post and came to join Dennison. "What brings you here? We thought you'd be in Naples by now!"

Dennison grunted and left Binnie to explain. She did so briefly and then looked at Dennison.

"Time to show Will the cavern." She put a hand on her son's shoulder. "I hated it when Dennison showed me first. But it's a secret for the family so you'd have to know sooner or later. There's a dry cave only accessible at low tide that your father used for landing his . . . contraband. Daniel knows of it. It was an odd piece of his jigsaw and he spent a ghastly night there when he borrowed *Scallywag*. Now he's used the cavern to dump Dennison and go on to see Violetta by himself." She shrugged. "He must have had his reasons, of course. Anyway, I put some heavy barrels over the trapdoor and Dennison was trapped down there until I heard the thumping half an hour ago."

Will half stood up, agog. "A secret tunnel!" he said, looking about eleven years old.

"Sort of." Binnie felt her heart lift in response. "Come on. Let's have this famous brunch, then Dennison can show you." She turned up the gas and gave a final crisping finish to the sausages, took toast from the grill and put it on the table. "What a comfort food is!" she said. "Come on, Dennison, you've got some catching-up to do."

Dennison smiled unwillingly as he sat down in front of his plate but still managed to mutter something about a "danged pirate".

Will said, surprised, "I thought you approved of Dad?"

"I meant that Dan'l Casey." Dennison hacked a sausage in half. "Your father was a master of the seas — something quite diff'rent and don't you forget it!"

Will caught his mother's eye and made a face. She smiled. Those awful few minutes, when she had been so certain Daniel was dead, were gone. There would be no corpses! Her smile widened.

They all went together to pick up the schoolchildren.

Will had spent nearly all his precious five hours in the cavern, wading past his waist in an effort to find the edge of the Curtain. He saw the secret landing place as an enormous asset. "This will attract the scuba divers, Ma. It will be dark when I get back this afternoon but I can investigate it tomorrow morning."

"The *Mermaid* won't go under the Curtain, Will. Not even at low tide," she warned.

Dennison wanted to go home. "Got nets to mend and things to think about," he grumbled. "Soon as that varmint shows 'is face, I'm laying into 'im again!" He saw Binnie's expression and subsided. "Not that 'e'll come back 'ere again. *Scallywag* and Daniel Casey is gone for good!"

Binnie refused to consider that but said, "Look, Dennison, if he has taken the boat then I can claim on the insurance. Please don't get het-up about this. I can tell you now that Daniel thought you were going to try a bit of rough justice on him. He put you ashore — safely, remember — to avoid that. Now he's gone to see Violetta. He's checking on what you found out. You can't blame him for that."

Dennison grumbled and muttered until they reached the short jetty at Keyhole. Then he was gone, marching past the children and across the apron and disappearing into the dunes before Binnie had even stowed the bags under the seating. Above her, Will helped Roger and Colin on to the top rung of the ladder. "The only word I understood," he called to his mother, "was 'budget'. What on earth has the Budget got to do with Dennison?"

Roger took his place and looked back up at Will. "It's two swear words into one," he explained kindly. "Bloody and bugger. All Skallions know that."

"Well, you've taught me something today, young sir!" Will tipped his driver's cap in Roger's direction.

Colin laughed. "He should know, Will," he said. "Granddad has always called our Roger a little budget!" He held Binnie's shoulder and stepped down

294

into the *Mermaid* with great dignity while Binnie and Will exploded with laughter.

They were still laughing and Will was checking his list and spluttering, "All present and correct," when a great shout came from the dunes.

"Dennison," said Binnie. She looked at Will, wide-eyed. "Does that mean *Scallywag* is back? Oh my God . . . Daniel . . ." She scrambled to the side and grabbed the ladder. "Wait for me, Will?"

Will said, "Course," which was immediately taken up by the children. As she ran across the apron, people seemed to appear from everywhere. Will shouted, "Let someone else drag him out of the water this time!" And then she dropped down from the dunes and on to the wet sand, and there, by the tide line, was Dennison bending over . . . not Daniel. She knew immediately who it was. So much hair. As if all his strength had gone from growing his body into growing his hair.

She stopped where she was and half a dozen people passed her. Someone rolled Alf over on to his stomach and straddled his back and began to pump on his ribcage. Walter peeled off and went for the phone and the ambulance. The others gathered close as if protecting him; someone held his head free of the sand. Dennison touched a bare foot, tears streaming down his face. Binnie had seen that before when he had first accepted that Theo was dead. She would have liked to have joined them and tried to comb out the wet sand clogging the long straggling hair. But she was not a true Skallion and had no right, so she stayed where she was.

They were still trying to get the water out of his lungs when the ambulance men ran down with the stretcher. They cleared a space and kneeled by him. Then one of them rolled him on to his back and brushed down his eyes. He looked up at the anxious faces. "He has been dead for some time," he announced.

Binnie put her hand across her mouth to stop the groan that rose in her throat. She had a reason for grief now. Here was the corpse that she had almost foreseen that morning and had been too blind to recognize had to be Alf's.

She felt grief like a physical lump, rising, rising, threatening to engulf her. She must not collapse, not here, not now. They all had to concentrate on Alf. There was a long moment of complete silence; the silence of respect. Then the ambulance men unrolled the stretcher and bent to lift Alf's body on to it. And in that moment, Binnie heard it. It was, of course, the sound of the sea. But it was the sea in all its moods: there was a whistle of wind, and beneath that a small slapping of waves against hulls of countless boats; followed by the faint roar of distant surf, settling down again to a much gentler breeze. She waited, longing to hear another song so that she would know without doubt that Alf had found his Marigold. But someone called her name and there was Maggie Govern, running down the dunes with Matthew behind her.

They enfolded her from either side and led her back to Ditchdrain Street.

CHAPTER
TWENTY-ONE

Matthew went down to the short pier to tell everyone that Alf had been taken back to hospital. He had a quiet word with Will and asked him to return to Keyhole after he had dropped Roger and Colin at Portcullis.

"Your ma will be all right with Maggie," he said. "D'you want me to come with you?"

Will swallowed. "I wouldn't mind," he said. "Perhaps you could have a word with the parents. They ought to know, surely?"

"All right." Matthew waved towards the lighted window above them and Maggie leaned out and waved back. Will undid the mooring rope and Matthew guided the *Mermaid* towards Postern.

At Harbour Lights, once started, Binnie found it impossible to stop crying. The sobs welled up uncontrollably and exploded in her throat and she was quite unable to drink Maggie's "nice hot cup of tea" or munch on one of her shortbreads.

"Don't take it so hard, my maid," Maggie said anxiously. "All you're going to do is give yourself a nasty headache and Alf would not want that. Alf would not want you to grieve anyway."

"I'm not," Binnie blubbered helplessly. "I'm grieving for myself. For the stupid fool I am. Wanting to see Theo's body so that I could weep for *him*! And now . . . it's almost as if I wished this to happen!"

Maggie was put out. "I've heard you say some daft things in the last three months, my girl, but this takes the biscuit! Now just you stop all that wailing and get this tea down you and don't let me hear any more about bodies and wishing death on people! It's so obvious that idiot Alf went in the sea after his budgeting wife!" She was slightly encouraged by Binnie's spluttering laugh at this point and went on, "You'll be telling me next you can hear them both singing!" She was startled when Binnie threw back her head at this and wept afresh — "like those men at the Wailing Wall in Jerusalem," she told Matthew later that night.

When Will and Matthew arrived she suggested that he and his mother should both sleep at Harbour Lights. Will, looking at Binnie as she rested her head in Matthew's armchair, tears pouring unchecked down her face, was all for it. "That would be great, Maggie. Thank you. Thank you both. For everything." He leaned down and raised his voice. "It will be great, won't it, Ma?"

Binnie felt like an ancient, deaf crone. She blinked and focused on her son with some difficulty. He repeated his words more loudly still. "Maggie has offered us beds for the night, Ma."

Binnie squeezed her eyes shut and howled again.

"We can't stop," she slobbered. "I've just remembered. I put Maggie's leg of lamb into a low oven just like Alf told me . . . Oh, Alf . . . Alf . . ." and she was away again.

So they went home and though at first Binnie huddled beneath the cowling, her hands to her face, the nearer they got to Trapdoor the less she wept and by the time Will anchored by the ridge of rock at the side of the beach, she had controlled her shuddering sobs enough to jump and clamber down to the sand.

It was a dark night. The drizzle was just a sea-fret now, but it wrapped them around like a damp blanket and the sea-lapping silence was unutterably soothing.

"No stars. Not a light anywhere." Will put his arms around his mother. "I've got the torch. Will you be able to get through the dunes all right if I go ahead and keep the light on the ground?"

"Of course. This is home. We know it like we know our own bodies, our own clothes. If we can dress in the dark we can find our way through the dunes."

"Oh, Ma, that's the first sensible thing you've said since . . . since . . ."

"Since I realized that Alf was dead." Binnie butted her head into his chest. "Don't be afraid to say it, Will. And don't be afraid at my incipient hysteria!" She snuffled a laugh. "Darling boy. This is an accumulation of tears. I should have let them come gradually instead of like a waterfall!"

They moved together at first into the hillocks and pits of the dunes. And then Will went in front and kept the torch on their feet. When they reached Jacob's

Ladder, he went ahead of her and lit all the candles in the hall, then fetched the storm lantern. She stood still, looking across at the darkness of the virgin garden, trying to think of nothing. When Will came leaping back up the steps again with the lantern, she touched his face with such love he too could have wept.

"I can smell the lamb from here," she said prosaically. "I can see and sense the garden and I can hear the sea beyond. And now I can touch my son. How . . . *useful* our perceptions are!"

He put the lantern down and hugged her hard. She felt the tears on his face and leaned over to kiss them.

He whispered, "We never do this. Perhaps we should."

He set her down and she laughed. "Perhaps. But we have our special ways too. Let's go and eat and taste together."

She picked up the lantern and they went down and into the house.

There was a post mortem on the mainland and the body was released for burial; the date for an inquest would be announced later.

The dry facts were relayed by Matthew to Will day by day. They obviously had nothing to do with Marigold, yet Alf had been half Marigold so, curiously, they seemed to have nothing to do with Alf himself. As his body was transported to Penzance and then back again, Will and Binnie felt themselves closer to him when they stood at the end of their garden and looked out on the dark smudge that was Casement.

Dennison came back with Will after one of his morning runs and spent a day digging and clearing the stones in the garden. Binnie kept an eye on him and saw that he too paused regularly and looked out at Casement. She went back with him that afternoon and walked with him to the lookout. Between them they carried supplies and one or two bottles of Theo's contraband brandy. He put them on the trestle table where the orange rim from the drowning sun picked out their mellow light.

Binnie tried to make some joke about not drinking them all at once. He looked surprised. "I en't a-going to drink them, missis. That's one for the Captain and one for Alf . . . stupid beggar."

He said nothing as she coughed and spluttered on tears again, and when she blew her nose fiercely and apologized, he said, "You got a lot to catch up on, missis. That's what I reckoned that day we first met." He met her eyes fleetingly and she was tempted to believe he understood everything. But then he added, "Best get back to the pier 'ead. First Mate will be waiting there by now." She treasured Dennison's naming of Will as First Mate.

The end of the month was in sight. It was incredible that so much had happened during November; somehow it was a relief to them that the month was nearly over.

That Saturday, Will spent time fiddling with the radio he had brought with him. He made notes about the weather forecast and took the set out to the kitchen for Binnie to hear the stark report of Alf's drowning. He then switched on the two-way radio that Alf had supplied for Binnie's first weekend here on her own in October. She brought in two mugs of coffee and watched him trying to raise a response without success.

She said, "I rather think Alf kept his radio in the *Mermaid*. It's probably bleeping away down at the anchorage right now." She tried not to think of the sheer poignancy of this.

"Of course! And we must leave it there, Ma. In case we need to keep in touch when I'm doing the run." He switched off and took his coffee from her. "What's the matter with mobile phones? Nobody over here seems to use them."

"Apparently there's no signal. Natalie couldn't believe it!"

Will fetched his tiny receiver and punched in a few numbers. "You're right. I tried Dorrie and Natalie — nothing." He sipped his coffee. "Never mind, you can communicate with the boat. Perhaps Walter Polpen or Matthew has a receiver you can radio. Put it on your list to follow up. Next to planting the seeds in trays and choosing an outfit from Maggie's catalogue!"

She was going to tell him that she had no intention of going to the Christmas ball but something stopped her.

The following Monday he told her Walter Polpen at the post office — "Where else?" — had indeed got a radio receiver, and she wrote down the frequency and stuck it to the freezer door.

Will hugged her and said, "See? We're getting organized. Properly dug in. I had a cheque from someone on Oriel this morning. Twenty-five pounds. It includes Alf's ten weeks. Look — here's a note. They think I should have Alf's money."

She said, "He told me you would have no difficulty getting the fares." She looked at him but did not weep.

He gave her an upside-down smile. "Well done, Ma!"

They drifted into December rather like a rudderless boat taken by the currents. Every day Binnie raised her brows at Will when he came in at ten o'clock to the scent of bacon and sausages. He would gently shake his head, which meant still no news of Daniel. Then he would tell her all the news he had assiduously collected during his pick-ups and drop-offs.

Gladys Polpen was planning to attend the ball in a trouser suit. Binnie raised her brows; Gladys was rarely seen in trousers, even informally. "Rather gaudy, Ma. I think Maggie is a bit put out. Gladys is going to steal the show." He added sadly, "Apparently Dennison has gone in for black. He is fishing with a rod off the southern point of the beach where he can see any boats arriving at the long pier. He wears black trousers and a black jacket and yesterday he had found an old black homburg hat and he was wearing that right down over his ears."

"Poor Dennison." Binnie sighed. "If only Daniel would bring back *Scallywag*. He shouldn't have taken it. That's the second time. No wonder Dennison hates him so much."

On Thursday, Will had more important news. "The vicar has fixed next Wednesday for Alf's funeral. They had to see me first because of the *Mermaid*." Will eyed his mother cautiously. "I didn't know what to say. But there wasn't much choice. I'm doing it."

"Doing what? Come on, Will. I've already spoken of Alf several times without dissolving. Surely it's not that bad?"

Will said, "I'm not sure. I rather think it's wonderful. It's Walter's idea and everyone else is for it. Even Dennison. They want to take Alf to Casement and do a burial at sea."

"Oh, Will! That really is wonderful. That's giving him the respect and honour that is his due."

"Yes. It is rather marvellous. They want me to pick up the children as usual and anyone else who wants to come but obviously they will go in other boats once we get to Keyhole. Alf will be in the *Mermaid* with Matthew and Maggie. And Maggie thought Dennison too. And you, if you will come."

"I'm not family," she demurred.

"Neither am I. We're . . ." he swallowed, "we're the crew." He cleared his throat. "They want me to be at the wheel, you one side of me and Dennison the other. Dennison says he won't come in the *Mermaid* but we'll see. I agreed with them that Alf would like it."

Binnie was silent for some time, and then nodded. "Alf would have been hard put to it to choose between you and Daniel. He really got on with Daniel." She smiled. "You know, love, nobody really got to know your father. He was always on the move, it seems. But

Alf got to know him through Daniel. And he liked Daniel."

Will smiled too, then coughed. "Don't you think we all felt that? Daniel was our link with Dad." He coughed again, then blew his nose. "So, you're all right with those arrangements?"

"I think so, Will. I hoped for something special and significant for Alf. And this couldn't be bettered. It's rather special for us too, isn't it? It's so good of Matthew to — to let us be there — part of it." She dished up his breakfast. "Let's hope the weather stays calm that day."

The next Monday Binnie went with Will to meet the *Queen of Skalls* and collect her very ordinary dress. There were a great many people on the long pier that morning; she recognized the sister in charge of the cottage hospital, and the caretaker at the school who often marched the children down for their boat trip home. Walter and Gladys Polpen were busy taking in goods, as usual on a Monday, and, of course, Maggie was with them, ready to take her letters and parcels home.

"No sign of Dennison?" Binnie asked.

Maggie shook her head. "Gone to earth in that lookout of his. Matt was anxious for him at first. Thought he might try to follow Alf. But Sister reckoned that if he hadn't done it straight away — that same afternoon he found Alf — then he wouldn't do it at all." She paused momentarily then said, "You all right to come with us in the *Mermaid*? I did wonder whether you could talk Dennison into coming too."

"Will and I — we're really honoured. I mean that, Maggie. I felt Alf was a special friend. But I'm still such an outsider."

"You were a special friend, my girl. No doubt about that. He thought the world of you. You took him seriously, see. The tourists — they lapped up his stories and thought he was one of the original Skallion characters. And us — well, we didn't take much notice of him. But you listened quietly and believed him." She glanced curiously at Binnie. "Did you really believe him?"

"I believed that he believed it." Binnie smiled sadly. "And something happened that morning. I think he was trying to tell me what he was going to do. But I didn't understand." She nodded. "Yes. Yes, I did believe him, Maggie."

And Maggie, tough Maggie Govern, who was in one of the gig teams, sniffed loudly and turned back towards Harbour Lights. "Come and have a coffee when you've got your stuff," she said brusquely. "And then go and see that idiot Dennison and talk him into coming next Wednesday."

Binnie left her parcel with Maggie, clambered through the dunes and crossed the road, then took to the slippery grass slopes that led to the lookout. Dennison had apparently finished mending nets and had spread them over the rocky outcrops. He was standing by his paraffin stove, boiling water for tea.

306

"Saw you coming," he said. "I en't got no biscuits or anything."

"I brought two doughnuts," she panted, hanging on to the lintel. "Tea will be nice. Thirsty work, climbing that last rise."

"Aye." He opened a deck chair for her and she almost fell into it. "You've come to talk me into going on Wednesday. You can save your breath to cool your broth."

She smiled at the old saying but said straight out, "Why? You and Alf . . . you understood each other. He would like you to be there."

He shot her a warning look. "Thought I was a fool. An' I thought 'e was a fool."

"There you go then. You were of like minds!" She held his gaze and at last he smiled unwillingly.

"I en't coming in that old tub of his and that's that." He made the tea in a battered metal teapot and immediately poured it out. No milk, just very pale tea. "I'll make a deal with you, Mrs Cap'n. If I get *Scallywag* back in time, I'll be there."

Binnie picked up her cup and let the steam soothe her face. She said slowly, eyes closed, "Dennison, I'll be honest with you. I don't think we shall see Daniel Casey or *Scallywag* again. I think he has taken your words to heart and given himself up. Heaven knows what will happen to the boat."

There was a pause; she opened her eyes and saw that he was standing by the window staring out towards Postern. He turned suddenly and shook his head at her.

"You know I en't got an opinion of Master Casey. But 'e wouldn't steal my boat. Not for good. An' if 'e's gone to make a deal with the drugs men, we've got 'em, missis. 'E'll show 'em the Curtain and they'll wait for the tide and they'll go in as often as they can in the time they got. They'll unload thousands of pounds' worth of stuff. Then they'll try to get up through the cellar." He sipped his tea. "An' we know they cain't do that. And by that time you will have got a'old of the coastguards and there they will be. Rats in a trap."

"What about *Scallywag*?" she said faintly.

"Either the old *Scally* will be back in Naples port or our Mr Casey will be outside, sailing 'er." He sat on the edge of the table. "I worked it out when I was fishing. 'E's going to bargain with the authorities, whoever they are. 'E's a cunning one, is that Mr Casey. 'Is freedom for trapping the smugglers."

"But if he did kill Theo —"

"I know. Justice won't have been done. An' it's up to me. An' don't you go tellin' me I cain't do nothin'. 'Cos I know what I can do and what I cain't do!"

"Dennison —"

"An' if it works out like I just said, then I'll be at Alf's funeral. I'll be at Casement at midday with the rest of you." His expression became challenging. "All right, Mrs Cap'n?"

She gave up. "All right," she said.

That night she dreamed that *Scallywag* berthed in the cavern at low tide and Daniel showed her what he had found in the waters around Sicily. In the shallow

308

hull of the boat was something wrapped in a blanket. Just as Marigold had been wrapped in a blanket.

In the dream she knew it was Theo's body and Daniel had brought it home so that she could grieve properly. She woke with tears on her face.

CHAPTER
TWENTY-TWO

The school was closed on Wednesday to allow the children to attend Alf's funeral. Will and Binnie were starting all the pick-ups at nine thirty. Will was expecting a very full boat; Alf was regarded as eccentric, even by the Islanders, but he was deeply respected too.

Binnie woke early after a heavy and unrefreshing sleep. Monday night's dream was still haunting her. She had had hopes that Dorrie and Natalie might arrive for the funeral and she had spent all yesterday making up beds and preparing meals. Now the day was here and there was no word from them. She had piled more rock-laden barrels over the locked trapdoor. Will talked soothingly to her but it was no good.

She tried to laugh about it. "Give up on me, Will. I'm just a mess at the moment."

He said, "Dorrie and Nat weren't close to Alf like you were, Ma. They're coming for Christmas, anyway."

"It's not that, Will." She frowned, concentrating. "It's Dad. After all this time, he's getting to me! Ridiculous!"

"Well . . ." Will was at a loss. "How about putting all your feelings — for Dad — into Alf's funeral, Ma? It could help you." He indicated the window. "It's pretty foggy today but not cold. And dead calm, thank goodness. I think Alf would like this weather; it's grieving for him but it's not angry." He hesitated. "And if you wanted a little weep, no-one would notice."

She grinned and shook her head at him, then looked at the grey blanket of mist pressed against the kitchen window. She hoped it would clear before midday, otherwise she could imagine half the boats getting lost.

They locked up at nine and walked through the dunes, picking the few remaining thrift blossoms as they went. Binnie had filled a lobster pot with every beautiful seashore plant she could find; she threaded the thrift through the wires as they started out towards Portcullis. Everyone who came aboard *Mermaid* that morning brought flowers; by the time they moored at the short pier in Keyhole, the boat was full of them. The mourners disembarked and made for the other craft lined up along the quay. "Like Dunkirk," Binnie murmured. "And the fog is lifting."

Will said, "I don't think it's lifting much, Ma. It's just that the daffodils are practically fluorescent in this light."

All the Islanders had stripped their really early daffs that year to make a cortege fit for a king — fit for Alf Trevose. Two gigs were lined up, flowers tied to the gunwales. The boats made a semi-circle around *Mermaid* and waited in the dim light. The hearse appeared at ten thirty, driving slowly down Ditchdrain Street, preceded by the Reverend John Tresillian of St Andrew's church on foot, Maggie and Matthew walking behind him and leaning heavily into each other. A shabby figure topped by a black homburg trailed behind the hearse.

"Dennison," Will breathed as he and his mother waited on the quayside, very still, very straight. Binnie lifted a grateful hand towards him and he nodded at her curtly, almost as if he resented being unable to keep away.

The hearse drew up and manoeuvred into reverse. John Tresillian stood by, holding his prayer book. Matthew came forward, shook Will's hand and kissed Binnie's cold cheek. Maggie did the same.

"Get down into the wheelhouse," she said. "The pallbearers have ropes."

Will handed his mother down the ladder, then followed. Maggie and Matthew joined them. They all waited while a silk-covered sling was laid on the ground. It was as if every person in all the waiting boats hardly breathed while the coffin was brought out of the back of the hearse and placed carefully inside the sling. Six men worked in pairs, carefully, precisely, one in each pair holding a longer length of rope so that not once did the coffin tilt. It bumped softly against the rubber fenders as it descended the wall of the pier; slowly it reached Matthew's outstretched arms. He guided it oh-so-gently to the top of the engine housing and then gathered in the black silk-covered ropes and coiled them on the lid. The six men descended the ladder and at the last minute, so did Dennison, bringing the mooring rope with him.

Will put the engine into reverse and then chugged slowly towards Postern and the outer islands. And as

312

the *Mermaid* forged through the fog and the oarsmen in the gigs reached and leaned rhythmically alongside, someone in one of the following boats began to sing, "Eternal Father, strong to save, whose arm hath bound the restless wave . . ." The words were muffled by the fog and the timing was not always synchronized throughout the little fleet, but Binnie thought it was all the better for that — as if the sea itself was singing.

They reached the gaunt fortress of Casement Island just before midday and made a circle, dipping and swaying irregularly. The Reverend John Tresillian stood at the side of the coffin and kept the flat of his hand on the wood as he read the service from the prayer book. Binnie had wondered whether a burial at sea might be rather dramatic and had dreaded it; but in fact the wording was the same, solemn and sonorous until the committal. Then, of course, came the words, "We therefore commit his body to the deep . . ." and the pallbearers lifted the ropes of the sling and held the last remains of Alfred Nelson Trevose against the side of the boat, then lowered him into the sea. Everyone stood as if turned to stone, rising and sinking with the boats.

Binnie lifted her eyes and gazed at the spot where not so long ago Daniel and Will had jumped on to the island to look for Alf. The sea was moving across the face of the rock, sweeping the bottom "step". It began to drain away. A shape was there. Binnie put her hand to her mouth. John Tresillian announced a hymn. The water sucked and began to return. It was as if the shape were made of water; sculpted by the sea. She stared, eyes wide, knowing that if she blinked it would be gone, certain, quite certain it was Alf. The water climbed the next step and began to recede again. Waveringly, the man — it was a man — took shape again. It was not Alf. It was Theo.

"The day Thou gavest, Lord, is ended . . ." The desolate words and melody took shape at the same time. The boats rose with the wave and then dipped. Theo was no longer there. Will's arm was at her waist, holding her hard against his side. ". . . The darkness falls . . ." He leaned close. "Are you all right, Ma?"

"Dad was on the rock. The first step. He was there." She spoke in short gasps and he hushed her gently.

"It's the middle pinnacle, Ma. D'you remember? The one I held on to? I see what you mean, it does look like a — a person."

"And rests not now by day or night . . ." There was a pause before the next verse. The boats dipped into a trough of the wave and she saw that Will was right: the pinnacle of rock that provided a handhold for any would-be islander stood streaming with water, which curved its starkness into . . . a shape. Even so, as the third verse started up, she said, "He could have gone behind the pinnacle, he could still be there."

"Ma, think about it."

She sobbed. Other people were sobbing. She said, "Yes. Yes, he's dead. But he's here . . . he's here, Will."

Will gripped her tighter, as if he would squeeze such mumbo-jumbo out of her physically. "In that sense, Ma, he's always here."

Binnie kept her eyes fixed. Nothing else took shape against Casement's rigid rocks. The final stanza rang

314

out, was caught by the wind and taken to the island walls. ". . . till all Thy creatures own Thy sway." She shuddered and turned her face into Will's arm as the young priest began the final prayers. And then from each boat, the flowers were put over the side. Will lifted the garlanded lobster pot and laid it on the water; it floated for an instant and then sank, but the daffodils stayed and were still rising and dipping, rising and dipping as they turned back.

Matthew started the engine and Will took the wheel. "Go and sit down by Maggie, Ma. Let Dennison come up." She did as she was told. One of the pallbearers leaned across. "Could you manage a thimbleful of brandy, Mrs Cash?" She shook her head.

Maggie spoke rallyingly, "A nice cup of tea — that's what we need." She eyed the circulating brandy flask with disapproval. "That's what we *all* need."

Binnie smiled her thanks; she was still living her nightmare. She said to Maggie in a low voice, "I had a dream the other night."

"I thought there was something." Maggie smiled. "Don't tell me. It was a mermaid song, wasn't it? And you were listening to it just now." She took Binnie's hand. "I'll tell you something. I heard it too. Not Marigold. Alf. He used to make sea sounds and they were so real you'd swear you were standing on the shore." She patted the back of Binnie's hand. "I looked across at you and I knew that was what you was hearing too."

Binnie hesitated, then nodded. She hadn't paid attention to them, but she knew that Alf's sea songs

were being sung. They were real and her sighting of
Theo's body, held in water like a fly in amber, was not
real. She turned her hand palm upwards and took
Maggie's fingers into it.

"It's all right now."

Maggie sighed. "Well, he's with his Marigold now
and no mistake!"

"He's safe," Binnie said.

They walked up Ditchdrain Street to the Dancing Bear,
where Natalie and Will had found sanctuary their first
day on Skall. Dennison stayed long enough to eat two
very large pasties and drink an unaccustomed glass of
sherry before going off into the fog. Matthew and
Maggie took charge and made sure everyone from the
outer islands ate enough to last the week. The children
were subdued, overawed by their experience, and Will
put on his ferryman's cap and clowned around for
them till he raised smiles.

As darkness fell people began to drift away and
everyone for the *Mermaid* gathered by the door.
Matthew checked them and pronounced, "All present
and correct." Will led them down the street and on to
the short pier.

Maggie had gone on ahead to fetch Binnie's order of
bread and milk, and came out carrying a large
cardboard box. "I'll give this to young Will," she said,
breathing heavily. "There's a message from Dorrie. You
might want to phone her back. I'll tell Will you won't
be a minute." She grinned ironically and went on down
the pier.

Binnie lifted the receiver and dialled. It was good to hear Dorrie's voice coming across as if she were in the next room.

"Mum. Are you all right? I'm so sorry about poor Alf. How did the funeral go?"

"Well, I just can't believe he's gone. But it was very special. We couldn't see much but we could hear him singing, of course. And . . ." she hesitated, "darling, I think I saw Dad. Standing up on the rocks but within the water."

There was a silence. Then Dorrie said cautiously, "Did Will see him?"

"I don't know. He said it was a rock that looked like a person. So he saw something."

"Mum, this doesn't sound like you. You're so down to earth."

"I'm not when I'm here, Dorrie. A lot of people here live on the edge of things. Dad did. And recently I feel he's . . . near."

"You're feeling like that because of Alf's suicide."

Binnie said, "Suicide? You know better than that, Dorrie! Alf walked into the water to be with Marigold, not to kill himself."

"Mum, what's the difference?" She added quickly, "Don't answer that! Think of what is happening next week — the Skall ball. Can we come early and go to that? And what shall I wear?"

"Yes. It is the end of next week. The nineteenth. And yes you can come. And wear a skirt or a dress and make it long." Binnie tried to sound as practical as she had always been; it was so obvious both children thought she was going mad and she knew she had never been so sane in her life before. "And who is this 'we' you mentioned in your letter? Not Gabe, by the sound of it."

"Gabe? No, Mum, I told you I don't see Gabe now." Another pause, then a deep breath, then Dorrie blurted, "Mum, I hope you won't mind. I'm coming with Miles." And in case there should be any misunderstanding she added, "Miles Thoroughgood."

Binnie held on to the phone and stared through into Maggie's living room. She remembered what Natalie had said not very long ago. Lady Dorothea. She tightened her diaphragm against a spurt of laughter at the thought of Natalie's smugness when she learned about this. She said, "Should I mind? Is there trouble with Lady Barbara?"

"Not at the moment. Because she doesn't know we're coming to see you at Christmas. And, of course, if we come to the ball we'll be leaving almost a week before Christmas." Dorrie cleared her throat and admitted, "So she might mind."

"She just might." Binnie couldn't resist grinning. After all, Dorrie could not see her face. She said, "Barbara and Sir Henry could come if they wanted to. I think — I'm almost certain — that the hotel on Postern will be fully open by then. It's pretty luxurious. I think they'd love it."

"Well . . . we'll see. There's the business, of course."

"Two days? Christmas Day and Boxing Day?"

"I know. But flights and things . . ."

318

"All right. See what you can do. I have to go. Will is waiting with a full load. I don't know what to say about Miles. I will try to phone from Maggie's at some point. Otherwise . . ."

"See you in a couple of weeks, Mum. Love you." And Dorrie was gone.

Binnie walked slowly down to the pier. Maggie and Matthew were still helping people down and into Will's waiting arms. Maggie hissed in her ear, "Dennison's aboard. Seems to think he'll stay the night on Trapdoor. Don't know what you think about that."

Binnie was surprised. She looked down at the boatload of people and saw him almost crouched by Will beneath the cowling, as if he were hiding from her.

She said, "I don't mind. Neither does Will, obviously. Probably needs a bit of comfort." But she knew very well he would sleep across the doorway in the hall.

Maggie said, "Well, at least if he's with you he won't be trying to walk into the sea after poor old Alf."

"True." Though, again, Binnie thought she knew differently. She remembered only too well how he had outlined Daniel's plan for capturing the fictitious drug smugglers.

She climbed down the ladder and dropped into an empty space next to Roger's grandparents. Will put the *Mermaid* into reverse and headed for Postern. It occurred to Binnie that he had taken to handling the heavy old boat as if he'd been doing it for years. Just like his father.

CHAPTER
TWENTY-THREE

Will tried hard to lighten the atmosphere as he threw out the anchor and directed the torch on to the rocks.

"We've been doing this for a while, Dennison," he said. "Plenty of fenders." He pushed the old car tyres over the gunwales, then pocketed the torch and leaped into the darkness.

Binnie put a hand on Dennison's shoulder and said in a low voice, "It's very easy, Dennison." She reached across and took Will's outstretched hand and stepped beside him on an upward wave. He shone the torch beam ahead of her and she moved on to leave a space for Dennison, and Will held out a hand for the black-clad figure standing uncertainly on the seating.

Will said conversationally, "I went through the charts with Matthew Govern and plotted a course very close to the promontory here. Deep water throughout each tide."

Dennison gathered himself together visibly, grabbed at Will's hand and jumped much too energetically. He staggered against the small headland and pushed himself upright with an obvious effort.

Will said, "It saves launching the dinghy every time and getting wet up to the waist!" He gave a small laugh and shone the torch ahead of them. "Can you see all right, Ma?" he called. Then to Dennison. "Just follow my mother."

Somehow they all got down on to the little beach, Dennison breathing heavily. "Right," said Will. "Let me bring up the rear and I can shine the torch ahead of you, Ma. We've done this in the dark before. It's not too bad."

Dennison spoke for the first time since he had left the Dancing Bear. "I'll go first. Get the storm lantern lit." And he was gone, evading Will's frantic flashing torch.

Binnie said gently, "He's probably done it dozens of times before, darling, in all weather conditions and laden with bottles of brandy!"

Will exploded. "Why on earth is he *here*? When he left the pub so early I assumed he'd had enough of all of us! Then I found him sitting in the *Mermaid*. Said not a word."

She said, "Keep your voice down, Will! I've told him he can come over whenever he wants. Don't forget he was Dad's right-hand man, even cooked for him."

"But I thought he was spending every minute at his lookout in case *Scallywag* came back!"

Binnie stared up at him through the darkness. "You don't suppose *Scallywag has* come back?"

"Course not. Otherwise he'd be dragging Daniel out of it and knocking him for six! He certainly wouldn't be here looking for board and lodging, would he?"

Binnie said nothing. She had imagined Dennison was simply checking on safety measures down in the cellar. If he had actually seen *Scallywag* he would be doing more than that.

She shivered and turned towards the dunes. "We'd better get on." She shouldered one bag of provisions and Will took the other and they trudged up towards the house in the wavering light of the torch.

When Binnie woke the next morning there was enough light to make out the shape of the furniture in her bedroom. She checked her watch: just before eight, so Will had already left. She pulled back her curtains and was faced by the silky grey of the fog slithering around the rocks on which the house was built. She stared out to where Casement must be and thought of Alf with a certain sadness but without the deep grief that had been with her since the discovery of his body last month. Looking back, there was an inevitability about what had happened. Once Alf had gone to Casement that last time, his intention had been so obvious. She imagined him staggering out of the hospital and through the dunes to the beach . . . She closed her eyes quickly and turned from the window. One way or another he would have joined Marigold. Whatever anyone had done or said. He had, after all, been more than just determined; he had been quietly assured.

She turned from the window and dressed quickly, bundling her hair to the back of her head. Only when she was going downstairs did she remember Dennison; that was because the candles had been extinguished — Will always left them lit for her.

There was no sign of him but she knew where he would be, and after she had lit the gas under the kettle and put bread in the grill she opened the cellar door and called down to him.

"Breakfast, Dennison!"

There was no reply but the storm lantern was on the floor of the cellar, casting a circle of light around it and she could see that the trapdoor was open.

Her voice went up a register in a spurt of panic. "Dennison — are you there?" and immediately his head appeared in the opening.

"Sorry, missis. Knows you don't like this place so checked it out early, like."

She swallowed, refusing to ask whether he had found anything, refusing to admit her own fear.

"I'm doing tea and toast. We'll have a proper breakfast when Will gets back."

She retreated into the kitchen and busied herself at the cooker. By the time Dennison joined her she was drinking tea, warming her hands on the mug, gazing at the red eye of the furnace, trying to fix her mind on the Christmas ball, Dorrie and Miles, Natalie and Ernest, and whether to begin insisting that Will should return to Leeds in January. And again Dorrie and Miles. She smiled to herself. She must not assume too much; it was almost too neat. Miles and Dorrie had known each other for years and probably she still saw him as a supercilious teenager; maybe his image of her had stopped at the scornful twelve-year-old who called him "a stuck-up stick-in-the-mud". And yet Natalie had practically foreseen it and — it would be so marvellous and somehow . . . *right*.

Dennison sat opposite her and reached across to pour tea into his mug. His pale translucent eyes looked at her and he said directly, "You saw it too, din't you?"

She looked up startled. "Saw what?"

"*Scallywag*. Yesterday. I saw you staring as if your eyes were going to pop out!" He frowned impatiently at her incomprehension. "When they was lowering Alf into the sea. You was looking and looking."

She dropped her gaze and dragged her thoughts away from Dorrie and Miles. "Yes. But not at anything real."

"You think I dreamed it too?" He was still impatient. "You think I could dream up *Scallywag*'s spinnaker? We both saw 'er. We both saw that sail. She shot out of sight behind the island — you saw 'er!"

She looked back at him, held his gaze. "No, Dennison. I did not see *Scallywag*. I promise you I would tell you if I had."

"What was you looking at then, missis?"

She took a breath and expelled it through puffed cheeks. "All right. I will tell you. I *thought* I saw Theo — the Captain — standing on the rock above the landing place. But it was covered in water. I dreamed it — I dreamed it two nights before. There was nothing there." She paused and frowned slightly. "And it wasn't during the committal. It was when they were singing the last hymn."

He was uncertain then. "Could've bin . . . but I saw that sail and I would know it anywhere. There's a patch midway."

"Daniel did it." She nodded, remembering. "I know what you mean. But a triangular slip of a sail disappearing around that steep rock cliff? Come on, Dennison. It could have been surf from a wave. Anything."

"The sea was sweeping past, not breaking anywhere."

She remembered. "True," she said. "But then, wouldn't we have seen it when we got back to Keyhole?"

"That's what I thought. I went down to the beach as soon as I'd ate. No sign. Went to the lookout, couldn't see a thing through the fog. Then I knowed zackly what 'e'd do. Come here. Wait for low tide and go in under the Curtain. 'E knows better'n what 'e did before. 'E'd 'ave matches and a lantern and food and clothing. An' 'e'd wait for the others to come."

She held his transparent gaze. "And there's no sign of him?"

"Low tide middle of the night. 'E went out then. S'long as you know what you'm doing, it's safe enough inside the Shark's Teeth. 'E'd anchor there and wait. 'E'll lead them in this afternoon when the sea's low again."

"Sorry, Dennison. I don't believe that." Binnie held up a placatory hand. "I don't mean you're lying. I think you've got the wrong end of the stick." She took a deliberate sip of her tea. "I think Daniel may well be in custody now. And with the publicity that will bring, the real smugglers — if they exist — will keep right out of it." She picked up a piece of toast and munched, and after a while Dennison did the same.

"You got your ideas and I got mine," was all he said.

But when she had told him that she was going to be cooking today in preparation for her daughter's arrival, she added, "You put the barrels back over the trap, didn't you?"

A small smile creased his wrinkles. "I did that, missis." He took another piece of toast. "But 'tis only you and me got keys anyway."

By the time Will got back, Binnie had made an enormous Cornish heavy cake and Dennison was clearing more brambles from the garden area. She slid a pan of baked mackerel from the oven and called Dennison. Will jerked his head and raised his brows and she said, "He is expecting Daniel to come in on *Scallywag* at low tide."

Will rolled his eyes but served the biggest mackerel to Dennison and said to him, "The Plaister grandfather was waiting with the boys at Portcullis this morning. Sent his regards to you. Reckons he hasn't seen you since Colin was born."

Dennison sat down and began to eat. "Silly old fool," he commented. "Scraping a living with a few sheep."

"He thinks a lot of you too," Will came back unsmilingly. "Asked if you'd like to be dropped there for an hour this afternoon. Have a chat."

Dennison stopped chewing for an instant. "Oh." He looked down at his mackerel. "Well, I suppose . . ." He shook his head. "Not yet. Tell him I'm busy. I might drop in after Christmas."

Will's mouth formed words Binnie thought might be unsuitable and she said quickly, "Dennison may well have spotted *Scallywag* yesterday. Coming from the direction of the Eastern Isles."

Will did not even look up from his breakfast and Dennison made no comment either. Binnie removed two thread-like bones from her fish and said, "I told him that I thought I'd seen your father."

"But then you realized it was the rock formation on Casement," Will reminded her in a level voice.

"Yes." She ate slowly, thinking. She said, "You don't suppose the two were connected? If Theo heard about Alf and really wanted to pay his respects, might he have —"

Will said violently, "Dad is dead, Ma!"

And Dennison said, "The Cap'n hardly knew Alf. He din't 'ave a lot to do with the Islanders. Didn't really consider them to be Skallions. 'E could trace 'is ownership back three generations."

This long speech seemed to absorb some of Will's sudden anger. He looked at his mother almost pleadingly. "Ma, you came here to find *out* about Dad — not to actually *find* him!"

She said quietly, "I came to discover my own feelings about him — whether I loved him enough to be able to grieve at his going. Of course, I was going to grieve simply because he was your father. But grieve for myself as well." She shook her head helplessly. "It's so difficult to explain."

Will said flatly, "It doesn't tie in with suddenly resurrecting him, Ma."

"No." She extracted more tiny bones and lined them up on the edge of her plate. "Anyway, I don't think I'm doing that, exactly." She flicked an embarrassed glance towards Dennison. "It — it's more to do with his presence. And — and what it means to me."

Will also looked at Dennison, who appeared to be oblivious to both of them as he chased the last of his mackerel around the plate and sat back with a sigh of repletion.

Will said slowly, "You just suggested that perhaps Dennison's sighting of *Scallywag* could tie in with your sighting of Dad's . . . *presence*! Maybe *Scallywag*'s sail was just a presence too."

For two pins Binnie could have wept with frustration at herself. She had thought by making the decision to come to Skall she had been following a definite purpose. Everything had seemed simple and basic.

She looked at her son, her brown eyes full of distress.

"I'm sorry, Will. I must be losing it completely. Shall we change the subject?"

Unexpectedly Dennison said, "Yes. Badgering on at your mother like that. Tide's already started back. I'll go up top and look down at the Shark's Teeth. Then we'd best barricade that trapdoor with a few more weights, and the same with the cellar door."

Will started to ask questions but Dennison ignored him, pushed his feet into his wellingtons and was gone.

Binnie said, "Don't ask, Will. Dennison's thought patterns are even more convoluted than mine! And just as cock-eyed too." She levered herself from the table, suddenly tired. "We know what has happened really. Daniel and the boat are in hock somewhere. And that's that. Dennison wants a big dramatic finale with police and helicopters. And I simply want a happy ending. Neither of us will get either of those things. And we have to learn to live with . . . nothing."

"Ma, come with me this afternoon," Will said suddenly. "Don't hang around here with that crazy man. Come and talk to Maggie about the ball. Phone Dorrie at work and have a chat with her. Walk up to the vicarage and have a chat with that Tresillian chap about the memorial service for Dad."

She smiled. "You really do think I've lost it." She shook her head at his protestations. "I'll come. Did I mention that Dorrie isn't bringing Gabe to the ball?"

"Who is it then?" Will opened his eyes wide. "Don't tell me my stepmother was right and she and Miles might be an item?" He looked at his mother and said slowly, "Lady Dorothea, eh?"

She kept her expression solemn. "We shall have to behave ourselves!"

She nearly added, no more ghosts for me, then thought better of it and was glad when Will said, "Good old Ma!"

They left early for Keyhole. Dennison was still keeping watch up on the "ramparts" but in the fog it was hopeless. They could just spot him, but where sea began and fog ended was another thing. They waved and he waved back.

"I suppose he's all right," Will said grudgingly as they giant-strode through the dunes. Binnie did not even reply; Dennison would do exactly what he wanted to do.

. The sea was still calm and *Mermaid* chugged across to Keyhole in record time; Roger and Colin, usually the first to arrive on the short pier, were not in sight. Will waited for the children while Binnie went to Harbour Lights to say hello to Maggie. When no-one was there either, she wandered across the apron towards the road and began to walk towards the school. The fog was moving here, leaving occasional clear patches on her left, and she paused and moved on to the marram grass at the start of the dunes. The tide was at its lowest and she could just see some of the small boats beached on the wet sand. She pulled her hat further over her ears and stamped her feet, thoroughly chilled after the trip across from Trapdoor.

The school bell came, muffled by fog; the first of the children would appear at any moment. It was Thursday, the weekend almost upon them, and they would be like young animals released from a cage. Only one more day of school before they broke up for Christmas. She smiled to herself, then turned and went back to the road to meet them.

She saw it much as Dennison must have seen it the day before: a triangular blob, white against the grey of the mist. Unmistakably a sail. Then it disappeared. Binnie knew why. The sail had been furled, the mast dropped. Someone would be strapping it down now; jumping out and pushing the boat up on to the beach.

She put her gloved hand to her throat and stared. The fog separated into droplets and became even more impenetrable. She took a step down into the valley of the dunes and began a staggering run towards the beach. Behind her she heard the shouts of the children as they came down the road. She stumbled and fell into a wall of sand, pushed herself up and went on. As the dunes gave way to the flat beach she began to gasp his name and her voice was swallowed almost instantly into the mist. She could hear herself, not only inside her head but as a sibilant whisper before the fog swallowed the single name. Theo. Theo. Theo.

The sand firmed with sea salt and she passed the first of the beached boats and paused to hold her side and get her breath. When she lifted her head a shape was forming twenty yards away; it was as if the fog was gathering itself together and she was seeing Theo as she had seen him held in water back at Casement only yesterday. The thought flashed through her mind that she really was losing it — she was going mad. The Skalls had broken her marriage all those years ago, and were trying to break her now.

There was a boat within arm's length and she reached for it and held on tightly as she bleated, "Theo? Is it you?"

The figure came closer; it was familiar.

A tentative, almost apologetic voice answered her. "No. It's me, Binnie. It's Daniel."

She gave a huge sob of relief and hurled herself forward. He caught her and held her against him. He was soaking wet and unmistakable.

She was laughing and crying. "I am so thankful. Of course you couldn't be Theo: Theo is dead! And I thought you were gone for good. Thank God — thank God!"

He relaxed his hold slightly. "Are you all right? Why are you here? What has happened?"

"I came with Will. Oh, Daniel, is it over? What happened? I was glad you landed Dennison in the cavern — he might well have killed you — but I still thought you would go to the police in Italy. I couldn't be sure from your letter whether you remembered what had really happened or — or what!" She realized he was letting her go and she leaned back from him and tried to read his face.

His voice was subdued. "Listen, Binnie. You have to go home now —"

"You'll come too?" she interrupted, eager as a child.

"Not yet. I have to see Dennison. Tell him *Scallywag* is back."

"He's at Trapdoor. You can come back with us — or, better still, sail across. Then he can take charge of his precious boat." She laughed. She was suddenly so happy. "It *was* you at Casement, wasn't it? You always got on so well with Alf and you went there early so as to . . ."

His voice was so low she had to concentrate. "You thought it was Theo. Didn't you? Just as you thought it was Theo just now. You came over here to find out about him, to find out about yourself. And you've done that."

"He's dead, Daniel. That's what I've discovered."

She realized he was moving away from her and she took a step towards him. He held up a hand.

"Don't follow me, Binnie. Theo isn't dead. That's what I remembered. We were stupid — thought we were so clever — acting like schoolboys. I can't go back with you. I'm sorry . . ." His voice trailed away as he backed into the fog.

She felt behind her for the support of the boat and could not find it. A long way off she could hear the children. Someone was singing "The Twelve Days of Christmas"; someone else was yelling, "While shepherds washed their socks by night . . ." She felt sick. She called out his name but there was no reply. Then she wondered whether the whole thing had been another illusion and she went forward over the damp sand until it became wet and she found *Scallywag*. She ran her hand along the painted line of the hull. She had imagined nothing. It was real. And Theo was not dead.

"The Twelve Days of Christmas" came to an end, someone yelled, "Yahoo!" and someone else yelled back, "Ballyhoo!" and there was laughter. It seemed to be getting nearer and she thought they must be coming through the dunes to look for her, then realized she had been unconsciously retracing her steps towards the sound.

She reached the road; the stragglers had a torch between them and they were flashing it and laughing as the light bounced back from the wall of mist. She followed the light. She did not know what else to do. She had to find Will and get back to their island and away from Daniel and . . . and Theo. She wondered where Theo had holed up; perhaps at the lookout. Yes, he would know that Dennison would always look after him. Oh God. Theo was not dead and had not been dead all the autumn and winter. She and Natalie were not widows . . . Natalie . . . she would have to get in touch with Natalie. Oh God.

A voice said, "There's Mrs Cash!" and Roger appeared with Colin in tow. "We were kept in, Mrs Cash. Did you come looking for us?"

She parried the question with her own. "Why were you kept in?"

Roger said matter-of-factly, "Col wet his trousers and Miss had to wash them and dry them on the radiator in the schoolhouse so no-one would know."

Colin said furiously, "Now you've told Mrs Cash!" He tried to punch his older brother and Roger kept him at arm's length and reminded him that Jack Winter was the worst wetter in the school.

Binnie saw tears on Colin's angry face and pushed away her thoughts as usual. "My goodness, that's nothing to worry about, Colin. Skallions didn't even have proper toilets when I came here first!" She stooped down. "Anyway, I don't count." He wiped his face with the back of his hand but seemed mollified. She said, "Would you care for a piggyback, young sir? We could probably catch everyone up then."

After a second's hesitation, Colin accepted her offer and scrambled on to her back, arms tight around her neck. "Come on, Roger!" she said, and pretended to gallop after the glow of the torch. Almost immediately, she began to warm up. She told herself she would be all right now. Will and the *Mermaid* would be waiting and the children would be chattering about Christmas. And at the end of the run, Trapdoor awaited them. Trapdoor was her sanctuary.

CHAPTER
TWENTY-FOUR

By the time Binnie had scrambled across the rocks and trudged through the dunes, she knew she was not well. She made tea quickly and drank hers with two aspirins. She had planned to tell Will and Dennison that Theo was alive and probably holed up at Dennison's lookout, but she knew that Will would not believe her and Dennison would want a lift to Keyhole immediately, which would make Will angry. And now she was beginning to wonder exactly what had happened and what had been said on the dark and fog-filled beach. Her head was spinning; had it been spinning then?

She said, "Will, I was going to do some lamb chops for supper. Can you manage? I really must get to bed."

He was concerned. "I thought you weren't right. Probably thoroughly chilled at the funeral yesterday. I shouldn't have taken you across this afternoon. Thought it would do you good to have a natter with Maggie . . ."

He kept this up while he dragged in the bath and filled it from the copper.

"No fire in the furnace," she put in. But, as she might have guessed, Dennison had cleaned and relit the furnace. After a very hot bath, she dried in front of the fire and staggered upstairs to find two hot-water bottles between her sheets.

"Oh, Will, thank you so much . . . feel just dreadful." She looked at him. "I rather think Daniel told me your father is alive, darling."

And, just as she had thought, Will did not believe her and swept it all aside on a tide of indulgence. "Don't worry about it now, Ma. Just lie down while I empty the bath. Then I'll get something to eat and bring it up on a tray. Poor old Ma. You've been under a strain . . ." He couldn't have been sweeter; it made her cry.

She managed to say, "Tell Dennison the *Scallywag* is back on Keyhole beach."

She was asleep by the time her tray arrived.

In the morning she felt better but very weak, as if she had been ill for some time. The pillows and sheets were damp and her hair sticky with sweat. She thought that in a few moments she would fetch some hot water and shampoo and maybe shiver her way through a strip-wash but then she went to sleep again just for a short time and woke to discover it was afternoon. There was a jug of water on the bedside table, slices of lemon floating on its surface. She poured a glass and drank thirstily, poured another and lay back luxuriating in the warmth of the bed and an unexpected feeling of well-being. She remembered yesterday and poor little Colin; then *Scallywag* and Daniel; then . . . Theo. It *had* all happened. She had not imagined Theo into existence. It was still a complete mystery, but no-one had been murdered and no-one was a murderer and for now that was absolutely all that mattered.

She felt herself going to sleep again and pushed back the clothes quickly. Her legs felt like cotton wool and her arms ached when she pushed herself off the bed but she needed to get to the lavatory in the lean-to as quickly as possible. The house seemed to be empty as she negotiated the stairs and the hall. In the kitchen the sink was full of crockery and a jug held cutlery soaking in soapy water. That must mean that Dennison had gone on the school run with Will. She stumbled into the lean-to and noticed that the door to the cellar was ajar. On her way back she shone a torch down the steps and saw that Dennison had rolled away the barrels from the trapdoor, so he must intend bringing *Scallywag* into the cavern at low tide. She shut the door and on an impulse slid the two bolts across, top and bottom. It was three thirty; ebb tide at four today. She fetched hot water from the copper and began to wash up.

The light was going but from the kitchen window the rocks were defined; the fog had gone. She wiped away the condensation and stared out beyond the Shark's Teeth. Alf was dead, but he had chosen that way and no-one else had died. Dorrie would come next week and perhaps tell her that she and Miles were an item. Will would go back to Leeds in January and she, Binnie Cash, would have to move again because Trapdoor Island was not hers after all. She waited for an emotional reaction to that fact, but there was nothing. Perhaps she did not really believe it herself. She smiled slightly, recalling that when she had thought Theo was dead she had been slowly but surely warming to him, or his memory. Now — if he were really alive — she had no right to that kind of feeling any more.

She fetched more water and washed her hair, then dried it in front of the furnace and twisted it to the back of her head like a big doughnut. Strands sprang out from the rubber band and curled around her face. She washed, then made tea. The thought of her last meal, yesterday's mackerel, was not pleasant; she needed plain bread and butter, cut thinly. And more tea; a lot more tea. She sat at the table with her third cup. In a minute she would go back upstairs and have a short sleep until Will and Dennison came back, and then she would come back down and cook something.

It was then Binnie heard a noise in the cellar. After the initial shock she relaxed. It would be Dennison. He had, of course, gone over with Will in order to bring the *Scallywag* back and he had sailed under the Curtain at low tide and come up through the trapdoor. She heard him climbing the cellar steps and then trying the door and, of course, finding it bolted. She was about to stand up and open it when she heard a muffled curse followed by an enormous crash as someone tried to break through. She froze. She had not lighted the lamps or candles and she shrank into her chair, making herself as small and inconspicuous as possible. The curse had not been Dennison's; it had been Theo's unforgettable growl of disgust.

She held her breath, waiting for the next crash. Her heart hammered urgently. He was not a patient man and the door reverberated two seconds later, followed by his voice bawling for Dennison. It occurred to her then that he did not know she was there. It gave her a choice. She could thrust her feet into wellingtons, wrap an oilskin over her dressing gown and go down to the beach to wait for the *Mermaid*. She could not see the clock through the darkness but the *Mermaid* was already overdue. School finished today for Christmas so there must have been a lot of tidying up to do and the children were late.

The anger that was emanating from behind the cellar door seemed to abate. Binnie breathed slowly and began to ease herself upright. The next time he yelled she would move across the kitchen and into the hall. But he did not yell, and she stayed where she was, awkwardly holding on to the table, while he seemed to be waiting for . . . what? Did he know she was there? Had he sensed her presence in some way?

Then he said, "Dennison, are you there? You bloody well should be!"

Another silence. She wondered frantically why Dennison should be there in the kitchen at four thirty in the afternoon when he knew his precious *Scallywag* was waiting for him on the beach at Keyhole.

Theo heaved a sigh that almost rattled the door.

"Dennison. Let's start again. It's me. The Captain. I am not a ghost. I am not dead. But if you don't put a move on and let me out of here, I might well be!" A pause. Another sigh. "Dan Casey brought me back in *Scallywag*, dropped me off in the lee of Keyhole, then went on round to the beach. I climbed up to your place. No Dennison. So I went back, got the *Scallywag* and went under the Curtain at low tide. We need

340

supplies. Then we can get out of here and be dead again! Come *on*! Let's go, man!"

Under cover of his voice, Binnie had moved swiftly into the hall but when he finished she came back and stared at the bolted door. Then she crossed the kitchen floor and said, "Is Daniel in on this, Theo? Is he going back with you and Dennison to be dead again?"

The shock was palpable and lasted over a minute. Then Theo said in a low voice, "Binnie. Dan said you would be with Will on the school run."

She could feel the anger boiling up inside her. "Well, I'm not. Is Daniel going back with you and Dennison to . . . wherever? Answer me, Theo!"

"I don't know." He cleared his throat so that she knew he was lying. Then he said, "Binnie, open the door. Please. I need to know some things and I can't talk through a lump of wood."

She shot the bolts and stood back. He came into the kitchen sheepishly, like a naughty schoolboy. She had seen it all before. He came to a halt three feet from her, and stared. His expression became still; she had not seen him for a long time and now she saw that he had aged. His face had been so open, anyone could have looked into it and he would not have cared. Now it was narrower and closed. He was thinner. He looked furtive, which in the circumstances was not surprising, but it gave him the face of a ferret. Where was her corsair now? She blinked and realized that she could weep or laugh and she didn't know which to do.

He drew in a breath. "My God, Binnie. That hair. I'm glad you haven't dyed it. What a . . . *woman*. And in a dressing gown too. What are you trying to do to me?"

Suddenly she did not want to laugh or cry. She said with a touch of contempt, "I've not been well. A twenty-four-hour thing. But I'm not dead, Theo. And I haven't been dead!"

He said, "I can explain everything. You'll understand. Dan seems to think it's something to be ashamed of — I said you'd understand." He spread his hands and gave a little laugh. "I can't believe this, my darling. I'm standing here where I carried you over the threshold and you're here again. Oh God, Binnie, this has got to mean something!"

She said shortly, "What is it you need? You'll have to be quick if you want to get out under the Curtain."

"Now that you know, there's no hurry, darling. Is there some tea left in that pot?" He moved towards the table. "If you knew the times I've dreamed of this. You and me. Here. Together."

"Don't sit down!" she said sharply. "Will and Dennison will be arriving home at any moment."

She could barely see him in the darkness but knew that he was sitting down with great deliberation. She picked up a spill, lit it at the open furnace door and took off the glass shade to light the kitchen lamp. Then she went into the hall and began to light the candles in the sconces, leaving the kitchen door open. When she went back in, Theo was practically lolling on the hard kitchen chair. She dippered water into the kettle and put it on the stove.

He said at last, "Don't worry. We'll be out of your hair tomorrow morning. But I must see Will now. You can't stop me, Binnie. He is my son."

She said nothing, just got on with the mundane tasks of making tea and cutting bread and butter. She fetched bacon and eggs and laid the table.

He watched her. "You've laid a place for me, Binnie. That's decent of you." Then he said, "You don't seem in the least upset. Does that mean you wanted me dead?"

She said, surprised, "Surely if I'd wanted you dead and discovered you weren't dead at all, I would be very upset?"

"Well . . . yes." The kettle was boiling and he stood up and made the tea. "So what's going on in that beautiful white head of yours?"

She was surprised again. "Were you always like this? So patronizing? I'm much more interested in what is going on in your head, actually, Theo. But I can wait. And if you're thinking of making up another pack of lies, I rather think Dennison might be in a position to put you right."

He poured the tea into two mugs and pushed hers across the table.

"Dennison does what I tell him, Binnie. And you're beginning to sound like Natalie. And I sold you as a sweet little mother-hen."

"Sold? What on earth do you mean?"

"Publicized you. Put you about. I said that if something went wrong, we would come to you and you would take us in until we got sorted out. And I understand that is exactly what Dan did. He fancied you like mad from a couple of old snaps I'd got. So he pretended to lose his memory and turned up at Cherrington. Yes? Isn't that how it happened?"

She tried to stay calm. "Not exactly."

He laughed. "The Grand Plan was that we were both going to die. We'd got into a nasty situation and wanted out, and it was the perfect way. Violetta was our witness and she was going to meet us on shore with a hire car filled with clothes and food. Except that she didn't. She thought she saw Dan hit me. And she made them put her ashore, then hightailed it to her grandparents' house and laid low for ages. Dan and I got separated and he came to find you."

"What about you? When she wasn't there with the car and things, what did you do?"

"Tried to find Dan, of course. Then went back to the boat, told Alberto — the boss — that Dan had tried to murder me and got himself drowned in the process. And resumed negotiations."

"The negotiations being?" She heard the coldness and underlying contempt in her voice.

"Dennison has probably put you in the picture there. It was all going on before our Grand Plan." He rolled his eyes humorously. "Using the cavern as it was originally intended, only in a big way." He saw she was not responding to his conspiratorial smile. "Come on, Binnie! I'm a smuggler. You must have always known."

"Actually, I didn't. Natalie told me and, of course, I saw for myself in the cellar. So we're talking about brandy. Cognac. Are we?"

"Anything really."

"I see. Heroin? Cocaine?"

He shrugged. "Smack mostly."

"And you tried to back out and then didn't."

"Exactly. There was no way I could back out without Violetta's help. They'd have got me one way or another. I was on my own, Binnie. You've got to realize that."

"Oh, I do." She studied him, then said, "How much does Dennison know?"

He shrugged again. "He knew about our Grand Plan. Dan tells me that when you convinced poor old Dennison that I was dead he was pretty well messed up. Then he went to find Violetta. Heard her story and came back here to kill Dan." He grinned. "Pretty melodramatic stuff, Binnie! Brightened up your life for a while, didn't it?"

"What do you mean?"

"Well, Dan making sheep's eyes at you. Trapdoor all yours at last." He tipped his head back to finish his tea and poured another. "Sorry about Trapdoor, darling. You can't stay here, of course. But I'm going to be making a great deal of money in the near future. I'll find you another island."

"Don't bother." She checked the bacon under the grill, turned it and glanced at him as casually as she could. "I'd already decided this wasn't a terribly good proposition. I'm going to buy a house on Keyhole and become a seaside landlady. I like the people — the Skallions. They're not money-grabbers. They take time to listen to the sea in case there are any mermaids about. Besides," she risked a tiny grin, "I'm arranging your memorial service with the local vicar, John Tresillian. I need to be in Keyhole for that."

He said, "But I'm not dead, Binnie. This is me. Here."

"Oh, I think you'll have to stay dead, Theo. In order to work this smuggling business. I expect you've got an insurance scam as well." She flicked him another glance and saw him hesitate. "You'll have to watch your back, though, won't you? If your boss — what did you call him, Alberto? — if he gets fed up with you, he might make fancy into fact. Not a big problem, probably. You've paved the way for your own demise quite well."

Theo made a dismissive gesture. "They can't do without the cavern, Binnie. That's my real insurance." He grinned and, standing above him, she thought he looked more like a rat than a ferret. He said, "Anyway, my love, if you want sufficient money to buy a house on Keyhole, you'd better pray my little scheme works."

She pretended surprise. "I thought Daniel would have told you. Natalie has sold the house in Cornwall. It fetched an enormous price. We've split it between us." She lied without thinking; it must be catching.

But it worked; he sat up straight and said, "You and Nat?"

She said, "Yes. She's taken to Will. She and her husband are coming over for Christmas. They'll be staying at the hotel on Postern. We'll probably join them now." She flashed another smile. "Should be fun." She left the cooker and sat down at the table. "One of the really good things about your death is how it brought Natalie and me together. I could understand so well why you got rid of your responsibilities, Theo, and turned to her. She's such wonderful company. When she and Maggie Govern get going it's really funny. You'd thoroughly enjoy it!"

"Are you trying to rile me, Binnie? Rub it in that I'm a true Skallion but not accepted by other Skallions. And you two complete outsiders are at home here?"

"Something like that. Yes."

"You've changed. You're hard."

"I think I am," she said with a certain pride.

With sudden urgency he leaned across the table. "Listen, Binnie. Stay with me. We could fall in love all over again. You're still beautiful and I'm still your pirate. The Italians would adore you. You give me — what's the word? — gravitas! I'd get some respect from them. And we could have fun again, darling. Up to the ramparts every morning to look towards America. I could show you how to swim under the Curtain even when it's covered. I still love you, Binnie. And you love me. I know you're not going to admit it, but you do. You've hardly taken your eyes off me since I came through that door." He seized her hand and she did not pull away. "Listen. I was going to send you back — you and Will. Get you out of the way. But we'll let Will go back on his own. And we'll be here for Alberto. The king and queen of Trapdoor! What do you say?"

"When are you expecting this . . . gentleman?"

"Alberto? He's coming on the next ebb tide. I shall take *Scallywag* under the Curtain and show him the way in. He'll come up and meet you. Have breakfast. Then he'll leave."

"And we keep the . . . stuff. In the cavern?"

"Yes. Can't risk it being in the cellar. It'll be collected gradually. Fishing boats. Seal watchers. You know the sort of thing."

"I think so." She withdrew her hand. "Do we deal with the money?"

"That's the bliss of it. No. The business is done in Naples. We get a lump sum." He grinned. "Do you see, Binnie? We need not even be here. Dennison will act as guide. And after the first consignment, everyone will get the hang of the tides and the Curtain."

"So if the worse came to the worst, you would disclaim all knowledge of the stuff — even of the cavern?"

"Certainly." He grinned. "Cast-iron alibi, I think it's called."

"Yes. Especially if you stay dead." She stood up. "I think that's Will arriving now. I'll go and get dressed while you put him in whatever picture you're looking at." She paused at the door. "By the way, where does Daniel fit in with all this?"

"After the way he duped you, I rather think he's had it." He was grinning almost from ear to ear. She nodded and went into the hall just as Will came in, closely followed by Dennison.

"Ma, what are you doing downstairs? I thought you'd still be in bed. Are you all right?" Will's face looked almost wild. He swivelled his eyes towards the kitchen door.

She said, "I'm fine. Nothing like a bit of a surprise to pull everything together." She smiled and nodded at his frantic mime. "You obviously know we have a visitor."

"When *Scallywag* wasn't there, Dennison thought
. . . yes, we thought you might have let him in." Will
said again, "Are you all right?"

"Of course. I'm going to get dressed. There's bacon
under a low grill and I'll do eggs when I come down.
Your father wants to talk to you. You're very late."

"Dennison nearly had a fit when *Scallywag* was
missing again! And it was the last day of school."

Dennison muttered, "Sorry, missis," and sidled past
her into the kitchen. Theo gave him a bluff greeting and
they heard Dennison say, "Good to see you, Captain."

Binnie lowered her voice, "We'll go back to Keyhole
as soon as we've eaten, Will. We need to be away from
this place before the next low tide."

"Yes. All right. Pack a bag then while you're upstairs,
can you?"

"Of course. Go on in now, Will. Remember, he is
your father."

She took the stairs slowly, suddenly feeling almost
ancient. She thought it highly unlikely that she would
ever set foot on Trapdoor again. She wondered what
Dennison had told Will and what Theo would tell Will.
Poor Will. Poor Dorrie.

It took ten minutes to dress and pack for herself and
Will. She took another few minutes to tidy both their
beds. Then she went downstairs again.

Dennison was at the cooker, frying eggs. Plates of
bacon were already waiting on the table. Theo was
being what he considered to be paternal. Dennison
was, as usual, silent. Binnie wondered whether she was
imagining that he was also embarrassed.

"Dennison is a proper sea cook," Theo told Will. "If you came with us, old man, you'd always be well fed, I can guarantee that."

Binnie felt a clutch in the region of her heart; Theo working on Will — that hadn't occurred to her.

Will accepted an egg straight from the frying pan and sat down with it. Theo drew out a chair for Binnie with an exaggerated flourish. "I didn't realize you'd been really ill, my darling. Come and sit down and eat something. I'm trying to recruit my son to a life of piracy on the high seas!"

Will glanced at her almost apprehensively and she grinned at him and said, "It's sad, isn't it? Such an elderly pirate!" But she sat down and began on her meal, unexpectedly hungry. "Thanks, Dennison. This is just what the doctor ordered." She patted the chair next to hers. "Come and have yours while it's still hot."

Theo looked at her sharply. "Not trying to encourage my crew to desert, are you, Binnie?"

She turned her grin on him, still chewing appreciatively, making a point of swallowing before she replied.

"It didn't occur to me, actually. If, by crew, you mean Will and Dennison — maybe me as well? — then I think we're all free to make up our own minds." She widened her grin. "I'm not coming, of course."

He managed to look regretful. "I hoped you might respond to my proposal. But I can quite see it wouldn't do for you, love. You were always tediously honest. Now, Natalie — she'd have to think hard about it."

Binnie actually laughed. "I don't think so. Ernest is in the grocery business — Foodezee. Probably a millionaire."

He shrugged. "Which leaves Dennison and Will. No question about Dennison. What about Will — would you be happy if Will joined the crew?"

"No."

"Is that it? Aren't you going to point out to him the perils of the high seas? What about the promise of gaol?"

"He knows about that."

"So, you really are leaving it up to him?"

"Yes."

Will finished his meal and leaned back in his chair. "Do stop talking about me as if I'm not around. You all know we're going back to Keyhole in the *Mermaid*. There are messages from Nat and Dorrie that they've both decided to arrive in time for the ball." He looked at his father without a glimmer of a smile. "I'm not sorry, Dad. Not a bit. Can't miss the Skall ball. And neither would you if you were a true Skallion." He scraped his chair back. "Mind if we leave you with the washing-up? Presumably you won't go to bed tonight so you've got plenty of time."

Theo looked at him in disgust. "All true Skallions are smugglers or wreckers, my boy. Don't you forget it." He forced a laugh. "And Dennison will wash up while I get ready for our visitors."

Dennison drank his tea. "Sorry, Captain. I'm too old for all this now. I'll keep on with the fishing. Do odd jobs for the missis." He glanced at Binnie. "What I saw of Italy, I din't like. And I don't fancy being dead, even with you alongside o' me."

Binnie was startled out of her iciness for the first time since Theo had come into the kitchen. She stared at Dennison.

Theo snapped, "You'll do what you're told, man! I've looked after you for years. It's pay-back time. Got it?"

Dennison said, "That Vi'letta — she were certain-sure Dan Casey knocked you off that cruiser. Certain-sure she were. And it got me thinking. I b'lieved 'er. But what if she were mistook? What if it were you pushing off Dan Casey? In bad light you could pass for each other. An' you swam ashore all right. Dan Casey didn't. Dan Casey almost drowned. An' 'e was dragged out of that sea with a lump like an egg on 'is 'ead. Ended up in a special 'ospital. Couldn't remember nothing."

Theo said, "Are you saying I tried to kill Dan? Dammit all, we were friends as well as partners. We both agreed we'd got ourselves into a hole, we both made the plan, we both said if we were separated we'd go to Cherrington. He remembered that all right, didn't he?"

"You din't do it, Cap'n? You din't try to murder your friend so you could do a deal with that Italian gangster on your own?"

"I did not!"

Will said almost sadly, "Dad. We know. One of the Italians has been trailing Natalie, making sure she didn't sell your house. Her husband had him arrested. He spilled the beans."

"No-one knew!" Theo blurted the words and then stopped. There was a long silence.

Binnie whispered, "Oh, Theo, when I arrived back in the autumn I thought I was getting to know you again. And now I do." She took a breath. "How could you? How *could* you?"

"It wasn't premeditated, for Christ's sake! We were on deck, ready to jump, and I suddenly knew Dan wouldn't — couldn't — go through with it, so I shoved him in with the end of a boat hook! And it didn't bloody work anyway, did it?" He turned to Dennison. "For God's sake, man, I shall need help with unloading the boxes! You can't leave now. We go back years, dammit. I helped you get your place, gave you a hand-out whenever there was a deal. What more do you want from me?"

Dennison turned away, crossed the kitchen and hall and let himself out into the darkness.

Theo was stunned. "He's gone. The ungrateful sod! When I think —"

"Dad, have you *been* to the lookout lately? It's a wartime pill box. There's no glass in the windows, nothing. Dennison lives on fish and what Maggie Govern gives him."

Theo said, "So I'm on my own, am I?"

"Looks like it."

Theo looked at Will and then Binnie. "I've still got the island — you can't take that away from me!"

Binnie said, "Go back to Violetta, Theo. Make another life."

"So that you can have Trapdoor?" he sneered.

Will said, "Shut up, Dad." He turned and went outside. Binnie followed, then went ahead of him and stood by the well.

She did not say goodbye and neither did Theo.

CHAPTER
TWENTY-FIVE

There was so much to be said but the three of them clambered over the rocks and squashed beneath the cowling without a word. Dennison went to start the engine and Binnie huddled into the oilskins kept under one of the seats. In spite of the walk through the dunes, hampered by bags and cases, she was cold. Only two hours ago she had been getting out of bed and wondering whether she was fit to do so.

The engine stuttered into life and Dennison pulled in the rope and pushed *Mermaid* away from the rocks. They hadn't bothered to throw out the anchor; it was calm enough, but they must have been in a hurry. Will held the boat steady as if she were a bucking horse and gradually she became accustomed to the butting of the swell. Then the engine sang a higher note and they moved away from the little promontory and the beach.

Binnie suddenly realized that some time during her twenty-four-hour fever the weather had improved. The pale evening sky showed a handful of stars and the air smelled differently. She remembered the long line of children meandering along the road to the short pier at Keyhole singing carols; it had been so foggy then; now it was definitely crisp, cold and Christmassy.

Will shouted anxiously, "You OK, Ma?" She nodded and he grinned suddenly and said, "In case you're worried about me, I feel great. My mother is not going doolally after all and I seem to have got rid of some kind of albatross around my neck!"

"Really?"

Binnie had forgotten about the resilience of the young. Will nodded, still grinning across at her. Dennison, on the other hand, looked literally crushed. Binnie put a hand on his shoulder for a moment but he did not acknowledge it. Probably he blamed her for taking the lid off that can of worms.

They did not talk again. When they reached Keyhole, Matthew was waiting at the short pier and looped the *Mermaid*'s mooring rope around one of the stanchions before reaching down an arm to help each of them up the ladder in turn. He led the way to the house and Maggie was there to welcome them inside as if they were survivors from a shipwreck. Binnie thought that in a way that was exactly what they were.

Maggie had made soup, which could be reheated when they felt like it.

She said, "Look, we know you've got a lot of talking to do. Matthew wants to check up on the Midwatch work."

"At this time of night?" Binnie put in, and Maggie said, "Yes," in the typically unequivocal way she often did. "So we'll drop Dennison off at the lookout." She stared at him sternly as if she expected a protest. None came. Dennison glanced up but his eyes were empty and beaten. Binnie started to object again and Maggie shook her head and swept on. "That will give the two of you time to sort yourselves out, have some soup and get to bed. I've put bottles in both beds and there's plenty of hot water for baths."

Will went round the table and hugged her and she beat him off because he was wet. He grinned. "You'll have to put up with it if you're going to look after us like this."

Binnie said, "Thank you, Maggie. Thank you."

Matthew brought Maggie's jacket over and helped her into it. He said to Binnie, "Will says you was ill, my girl, but you don't sound bad in spite of everything." He nodded at Dennison. "And we're pleased to see you, lad. We expected these two but we weren't sure about you."

Maggie zipped herself up and made for the door. "Daniel told us you'd do it. He said you knew what was right and what was wrong, and once you were certain of what that there Captain Theo, or whatever you call him, smuggled — drugs — you'd leave him to it." She motioned Dennison ahead of her. "You got more sense than I thought. Sit in the front with Matthew, if you like." It was the only treat she could offer him. He shot her a surprised look, then went out into the darkness without saying goodbye.

Will closed the door and struggled out of his oilskins, and after a moment Binnie did the same.

"Sorry, Ma." He drew a chair close to the fire. "I know I keep on, but are you sure you're all right? You had a pretty high temperature last night and every time I looked in on you this morning, you were asleep. It was a bit of a shock to find you more or less in control of everything when we finally arrived this afternoon."

Binnie smiled at him. "I'm cold — warming up now — but I feel mistress of myself again!" She laughed. "That sums it up, Will. I've been so darned *ambivalent* about everything. Was I mourning Dad or was I not? Should I take the whole Daniel thing to the police?" She spread her hands to the fire. "Now it seems the boot is on the other foot completely!" She glanced up into her son's young face, set grimly. "Thank God he didn't actually kill Daniel," she went on quickly. "He's just a silly weak man who seized the wrong opportunity. But he didn't actually kill anyone, Will. Daniel must have a rubber skull!" She tried another laugh but Will did not join her. His throat moved convulsively as he swallowed and she reached for his hand.

He said, "We'll talk about it again, Ma. I think you should go to bed now."

"Not before you've told me how you and Dennison knew that your father was alive and with me!" She pulled on his hand and he sat on the floor and leaned on her knees.

He sighed, resigned. "It was Daniel, of course. As we tied up at the short pier, he came over the apron at a run. The kids hadn't arrived. We guessed they'd be late as it was the last day of school. He was expecting to see you as well as Dennison. We told him you were ill." He paused between each staccato delivery and Binnie realized he was very tired.

He went on, "Daniel was pretty worried, we could see that. He'd gone down to the dunes to make sure

358

Dennison got his *Scallywag* back all right. No *Scallywag*. Either Dennison had it or Dad. So he came to meet us. And it wasn't Dennison. So it was Dad. And there was only one place he'd go and that was the cavern. And you were in the house. Ill."

Will stopped for breath then said slowly, "I was glad — so glad — at first. I thought . . . you and he . . . together again. And your apparitions hadn't been apparitions after all. You'd actually seen Dad." He made a sound like a sob. "Then I had to ask Daniel where Dad had been all this time, whether he too had lost his memory, what the hell had happened." He shuddered another sigh and pressed hard against Binnie's knees.

"Daniel did not want to go into it at first — just kept telling us we'd got to go — not wait for the kids even — just go. And of course we couldn't do that so he suddenly made up his mind and told us his memory was back. He remembered the yacht. It was a luxury cruiser, apparently. He could remember the name. *Dolce Vita*. He remembered Alberto. Actually a Sicilian, can you believe it? He remembered what he called 'the Grand Plan'. He is deeply ashamed, Ma. He tried to change Dad's mind. Right up to the very last minute when they were on the deck about to dive off. He said they should face Alberto and tell him the deal was off. That was when Dad hit him. And . . . well, you know the rest." He put his forehead against Binnie's knee. "All that stuff about Natalie — I made that up. Didn't want to let Dad think that Daniel had let him down. Daniel still thought he might persuade Dad to face up to Alberto. But in his heart he knew it wouldn't work."

He pressed his head hard into Binnie's knees. "I don't know what Daniel's told Matthew and Maggie. I don't know where he is now. I don't know how Dad thinks he can go on with this precious drugs deal when so many people know about it. It's such a mess, Ma. And we were happy by ourselves on Trapdoor. Weren't we?"

She murmured reassurances.

He moved his head so that he could look into the fire. After a moment he began again. "The kids arrived and we asked Daniel to come with us and he said no because he'd already said goodbye to you. We were at Portcullis, unloading Roger and Colin, when Dennison remembered he'd left the trapdoor to the cavern open so that he could land *Scallywag* and come up the ladder that way." Binnie felt him tremble. "We couldn't get the old *Mermaid* to go any faster, Ma. It was terrible. You were ill and vulnerable and the man you thought was dead was a murderer — well, a potential murderer! Dennison was in a hell of a state."

He gave a sound suspiciously like a sob and Binnie gathered him to her.

"Will, I'm here and I'm all right. I'm so much more than all right, darling."

"I said some awful things to you, Ma."

"Not really. You described the situation as you saw it. That's all. And — like you've just said — we've managed so well together, Will. We're friends. That's so important to me. Through all this I've had such friends and you have been the best one."

"No, Ma. Daniel has been your best friend. But . . . yes, we've made a good team. Haven't we? Haven't we, Ma?"

She smoothed his hair and kissed his forehead. "We have indeed. You must know that, Will."

He was quiet for a moment, lifting his face like a child when she dabbed at him with a tissue. Then he said something in a low voice that she did not hear.

"Say that again, Will."

He whispered, "I've got his genes, Ma."

She was shocked. "Oh, my love . . . and his genes were so splendid." She laughed at herself. "He was pretty wonderful, Will. And then he let it go. Something you won't do because you've got my stick-in-the-mud genes and they'll keep you on the straight and narrow." She was laughing openly now, cupping his face and demanding his total concentration.

They talked for a while longer, then he scrambled to his feet and insisted on getting her a bowl of soup. "I bet Maggie's got a thermometer somewhere but I don't know where. Do you feel hot?"

"Just wonderfully warm." She smiled at him. "And very happy, Will. I really have got my life back. No more guilt about you and Dorrie being deprived of a father." Her smile widened. "Sounds almost as if it were heavenly intervention!"

Will finished his soup and fetched bread and cheese. He was looking better by the minute. He said soberly, "What about Daniel, Ma?"

She shook her head slowly. "I don't know about that, love. He looked for me because of some subconscious need for sanctuary. Things are different now. His memory is back. Fully, I wonder? Is he remembering someone close to him? He could be married . . . have children. I think we have to let Daniel go. As he said, we've said goodbye. He may have gone already."

"He won't leave till he knows you are safe."

She looked at him, surprised. He said, "Perhaps he's at the lookout. Could be that Maggie and Matthew want to tell him that you are here."

Binnie thought about it and nodded. She stood up, took her bowl into the kitchen and rinsed it beneath the tap. Then she went to the stairs and said over her shoulder, "Then he will be free to go." Momentarily she remembered the amazing times — only twice, after all — when they had been swept away by a passion that even now she could not identify. She would prefer to remember those two weeks when the three of them had lived together on Trapdoor and made a routine that brought order and contentment to all of them. She said, as much to herself as to Will, "I can cope with that. I'm whole again. I don't need to bury my head in any sand!"

Will had no answer to that. Slowly she climbed the three flights of stairs to the top of the house. She was too tired for a bath and stood at the window looking out over the harbour and into the darkness towards Trapdoor. She thought of Theo alone there, really alone; she waited to feel some kind of pang.

Then she smiled. He had plenty to be getting on with if he wanted to meet his precious gang of smugglers in six hours' time when the tide dropped enough to reveal the edge of the Curtain. And anyway, first of all he really should get on with the washing-up!

She undressed, slid between the sheets and found two hot-water bottles. She had no doubt at all that tonight she would sleep long and dreamlessly. She closed her eyes.

CHAPTER
TWENTY-SIX

The newly appointed manager at the Postern Hotel had badly wanted to open fully for Christmas that year but with only two enquiries, and those from widows who specifically required "congenial company" — whatever that might mean — it seemed, in hoteliers' terms, an entirely non-viable option. And then Lady Thoroughgood telephoned from some estate near Bristol. She had no requests, simply requirements.

"There will be four of us. My husband, Sir Henry, my son and his girlfriend and, of course, myself. We shall therefore need four bedrooms with sea views. I take it the beds will all be at least four foot six — we are not small people — and that there will be room service, drinks facilities, all that sort of thing. We do not need, or in fact want, entertainment, but some kind of private boat hire that will enable us to go from island to island."

The new manager, who was young and inexperienced, assured her he would do his best on all counts.

Lady Thoroughgood said, astonished, "Best? I would hope so!" He heard her breathing into the receiver as he gabbled reassurances. She interrupted to tell him sternly that there might be others in "their party" but they would reserve separately. "I really cannot be responsible for people I do not know and who, I have to say, sound somewhat eccentric. However, there are connections which naturally one cannot ignore completely." The connections had a great deal to do with Ernest Broadbent being a grocery millionaire with enormous car parks in his various establishments that might need professional cleaning in the future.

The manager's name was Robert Newsome. He had dropped out of a degree course in physical education and gone for three months' "initiation" into "leisure activities". He wasn't quite sure how he had then transferred to hotel management and found himself in a partially refurbished hotel on an island he had never heard of with a skeleton staff and a carpenter who was much better suited to the manager's job than he was himself.

After the conversation with Lady Thoroughgood, he removed the snow-white handkerchief from his top pocket, wiped his face, replaced the receiver and stared out of his office window at the view of the sea, which at that moment looked like liquid steel. Six definite room bookings, including the widows, and perhaps another two, made during the opening week and in mid-winter . . . company management could surely not be displeased at that. But a boat? They were such an independent, not to say prickly lot on the islands. Even their name, Skallions, sounded a mixture of harshness and sheer impudence. He really could not see anyone from Keyhole or Postern willing to put a boat at the twenty-four-hour disposal of the hotel.

He was chewing his lip and drumming his fingers on his virgin desk when the telephone rang again.

A voice said, "My name is William Cash and I am speaking from Harbour Lights in Keyhole. Am I talking to the manager of the Postern?"

Even Bob Newsome had heard the name Cash. Matthew Govern, who was practically carpenter-in-residence, had succeeded in curdling his blood with tales of Pirate Cash, as he called him, who had his very own island called Trapdoor — which sounded sinister enough in itself. But surely he hadn't been a William? However, Lady Thingammy had mentioned some eccentrics . . .

The caller said impatiently, "Are you there? This is —"

"Sorry. Yes, I am here. Robert Newsome, the manager." The managerial course had given him a phrase to add to the baldness of an introduction. He remembered it at the last minute. "How may I help you?" he almost gasped.

"My mother and I would like to stay for two days over Christmas."

Well, that answered one question: this was not Pirate Cash but perhaps his son. And these absolutely must be the extra bookings half promised by Lady Thingammy.

"Certainly, sir. Rooms with views, of course. And four-foot-six beds?"

The voice became disconcerted. "Well . . . that would be grand, of course. Thank you." There was a pause and then the voice said boyishly, "We have friends and family coming to stay with you. Otherwise, of course, we would be spending the whole of Christmas here in Ditchdrain Street. The Governs are almost family by now and . . . anyway, they have relatives coming for a night from the mainland so will be pleased to have the extra space."

"Er . . . of course, sir."

Bob Newsome took details and replaced the receiver. The pirate's son didn't sound odd at all. And he must be staying at the carpenter's house. Just as Bob stood up to go and have a word with Matthew Govern, the telephone rang again. The area manager had told him there was no hope of installing a receptionist until well into the New Year. If things went on like this, however, he would need someone.

This time the voice was high, clear, just as dictatorial as Lady Thingammy's but much younger.

"I'd like to book two rooms from the seventeenth December until some time in the New Year. Don't know exactly how long but I expect you've got loads of space. And may I enquire whether there will be transport over to Keyhole most days? Especially on the nineteenth? For the Skall ball, you know."

Bob had heard there was a hop at the church hall, but could it possibly be a tourist attraction? He took down the particulars. Mr and Mrs Ernest Broadbent — which sounded vaguely familiar. He had replaced the receiver and rounded up the staff for an unexpected pep talk when it came to him. Ernest Broadbent had been mentioned more than once during the hotel management course. He was chairman of one of the biggest food outlets in the United Kingdom, Foodezee.

Bob Newsome stopped talking to the six girls and two lads who comprised the staff of the Postern Hotel and put a hand to his mouth. This might be some kind of inspection laid on by the hotel people. He stared at the teenagers in front of him, suddenly aghast. And the door opened.

It was Matthew Govern, short, stalwart and reliable.

Bob blurted helplessly, "Just had eight new bookings! And one of them is Ernest Broadbent. He's only the Foodezee man!" The last was a wail of despair.

Matthew grinned and nodded.

"I knew they were coming for the ball. Thought it would be a nice surprise for you. I don't know about Natalie's husband, Ernest, but she will keep him in order, never fear, my 'ansome. I don't know the Thoroughgoods either, but from what Binnie said they've got hearts of gold. The others, they're good people." He turned to one of the girls. "Binnie will want to help you with the washing-up, Tracy. She's used to keeping going but just at the moment she's not well and she sits around a lot staring into space. So if she offers to lend a hand, let her, there's a good maid. She needs to be busy again." He joined Bob Newsome at his table and grinned at them all. "You'll do a marvellous job. Right now that would seem to be making eight beds, cleaning eight rooms and eight bathrooms! Go to it, my lovelies!"

He pointed a finger at one of the young boys. "Now's your chance, Greg. Not many chefs can use their wooden spoons on just eight people at a time. Remember all that stuff you learned at the Penzance school and just go for it. Menus on Bob's desk in an hour, then I'll take the order over to Keyhole and the *Queen* will bring it in next sailing."

Bob stared up at him as if he were a vision, which indeed at that moment he truly was. Bob was fairly certain that after hearing what he had had to say they would have gone off either as terrified as he was himself or sullenly resentful at having their leisurely lives disrupted by unexpected guests.

Matthew continued to grin. "Expect the best from people and you usually get it," he recommended. "Just so long as they see you putting in as much effort as they do. So roll up your sleeves and work with them. Tell them to call you Bob. Loosen up, as the youngsters say these days!" He laughed and leaned on the table. "I was going to suggest panelling in the dining room but we'll leave that till the New Year and dab a bit of paint under a nice dado — what do you think?" Matthew knew very well that if he had suggested spreading ice cream on the walls it would have been just as acceptable.

"No spine at all," he told Maggie that afternoon. "Let's see what Christmas with Binnie's little lot will do for him."

"Let's see what it will do for Binnie," Maggie said soberly. "I reckon she must've been carrying a torch for that rotter of a husband of hers. Otherwise why doesn't she get up to Dennison's lookout and see that Daniel Casey? I don't understand it."

"She 'asn't got her island nor 'er home. She lost a good friend in Alf. Those two spoke the same language. An' it's one thing to mourn a dead 'usband, to bury his

369

misdeeds and remember only the good ones. It's quite another to find he ain't dead at all and his legacy ain't no legacy after all. She is being forced to remember every solitary misdeed from the past and many others since then."

"Yes, but none of it is her fault, Matt. And she's taking it all on 'erself."

"Rubbish!"

"'Tis true. She said to me only yesterday that if she hadn't dashed off to see the island as soon as she knew it was hers, none of this would have happened."

Matthew said grimly, "Alf would still be dead. That Theo Cash would still be alive. And I reckon there's a damned good chance Daniel Casey and Dennison would both be dead. What Daniel did he did for her, not for himself. And so did Dennison partially."

Maggie looked at him as Bob Newsome had looked at him not long ago. Then she pecked his cheek. "Tell her that, my lover. And while you're at it, tell her about Midwatch cottages. In fact, take her over there one day and let her see what you been doing."

Matthew returned her stare; he could not remember the last time she had volunteered a kiss. She looked back at him challengingly and he grabbed her.

When Binnie came in from a late afternoon walk to St Andrew's church they were wrestling around the kitchen, laughing and spluttering helplessly. She crept upstairs without them seeing her.

Since they had arrived back at Harbour Lights, nothing had happened; she should have got better immediately

370

and she had not. Dear Will looked after her and Maggie and Matthew were wonderful, but something was missing.

What had she expected, for goodness' sake? Had she really thought Daniel would come to her side and everything would be swept under the carpet and they would live happily ever after? What if he had indeed remembered a wife and family somewhere else? In which case why was he hanging around on Keyhole? Why didn't he get himself off and leave her to find another life? She knew full well that she was in what Lady Barbara referred to dismissively as "a bit of a state". Yet that was wrong too because she wasn't in anything at all; to be in a state would mean there was something she could do about it. And there was nothing she could do about the way she was feeling now, simply because she wasn't feeling anything.

That afternoon she had forced herself out for a walk in the wintry sunshine, but she hadn't wanted to go. Yet neither had she wanted to watch television or chat to Maggie or help with the high tea or anything. She knew that Will had gone fishing with Dennison but when he suggested she join them for half an hour, she had known she had not wanted to do that, though she missed Will's companionship more than anything. She lived in a world of negatives.

She sat on the edge of her bed and stared across at the window. The sea looked molten and heavy, so heavy it might even take her weight; maybe she could walk across it to Trapdoor and cook something in the heavy iron frying pan for when William got back from the school run. Yet there was a reason for not doing that either. She could not quite remember what it was except that Theo's name for Trapdoor had been No Man's Island. He must have meant No Woman's Island.

She sobbed a little laugh and picked up her nightie from the pillow, shook it out and refolded it. This morning she had heard Will phoning the hotel at Postern and booking them in for the Christmas weekend. She didn't want to go there, but she didn't want to stay here and be a nuisance to Maggie . . . more of a nuisance than she was now. And she would be able to see more of Dorrie if they all stayed there, which Will said they would.

Dorrie. Dorrie and Miles Thoroughgood. That was positive and surely still quite wonderful, like a fairy tale with a happy ending. Not that Gabriel had been that bad. She had felt almost close to him at times, as if she had known him in another life. Which, in a way, she had. Gabriel was charming but very shallow and with one enormous flaw in his character. And Theo had been like that, though she had not realized how enormous the flaw was until recently.

She stood up and walked to the window. The light was fading fast, which meant that Will would appear at any minute, and she should go down and help Maggie and talk to Will and ask Matthew about the hotel and . . . She walked back to the bed and slid beneath the covers. She did not take off her slippers. She pulled the pillow almost over her head and closed her eyes. It did not occur to her that she was ill — "properly ill" as

Maggie would say. All she knew was that the only emotion she could muster was fear.

Will came into her room without knocking, switched on the light, saw her and yelled over his shoulder, "She's here! Don't worry. We'll be down in a minute."

She said, "Switch off the light, Will. It's hurting my eyes."

He switched it off and came to the bed, drew up a chair and sat right next to her. "Maggie didn't see you come in, Ma. She was frightened to death."

"Sorry." Her voice was muffled by the pillow and he moved it gently away from her face.

"Ma. Can't you talk to me? We went through all that stuff back on Trapdoor . . . together. You, me, Dennison. And Daniel over here, not wanting to tip the scales one way or the other. Leaning over backwards because he was so damned certain you were still in love with Dad." There was a pause. Binnie could not think of a single thing to say. Will had put it succinctly. That was exactly how it had been. There was nothing to add, no comment to make.

He said sharply, "You're not, are you?"

She roused slightly at his tone and said, "What?"

"You're not still in love with Dad? You must have seen that he's not just a swashbuckling pirate. He's mean and underhand and downright evil. You did realize that he is into drug smuggling, didn't you? Ma! Listen to me!"

"I did realize. And I am not in love with him. And I haven't been for a very long time. Now please, Will, let me go to sleep."

"You don't sleep. I've heard you moving about in the night."

"Will, please."

"Listen, Ma. This can't go on. You're like a zombie. I don't get it. Dad's out of the picture. Daniel is in love with you — obsessed, if you want to know. And I thought you quite liked him. What's the problem?"

"I want to sleep."

He sighed deeply. Then he said in a low voice, "Ma, how do you think it is for me? I've got Dad's genes. Do you think that's a pleasant thought?"

She roused at that. "Don't be silly, Will. We've already sorted that out. You don't *use* people or circumstances or situations. You love the islands and the sea but you don't see them as a business proposition." She had half raised herself on one elbow, now she sank back. "Anyway, what you saw — what we all saw — on Trapdoor will keep us from similar harm." She closed her eyes. "That's why Dennison came back with us."

He was silent and she thought he might get up and leave her but he stayed. After a while she undid her hands, which were twisted together beneath the sheets, and reached for one of his.

"I wonder whether Dorrie was displaying the presence of some of my foolish genes when she hooked up with Gabe. But she's with Miles now. And you . . . oh, Will, you remind me so much of Alf sometimes."

He spluttered. "Alf? Thanks, Ma. Should I start growing a beard?"

"It's your feeling for the sea, darling. The sea and the islands. You love them and you respect them. Just as he did."

He was quiet again, massaging the knuckles of the hand that lay so limply in his. Then he said quietly, "I love you, Ma. You are going to get better and come back to us, aren't you?"

"I don't know. I want so much to sleep. Could you explain to Maggie?"

"Yes. Of course. But try to think a minute, Ma. Please. Tell me how you are feeling. Talk to me."

She was so long replying he thought she had actually fallen asleep. But when she spoke eventually her voice was surprisingly clear.

"He used me, Will. And I thought Daniel had used me too. Life . . . used me. And I think I am used up. I don't think there is anything . . . inside . . . any more. It's all been used up." She made a sound like a tiny laugh. "The funny thing is, I didn't know it was happening. Not until that afternoon. Not until then."

He said nothing. He was crying and didn't want her to know. In the darkness he stretched his facial muscles hideously in an effort to control anything like a sob. But the tears ran the length of his face and dripped from his chin.

It was probably fifteen minutes before he felt he could move. He put his free hand on his mother's head and felt the heat coming through her hair. Her breathing was even but shallow. She was asleep at last.

He took her hand and put it beneath the covers, then crept out of the room. Maggie met him at the bottom of the stairs.

"What is it, Will? Can't you talk her into coming down? She's hardly eaten a thing since she arrived."

He said, "When all this happened, she was ill. She had a really bad fever the night before. I think she's got it again."

Maggie saw the marks of the tears on his face. She took his arm and led him to the table. "Come on, my boy. Lamb. And it's not from Portcullis Island either! Help yourself and I'm going to put some on a plate for your dear ma. Perhaps Matthew should go and telephone Dr Kennan. It'll be easier for her to know she's properly ill. She probably thinks she's going mad. And that's the worst thing of all."

Will let himself be taken over by both Governs. When Dr Kennan arrived, Will went upstairs with him and held Binnie's hand while her temperature and pulse were checked.

"A rip-roaring temperature," the doctor announced cheerfully. "Galloping pulse." He grinned. "I think you'll live. You've picked up the same bug as they've got on Portcullis. Nothing much I can do for you because it's a virus. Keep warm — bed would be best for that, if you can bear it — plenty to drink. I'll give you some of my specials." He poked around in his bag and came up with two bottles of tablets. "Vitamin C. They're quite tasty. And some relaxants. Help you to sleep. Oh, and a nice vapour — breathe it in, good for the chest. And this." He extracted a paperback book. "It's a history of the Skalls. Should stand you in good stead if you run out of conversation with your partner at the ball."

Binnie almost smiled. As if she would be going to the ball with a virus. She saw it was the same book she had kept at Cherrington.

Will smiled properly and pecked her on the nose. "Now you *can* go to sleep. Pleasant dreams, Ma."

"She won't have a single dream after one of my tablets," Dr Kennan said even more cheerfully.

He was right.

CHAPTER
TWENTY-SEVEN

Will looked in on his mother at midnight. She was lying on her side, so perfectly relaxed it made him smile. At eight thirty the next morning, he took her some tea and toast and she was still in the same position. He stared down at her and thought she looked better, then wondered whether he was imagining that her mouth was slightly upturned as if she was smiling in her sleep. He clutched the tray to his chest and kept staring; it must be over ten years since he had crept into bed with her at weekends, and Dorrie had brought them cool tea and hard toast and Ma had said it was like being at a four-star hotel. Dorrie had said disgustedly, "You used to say it was like living in a gingerbread house in the middle of the forest! And now it's a posh hotel! Mummy, just face facts — it's an old game-keeper's cottage, and it's not even ours!" And Binnie had laughed and only Will had known that she was a little bit scared. Since that time he had gone to Leeds and Dorrie had moved in with Gabriel and their mother had been on her own. Maybe a lot scared.

He leaned over the tray and said softly, "Ma, whether you like it or not, I'm not going to leave you on your own again. We might be back to square one — no home, no money — but we're still a family and don't you forget it!"

She did not open her eyes but he could have sworn that her mouth definitely twitched upwards in a smile. He smiled back and crept out of her room, still clasping the tray to his chest.

She woke slowly, not even opening her eyes until she had fully relished the warmth and softness of the bed and the complete relaxation that was melting her limbs. The heaviness, the indefinable ache everywhere, had gone; her body lay gratefully where she had put it last night. Her lids fluttered while she focused her eyes; the room was full of grey light. Was it dawn or dusk? Time meant nothing. Somewhere Will would be waiting for her to be better. He had been with her several times during the night, she was certain of it, and she turned her head carefully so that she could see the door and the brass handle.

After a while she eased herself on to her back and then on to her left side so that she could look at the clock. It was just two o'clock. That meant she had slept for eighteen hours, apparently without moving and — as Dr Kennan had promised — without dreaming.

At two thirty Will still hadn't appeared and Binnie decided he must be fishing off the point. She swung her legs sideways out of bed and sat up. It was unexpectedly difficult; she had felt so well when she woke first. She reached for the water with lemon floating in it and drank thirstily from the jug. Will had made it just as he had made the other jug back at Trapdoor. That seemed like another life.

Her duffel coat was hanging behind the door, which was unusual until she remembered sneaking up the stairs the day before yesterday, not even pausing to take it off and hang it on the hall stand. She drank some more water and stood up to test her legs. They held her. She moved to the window and looked out. It was all so blessedly familiar to her already. How long had she been here on the Skalls? Three months. A quarter of a year. And so much had happened. Or rather not happened. Here she was, without a home or a proper income or even a proper job any more. She felt a flutter of panic. It was going to hurt when she left, really hurt. But she couldn't stay here when Theo was less than an hour away. If only . . . if only . . . She put a hand to her mouth, horrified. Had she been about to wish that Theo really was dead? Oh God, oh God, oh God, what was happening to her? She pressed her hand hard against her mouth until her teeth hurt and then squeezed her eyes tightly shut. What was going to happen to her? Lady Barbara would probably find her a job again. But she didn't want to go back. She wanted to stay . . . oh, how she wanted to stay.

She took a huge breath through her fingers and then spluttered a stupid laugh at the noise it made. The moment of desperation passed. And, through the window, there below her, just as he had been two months before, was Dennison. It was a moment of pure *déjà vu*, and she turned and picked up the binoculars from the dressing table and trained them on the small lone figure crouched like a gnome at the very end of the short pier. It was definitely him. No sign of Will either. She felt a little jump of fear. If Will was on Keyhole he would have been here, bringing her a tray of tea. She removed the binoculars and stood straighter, trying to concentrate properly. Will was not with Dennison and Dennison was on the pier waiting for someone. Will? The only other person Dennison would wait for was Theo. Surely not Theo? She drew back as if she could be seen.

It was cold in the bedroom and she automatically felt the radiator in front of the window: that was cold too. She fetched her duffel coat, stooping slightly to use the bed and the back of a handy chair and noting with slight dismay that she was very weak. She struggled into the heavy coat and buttoned it over her nightdress, then went back to the window and picked up the binoculars. Dennison was standing now, waving. She steadied the heavy glasses and inched them slowly upwards. Tacking in a wide arc from the sea came *Scallywag*, sails and spinnaker stretched to the wind that must be brisk out there. The whiteness of the boat against the grey sea and sky was beautiful. Binnie kept her within the frame of her vision as she swept around and headed for the short pier; the crew was in full view. Two men. One was Will. She lowered the binoculars and continued to stare through the window. *Scallywag* had been with Theo. He had taken her from the dunes and sailed at low tide into the cavern. And here she was again, back at Keyhole.

Binnie put the binoculars back on the dressing table and glanced out of the window again. The sails were down and Dennison was catching a line and running it around a stanchion; Will was climbing the iron-runged ladder to the pier head. He shook hands with Dennison — it looked strangely old-fashioned, as if they were sealing a bargain — then Dennison was going down the ladder with the agility of a monkey and the other man was coiling the rope flung by Will and pushing them away from the pier. Dennison started the engine, pushed down the outboard and they moved out from the pier towards the dunes. As they rounded the end of the long pier, the other man looked back and up, directly at the window where Binnie stood. She knew that unless she opened it and leaned out, she was invisible from the sea. Nevertheless, she gasped and stepped back quickly. Then she took off her coat and hung it back behind the door and got into bed. Her heart was beating hard and her legs were trembling. Theo was out there somewhere. They had taken his boat. He would come for it.

Ten minutes later, Will knocked and came in. He was carrying the tray, this time loaded with tea things. He stood just inside the door, pretending amazement.

"Ma, you look wonderful! What has happened?"

"Don't be silly, Will. I'm better, that's all."

"But so soon!" He pulled out the bedside table and put down the tray. Maggie had toasted some teacakes and they were oozing butter and fragrance next to the teapot. Binnie felt her mouth water. She really was feeling better.

She said, "I told you. I needed to sleep. And I've only just woken up."

"My God. That's something like eighteen hours!" He poured tea and passed her a teacake on a plate with a paper napkin printed with a Christmas tree. "Maggie wants me to tell you that these serviettes are not last year's! She's broken into her Christmas store for this year specially, to put you in a jolly frame of mind. And tonight the St Andrew's carollers are coming from top to bottom of Ditchdrain Street so you need to come downstairs and greet them properly!"

"Royal command?"

"Definitely!" He bit into his teacake and patted her knee through the duvet. "Oh, Ma, it's so good you feel better. You should have given in to it the moment we arrived instead of bottling it up so that it was ten times worse than before."

"I didn't bottle it up, love. It was there, but I wasn't with it. I mean, I sort of stood aside from it for a while."

"Well, that sums it up all right. Maggie thought you were pining for Trapdoor. Matthew thought it was Dad." He laughed, watching her carefully for a reaction.

She returned his look. "Are you all right now? How do you feel? I don't mean the genes thing — I hope you're all right with that. But . . . us. Dad coming back like this."

"Pretty bad." He chewed thoughtfully for a moment. "I hated him at first — wished he really was dead. Then I hated him more for making me feel such a ghastly thing. Then . . . Dennison said something and I felt better about it." He swallowed, took another enormous bite and concluded, "Actually, Ma, I do feel better about it now. What you said about genes and things . . . and Dad being weak rather than evil . . . a bit like Dorrie's Gabriel, from what I know of him . . ."

He coughed and Binnie said, "Wait till you've finished your teacake."

He swallowed again and grinned. "That's it, really. You gave me something I could still almost admire, Ma. And the other thing, the disastrous side of Dad — well, I've just got to look out for it and sit on it the instant it rears its head!" He laughed, but she knew he was serious and she nodded, still waiting for him to tell her about his sail this afternoon.

He said, "Have another teacake, Ma. Maggie said she wouldn't be dishing up until later tonight so you've got plenty of time to work up your appetite again."

She nibbled obediently. "I don't know whether I can face a big meal. Can you bear to bring me another tray? Then you could help me out with it!"

"I will, if that's what you want. Maggie has made a Lancashire hotpot for this evening and it smells out of this world."

"She's marvellous. D'you think she'd be hurt if I had it up here?"

"No. But I think you should come downstairs for an hour, Ma. The carollers and everything. Make you feel part of Skall again."

She said, surprised, "But I'm not, am I? Oh, I suppose we'll be staying for Christmas but then we'll go home, Will. Pick up the threads. By this time next year it will be like a dream." She forced a laugh. "Rather, a nightmare."

"Ma. You don't mean that."

"Darling, be sensible. We can't stay here. For one thing, we haven't any way of earning money. For another, can you really say you want to stay when Dad is just over the water and you know what he's up to? The situation is completely . . . I don't know . . . untenable."

Will made a thing of stacking plates and cups on the tray. "What if . . . he wasn't there? If he went abroad to live. Somewhere a long way off. And what if something turned up so that we could stay on Keyhole and make a living and I could go on ferrying the kids to school and you could have a proper garden and grow spring flowers for the market?"

She said, "My mother used to play that game. The 'praps game'. That was what my father called it. It drove him mad. He used to say she lived in a hypothetical world." She took his hand. "Will, your father isn't going anywhere. He's on to a good thing, leading the sort of life he loves. Why would he move?"

He said in a low voice, "He might have no choice. Too many people know about him now."

"Daniel told Matthew and Maggie. They won't let it go further."

"He might still leave, Ma. With his wretched Alberto."

She stared at him, suddenly frightened.

"You were out this afternoon in *Scallywag*. So you must have gone to Trapdoor."

He said immediately, "Yes. We went to see whether Dad was all right. And to ask him to leave."

"I'm not that gullible, Will!"

"I know it sounds crazy, but don't forget when we left him he was in the middle of a criminal act! And things were not going according to plan." Binnie continued to look at him disbelievingly. He said, "Supposing they had beaten him up, Ma. Supposing he had been injured and was lying there." He saw her expression change and went on quickly, "We simply wanted to know what was happening. And he's not there, Ma. The place is empty. Gas all disconnected, furnace out. We looked through the trap — tide almost out, no bits of debris floating about. And what's more, no new goods. No boxes, containers, nothing that wasn't there before. Ma, he's abandoned the place. He's probably on his way to South America right now."

She said carefully, "The thing is, Will, we left *Scallywag* in the cavern. It belonged to your father and it was the only way he had of getting off Trapdoor."

He shrugged. "He's gone. So he must have left with Alberto or whatever his name is." He stood and picked up the tray. "Matthew took us over after lunch. We searched the house — nothing. No overturned furniture — nothing. But *Scallywag* was still below. So we waited and as soon as there was enough water we floated her out." He went to the window. "Matthew is tying up now." He looked round at her. "All right, Ma,

I know *Scallywag* belongs to Dad. But if you had seen Dennison's face . . ."

She sighed. "I can imagine." She sat on the edge of the bed, gathering her limited strength. "D'you know, in all this, you haven't mentioned Daniel's name once."

"I gather you don't want to hear it." He made for the door and stood very still for a moment. "You know, Ma, he's done nothing wrong in his dealings with us."

"Dad said . . ." she spoke so quietly he had to strain to hear her, "Dad said he sold me to Daniel. And before you say anything, I know what he meant and I know Daniel had amnesia. But he still found me, didn't he?"

"Oh, Ma. Do you find that unacceptable?"

"Worse than that, Will. It's all part of being used. It spoils things. The two weeks we all spent together on Trapdoor seemed so good. Now it doesn't. You were right to be so angry with me. I let myself be fooled. I was a fool." She raised her brows at him. "I want to forget it, Will. Bury my head in sand again!" She laughed, then said, "Look, I'll have a bath, if there's any hot water, then I'll come downstairs and eat some hotpot and listen to the carols, and we'll forget this conversation too. All right?"

He opened the door. "All right," he said uncertainly.

She laughed again. "I think you did the right thing about *Scallywag*. And I'm so happy for Dennison."

In spite of her weakness Binnie enjoyed that evening more than she had enjoyed anything since Theo's return. Maggie laid a small table by the fire and the

387

four of them ate their hotpot and Matthew talked about Alf and how he had taught Matthew to swim as a small boy.

"He did used to stand on the roof ridge of the Peruvian, run down it until he was going faster'n his legs, and jump right out over the rocks and into the sea. My life, he looked like he were flying. But when he were about fifteen or thereabouts, he jumped wrong. Caught his back as he went down. Just a glancing blow. But he never growed any taller after that."

Will said, "Good God. He could have drowned or been paralysed or — or anything!"

"It was a miracle he weren't drowned. He was knocked out. But he floated up on his back. Doesn't usually 'appen like that, you know. He always said it was a mermaid what 'eld him so he could breathe. That was the start of it."

"Knocked the sense out of 'im, I reckon," Maggie said. "'E would never 'ave 'is hair cut or shave. He was always listening to the sea. Well . . . you know that as well as we do. You got very close to him, Binnie."

"He was special. I knew that much." Binnie put her knife and fork neatly on her empty plate. "That was delicious, Maggie. Thank you so much. I'll do the cooking tomorrow."

"Not just yet, my girl." Maggie gathered the plates on to a tray. "If you're up to it, my Matthew wants to take you out to see what he's been doing at Midwatch cottages. Remember them?"

"Of course." Binnie smiled, surprised. "That would be really nice, Matthew. Thank you. I'd really like to see your work. How's it going over at Postern?"

"Oh, 'tis all done now. I've sorted them out. Them over on the mainland, the consortium or whatever they call themselves, didn't dream poor old Bob would have any visitors. Now it looks like he'll have ten of you! I told him — this is your chance, boyo, I said. You got a good staff who en't afraid of work and you got a nice enough way with you. These people want to be well fed, warm and feel at home yet not at home. You can do it, I said. And I think he believes me." He looked at Binnie. "There's two ladies coming who won't know anyone, not even each other. Make sure they're happy, won't you, Binnie?"

"Of course I will, Matthew." She smiled unreservedly. "Skallions have got a reputation for being a bit awkward but the ones I know are warm and caring. I'd like to be the same."

"You've got a head start," Maggie told her. "After all, you're a Skallion now. No doubt about that."

It was at that point that they heard the first of the carollers. From far off — the very top of Ditchdrain Street in fact — the piercing note of a flute reached their ears. John Tresillian had been practising. He pitched the note and immediately Walter Polpen's voice could be heard: "Oh, here we come a wassailing upon the midnight clear . . ." Maggie and Matthew went outside to wait for them.

"Go on out with them," Binnie said to Will. "I'll go up to the top door and listen from your bedroom window."

She climbed the stairs slowly and with some difficulty. The singing was all around the house now. People had come out of the Dancing Bear to join in. In spite of herself she felt the usual stab of excitement at the idea of Christmas. Natalie and her Ernest — or Ernst, maybe — would be arriving on the next sailing of the *Queen* and, soon after, Dorrie would arrive with the Thoroughgoods. It would be as if they were a huge family coming together to celebrate. For a little while at least she could pretend her life was . . . was what? What did she expect of life?

The carollers were descending the steep hill now and Binnie unlocked the top door and went outside to watch them group along the short pier to sing to the sea. It was a damp evening; cloud coming from the west was swallowing up familiar landmarks, shrouding lamps and lighted windows. She recognized Walter and Gladys, and some of the nurses from the cottage hospital. Maggie and Matthew came from the house, shrugging into jackets, holding a storm lantern at shoulder height. "While shepherds watched their flocks by night" drifted from one pier to another; the last time Binnie had heard an alternative version of that had been on the dunes road, from the schoolchildren. So successfully had she blotted out all thoughts of Theo and Daniel that she could actually smile at that memory. They finished that carol and started on "Hark!

the herald-angels sing". She took a few steps down the road towards them and then stopped.

Daniel, wearing the duffel coat he had bought to go off with Dennison in *Scallywag*, was standing at the back, looking over John Tresillian's shoulder at a carol sheet held under a lantern. His hair was white in the lamplight, his shaven face gaunt. Binnie felt her heart lurch. For a moment she lost her balance and leaned against the wall of the house. She watched Daniel. The flute gave them a note and they all began to sing. She did not take her eyes off him: his face, his being, his presence there at this moment, when this world was magical and anything could happen. She knew that soon the intensity of her gaze would draw him to her. She watched.

And then someone stood behind her. It was a man and his shadow leaped over the wall and obliterated hers. She turned. The granite of Matthew and Maggie's house cut through the thicknesses of her coat and indented her shoulders. She had known he would come back for *Scallywag*. And for Daniel, who had betrayed him.

She made a whimpering sound. "Theo — oh dear God! Why — what has happened?"

And then Will's voice said, "Ma, it's me! I thought you'd like to go down and sing with everyone. Come on!"

She felt herself slipping away somewhere. Will's arms were holding her up. He was saying something about trying to run before she could walk. He was practically frog-marching her back into the house and along the corridor to the bedroom.

She sat on the bed, fighting nausea. It was all right. It hadn't happened. But it could happen. She knew suddenly that Theo would never let anything like a normal relationship develop between Daniel and herself. He had dripped his poison between them already. *I sold you* . . . The hated words echoed in her head.

She took a huge breath. "Will, I'm sorry. I thought — I thought you were Dad."

"I know. I just did not realize how terrified you are of Dad. My God, Dan was right. He said there would be no peace for you until Dad had gone for good!"

She got off the bed somehow. "I have to go to the bathroom," she managed to gasp. And there she was sick.

When she had finished, she stood up and washed her face, then stared at herself in the mirror. And suddenly she remembered. It was as if, behind her reflection, there was another, dimmer but clear enough. A girl in a gingham dress, which was tucked into her knickers; a boy in short trousers, but well below his knees. The girl was dark, her hair in a single plait; the boy's strawberry-blond hair fell into his eyes. It was Cherrington; the beach; the slipway. They were paddling.

CHAPTER
TWENTY-EIGHT

Binnie felt better afterwards and tried to laugh at herself. "Don't tell Maggie, for Pete's sake! Such a waste of a lovely meal!" She sat back on the bed and put her hands palm up. "Look, I'm fine again." Will frowned and took her hands in his, and she said contritely, "Sorry, Will. I thought your father had come back for *Scallywag*."

Will helped her off with her coat. "You thought he was after Dan, didn't you? I saw him with the singers. You saw him too."

"I don't know what I think." She looked at him helplessly. "I don't want to see him, Will. He reminds me of what an idiot I've been."

"Ma, he wasn't part of it —"

"They cooked it up between them. You know that, Will! And we shall none of us ever know whether he really had lost his memory!"

"Listen. Ma, just listen. He still hasn't got his memory back properly. So far as he knows, he has nowhere to live. He's staying in that ghastly so-called lookout place with Dennison until . . ."

"Until when? Until I fall into his arms again?" She put her hands to her face. "Oh God. When I think . . .

It was so good to have a friend, a proper friend, and all the time he was using us. You too, Will. He thought Theo was dead and the island was ours and he was on to a good thing."

"Ma." Will took her hands from her eyes. "Stop talking like this. You're only beating yourself up, no-one else. And if he had thought that, then why is he hanging around now? He knows we're practically on the breadline. Why isn't he pinching the *Scallywag* and following Dad?" He sighed. "Ma, you're not making sense."

"I know. Sorry. Sorry, Will." Remembering the foggy afternoon when Daniel had emerged from the sea and almost taken her by storm, she shivered. Perhaps that's why he was still here, because he had some crazy idea of owning her. After all, Theo had given him permission. Theo and Daniel. So alike. If Dennison hadn't descended on them and battered Daniel to the ground, she would gladly have let herself be swept away by that passion. And that would have been the end of them, because Theo would have found them and killed them both. None of this could be said to Will, of course. She swallowed hard and took a trembling breath. "You're right. I know you are really. Even so, love, I cannot see him. Forgive me if I am putting you in an awkward position but it won't be for long. As soon as Christmas is over, we'll go back to the gamekeeper's cottage and settle in until the New Year. Then I can sort out whether or not I've got a job down at the Manor. And if not, I shall get a flat in the middle of Cherrington and a job within walking distance and

— and I think I'll join a choir and maybe a social club of some sort and —"

"Ma, you're gabbling. Just forget all that rubbish and listen to me. I will make sure Daniel does not get within twenty yards of you while we're on Keyhole. Is that all right?" She nodded dumbly because there was nothing else to do and Will went on gently, "Just let everything go. Think of seeing Dorrie and the new hotel. And tomorrow, if you're up to it, Matthew wants to take you to see his work at the cottages." He waited and she nodded again and he smiled. "Good old Ma. Now get into your nightie and put your hair in curlers or whatever you do, and I'll bring you a sandwich and a drink."

She managed a smile.

She slept the rest of the evening and the night through again and — just as the old wives guaranteed — things felt better the next morning. The leaden skies lifted at the same time. Binnie stood at the window and watched without panic as *Scallywag*'s sails caught the breeze and headed away from the short pier. She knew Will was not on it but there were two figures in the small hull. Dennison and Daniel. Even as she watched, the sails swung across the boat and they made for Postern. Her heart lightened; both of them well away, at least for a few hours.

Maggie, Gladys Polpen and several other local women were all at the church hall decorating it for the ball on Friday and Matthew was keen to "get going" up to Midwatch.

"I know you got to take it steady, my maid," he said, shovelling toast rack, teapot and butter dish on to a tray, "but the other widow — that there Natalie — will be here tomorrow and though she's staying over Postern, there don't seem to be much peace and quiet when she's within a ten-mile radius!" He gave Binnie a comical look. "I wouldn't mind a bit of your company myself, and your young William wants to do a meal for us all tonight — caught bass the other day, din't you, m'boy? — fancies isself as a bit of a chef, I reckon!"

She thought of standing on a wind-buffeted headland, admiring Matthew's handiwork, which wouldn't mean much to her as she had not seen the cottages in their original condition.

She said, "That will be great, Matthew." Then she smiled. "I shall really enjoy having a run over the island too." Will glanced at her and nodded approval, which made it all worthwhile. It occurred to her she hadn't been much of a mother lately.

They drove sedately along the road to the school and then took a right turn, which snaked via hairpin bends to the top of Keyhole. Matthew stopped the car so that he could point out other islands.

"On a good day you can see the Wolf Rock from here," he told her. "Makes you feel you want to grow wings and take flight, doesn't it?"

"You got that from Alf," she said.

"I got lots of things from Alf," he agreed.

"So did I." Tears threatened. She said, "I've got this silly feeling that if Alf were still here I'd be all right."

Matthew took her arm. "Come on, my maid. You bin working hard and then there's that Daniel running off and leaving you. Now Alf wouldn't have let that happen!" He shook her arm as if to jolly her back to herself. "Alf always said you two was meant for each other — well, he didn't know as much as he thought, did he? Did he, eh?"

Binnie forced herself to reply. "Theo would have always been there between us. Alf didn't know about that, of course."

"No. None of us did. Now Natalie — we knew she was still carrying a torch for Theo Cash. He were a sort of schoolgirl hero for Natalie. But not you. Not you, my maid. You've spent a lot of time without him now. Time to realize what a — a — rotter he were. A downright rotter. 'Tis an old-fashioned term but it suits him down to the socks."

She glanced at him, surprised, almost shocked. He met her gaze and smiled apologetically. "We can't 'elp talking about it — me and Maggie. We don't approve of 'usbands who leave their wives and children." He laughed. "That makes us really old-fashioned, don't it?" He released her arm and started up the car again. "Anyway, let's get on now. This part of the island is called Little Keyhole. No church, but there's a Methodist chapel and another reading room — they has whist drives there at times. The sea's rougher this side and a lot of the visitors like to surf so there's a surf shop open in the summer. 'Tis manned by these young men who can walk on water. I mean that, 'cos when they water-ski, they step off the skis straight on to the water and ski on the soles o' their feet!"

Binnie groaned. "Sounds painful."

The road dipped down into a shallow coomb and ran by the side of a clear stream. Matthew pulled in again to point out other landmarks: a short cut up to Dennison's place, a coastal path that served two other beaches, a lagoon towards the tumble of rocks that marked the end of the island.

"Twitchers like that lake there," Matthew said, pointing. "Atlantic tern, puffins, cormorants, ducks, even swans. Plenty of visitors all round this side."

Binnie said, "It's beautiful, Matthew. I had no idea there was this wild country so close at hand. I've walked along the tops but never seen this part. And such a contrast to the calm and quiet of the harbour."

"Most of the islands got two different faces, you know. Even small ones like Postern got their calm side and their rough side. Nat'rally the old settlers made their houses on the calm side. But then in the past eighty years, visitors have wanted to stay on the rough sides for the water sports and the birds and seals and what 'ave you."

She was fascinated. "Is it far to Midwatch now? Shall we walk?"

"You up to it, my maid? The breeze is fairly breezy. But it might put some roses in your cheeks!"

They got out of the Standard and walked on down the coomb, past a shuttered shed that displayed tattered advertisements for surf boards, wet suits and parascending, and then to the right where the road ran

398

parallel to the coastal path. Below them was a small beach, and the crystal-clear water from the stream crashed through ferns and rocks and made a deep channel in the sand on its way to the sea. Binnie could imagine children building their sandcastles around it, making bridges from the flat stones that lined the cove. Dorrie's children, maybe; or Will's. More tears threatened. She was shocked at herself. She must be as weak as a kitten. She blinked hard and drew level with Matthew.

"Long way for you to drive to work," she commented breathlessly.

"Well, course, I never bothered to stop and look at the scenery." He grinned. "That's what's good about showing people around. You see it yourself too." He rounded another hairpin bend and there in a fold of the bracken-covered slope was a group of six small cottages, obviously holiday lets.

She was surprised. "I thought they were old dwellings — fishermen's cottages, that sort of thing. These were built . . . what? Ten years ago?"

"Not much longer. True. Jerry-built, as you see. That's why they're always calling me in. And when there was the last crisis, the old caretaker was still living here. Couldn't leave him to the weather, could I?'

"Oh, Matthew, you are good." But she was still surprised. Doubtless the work Matthew had put in was first class, but she had expected something, well, different.

He said, "I got the keys. Let's have a look round."

He showed her two of the cottages. A two-bedroomed one with an open fire and calor-gas cooker. And a four-bedroomed one with central heating and a washing machine.

"They're smashing," she said with forced enthusiasm. "Just imagine arriving here from the airfield or the harbour, tired and fed up and finding this little haven."

Matthew nodded. "They are popular up to a point. But they had this bloke as caretaker and he had no idea of being friendly, telling folks where to go, helping them out with the shopping. An' 'e were no good when it came to repairs. They still had to get me in when anything needed doing." He walked across an overgrown lawn to a bungalow tucked into a rocky outcrop. "This is his place. Probably in a bit of a state, but worth looking at."

He unlocked a door set into a big porch that ran the width of the house.

"All double-glazed," he said, sounding like a house agent. "Lovely environment for plants. He had deck chairs stacked here." He made a sound of disgust and went on into the hall of the bungalow. "Not exactly imaginative, is it?" He walked the length of the hall, opening doors as he went. "Sitting room, dining room, kitchen, bathroom, bedroom one, bedroom two. But handy. I like the way the sitting room can open out into the dining room and the dining room into the kitchen. All one side of the house — see what I mean?"

"Yes. Yes, very, er, handy. As you say."

"I've suggested to the owners that it's about time for a new kitchen and bathroom. They haven't exactly said yes but then they haven't said no either. D'you think the new manager would be able to cope with them as they are?"

He ushered her to the open door of the bathroom. It looked perfectly serviceable to her. After all, white bathrooms were back in favour again.

She went to the sink in the kitchen and looked out at the view from the back of the house where the land leaped upwards. She said, "You could slide down there on a tin tray. Apparently, Theo used to coast down the dunes at Trapdoor on a belly-board."

There was a silence.

She turned and smiled. "Come on, Matthew. What are you getting at?"

"Getting at? I en't getting at anything. Just showing you around, like. As you're hoping to go into the tourist business, I thought you might be interested."

"Of course I'm interested. But only as someone who admires your carpentry skills." She reached out and put her hand on his arm. "Matthew, I'd better explain. There's been a change in my prospects. Now Theo's alive after all I haven't inherited Trapdoor. And I've got no money. So my interest in the tourist business is purely objective."

He stared at her. "My dear life, I never thought . . . But of course! The bugger's alive so there's no bloody inheritance at all!" He stopped and then apologized profusely and she reassured him, smiling sympathetically. At last he recovered his composure. "What a shock for you. Oh, Binnie. No wonder you look as if you've seen a ghost all the time! That Natalie won't be too pleased neither, will she?"

"No." Binnie had to smile at the thought of Natalie's reaction.

"Well, well. I can't get over it. Maggie thought we'd have to try to talk you out of Trapdoor. And here you are . . . no Trapdoor!"

She nodded. "No Trapdoor indeed. And why would either of you want to talk me out of it? I thought you were all for it."

"That were Alf. He were never practical, were Alf. Now Maggie is a different kettle of fish. Maggie's practical down to her toenails. And when the manager here left she said straight away that it was your place. She's right, you know. Trapdoor would never make you a living, my maid. But this place . . . you live rent free and there's a small wage goes with it — a percentage of the rentals, actually. It's not usually full but with you at the helm it would be different. You'd look after people properly, get them interested in Skall, take them along to the reading room when there's something int'resting. You'd have all those houses full up for a long season too. And Keyhole is a better place to live in than Trapdoor in the winter." His face was red with enthusiasm and with the will to make her see his point of view. "Say you'll apply for it, Binnie! Maggie and me, the Polpens, everybody, will send references. Keyhole is your place, my maid. You'll be able to forget that 'usband of yours and be happy here!"

She stared back at him. Her mind was racing. She felt better; the ache in her back had almost gone.

Matthew was right on all counts: Trapdoor had been a strange haven but it was not a place for a seaside landlady. And that was what she wanted to be. She recalled the little bay they had just left . . . Dorrie's children and Will's boys . . .

She said, "Oh, Matthew, I can't believe this. It would be a proper home. Do you think I stand a chance?"

"No-one else on the islands will apply. They're too tied up with family. Everyone on Keyhole has other fish to fry. Yes, I think you stand a chance." He was grinning. As far as he was concerned she was already installed.

She said, "I've been wondering what on earth to do. Home as soon as I can and back to work . . . I felt as if I was in one of those padded cells where there's no door. Oh, Matthew, how can I ever thank you?"

"By becoming a proper Skallion, having a rattling good time at the ball on Friday, making all your family and friends walk the length and breadth of Postern on Boxing Day."

"Listening for mermaids," she said, starry-eyed.

"Just walking off the after-effects of lunch," he said, openly laughing at her. He sobered suddenly. "Oh my life! Alf would be an 'appy man over this. Of course you'll be listening for mermaids. And for his daft sea songs. And I don't doubt you'll hear both!"

She walked through the bungalow again and then a third time. The porch took on the grandeur of a conservatory. She remembered the two wicker chairs she had in the kitchen of the gamekeeper's cottage.

They would be ideal, sitting amongst the geraniums and busy Lizzies.

"I expect you'll start a little kitchen garden on that plot at the back," Matthew ventured, well pleased.

Tears almost welled again because it had been Daniel and Will who had worked so hard on the plot at Trapdoor. But then she almost ran around to the back of the bungalow, and sure enough there were the remains of a garden stretching from the back door up to the gentle slope that then steepened into the thrust of the hill beyond. She bent down and took a handful of the damp earth; it crumbled satisfyingly between her fingers. "Broad beans," she murmured dreamily. "And then kidney beans. And carrots and onions. And big fat cabbages like footballs."

Matthew came behind her, breathing heavily. "You should mention that in your application, my maid. The owners would like to think of you supplying fresh vegetables."

"I hadn't thought of actually supplying stuff. But why not?" Binnie stood and turned to him. "Matthew, it would be wonderful! You don't know how wonderful. When you first started work here, I imagined old cottages falling to bits. And I couldn't cope with that. But these . . . this . . ." She swept the area with her arm. "I shall love the solitude through the winter — just as I loved it at Trapdoor. And in the summer it will be *fun!*"

He was delighted. "Let's walk up to the tops. Then you can see Dennison's lookout and know how long it would take you to walk into town."

So they scrambled up the steep hill where the footpath became a muddy trough between grass banks and eventually led out on to a windswept ridge. They stood there, gasping for air, laughing and not knowing why. The wind was taking clouds over the island fast so that the light constantly changed. Below them lay the cove, suddenly spotlit and golden. Behind it, the road led back into the hills darkly and they could only just see the car from the light's reflection on the windscreen. They turned in unison, following the coastline, rocky at first and then tumbling into the dunes that eventually skirted the little town and harbour. The town was invisible from here — even the church tower was folded into the hills and valleys somehow — but as they turned the lookout appeared, bleak and stark in the winter landscape.

Binnie shouted into the wind, "How on earth does Dennison keep inquisitive little boys from invading his privacy throughout the summer?"

Matthew laughed. "He's got his ways! Doesn't say much, as a rule, but when he does, he's blunt and to the point!"

"I'll have to have a word with him. He mustn't frighten off my families!" She was half-serious and Matthew nodded sagely.

"He could be part of the attraction," he came back in the same vein. "An old original hermit fisherman!"

And it was while they were still laughing that, on the invisible horizon, a puff of smoke appeared. Even then it was possible to see that the smoke contained an orange glow. The glow exploded up and out, fuelled by flames from underneath it. It looked almost like the pictures of an atomic explosion, gathering itself into a mushroom shape. And then came the vibrations travelling along the seabed and shaking Keyhole, gently but inexorably.

Matthew grabbed Binnie and held her protectively.

"God'lmighty!" he said, his voice quiet, awed. "There's no record of any kind of volcanic activity. But that's what it must be. 'Ang on to me, my maid. We'll be all right."

She did hang on to him, burying her face in his shoulder. She said nothing but she knew this was no natural eruption. This was the cavern beneath the house on Trapdoor Island, exploding. She dug her gloved fingers into Matthew's jacket and hung on to him desperately. Her mind leaped ahead, constructing scenarios, discarding them. This was no accident either; this was something to do with Theo's nefarious activities. She closed her eyes against the livid glow. Was Theo a victim of his own cunning? Or had he himself organized the complete destruction of all the "evidence"?

Matthew said, "It's a one-off, girl. Don't worry. You're shaking like a leaf."

"It's just that I'm feeling the cold." She lifted her head and stared past the lookout to where already the glow was consumed by flames. She said flatly, "It's Trapdoor, Matthew."

He was silent for a moment, staring hard. "I reckon you're right, m'ansome. And I don't reckon it's a volcano — they was extinct a long time ago. I reckon

406

some of your late 'usband's brandy supplies 'ave gone up in flames." He sounded puzzled. "Someone must've started it, though. What's going on?" He looked down at her. "My dear life, where's that fool Dennison?" He let her go and began to run and stumble towards the lookout. She caught him with difficulty.

"Matthew, stop! He's not at the lookout! I saw him heading for Postern earlier this morning." They paused, panting for breath again. "Let's get back to Harbour Lights."

They stumbled back down the slippery path to the group of summer cottages and on down to the road that ended by the cove. As they ran to the car, Binnie knew a moment of sheer terror. Daniel had been with Dennison in *Scallywag*. And Postern need not have been their final destination. For a ghastly instant, before she could cut it off, she imagined Daniel and Dennison pulling *Scallywag* into the cavern just as Theo or Alberto, or whoever it was, detonated the explosive devices they had left behind them.

Matthew settled himself beside her in the driver's seat. "You're still shivering, Binnie. Cain't be the cold after that tramp back here!"

She moved away from him and tried to laugh. "A goose walked over my grave, Matthew."

"You were thinking that your husband might have been mixed up in that explosion." He nodded. "It certainly would be a case of the biter bit, wouldn't it?"

She said nothing and he ground the gear into reverse and turned the car towards home.

CHAPTER
TWENTY-NINE

Everyone was huddled into the two bars at the Dancing Bear, asking each other what could have happened and concocting scenarios based on old films of the San Francisco earthquake. Will fought his way through to his mother.

"A bit like your game of praps," he suggested, making a face. "You know what I've been thinking, don't you?"

"Dad?"

He nodded. "Yes, Dad."

"He wouldn't blow up his own secret cave, Will."

"No. But if he was telling us the truth — and we can never be sure of that — then his precious Alberto, or whatever his name was, could have blown the lot to kingdom-come and Dad with it."

"Yes." Binnie shook her head, not believing it. "Anyway, what's happening?"

"The rescue craft has gone out. Everyone realizes it's Trapdoor. They don't know whether anyone is there or not. I've told them not. But there's no sign of Dennison."

She said in a low voice, "Dennison and Daniel were in *Scallywag* earlier. Making for Postern."

He stared at her for a moment, then said, "Fair enough. I got hold of Daniel last night and told him to put some space between himself and you. He must have got Dennison to take him over to Postern." He paused, then added, "But in that case why hasn't Dennison come back and beached *Scallywag* as usual?"

It still wasn't quite what Binnie had been thinking.

She said, "When did the rescue boat go?" Meaning when will it be back?

"Not sure. I was in the middle of skinning the fish and when I heard the bang I rushed to the window and saw the fire. Then Maggie stuck her head round the door to say everyone was up here so . . . I came too." He changed topics suddenly. "What did you think of Midwatch cottages?"

Binnie saw a seat by the window and eased into it, making room for him. She understood he did not want her to think too much about the explosion.

"I thought they were marvellous." She did not have to feign enthusiasm. "And our bungalow is perfect."

He said, "Our bungalow, is it?" He took her hand. "Oh, Ma, wouldn't it be marvellous? I knew you'd jump at it. Listen, don't let this — whatever has happened — change your mind, will you? Dennison would be so pleased to think of you within sight of his lookout."

"So you do think Dennison is involved?" She moved her head towards the window and then turned to peer outside. The wind was blowing the smoke from the Ditchdrain chimneys in horizontal streams across the pier. The flames on Trapdoor would be fanned by this wind and there would be nothing left of the house.

Will followed her gaze. "I don't know what to think, Ma." He paused, then bit his lip. "I shouldn't tell you this, I suppose, but he used to be a miner. He knew how to set a charge."

Momentarily she was surprised that Dennison had opened up to Will about his past. But then she shook her head. "Surely not to make that sort of explosion, Will? My God, it was huge! You'd need to be an absolute expert to make that kind of bang! Matthew thought it was a volcanic eruption. We could see everything, we were almost next door to the lookout."

"You're right. Dennison of all people, an explosives buff? I don't think so!" He tried to laugh. Then added, "Natalie will be furious she missed it by a day!" And the laugh became genuine.

Walter Polpen leaned over their table. "We're all very sorry about your place at Trapdoor, Mrs Cash. But I don't think I'm jumping the gun when I say that the little bungalow and the job at Midwatch is yours if you want it. We'll all help you to settle in ready for the next season and if your son can stay for a while it shouldn't take long before you can actually live there."

"Mr Polpen, I think it's ideal. I'm going to write my application tonight and it can go over on the *Queen* tomorrow. Will and I — we're really excited about it. Matthew says you'll give us a reference. We're so grateful —"

"Don't say any more, my 'ansome. You're one of us now and we look after each other. You were good to Alf

410

and you're still good to Dennison. Deeds is better than words, Mrs Cash. A great deal better."

Matthew elbowed him out of the way. "News on the radio phone. They've landed on the beach at Trapdoor, got up to the house but it's no good — there's nothing to save. I'm right sorry, Binnie, Will. They think it was a small explosion — could've been that dynamo Alf got. But then the brandy and the fuel . . . it's just out of hand. They'll have to let it burn itself out. Did you have anything precious there?"

They both shook their heads. As Will said afterwards, "We had a lot of good memories but they got lost the moment Dad arrived."

Maggie appeared at Matthew's shoulder. "Go home and put the kettle on, Binnie, will you? My tongue is sticking to the roof of my mouth." She smiled. "I'm that glad about you staying on. I'm that *glad*!"

"Oh Maggie," Binnie smiled too.

"Come on, m'dear. We'll have our tea like we always do and watch the dark come in. Then our young Will here will serve us dinner!" She put on an accent and twiddled her fingers in imitation of a French waiter and Matthew suddenly hugged her against his side.

"She en't a bad old dutch, is she?" he asked.

Binnie could have wept then. She knew so little about the Governs. They had no children and they lived away from everything most people felt they needed. But theirs was a proper marriage. She remembered the two weeks after Guy Fawkes' night when she and Will and Daniel had shared their lives so easily and amiably. And quite suddenly, sitting there in the crowded pub, practically destitute but with some good and realistic prospects in view, Binnie understood something. She almost spoke the words aloud. Alf had been right: she and Daniel were meant to be together; the butterfly that might have been their chance for happiness had been within landing distance. And they — she — had let it go.

The next morning there was a record turn-out on the long pier to meet the *Queen of Skalls* as she trumpeted her way through the fog, which had come in with the wind during the night and settled over the Islands, "like a big fat duvet" as Maggie irritably put it. "I never liked the things. Give me a sheet and blanket any day," she added.

All the flights were cancelled so the *Queen* was carrying more passengers than usual. As they filed down on to the long pier there was no missing Natalie. She was wearing grey faux fur from head to toe and looked dressed for the Arctic. Binnie and Will waved at her and she waved back, then half turned and spoke to a small man who was following her. He sported a long overcoat and a Cossack hat. Will spoke out of the side of his mouth. "Surely not the famous Foodezee man?"

Binnie flashed him a look and said, "Behave yourself. He must have an amazing personality because he is not carrying one article of luggage!"

Remembering Natalie's departure from Keyhole last October, Will nodded. Then the two of them surged forward to be engulfed in the pale grey fur.

"Oh, I feel I'm coming home for Christmas!" Several heads turned at Natalie's loud exclamations. "How is dear Maggie? It was dreadful about Alf but I know you and Daniel will have taken on the school trips, dear boy." She released Binnie and hugged Will to her. "Life here has a way of going on, doesn't it? D'you know what I mean, Billy? Oh, it's so good to see you! So much to tell you, darlings — so much. And you must have loads to tell me. Are they going to race the gigs on New Year's Day? Because if so, I want to be in Maggie's crew. I absolutely refuse to compete against her. She's too good. Where is she? I expected her to meet us. Will it be all right if we have a few hours at Harbour Lights before we go over to Postern? I feel like a bottle of champagne that's been shaken and is striving — absolutely striving, Billy darling — to be uncorked!"

Will and Binnie found themselves laughing the whole time. Binnie turned expectantly to the small man by Natalie's side.

"It's obvious we are not going to be introduced properly. You must be Natalie's —"

Natalie broke in. "Ernst, darling. Probably of Hungarian extraction. I telephoned the manager at the hotel from Penzance and ordered goulash for this evening. We simply must establish an air of mystery. 'Foodezee'? Ghastly name. So the chairman has to be mysterious. What could be a good derivation of Broadbent? Ernst . . . Ernst . . .?"

He said, "I'm pleased to meet you anyway. Nat is terribly wound up but she'll gradually run down. And I take it the luggage will wait here until we can get a boat over to the other island?"

"Darling!" Natalie protested but she smiled happily at Binnie. "He is very masterful," she said, only half joking.

Binnie took to him. She was surprised at herself because the men in her life — Will, Miles, even Theo in the old days — were constantly bantering in general conversation. Ernest — or Ernst — was not like that. There was a basic sincerity about him that might indeed have been acquired over years of business transactions. She could see that Natalie might find his straightforwardness boring occasionally but she hoped very much that his common sense would be appreciated too.

She was surprised when he took her arm as they walked down the uneven surface of the long pier.

"I'm a good bit older than Natalie — and you, Benita. If you don't mind giving me your arm and making it look as if I am offering mine, I would be most grateful."

"I'm pleased." She smiled down at him. "I dare say you are more used to a red carpet than these huge granite slabs."

"Not quite." He smiled back, apparently completely unembarrassed by their difference in height. "But I am certainly an urbanite down to my fingertips. This Christmas is going to be quite an experience. Natalie has talked of nothing else but the Skalls ever since her holiday with your son. I am looking forward to a very eventful time."

414

"Well, it's not really like that," she temporized, then added, "though we did have an enormous explosion yesterday."

"What?" He looked up. "Are you all right?"

"Perfectly. We'll tell you all about it. Will is going to take you over in Alf's old *Mermaid* — which is now Matthew's, of course — and we'll both come up to the hotel and see you settled. Matthew is already there, quite determined that you should have a VIP welcome. It seems the manager is very young and very nervous, and is under the impression that you are coming to inspect the hotel!"

Ernst gave a small, barking laugh. "The consortium is, as yet, nothing to do with us, but if we find it a good hotel I will certainly write to the chairman and congratulate him on his latest acquisition!" The laugh became a chuckle. "I might even get the provisions order for the whole chain!"

They came to the front door of Harbour Lights and were welcomed in by Maggie. It was immediately obvious that she did not approve of Natalie's furs but was tactful enough not to mention it.

"So this is the husband." She took Ernst's hand and seemed to be weighing it in hers. He said nothing after the introduction but looked her straight in the eye and after an interminable two seconds, she said, "You'll do. You'll keep her on track. She's got a good heart, you know."

Ernst, as Natalie had introduced him, threw back his fur-hatted head and laughed properly.

"I do know, Mrs Govern. And don't worry about the Ernst, will you? In private she still calls me Ernie."

Natalie shrieked a protest but Maggie said, "I'm glad. And please call me Maggie. And if I may . . .?"

He said with an air of resignation, "Yes. All right. Ernie it shall be. Just for the Skall Islands."

After showing them the table bearing a sandwich lunch, she excused herself. She and Gladys were now making cakes for the Skall ball.

"The church hall looks a treat. And we've got plenty of drinks." She looked sadly at Binnie. "Wish we could have rescued some of Theo Cash's ill-gotten gains, but perhaps best not."

"Certainly best not," Binnie said in a deliberately firm voice. "And we'll be going to Postern this afternoon, Maggie. Home by tea-time with Matthew. Is that all right?"

"You know it is, my girl. You need to tell Natalie here what has happened." She ignored Natalie's vociferous questions. "Not that it will affect her like it does you, o' course. But she will need to know." She paused, then added as much for the Broadbents as for Will and Binnie, "My brother and his wife won't be here till Christmas Eve. They can't make it in time for the ball. And, anyway, you could still stay here with us."

Will said swiftly, "I've booked us into Postern, Maggie. Dorrie is coming over and Ma will want to hear . . . things."

"Don't tell me!" Natalie said, wide-eyed nevertheless. "I predicted it, didn't I?" She turned to Ernst. "Darling, I said that Doreen would marry into that old

416

squire-type family and she would eventually become Lady Thoroughgood! Now what do you think of that?"

"The event? Or your crystal ball success?"

"Darling, sometimes I could kill you. But whatever. Isn't it marvellous?"

Ernst smiled and looked around him. "As a matter of fact, I think everything I've seen and heard so far is rather marvellous."

It was Will who said, "Ernst, you are going to go down very well in the Skalls."

Over lunch they told the Broadbents everything. Nothing was held back. Natalie listened, transfixed, and did not interrupt once. There was a long pause when they finished. Binnie noticed that Ernst had put his hand over his wife's.

Then Natalie said with some bitterness, "He couldn't do anything right, could he? He had the chance to make it up with both of us and he missed that. Dammit, he couldn't even murder someone properly!" She saw Binnie flinch and put a hand to her mouth. "Darling, I didn't mean it like that, I really didn't. It's just that . . . well, he might well be properly dead now, but he's managed to gyp you out of Trapdoor yet again because we shall never really know, shall we?" Binnie said nothing. Natalie said, "What will you do now, Benita? Oh God, this is terrible."

Ernst said, "The sale of the Cornish house has gone through, darling. And whether he is alive now or not, he is still officially dead, which was what he wanted. So you have half the money from that, Benita. And I was thinking of setting up a small provisions store on Keyhole, which obviously will need a good manageress."

Binnie laughed. "Oh, Ernst, you certainly think on your feet, don't you?" She looked at Natalie. "So much has come from all this, Nat. Our friendship. Our realization that poor Theo certainly was a pirate, and pirates are, after all, criminals." She sighed. "So much we could say about all of it — and doubtless will the older we get! I don't know what to say about the house sale. We must think about that. But the good — the wonderful — news is I've probably got a job, Ernst. And it includes a home. And it's far more practical than Trapdoor ever could have been."

She began to tell them about Midwatch. Her voice quickened with renewed excitement. Will chipped in. Natalie clapped her hands and Ernst smiled.

They moored below the Old Peruvian at three o'clock that afternoon. The fog had lifted off the sea and sat like a giant saucer just above them so they could not see the top of Postern, not even the chimney-pots of the Peruvian. At the base of the jetty a tractor and trailer awaited them, the only motorized vehicle on the island. Natalie and Ernst were helped into the trailer, which was covered by flapping canvas and had obviously been recently used for muck-gathering. Natalie clutched her furs out of harm's way; Ernst climbed inside as if it were a Daimler. The luggage was packed around them: two trunks and a case inside, another trunk roped on to the tractor itself. Will and Binnie walked circumspectly behind. The little track that led across to the Postern

418

Hotel was muddy and slippery. They clutched each other and laughed. They were both heartened by Natalie and her husband; both trying to forget that *Scallywag* had not shown up on the dunes last night or this morning. Binnie constantly wondered whether Daniel was on Postern. Was it really possible that he might be *dead*? Wouldn't she know with some kind of sixth sense if he really were dead? Her whole being would be deprived of him — she would know that. She would feel it as a gaping emptiness. The world would look different, cold and hard.

Then she shook her head irritably, knowing that would not happen. She had believed Theo to be dead and he had been alive all the time. It was much more likely that Daniel and Dennison could be abroad now, starting another life. She would not know. She might well have to live the rest of her life not knowing. She breathed deeply and clenched her hands. No-one died of a broken heart.

The Broadbents were welcomed like royalty. The young manager — "Please call me Bob" — led the way to their room, which overlooked the sea and contained two enormous beds — "I understood from Lady, er . . . um . . . that single beds were not required" — indicated the facilities with nervous pride and then suggested complimentary drinks in the lounge before a late lunch.

"Darling — Bob, I should say — we've already lunched with Bill and Benita." She noticed his blank look and added, "I thought we were probably all on first-name terms. This is Benita Cash and her son, Billy. They own Trapdoor Island, or what is left of it. Benita is a kind of sister really." She looked at Ernst. "I suppose we must be related in some way as we were married to the same man?"

He said equably, "I suppose so, dearest. Now shall we meet your sister and nephew in the lounge in ten minutes? While we settle in." He glanced at Bob. "Everything is very satisfactory. I take it someone will bring the luggage up shortly?"

Bob tied himself into more knots while he reassured them, and then escorted Binnie and Will downstairs again. In the lift he relaxed sufficiently to say, "Of course, Matthew Govern has explained the situation to me but I still think that Ernest Broadbent will have his eye on me. It is very tricky because the management had no idea there would be bookings this Christmas and we have just a skeleton staff."

Will said, "Bob, try to relax. The Broadbents are in love with Skall anyway, so you are all right there. And though Lady Thoroughgood might be rather overwhelming at first, her bark is worse than her bite."

Matthew was waiting for them in the lounge and took them on another round of inspection, this time of his renovations. He was explaining about the panelling in the dining room — "Postponed it till after Christmas but it will look great" — when a young girl in a navy blue suit that did not quite fit her pushed her head around the door.

"Matthew! Someone at the recep for you. Some tale about Trapdoor. Couldn't make 'ead nor tail of 'im but said you'd understand."

Matthew raised his brows at Binnie. "This is Polly. She's from the Old Peruvian, standing in at the desk just over Christmas. Landlord didn't think much of it but, as I said, we all got to pull together . . ." He was making for the door as he spoke.

Polly said, "Not really my cup of tea, all this. Too posh. But poor old Bob, he has kittens every day three times a day. Not fair really, is it?" She smiled suddenly and went to the bar. "Let me get you some drinks. That's my proper job!"

Will grinned at her and Binnie said, "Will, I'll have an orange juice. I must just find the cloakroom . . ."

Polly called rather too loudly, "Opposite the desk there! Cain't miss it!"

Binnie walked across the lounge unsteadily. It was either Daniel or Dennison in the "recep", she was sure of it.

She opened the door on to the foyer, which was palatial with palms and squashy sofas grouped around coffee tables. Matthew was standing with his back to her; he was leaning on the desk, masking another man. Binnie slid sideways behind a palm. She should have trusted her instinct, she thought, and accepted that Daniel was not dead. She might not be able to see him yet but she knew it was him. His voice, low and unmistakable, came clearly across the foyer, lifted in protest at something Matthew had just said. She wanted to rush across the carpeted space between them and tell him that she had remembered at last; that she had been there, with him, in the sea when they were ten years old.

Matthew said slowly and very clearly as if talking to a child, "No-one can stop that there Dennison doing anything when he sets his mind to it. And I'll lay you odds he'll turn up again. Like a bad penny. He'll skim that ruddy *Scallywag* over the waves and into the harbour one of these days."

"I shouldn't have let him go," Daniel mourned, not arguing, simply following his one thought. "I'll go back to Keyhole with you, get myself up to the lookout where I can see what's happening once this fog lifts."

Matthew said flatly, "Binnie will be with us, Daniel. She and Will brought Natalie and Ernest Broadbent over just now. They'll be taking me back. Who else will be going across on a night like this? You'd best have another night at the Old Peruvian, old son. Try and get yourself together."

Daniel was silent. Binnie wished she could see his face. She wanted so much to go to him now, at this minute, and say — with Matthew as her witness — that she loved him. But she wanted to see his face. Had he gone into that terrifying world of forgetfulness again?

He said in a low voice, "She can't stand the sight of me now. Did you know that?"

Matthew said uncomfortably, "She's had a tough time, my boy. Lost a husband, found him, lost him again . . ."

Daniel went on as if he had not heard Matthew. "I promised Will I would keep away. She is frightened of me. I look like him, I was his friend and partner. She'll never trust me." He must have been sitting on a bar stool because he stood and Binnie could see him properly. He was wearing the duffel coat but no hat, no gloves. He looked awful. She pressed her back against the wall; she must not faint. Not now . . . not now.

He said, "I'm off. Don't worry, she won't see me. I've made a mess of everything. At least I can make sure she won't see me again."

He turned and went through the revolving door into the porch and then was swallowed into the fog.

Binnie pushed open the door marked "Ladies" and turned on one of the taps to splash her face frantically. She knew that Daniel Casey had come to the end of the line. And she had put him there. So it was up to her to bring him back.

CHAPTER
THIRTY

Matthew was still in the foyer; it could have been less than a minute since Daniel had gone through the revolving door. Binnie passed Matthew at a run and gasped, "Tell Will to wait. I'm going after Daniel!" Just for a moment she saw his face go from bewilderment to understanding and then joy, and she was reminded of Alf. Matthew and Alf were cousins, after all.

The fog was still coming down and the short afternoon was darkening rapidly. There was no sign of anyone at all. Very faintly she could see the lights of the Old Peruvian and she made for them, slipping on the muddy track but recovering each time so that she could gasp into a desperate run. She did not know Postern well enough to strike out across its hump but she thought she could remember Alf telling her that he listened to Marigold away from the harbour "on the wild side". Which — she prayed — meant there were no beaches there. Her only hope was that Daniel would go gently into the tide as he had done at Cherrington.

The track turned outward towards the sea and the Peruvian's lights disappeared for two whole minutes while she scrambled around the swell of land and began the descent towards the jetty. Then it was laid out before her and she paused, holding her side, trying to get her breath, looking . . . looking with the intensity of an analyst from one side of the harbour to the other. A door in the pub opened and a shaft of light beamed down on to the *Mermaid*, anchored at the jetty. Someone came out and reached up for the bell rope. The bell — a fog warning — tolled across the narrow strait between the islands. Binnie remembered hearing it from her bedroom at Harbour Lights and Alf explaining that it had been there "always", and in spite of all the modern technology the landlord always tolled it every half an hour when there was any fog about. Now, the sudden spot of light took some of her concentration and left the beach temporarily darkened on either side. She took a last deep breath and began to scramble down directly, at first through old brambles and then on to the rocks. She knew this was the place where she was most vulnerable. If she slipped and fell, Daniel would never know, but there was not one moment of indecision, no inclination to weep or wail or do anything to spoil her concentration. She was entirely and coldly calm; she knew that she was completely focused for the first time in her life. Perhaps the last.

She clambered down the rocks and jumped from the last one on to the soft sand, and almost immediately fell over something. She turned and picked up a bundle of cloth and knew that it was Daniel's duffel coat, bought from the post office a month ago when he had duped Dennison into taking him to Italy to find Theo. She dropped it and ran down to the water. He could not be far; he had not had time to get that far ahead of her and he wouldn't have run. He would have walked purposefully, just as he had before.

She saw the ripples in the fan of radiance from *Mermaid*'s riding light. She began to tear off her jacket and wellingtons, then ran to the jetty and clambered on to it. Daniel had gone in from the beach and had not yet reached the end of the jetty; as she drew level with the *Mermaid* she saw his straw-white head dipping in rhythmic alternation with his strong breast-stroke. She paused, holding her side, then shouted as loudly as she could. Either he ignored her or he could not hear. He continued to dip and breathe regularly and was moving fast. She took a slow, long breath, pelted to the end of the jetty and swallow-dived from it in an enormous arc.

When she surfaced she was momentarily disorientated. The fog seemed lower still at sea level, and the waves slapping against the jetty, and the *Mermaid*, which should have been directly behind her, seemed to be at the side. She spluttered around until she was facing them. And there was Daniel, treading water, ten yards away. And he said in a tone of mild surprise, "What's going on?"

Something seemed to snap inside her. She screamed. And screamed again. By which time he was within arm's reach, so she grabbed him furiously and tried to shake him.

"Binnie! What — what's happened?"

They both submerged; she kicked hard and surfaced and he followed.

"Turn around!" she shrieked. "Get back to the shore! Go on! Now. D'you hear me? I said *now*!"

426

He stared at her and then did exactly as she said. She watched him take half a dozen of his long powerful strokes and knew he was safe. She felt suddenly drained of all her strength. She turned on her back and concentrated on breathing. The fog came closer and laid over her like a blanket. She closed her eyes.

It was just as it had been the day she had thought Daniel was dead . . . the day that Alf had died. She was in the presence of something completely unknown, another dimension, another perception that had nothing to do with the reality of human life. And she thought it was her own death. And she lay very still and waited.

He came back for her. She never knew how long she let the sea take her but she did know that if he hadn't come back for her, she would have surrendered herself to the movement and the mist and the inevitability of eternity. If he hadn't come back . . . if her hair had not streamed out of its fastenings and drifted palely behind her so that he could find her . . . if he had indeed intended to drown himself . . . if . . .

She heard his voice, felt his hands on her head in the classic life-saving position, knew they were moving slowly and inexorably towards the shore, felt his hands shift to beneath her arms when he was in his depth and then the swifter drag of the water as he towed her on to the sand. He released her and collapsed on to hands and knees. With a supreme effort she turned on to an elbow and looked at him. He crouched there, spitting sea water, panting. He was wearing shirt and pants and socks. It reminded her that she was wearing the same and she began to shiver. And then to weep.

"I thought I was going to have to save you again, Daniel Casey!" she sobbed. "I cannot believe — I simply cannot believe — that you would do that to me. Not a second time. I could kill you myself. I could kill you here and now for doing such a thing, for even letting it cross your mind!"

He turned his head and looked at her, his eyes glazed with sea water like a seal's. When he spoke his voice came in bursts with each breath but was reasonableness itself.

"I was not trying to drown myself, Binnie. I was intending to swim across to Keyhole and make my way to Dennison's lookout."

She continued to stare at him. The things that had happened between them were still there. They would always be there. But they need not separate them, they need not be obstacles.

She said very quietly, "I was in the foyer when you were talking to Matthew and I was certain that's what you were going to do. And I thought it would be into the tide. Like before. And then, out there, it became true. Death was there. I sent you back to the shore so it couldn't be you. So it must be me. And I waited and then you came back, so it wasn't me." She squeezed her eyes shut. "Daniel . . . I think it must be Theo." She took a deep breath. "It was Theo. Daniel, Theo has gone."

He stayed, crouching like an animal. "Perhaps."

"In the explosion?"

428

He said again, "Perhaps."

"How?" She sat up. "Did you and Dennison plan to kill him?"

His gasp was rasping. "No!" He sat back on his calves. "Now is not the time to talk about this, Binnie."

"Yes. Yes, it is. Tell me." She demanded. "Now."

He stared at her. The fog was coming lower and she seemed to move as if still in the water.

He said slowly, "Dennison and I, we knew he was there. And once we'd taken *Scallywag*, we knew there was no way he could get off the island."

"So Dennison went back? Blew him up?"

There was a long pause, then he said slowly, as if working it out as he went along, "I don't really know. Dennison dropped me on Postern. Will said you would prefer it." She made a little sound but did not contradict this. "Dennison was to fetch me last night. But he has not come. Last night or tonight."

"Did you know he was going to Trapdoor? Did you know he was used to explosives when he was a miner?"

"No." He was surprised.

"Matthew told me." She got to her knees and stood up. "We'd better get to the Peruvian. It's December. Hypothermia." She looked around her. "Your duffel coat was on the sand by the rocks. And my clothes too." She shuffled through the sand. "You realize you would never have made it to Keyhole, Daniel. The cold would have got you. And the currents in the strait are killers."

"I've done it before." He moved slowly up the beach and gathered up his coat and other clothes. Between them they found hers. Without thinking they stripped off their soaking underclothes and struggled into the dry garments. He held her arm and they pushed themselves through rough sand and rocks to the top of the jetty. And there, just before they went through the door, he held her tightly against him and said, "So you saved my life. Again."

"I thought I did. But apparently there was no need."

"You were so angry with me."

"Yes." She paused, then put her arms around his waist, her head on his chest. "I'd only just started to realize that everything between us didn't matter. I loved you. And you were killing yourself. The man I love. Of course I was angry." She hung on to him; she was shivering violently. He moved them both towards the door. It opened and a man came out and clanged the bell, then turned and saw them standing there, clutching each other for support. He shouted to someone inside. They were surrounded and brought into the warmth and light of the ancient inn.

That night, drowsy with whisky and the heat of the fire in the tiny snug next to the public bar, they stayed at the Old Peruvian. The landlady knew all about them — as everyone seemed to — and put them into a double bed made like a bird's nest with an enormous feather mattress. Without any embarrassment she brought flannelette nightshirts for both of them and a big stone hot-water bottle on which Daniel immediately stubbed his toe.

"About time," she grumbled, holding up the bedding so that Binnie could slide between the sheets. "You should take a leaf from Alf Trevose's book. When he saw his Marigold behind the bar downstairs, he din't waste no time. Good job too 'cos they din't have much of it. Now cuddle down together and forget everything except your two selves. You've phoned your son and you've talked to Matthew Govern, an' I don't reckon there's much else to say."

She left them, clicking the door impatiently without actually banging it. They lay there side by side and could very easily have slipped into sleep without saying another word. But there came a sound from Daniel and then from Binnie and they rolled in to each other and clung together. They were laughing. Perhaps it was hysteria; it did not matter. They were gripped and united in sudden paroxysms of giggles, which, once started, were hard to stop.

"Two very naughty children," Daniel gasped. "Getting themselves soaking wet in the middle of winter."

"You're speaking words, Daniel," Binnie spluttered foolishly. "Mrs Goring said there was nothing left to say!"

He enfolded her and put his face into her neck. "Is it as easy as this? No more words? Just Binnie and Daniel, together for always? Can that really happen?"

She stroked the back of his head. His hair was dry and crisp with salt. "I don't know. I think there's a good chance it can. Even if Theo is still alive, we can do it, Daniel. I'm certainly not under the illusion of being in love with him!" She laughed at herself, then sobered suddenly. "What was much worse was when I was so hooked up on that dreadful feeling of being used — made a fool of. Pride, I suppose."

"I would never have used you, Binnie."

She shushed him. "I know that now."

He kissed her and they clung together in sudden fear at how close they had come to missing this moment. There were no more words and no need for them. They drifted into sleep together.

The next day the fog had taken over completely. Mrs Goring woke them at eight with the contents of a breakfast tray already cooling fast.

"Flights all cancelled," she announced. "Shouldn't think your Will would be daft enough to take the *Mermaid* back to Keyhole." She looked at Binnie, wild white hair, bleary eyes and all, and added, "Don't know, though."

Daniel laughed. "Better than swimming, Mrs Goring." He made a lap for the tray. "Knives and forks? Bacon arriving later?"

"Porridge will need cutting," she explained tersely. "Expect you will want to get over to the hotel and let them know your news."

"What news?" Binnie asked, struggling to sit up in the deep feather bed.

"That you're getting married, o' course!"

"Oh, *that*." She smiled blissfully. "I think they already know about that."

Mrs Goring sniffed. "Your clothes are dry. I'll leave them in the bathroom," she said, and left them to it.

The porridge did indeed cut into slices. Daniel forked a slice on to a plate and passed it to her. "Did you mean that? About the others knowing already?" He was grinning like the Cheshire cat.

"They will now. We've slept together, after all. We're both compromised up to the hilt."

He looked at her and stopped smiling. "I can't quite believe it. I was Theo's partner — his *partner*, for goodness' sake. You kept mistaking me for him. And you have shaken him off . . . why not me as well?"

She sighed and cut a piece of porridge with her fork. "I tried. Even when I knew I loved you, I still tried. And then I thought you were going to drown and I stopped trying." She put the porridge into her mouth and chewed manfully. He did the same. And then they gave up, moved the tray to the floor and came together so easily, so naturally, it was, as Daniel said later, as if they had been living together all their lives.

And she said, "You really will have to marry me now. Will you mind?"

"Not a bit."

She kissed Daniel very gently. "That was a butterfly kiss. From Alf." She smiled into his eyes. "You and I have got a home and a job and . . . a life to look forward to. Together."

"A home?"

Again, the smile. She whispered, "Don't pretend you don't know about the Midwatch cottages, my lad. I'm fairly certain you worked on them with Matthew."

"Yes, but I didn't think for one moment you would want to take them on. Do you mean it, Binnie? The season is short and the winters are long."

"They will be the best part. Oh, Daniel. We're going to be all right." She tipped her head to look at him. "Aren't we?"

"We are, my love. We are."

If they had hoped to surprise the others even slightly, they were disappointed. Mrs Goring must have telephoned the moment they left the Old Peruvian and Natalie greeted them with, "Aaah. Sliced porridge for breakfast, eh? Something different."

Binnie said, "Eaten in bed from a tray. Luxury."

"Slightly congealed. Tea and toast, chilled," Daniel added.

Will pumped his hand and Natalie hugged Binnie. "What did I tell you, darling? Right from the start I knew it was a match made in heaven."

"You thought it was a match made by Theo," Binnie reminded her. "But who cares? Will, are you all right with this?"

"Having Daniel as a stepfather?" Will made a face. "I suppose so. It's Lady Barbara I worry about!"

Bob Newsome, hovering nearby and feeling pretty good at the latest development, quivered slightly. But the fog was still bad and no-one could fly from the mainland for a while. He smiled again and suggested a pre-lunch drink, on the house. Yes, he was definitely getting into the swing of things.

CHAPTER
THIRTY-ONE

The fog cleared the next day, in time for the Skall ball.

"I knew it would be all right," Maggie Govern declared. "Coming up to the shortest day. There's often a change of weather then."

Matthew eyed her but did not argue. With the sky showing high and blue by nine o'clock in the morning it would have been pointless. Just before lunch, the small eight-seater plane circled above the tiny airstrip on Keyhole and made its decorous descent. The red postal van drove across the field and the rabbits hopped just in front of the wheels. "Get out of it!" Walter Polpen yelled through the driver's window.

Lady Barbara, first out of the plane, raised astonished eyebrows and spoke over her shoulder. "Your father always talked to the rabbits, Henry. Never thought I'd hear that sort of thing again!"

Natalie hissed, "That's her, isn't it, Benita? D'you think our dear Doreen will be able to cope?"

Binnie was far more concerned with how Natalie and Lady Barbara would mix. Not that it worried her; not that anything much worried her. She now felt that her happiness was like a wonderful fleece that kept out the fog and the cold, but was light and almost airy. As for

Daniel, from his weather-bleached hair to his mud-encrusted wellingtons, he seemed to glow.

"I could never come to terms with the word 'incandescent' when applied to a person," he had told her pedantically. "Now I know exactly what it means."

She had smiled and asked him whether they were being very selfish. He knew what she meant and reached for her hand. Trapdoor and its old Victorian house were strangers to insurance policies but the fire investigation teams had been over it none the less. There were no traces at all of human remains. Not a scrap of sail floated behind the Curtain of the cavern. Two men and one small yacht had disappeared. Binnie and Daniel had talked about it a great deal during the first wonderful day of what Binnie called their "togetherness". Then Daniel had said, "Look, my love, we have to let it go. Not far, I grant you. In some kind of pending place. Otherwise it will spoil everything." And she had considered and then nodded. So no more was said, and her question about their selfishness was not answered in so many words.

Now they went forward with the others and made introductions. Daniel grinned at Miles and said, "If you hadn't given me a lift from Bristol to Cherrington that day in September . . ."

Natalie ignored Sir Henry's outstretched hand and hugged him ecstatically. "You're the first upper-class, real-live sir I've met! And we're going to be practically related, d'you realize that? I'm Benita's husband's second wife, which makes Doreen — I mean Dorothea, of course — my stepdaughter!"

436

Sir Henry, fairly pleasurably astounded, said, "Well. That sounds logical enough, my dear. Though how that means you and I are related, I cannot quite see."

Natalie laughed. "If Dorothea and your son are about to be —" She screeched and closed her eyes momentarily. "Benita! Darling, that was my foot!"

"I'm so sorry, Nat, how clumsy of me." Binnie gave her a dire and significant smile. "May I introduce you to my one-time employer and great friend of my family, Lady Thoroughgood." There was a cool touching of hands. "And of course you know Dorrie. And this is Miles."

Natalie went into gushing mode again while Lady Barbara made some comments about fake fur being only just acceptable. "It is still giving out messages to some people." She glanced at Daniel. "Pleased to see you again, young man. I thought you might try another walk in the sea!" She smiled frostily so that he would know she was making a joke and after a startled moment Daniel smiled back. Sir Henry pumped his hand. "Winter cabbage doing well, Daniel! You had a way with vegetables. Beat old Parkes hollow. Got a garden here, have you?"

Daniel smiled. "As a matter of fact, sir, we have. You must come and see it while you are here. We've got great plans."

"We? We? D'you mean to tell me . . .? Hey, Ba! D'you hear this? Our Binnie and this lad here are making a match of it!"

"Not in the least surprised." But Lady Barbara looked suddenly pink and Sir Henry put an arm across her substantial shoulders and squeezed sympathetically. "Always were a romantic, Ba. Chocolates and roses. That's my wife, Daniel. A tip worth remembering. Chocolates and roses."

Daniel's grey eyes twinkled at Lady Barbara. "We've got early daffodils, sir. Will they be all right?"

Laughing and delighted they all moved towards the little mini-bus to Harbour Lights. There were two other ladies waiting for the service into Keyhole town. They turned out to be heading for Postern as well, and looked rather overwhelmed by the welcoming committee. Binnie, remembering her promise to Matthew, made wider introductions. They smiled, well pleased by the titles.

"Mrs Thelma Selway," said the dark one.

"Jennifer Smith," said the other one who was wearing an Icelandic cap with ear flaps so that it was impossible to judge her colouring.

Binnie, duty done, settled behind Miles and Dorrie.

"You know, I can see how the land lies," she said in a low voice, leaning forward. "But no-one has told me anything and for all I know you are just good friends. Natalie nearly put her foot right in it just now with your father, Miles."

"I know. She's amazing, isn't she? I'm so glad she has told me Dorrie's real name. Doreen. Very pretty."

Dorrie snatched off her knitted hat and tried to hit him. He held her arm and turned to Binnie. "We're engaged," he said, grinning from ear to ear and holding up her hand to display a single diamond. "I got tired of waiting for you and though your daughter is inclined to be hoydenish, she is young and can be trained."

Dorrie surrendered, pretending to smoulder. "You see what I have to put up with? No wonder I didn't tell you that I was chained to this for life!" She too turned in her seat. "Mum, say you're pleased. I know he's got responsibilities coming out of his ears and I am — well, the two of us are really — always going to have to take second place to the Manor but —"

"I'm pleased. Very pleased for both of you."

They both began to tell her their plans. They were going to take over the stables. The grooms had had quarters above them, which could be made habitable fairly easily. Long-term, they planned an enormous open-plan ground floor. Binnie listened with half an ear. Behind her, Natalie's Ernst was talking to Lady Barbara about the difficulties of keeping the many Foodezee car parks free of litter. Binnie glanced over her shoulder and saw that Lady Barbara was smiling happily. Sir Henry was confiding to Natalie that, yes, he did have one vice. He enjoyed a little flutter on the tables and Dorrie's old boy friend, chap called Gabriel, had introduced him to a rather decent club in the city.

Dorrie raised her brows at her mother. "What was it Alf called Gabe?" she asked.

"Dodger," Binnie replied, and decided she had better have a word with Sir Henry.

After a cup of tea at Harbour Lights, Matthew took them over to Postern, escorted them to the hotel and waited for them to get settled in before bringing them back for the ball. Meanwhile Binnie, Daniel and Will were toing and froing to the church hall with covered trays, which had to be arranged on trestle tables in the vestry. The cacophony from the main hall where Walter Polpen was connecting his disco equipment was deafening, but at one point, when for a moment there was blessed silence, the Reverend John Tresillian could be heard asking at the top of his voice what the bloody hell was going on. Maggie answered him sharply that it would be all right on the night. "This *is* the night, woman!" bawled the hard-pressed vicar. The electrical screeching cut in again and then suddenly the sweeping notes of "The Blue Danube" cascaded throughout the hall and into the vestry and all was well.

Binnie, Will and Daniel went back to Harbour Lights to change and wait for the others. Maggie and Binnie knew that they would be outshone by Natalie, but when Gladys Polpen joined them wearing her flowing trouser suit they were a bit put out.

"Everyone will have long black skirts like us," Maggie said mournfully in the kitchen. "We should have gone in for something colourful."

"You've got your gold lamé top," Binnie said. "And it looks marvellous."

"And you look smashing, love. I suppose you can take that bolero off if you get hot."

"Well, yes. But I don't think I will. This dress is strapless. People wouldn't approve."

"If they have to put up with much more swearing from the vicar, they won't notice strapless! Besides, all eyes will be on Natalie."

440

And then Will and Daniel joined them in their hired dinner suits. Binnie had never seen Daniel in a suit. She had kitted him out in jeans and sweaters from the limited resources of Cherrington shops, and as far as she knew, apart from the duffel coat he had bought from the post office, those were his only clothes.

She said, startled, "My God. You look impressive!"

"And you look absolutely beautiful," he came back, just as surprised.

"And I'm stunning," Will suggested. "And Gladys," he held out an arm and made way for her between the kitchen table and the wall. "Gladys is a symphony in sapphire satin."

"Go on with you!" Gladys replied. "How about a cup of tea before Matthew brings everyone in?"

There was a small round of applause. But Daniel had not taken his eyes from Binnie and she knew it. They sat at the kitchen table and she held his hand, and when the others arrived she said under cover of the chatter, "D'you remember what Alf told us about the butterfly of happiness?"

"I remember," he said.

"It's settled on us, hasn't it?"

"Yes. Oh, yes." He smiled at her.

The ball was a success. The family from Portcullis came and the boys danced with the girls from Oriel. The flower farmers and the fishermen talked of prices and transport to the mainland, and then were whirled into a Paul Jones and leaped haphazardly in time to the music.

Natalie, wearing a very short silver dress and sparkly lilac-coloured tights, danced with Ernst and Will in turn and then claimed Daniel.

"I have to talk to him, darling," she told Binnie. "I'm the only female relative of your generation and I need to tell him that you are the best thing he's ever known."

Actually what she said as they swung into the circle of dancers was, "Look, Daniel, tell me the truth. Can you remember everything now?"

"I think so. And now you're going to ask me whether I'm already married."

"Not at all," she replied equably. "But since you mention it . . ."

"No. I am not. And never was." He whirled her around three times then said, "There was someone, Nat. It was when she died that I went off the rails. Theo found me drunk in a taverna in Crete, sobered me up and gave me a job. Smuggling. I didn't care whether I was caught or not so I was good at it." He held her at arm's length and smiled. "You know the rest. And I hope you know that I intend to spend the rest of my life nurturing the butterfly."

"Is that what you call her? Doesn't suit her actually, but then love is blind." She said seriously, "You'll do. I always thought you would." She pulled him towards the vestry. "Come and rescue her from the food."

They all went to see Midwatch cottages on Christmas Eve. Binnie, Will and Daniel were booked into the Postern Hotel for Christmas Eve, Christmas Day and Boxing Day.

"Heavy, heavy," Will groaned.

"I tend to agree," Daniel said. "Let's make the most of today and walk back to the harbour, shall we?"

Will shook his head. "Miles and I are going to hang on a bit and do some fishing off the point. You two carry on."

So while the others piled into Matthew's Standard and Walter Polpen's Ford, Daniel and Binnie walked along the ridge and past Dennison's lookout, where the view of the horseshoe of islands was magnificent.

"Postern, Transom and Casement," chanted Binnie. "Then Portcullis and Oriel with Trapdoor one end and Keyhole the other."

"You can see the outlying islands too." Daniel pointed. "You pass them if you set a direct course to France. Some are just rocky outcrops but others are green. Granfer Billiton from Portcullis was chatting at the ball, and reckons he could take some of his sheep over in the summer for grazing."

"We must get some binoculars from the post office," Binnie said. "A day like this, we could probably pick out the bigger islands." She frowned. "Someone's out sailing. Who can that be?"

They stood, arms around each other, staring. Long before they could distinguish the blue line, they knew the boat was *Scallywag*.

Daniel said slowly, "My God."

Binnie said, "It can't be Theo. He wouldn't have the nerve to show himself over here. It must be Dennison."

"It need not be either of them. Come on, Binnie, let's get down to the dunes. If it's Dennison that's where he'll go."

They giant-strode down the footpath towards the beach, ran through the dunes and then stopped.

Scallywag was tied to a buoy, riding high enough to show off its blue line, the mast down and secured. Knee-deep in water, coming towards them, was Dennison.

He had not seen them. He held a bundle over his shoulder and he wore an old felt hat pulled right down over his ears. Daniel gave a small involuntary groan. "Theo's hat. He's had it ever since I've known him."

Binnie whispered, "Oh, no . . ."

Dennison waded out of the sea and began the long walk over the wet sand. There was something about his gait; had he been walking on grass he might even have skipped now and then. For some reason, Daniel and Binnie drew back into the shelter of the dunes. Dennison came nearer and suddenly they heard he was singing. Or rather, humming. Binnie looked wildly at Daniel.

"It — it's a sea song!" she said.

"A sea song? A shanty, d'you mean?"

"No. The sea sounds. Like Alf used to do." She listened again. "My God. Exactly like Alf used to do!"

Dennison heard them and stopped.

"That you, Mrs Binnie?" he called. "Is Daniel Casey with you?" They went to meet him and he stood there, grinning from ear to ear. "Dear Lord. The Cap'n said as much. I weren't too sure m'self but . . . 'ere you are. How did you know I were coming in today?"

"We didn't." Binnie wanted to hug the little man to her, she was so pleased to see him. "We're walking back from Midwatch and we spotted you from the lookout."

They waited. As usual Dennison saw no need to say more. He dropped his bundle, then reshouldered it. He looked up at them as if surprised they were still there and grinned again.

Daniel said, "So the Captain thought Binnie and I would make a match of it, did he?"

Dennison snorted a laugh. "Aye. He did. An' 'e weren't wrong."

"When did he make that comment, Dennison?"

"When we was drifting about in that fog. Thought it would never lift." He started up into the soft sand of the dunes, then added as an afterthought, "I were going to blow 'im up along with the cavern and all the stuff he'd brought in. Put in half-an-hour's fuse and went to tell 'im. Mad, 'e were. Wanted to go below and cut the fuse. I wouldn't give 'im the key to the trap. Told 'im we'd go together, same as it used to be. 'E grabbed me . . . bit o' board just outside the door, there was. We got on it and came down the dunes like a rocket. Straight into the sea." He ploughed on through the hillocks of sand, laughing. Binnie had not heard him laugh like that before. "Swam straight out to sea, 'e did, me on the board behind 'im. And then the whole thing went up. Sky-high." He stopped and turned to look down at them, suddenly solemn. "The sea trembled. I ain't never felt that before. The sea, trembling. I thought it was the end. Bits of red-hot timbers and the like falling everywhere. The Cap'n said as we would wait and then get back on the beach when it all died down. But it was just words 'e were saying an' 'e din't believe 'em 'imself! And then it 'appened. Just before dark." His grin came again. "*Scallywag* came for us. Came round by the point, sail still furled, mast down like I'd left 'er in the cavern. We thought at first she were coming straight to us, then she veered away and we saw she was caught in the vortex around the mouth of the cavern so the Cap'n swam into it 'imself, caught up with 'er before 'e were sucked under, and came back for me." His grin was triumphant now. "The Cap'n came back for me, missis."

"Where is he now, Dennison?" Daniel spoke quickly, afraid of the answer.

"I reckon 'e's where I took 'im to meet Violetta. I cain't tell you where that is, Daniel Casey. It's better no-one but me should know. She were that glad to see 'im. She got a big family and they will take care of 'im for a while." He looked at them, sharing the joke. "'E's dead again, d'you see? Deader than before, I reckon. 'E needs looking after. 'E missed 'is way somewhere, 'an't 'e? But," his voice took on a note of sheer pride, "'e came back for me."

He turned back and plodded on. They did not follow him. Daniel watched Binnie and she watched Dennison as he disappeared on to the road.

She said, "Thank God. I'm so glad Dennison has not got to live with the knowledge that he killed his beloved Captain."

446

"He would have gone with him," Daniel reminded her carefully.

"But he didn't." She put her head against his. "Stop seeing ghosts, Daniel Casey. No-one is dead except Alf and his haunting is in the sea and will always be a pleasure."

"I thought you would be frightened. In case Theo appeared again."

"No. Not now. Not any more."

"But we are back to square one in a way."

"How? You have been saved, your memory is back, we are in love."

"But as far as you are concerned —"

"As far as I am concerned everything has moved on at an amazing rate. I came to find out how I felt about Theo. I now know that I never really loved him. Isn't that important?"

"Absolutely." He put his arms around her and held her tightly.

She said, "I suppose he is a criminal and he should be brought to justice."

"I think justice is being done, my love. Maybe Violetta can offer some kind of rehabilitation?" They both laughed. "Meanwhile, we've got to think about Midwatch and next season."

She kissed him. "Christmas first," she said.

He wanted to tell her that every day would be Christmas from now on. It sounded trite. But it was true. So he said it.

Also available in ISIS Large Print:

Golden Days

D. E. Stevenson

Mrs Tim goes to the Highlands of Scotland and is involved in a plot to rescure a naval officer from the toils of a siren; but, alas, the best laid plans "gang aft agley".

The characters are skilfully drawn, from the fierce Mrs London with her heart of gold to the garrulous Mrs Falconer who always gets things wrong and whose muddled stories of her girlhood make excruciatingly funny reading.

The house party amuses itself with picnics and fishing excursions and is suitably thrilled by the flourishing ancestral feud of two rival clans, which has its origin in the dim past.

Mrs Tim observes her fellow men and women with sympathy and humour and records her observations with a racy pen. The result is an attractive and witty story of an unusual character.

ISBN 0-7531-7612-2 (hb)
ISBN 0-7531-7613-0 (pb)

Charlotte Fairlie

D. E. Stevenson

Charlotte Fairlie is a successful, elegant career woman. Still in her 20s, she has landed a job as headmistress of her old school. She is admired and liked by both staff and pupils — but she begins to feel there is something missing in her well-organised life.

Then one summer she goes to stay with a young pupil on the remote Scottish Isle of Targ. In the romantic atmosphere of the Highlands, anything can happen — and even the cool, efficient Charlotte surprises herself . . .

ISBN 0-7531-7614-9 (hb)
ISBN 0-7531-7615-7 (pb)